STORM
CYCLE

**Center Point
Large Print**

Also available from
Center Point Large Print

By Iris Johansen
The Treasure

By Iris Johansen and Roy Johansen
Silent Thunder

**This Large Print Book carries the
Seal of Approval of N.A.V.H.**

STORM CYCLE

IRIS JOHANSEN
AND ROY JOHANSEN

CENTER POINT PUBLISHING
THORNDIKE, MAINE

This Center Point Large Print edition
is published in the year 2009 by arrangement with
St. Martin's Press.

The text of this Large Print edition is unabridged.
In other aspects, this book may vary
from the original edition.
Printed in the United States of America.
Set in 16-point Times New Roman type.

ISBN: 978-1-60285-548-9

Library of Congress Cataloging-in-Publication Data

Johansen, Iris.
  Storm cycle / Iris Johansen and Roy Johansen.
    p. cm.
  ISBN 978-1-60285-548-9 (library binding : alk. paper)
  1. Women computer programmers--Fiction. 2. Archaeologists--Fiction.
   3. Egypt--Antiquities--Fiction. 4. Texas--Fiction. 5. Large type books.
   I. Johansen, Roy. II. Title.

PS3560.O275S75 2009b
813'.54--dc22

2009014188

For Jennifer Enderlin, editor extraordinaire . . .
Whose insight enriches our books,
whose friendship enriches our lives

STORM
CYCLE

ONE

The trees on the hill should be a perfect cover, Pelham thought.

He moved quickly up the incline from the side of the road, where he'd hidden his car. The sun was low in the sky. He didn't have much time before the Kirby woman would be running down the path toward the Science Building. For the last five days Rachel Kirby had been putting in twenty-hour workdays, taking only four hours to rest at her condo before she'd gone back to the lab to work. Today should be no different. She'd drive her car to the parking lot three miles from the Science Building and run the rest of the way.

Pelham knelt as he reached the trees and gazed down at the campus below. A few students were strolling on the sidewalk, and there was a girl sitting on the steps of the English Building working on her laptop.

Should he take them out? It would confuse the motivation. The police would think he was just a nutcase if he didn't focus solely on Rachel Kirby. But it would also raise a public outcry and make the chase hotter for him.

Oh well, he'd decide later. His instincts were

9

usually good when it came down to the final moment.

He opened his gun case.

W ait, Rachel."

Rachel turned at the front door to see Allie coming down the stairs. "I've got to get back to the lab, Allie. I'm late."

"Not too late to talk to me for a moment." Allie closed the door and leaned on it, blocking her way. "You've got to stop this, Rachel. It was bad before, but now you're being stupid. You're working yourself to exhaustion."

"I have a few problems to iron out. I'll rest when I get back on level ground."

"If you don't have a breakdown." Her sister smiled. "We can't have two invalids around here. Letty would quit on us."

"I haven't heard Letty complaining."

Allie's smile faded. "No, you wouldn't. Letty is like you. Nothing is too good for me. Even if it means that you're both strained to the max."

Rachel didn't want to hear this. She had known it was coming. Allie had been too quiet, and Rachel had been aware of her sister watching her, but she had hoped to avoid a confrontation. "We're not strained. I don't need much sleep, and I'm as healthy as a horse. And Letty wouldn't have her life any other way. She loves taking care of you."

"I know that. She's going to hate it when—"

"Shut up, Allie."

"Why? I'm not afraid any longer. I've accepted it." She looked her in the eye. "I want you to accept it, too, Rachel. It's time."

It was worse than Rachel thought it could be. "The hell it is. It's not going to happen."

"It's already happening. When I go through one of these downward spirals, it gets harder to walk, and I lose control of my hands. My toothpaste went everyplace but on the brush this morning. And my eyesight is getting worse."

"Your eyesight? When did this start?"

"Just in the last couple of weeks. I tried to tell myself it wasn't happening, but I've lost a little of my peripheral vision. It scared me." She made a face. "And then it made me mad. At any rate, it was a wake-up call."

"You know how GLD works. Symptoms come and go. It may be years before it gets any worse."

Allie nodded. "I know that. Next week it may correct itself, and I'll have a good period. But I have to be ready. You have to be ready."

Rachel closed her eyes. Dammit. Allie had been struggling with this disease since she was a child, but the past few years had been especially brutal. Globoid Cell Leukodystrophy, aka GLD or Krabbe's Disease was a rare disorder of the nervous system that most commonly attacked infants. They seldom lived past the age of two, but late-onset GLD patients such as Allie were all over the map in terms of symptoms and prognosis.

Allie brushed her hair away from her face. "You can't stop it by working yourself to death for me. That's not what I want. Do you want to know what I want?"

"It doesn't matter whether I do or not, you're going to tell me anyway."

"You bet I am." She smiled. "I'm lonely, Rachel. I want you to spend time with me instead of in that lab tilting at windmills. The battle is over. Let's make our peace with it and enjoy."

Every gentle word Allie was speaking was tearing her apart. "It's *not* over," she said fiercely. "I won't let it be over."

"You can't work miracles, Rachel. You've already gone above and beyond. You started a research foundation for me, for God's sake. Because of you, half of the computers in the free world are working on a cure for GLD."

"The foundation is close to a breakthrough. They'll come through. I just have to keep—" Allie was shaking her head. "Don't you dare give up now. I won't have it."

"I'll fight as long as I can. You deserve that from me. I deserve that for myself. But I'm not going to pretend anymore. Now will you stay home and get some rest?"

Rachel shook her head. "I'm fine."

Allie moved away from the door. "Then go on and tilt at some more windmills. But when you get tired, come home and be with me." She started up the stairs. She was moving slowly. It was another sign of the toll the disease was exacting, Rachel thought in agony. When she was going through a down spiral, all the energy and vitality that was Allie was shaded like a lamp with the light turned low. She was two years younger than Rachel and when she had her full strength far more attractive. Her huge dark eyes, peaches-and-cream complexion, and sleek red-gold hair gave her drama and fascination. But today her eyes were shadowed. She seemed thinner and more fragile than she had even last week.

"I'll try to take some time off tomorrow," she called after her.

"That will be nice." Allie looked back over her shoulder. "Stop frowning. It's okay, Rachel. I'm not trying to lay a guilt trip on you. I've made a good life for myself. I keep busy. I paint, I work on my cars, I do stained glass. But I love you more than anyone in the world, and I want you to be part of that life. I just had to tell you how I felt."

"You're wrong, Allie."

"Maybe. Don't work too hard tonight." She disappeared around the turn of the stairs.

Rachel stood gazing after her, feeling pain twist through her. It always amazed her how much inner strength was housed in that fragile body. Allie had always had a loving serenity that could occasionally erupt into a puckish humor that was completely different from Rachel's own character. Rachel burned with energy, and Allie glowed with soft warmth. Yet sometimes, Allie could be an overwhelming force.

A force that had to keep on existing, dammit.

Keep calm. Emotion wasn't going to help her keep Allie going. Only work and determination would do that and, in spite of what Allie had said, Rachel would give everything she had to give.

Stop standing here brooding. She was already late getting to the lab. Lately, everything had seemed to be falling apart, and this latest breach in the flow could be devastating. She had to stop it before it affected the foundation.

Before it affected Allie.

She opened the door and ran down the steps but didn't jump in the car as she usually did. She had too much emotion tumbling through her and she had to burn some of it off so that she could work tonight. She'd run the eight miles to the lab, and maybe it would clear her head. Her usual jog of three miles from the parking lot wasn't enough.

Not today.

Pelham's hand tightened on the rifle.

There she was.

Rachel Kirby had come around the corner of the path. She was running hard, her forehead knitted with concentration. In her navy blue running suit, she looked even smaller than her five foot two. She appeared almost childlike, with her delicate features and short brown-gold hair, her face glowing with energy and life. Beneath the canopy of oak trees, she could have been an innocent little girl called home to supper.

She was far from innocent.

That delicacy and air of youth and pseudoinnocence was just another of her weapons. There was nothing childlike about that cobra. She was filled with venom and power. She knew exactly what she was doing and thought she could get away with it.

Sorry, bitch. Not this time.

He lifted the rifle and sighted down the telescopic lens.

Just a little closer . . .

Lord, it was hot.

Rachel could feel the heat sapping her strength and breath as she ran down the path toward the Science Building. She had a stitch in her side that was like a dagger thrust. She hated running. Hell, she hated exercise. She ran because she knew it was good for her, and in her work, this daily run was the only way she could be sure of getting enough exercise to stay strong and functioning. But increasing the miles today had taken its toll on her, and the thought of Allie's words still haunted her.

Focus on something else. Like her job, maybe. Oh, yes, she knew how to obsess on that. Ask Allie.

With the computer systems she'd designed, at least there was a sense of order, clear-cut answers to the problems that came her way. Not messy like life.

This project, however, was different from the others. It was important. And sometimes, she was paralyzed by the thought that millions of lives could be at stake.

All those lives, but only one that truly mattered to her.

Just a mile more.

She smiled and waved at Professor Bullock as he parked his car in the lot. He hated her guts, but there was no use giving him ammunition by showing animosity. The best way to handle jealousy was to pretend it wasn't there.

"You're out of shape. You're panting like a pregnant mare." Simon Monteith was suddenly trotting beside her. "And why are you sucking up to that effete bastard?"

"Shut up, Simon. I wasn't sucking up to him. I was being civilized." He was right, she was wheezing, she realized with disgust. "And I didn't invite you to join me. Why aren't you in the lab? What do I pay you for?"

"My brain, my initiative, and for putting up with you."

"Why aren't you in the lab?" she repeated.

"Dinner break." He beamed. "And when I saw you gasping and suffering, I thought I'd show you how physically superior I was to you. I don't get much chance. Are you noticing how easy I'm finding this little dash? I'm not even out of breath."

"I'm noticing that you're twenty-four to my thirty-two. Dammit, you were still playing college football when I hired you two years ago." She added sarcastically, "Children always have more endurance."

"You used to have endurance. A year ago you ran the Boston Marathon. I was impressed. Then you went to pot."

"I doubled my miles today. Besides, I've been a little busy lately."

"Yeah, making Val's and my lives miserable." He paused. "How is Allie doing?"

"The usual." No, not usual. Today she had seen sadness and bewilderment and the beginning of resignation. "She said she missed me. She told me to give it up."

"And it made you feel guilty and torn and angry. So you decided to run from your house to the lab and get rid some of the emotion."

She didn't deny it. "And I had some thinking to do. I've been bothered by the amount of computing power we've lost in the last week. It's like our system has suddenly sprung a leak."

"Rachel, some loss of processing power is unavoidable. With power irregularities, network congestion—"

"Not this much. It's being siphoned off some-where. It probably just comes down to one line of code."

"Out of millions."

"Yes. And it's starting to make me crazy."

"Which means everyone around you is going to catch hell tonight."

"Quit."

"I can't. What would you do without me?"

"Get someone who wouldn't give me the guff you throw at—" Her cell phone rang, and she glanced at the ID. "Norton." She ignored the call until it went to voice mail. It was the third time he'd phoned in the last two hours, and she didn't want to deal with the bastard now. She'd get angry and upset, and she had to focus on the work tonight. "Has he been calling the lab?"

He nodded. "I told him you were in Jamaica lying on the beach and had thrown away your cell. Is that okay?"

She smiled. "Perfect."

"Except that since he's with the NSA, he prob-ably knows every move you make. Why is he in such a stew?"

"I halved his computer time."

He gave a low whistle. "That would do it."

"Too bad. This blasted leak is making me come up short. I wasn't about to take any time away from the medical research. I don't even know what project Norton is working on. He's probably trying to pave the way to build a new and better bomb. Screw him."

"He can cause trouble. The National Security Agency is nothing to fool with. There are all kinds of ways for Norton to undermine you. Those government dudes are pretty sneaky."

"I'll deal with it."

"I know. You always do. Just a comment." He looked away from her. "And, actually, I lied. I wasn't at dinner. I was at Jonesy's relay lab in Galveston checking on something."

Her gaze flew to his face. "You found the leak?"

"Maybe. I found a thread that may lead to it."

"What?"

"I'll tell you at the lab."

"Now."

He shook his head. "I think you need incentive to keep you going." He speeded up, leaving her yards behind. "This pace is too boring for me. I'll see you at the lab." He darted a sly look over his shoulder. "If you make it."

She muttered a curse under her breath as she watched him lope away from her. Simon had a puckish and sometimes devilish sense of humor, and she wasn't in the mood for it right now. Then she smiled grudgingly as she trotted after him. At least he'd taken her mind off the pain in her side, and his teasing incentive was making her speed up her pace. She wished she could stay pissed at him, but she had known Simon had that wicked slyness when she'd hired him. He was brilliant and, as he'd said, innovative, and those qualities often were accompanied by idiosyncrasies. And if that brilliance had led him to finding the processing-power leak she had been searching for, then she'd put up with anything he threw at her.

And Simon usually knew better than to step over the line in his little jabs. He must have found out something at the relay station. Eagerness surged through her at the thought. Even if he had a clue, it would be something they could work on.

And, hell, maybe Rachel needed him pricking at her occasionally. She would probably become obnoxious if she was allowed to have everything her own way. Most of the people surrounding her would say she was already there.

He and Val had worked to exhaustion for the last few weeks, and she hadn't been easy on either of them. She was lucky they didn't walk out on her.

The Science Building was just ahead, thank God. Simon was probably already lolling at his desk and waiting with that Siamese cat smile for her to walk into the lab. Bastard. She'd have to think of some way to make sure he paid. Maybe she'd work on getting in shape and leave him in the dust. His male pride would be—

A whistle of sound.
Pain streaking through her temple.
Falling.
Darkness.

. . .

Was she dead?

No, Rachel's head was pounding with agony. You shouldn't have to feel pain if you were dead. Unless you were in hell. And this smelled more like a hospital than hell. Though how did she know what hell smelled like? Brimstone was one of the popular descriptions, but she—

"Dr. Kirby? I'm sorry to—"

"Go away." She didn't open her eyes. "Unless you're my doctor and can give me an aspirin for this damn headache."

"I'm Detective Don Finley with Houston PD. I need a few words with you. I promise I won't keep you long."

"Am I dying?"

"No, ma'am. You're only suffering a mild concussion. The shot brushed your temple. You'll be fine."

"Am I in jail?"

"No, you're at Sharpston Medical Center."

"Then go away."

"The medical team said I could question you. I'm sorry, ma'am. If you don't talk to me, I'll only have to come back tomorrow, and the perpetrator will have a better chance of getting away. Five minutes."

He sounded determined, and she wasn't up to arguing with anyone at the moment. She flinched as she opened her eyes to look at him. Forties.

Thin, with receding pale brown hair. Cool gray eyes. "Talk."

"You're aware that you were shot by a sniper at the university?"

"No." She tried to remember that last moment of pain, but it was all a blur.

"You don't appear shocked."

"I'll be shocked tomorrow if my headache gets better. Come back then."

"At first we were afraid that we might be having another campus killing spree, but we've changed our mind. We don't believe it was a random shooting. You were the only target. Do you have any idea who would have reason to try to kill you?"

"Not at the moment."

"No enemies? No one hates you enough to kill you?"

"Lots of people hate me enough to kill me. I just didn't think they would. It takes a certain kind of personality actually to commit to violence."

"Give me names of possible suspects."

"Tomorrow will be soon enough." She had a sudden thought. "Wait. Send someone to watch my house. My sister, Allie, and my house keeper, Letty Clark, are alone there."

"You think they're in danger?"

"I don't know. But I don't take chances."

"If you'll cooperate, we'll cooperate."

She studied him. "Don't try to blackmail me.

Your job is to guard citizens. Now guard them. You said I was the only target. Simon and Val weren't hurt?"

"Your assistants? No."

Relief poured through her. "Good." She closed her eyes. "Keep an eye on them, too."

"Why?"

"Because I don't want to have to replace them if you let them get killed."

"We already have them under surveillance."

"I need to see Simon right away."

"You're not allowed visitors. They made an exception in my case."

"Then go away and tell the doctor I need more meds. I'll call you tomorrow."

She could sense him hesitating. She opened her eyes again. "You're not going to get anything else from me right now. I'm not going to turn you loose on anyone unless I'm sure there's a chance they're guilty."

"It's our job to determine that."

"No, the buck always stops with me, and I've accepted it," she said curtly. "I can't think, much less analyze the situation. You'll get your names when I can."

He frowned. "I'll leave, but I don't want to wait for—"

"Go away or I'll scream and they'll come in and kick you out. I may even throw in a harassment charge."

He stood there staring at her for an instant, then turned on his heel. "You're right. It may take too long right now to go through the list of suspects who might want to kill you."

She had antagonized him she realized vaguely as he left the room. Too bad. He was only doing his job. But she had no time or strength to argue with him now. She had to rest and heal and get back to doing her job.

Someone had tried to kill her. It was a strange and chilling thought. She had tried not to show the shock she was experiencing to that detective. Shock was a form of weakness, and she must never be perceived as weak. She couldn't let her guard down and let that cop see that she was afraid. There was no use whining when she had always known the risks of what she was doing and was prepared to deal with them.

She mustn't let this madness get in the way. Let the police find out who had shot her. It was probably some crackpot who had decided she was the cause of all his problems. She had to live. She had to work. There were too many people depending on her. Allie was depending on her. She would get through this as she had all the other barriers she'd had to leap.

Get over the pain. Heal. Get back to work.

Tough nut," Gonzalez murmured as Detective Finley came out of Rachel Kirby's room. "She

24

looked like a broken angel lying there until she opened her mouth."

"An angel she's not," Finley said emphatically. "But we need to know what else she could be. Call the president of the university and get a report on Rachel Kirby and her work there."

"I already called him and made an appointment." He handed him a few sheets of paper. "This is the initial report on her, Simon Monteith, and Val Cho. Nothing about her work at the university, just the bare bones. That last line is interesting. They have top secret government clearance."

"For the work they're doing?"

"Why else? It has to be something to do with that computer in the science lab. From what I've heard, that computer has a capacity that the Pentagon would envy."

"Get me details." He scanned the report, then headed for the waiting room. "Are Simon Monteith and Val Cho still waiting to see her?"

Gonzalez nodded. "They said they'd wait until she was well enough for them to see her. They seem upset. They must be pretty close to her."

"Then it must go only one way," he said sarcastically. "She said the reason she didn't want them shot was because she'd have to replace them. She's a real sweetheart." He was glancing at the scanty info on Rachel Kirby. "Unmarried, parents dead, one sister, Allie, two years younger. Send a car to set up surveillance on the sister." He'd tried to bluff Rachel Kirby, but if there was a chance her family was in danger, it was his job to protect them. And Rachel had known he would do his job. Even in her pain she had been able to see through him, dammit.

And Gonzalez was right, he realized, as he entered the waiting room. The young man and woman who worked with Rachel Kirby seemed genuinely worried. They were both in their twenties, dressed in jeans and sweaters, and were very different in appearance. Simon Monteith was big and muscular with blue eyes and close-cropped sandy hair. Val Cho was obviously of Asian descent, medium height, dark-haired, dark eyes, and strikingly attractive.

"I'm Detective Finley. I'd like to ask you a few questions."

"We don't know anything," Val Cho said flatly. "Don't waste your time talking to us. Get out there and find the son of a bitch who shot Rachel."

"Easy," Simon said gently. "He has to follow procedure, Val."

Finley sized up Val for a moment. "A bit defensive, aren't you? Got a problem with authority?"

Simon turned to the detective. "You might, too, if you'd spent the first ten years of your life in a North Korean concentration camp."

"I don't need you to make excuses for me, Simon," Val said curtly. She looked the detective in the eye. "Are we under suspicion?"

"No, we've checked, and you were both in your lab when the shooting occurred. I thought you might have an idea who might have done it. Dr. Kirby wasn't willing to cooperate." He paused. "And she was a little belligerent."

"You must have caught her in a good mood," Simon said lightly. "She's usually more than a little. Particularly when she's feeling helpless."

"Is that why she said there were people wanting to kill her?"

"Nah. Who kills someone because she's testy? Look, they let you talk to her. Can you get them to let Val and me in to see her? She'll feel better if she knows we're keeping things running."

"What things?"

"The lab."

"And what do you do in that lab? I understand it houses one of those supercomputers."

"It's not a supercomputer in the traditional sense. But still, Jonesy could eventually have the capacity to run the entire country."

"Jonesy?"

"Just our nickname for the computer. Matthew Alvin Jones donated the computer to the university. When you live and work with a computer as intimately as Val and I do, it becomes almost a person to you."

"I wouldn't think anyone could become intimate with a computer."

"You're wrong. You should see Rachel working

with it. She can make it do tricks that are pretty amazing. It's almost an extension of her."

"And what do you do in that lab?" he repeated.

Monteith chuckled. "Well, we're not trying to undermine Wall Street or concocting biological weapons. We just process and allocate data."

"Boring?"

"Sometimes."

"Good money?"

"Fair."

He glanced down at the dossier. "Then why would you give up an offer at AT&T that would have put you on a very lucrative fast track?"

"Money isn't everything. I like university life. Lots of beer parties and football games. It's relaxing."

Val snorted. "For God's sake, stop hedging, Simon. If you don't want to tell him, don't do it." She looked Finley in the eye. "It's a good job with potential to develop into something extraordinary. We're both learning a hell of a lot from Rachel, and we're grateful. Yes, she's tough as nails, but she has to be. She doesn't deserve some nut trying to kill her."

He leafed through the dossiers. "Her report says she received her Ph.D. in Computer Science when she was fifteen and her Doctorate in Medicine at twenty. Impressive. She worked in Japan for four years before she returned to the U.S. You were working in a government lab in Yokohama during that period. Is that where you met?"

"Yes."

"And later she pulled strings and brought you over here when she started working here at the university. You must be grateful."

"No, Rachel doesn't accept gratitude as a concept." She smiled faintly. "She says it gets in the way. The giver tends to feel sanctimonious, and the receiver feels a tinge of resentment at owing a debt. She brought me here because she wanted to do it. I came because I wanted to do it."

"Why you? Why not a U.S. student?"

"I'm brilliant." She glanced blandly at Simon. "And look what she got when she hired Simon."

"A bonanza," Simon said. "Not a Madame Butterfly who thinks she's a Nobel prize candidate."

"Madame Butterfly was Japanese."

"Whatever." Simon turned back to the detective. "Can you get us in to see her?"

"Maybe. She said she wanted to see you. Why do you have to have security clearance to work in the lab?"

"Ask Rachel." He stood up. "And you know the reason I have security clearance is because I'm not a blabbermouth. Now will you get me in to see her?" He paused. "It's important."

Finley hesitated.

Val took a step closer, her hands clenched into fists. "I know she probably made you angry. She has to wheel and deal so much that she has a tendency to be blunt as hell when she lets down her guard. But Rachel has to juggle problems you couldn't even imagine. Give her a break."

"Give *me* a break. I have my captain hot on my ass to find who this shooter is. Who's to know if that sniper might not decide to choose another target? School shootings are a nightmare. Every parent of every student at the university will be on the phone wanting to know why he wasn't caught and why we didn't know this was going to happen. I'm walking around in the dark, and I don't like it." He paused. "So you get me out of hot water and give me something to tell my captain and I'll get you in to see her."

Val hesitated. "What do you want to know? We have no idea who shot her."

"Too many candidates?"

"Maybe thousands. I'm not joking. We get thousands of applicants who want us to dole out processing power to their research. We might make or break careers. To some of these people, it may even be a matter of life or death."

"Processing power? I still don't know what the hell you're talking about. It can't be that important."

"Believe me, it's that important."

"And what exactly do you do in that lab?"

Val spoke simply, as if talking to a child. "You know the expression 'two heads are better than one'?"

Finley nodded. "Of course."

"Think about how much better three hundred thousand heads would be. Because that's what we have."

"What?"

"People all over the world let us use their computers when they're not using them. They do this by installing a small program that lets us send and receive data to and from their systems. Our computer, Jonesy, divides up problems and distributes them through the Internet to these thousands of smaller computers."

Finley nodded, trying to understand. "So you've got all these other computers working together on the same problem."

"Exactly. We get people to donate their computer's processing power to our projects. We measure this power in terms of computing cycles. The more cycles we can get, the better."

Simon smiled. "And it's not just from computers. Tell me, do you have children?"

The detective's eyes narrowed on him. "Yeah. A boy."

"Does he have a game console at home? Nintendo, X-box, PlayStation?"

"Sure."

"There's more computing power in that box than most businesses have. If the owners of those game consoles agree to leave them powered on and connected to the Internet even when they're

not being used, they can let us use their processing power—their computing cycles—for all
kinds of projects."

"And you get them to *donate* the use of their
computers?"

Val nodded. "Absolutely. It costs them nothing,
except maybe a few cents in electricity. And
Rachel's software is designed to only use the
donor's systems when they're not being used for
anything else. We use computing power from
home users, businesses, anywhere we can get it.
And they get to be a part of all kinds of worthwhile
causes. It's a win-win."

"What kind of causes?"

"All kinds of things, but it's fantastic for disease
research. In one of our projects, we're examining
millions of tissue-sample images and comparing
them with cancer-patient diagnoses and disease
progressions. It might help detect cancers earlier
and maybe even help cure some types. It's also
useful for comparing DNA strands with certain
traits and diseases."

"So you deal mostly with health-care projects?"

"Not at all. Jonesy is also helping to develop
alternate-energy sources. Another project will
combat global warming. And by analyzing meteor-
ological patterns over the last fifty years, we'll be
able to forecast the weather with more accuracy
than ever before. These are projects that might take
years with a traditional mainframe computer, but

with the help of your kid's PlayStation computing cycles, it might only take a few months in our system."

"Who chooses the projects?"

"Rachel. And *only* Rachel. It was part of her deal. The university isn't as interested in the good works projects as it is in Rachel's software. It could revolutionize computing."

"But haven't people been doing this already?"

"Not this well. There have always been several weak links in the chain, and Rachel has come up with solutions for almost all of them. Complicated problems need to be divided up, distributed to thousands of computers, then recombined. It's a tough thing to do."

"Unless you're Rachel Kirby, I guess."

Val shrugged. "She'd say it's tough, too. But her solutions are brilliant. Her software detects the computing potential of each of the thousands of systems and adjusts for the amount and complexity of calculations parsed out to them."

"Why the government clearance?"

"Rachel was forced to accept a government project from the NSA. They needed the computing time."

"Couldn't they commandeer it?"

"Yes, but they didn't want to go through regular channels. Jonesy had the power and privacy."

"What kind of power?"

"Right now, I'd say we control more computer

power cycles than the government computer systems in all of Western Europe combined."

"My God." Finley and Gonzalez looked at each other in surprise. Finley asked, "And Rachel Kirby is head of this program?"

"She *is* the program. She persuaded the university to let her run the lab when she heard it was being donated. They get the praise and prestige, and she does the work. She goes out and gets contributions to fuel the computer. Every medical and scientific organization in the world would give their eyeteeth to be accepted by Rachel. She only accepts ten a year."

"Including a government think tank from the NSA."

"She had no choice. They were pressuring the university, and we have to have Jonesy."

"And possibly the shooter could have been someone who didn't want this government project to succeed?"

"Maybe. You could say that about most of the projects. Someone always has an axe to grind or a slight to avenge." Simon said impatiently, "You can tell your captain that. Now, will you get them to let me see her?"

Finley hesitated, then turned on his heel. "I'll do what I can."

TWO

Rachel."

Simon. Rachel forced herself to lift her lids. "I didn't think that detective would get you in. The doctor just gave me a shot . . ." She didn't know how long she could keep awake. She had to be quick. "Allie. Make sure she's okay . . ."

"I'll go there right after I leave here." He took her hand. "It's going to be fine, Rachel. Val and I are handling everything."

"That's . . . scary."

He grinned. "I thought that would jar you out of that bed. I told you I believe in incentives."

"The leak . . ."

"See? Your curiosity probably kept you alive. If I'd told you right away about the relay, that would—"

"Simon."

His smile faded. "I found a discrepancy from the flow in the Galveston relay. It was very cleverly camouflaged, and I almost had to stumble on it before I noticed. Whoever is siphoning off our cycles is damn sharp."

"I knew that before. I made it impossible for any hacker to get into Jonesy. Did you pinpoint the entry?"

"One of them."

"*One* of them?"

"I think he has other backdoors he's made in the system."

"No way."

"I saw traces."

Rachel sighed wearily. "Dammit, it will take time to fix this. I'd better go to Las Vegas."

"You're not really going to see Demanski, are you?"

"There's no other way. He's sitting on a massive amount of unused computing power. That could really help us until we get our own system back to a hundred percent."

"You don't pick easy marks. I heard he managed to even make the Mafia back down once. Why him?"

"He has his Las Vegas casinos, three on the Riviera, one in Australia, and one in Macao. Besides, he has enough clout with the locals in Las Vegas to bring a bonanza of computer cycles to us if he only lifts his finger. I *need* those cycles." Her lips tightened. "That damn leak is crippling me. I have to get a new influx."

"You sound like a vampire after fresh blood. You'd better be careful Demanski doesn't decide to sink his teeth into you. I don't think he's one of the businessmen you can charm or browbeat into giving you what you want."

She scowled. "I don't use either of those methods. I just figure out how to make a donor feel it's to his advantage to do it. Demanski is difficult, but I'll work it out." Her smile had a touch of the tiger. "I've been waiting to tap him for a long time."

"That sounds a little personal. Have you met him before?"

"Once. When I was nineteen. He tossed me out of one of his casinos."

"Why?"

"I'd just taught myself card counting, and I was too good at it. He saw to it that I was banned from every casino on the strip."

Simon chuckled. "And now you want to get a little of your own back."

"Maybe. Or maybe he's just an excellent prospect to give us what we need." She shook her head. "If I can figure out one final piece to the puzzle of how to do it."

"Don't think about it tonight." He squeezed her hand. "Go to sleep. I'll go check on Allie, then go back to Galveston." He started to turn away. "I'll have more for you when you wake up tomorrow."

"Wait. Could you trace where our computer cycles went?"

"Yes. He was evidently in a hurry and wasn't meticulous about covering his tracks. You're not going to like it."

"Where?"

"Egypt."

"Hell's bells. The Middle East. That's all I need. If a terrorist organization is using our system to develop a new superweapon or to crack into classified databases . . ."

"Look on the bright side. It's Egypt, not Iran. Jonesy may not be supplying the brainpower for the development of another nuclear state."

"But someone could still use it to infiltrate and shut down power grids around the world. You know how powerful Jonesy's become."

"That's not the bright side." He moved toward the door. "And when you get out of here, we'll find a way to close all his backdoors and kick him out. Now if you want to worry about something, Norton called and said he was jumping on a flight from Washington. He was disturbed that you were shot. I think he's afraid it may interfere with his project."

"Heaven forbid that anything do that." She closed her eyes. "Come back and check me out first thing in the morning. Bring me something to wear. Don't tell Allie I was shot. Tell her it was an accident at the lab."

"She may find out. You're on the news."

"She doesn't watch the news. It makes her unhappy."

"It makes all of us unhappy."

"Not like it does her."

"I'll do my best." He left the room.

Egypt.

She tried to hold off sleep. She should think of all the ramifications so that she could prepare herself. It didn't have to be a disaster. But a hacker of that brilliance and capability had to be in demand, and the money in the Middle East had to be tempting to . . .

She was drifting away. Not now. She had to get a grasp on the problem and . . .

It was no use. Let go. Sometimes when she slept, she woke with the answer to a problem.

Egypt . . .

SAQQARA, EGYPT

Let's go back," Ben Leonard muttered. "This is crazy. Crawling through a damn tomb isn't my idea of any way to spend a night."

"We're almost there." John Tavak slid forward on his belly toward the wall of rocks ahead. He hoped he was telling the truth. They didn't have time for mistakes. But so far the other information about Kontar's tomb had checked out. Their guide, Ali, had only led them down to the main corridor before he'd scampered away like a scared rabbit. But the central room of the small tomb built in the time of Shepseskaf had been where he'd been told it would be. All artifacts had been removed from the primary burial chamber, but there was no sign of any digging in this area yet. If the secret shrine existed, then there was a chance it had not been discovered. "The wall is just up ahead, and the shrine should be just beyond it."

"How do you know?"

"The magic oracle of the Internet."

"And it told you about a shrine no one has discovered for thousands of years?"

"Sure. It whispered in my ear. That's why it's magic."

"Have I ever told you that I'm claustrophobic?" Ben asked.

"No. What a pity. We'll take you to a therapist when we get home." He'd reached the wall and was exploring the rocks with his hands. No adhesives, but the stones were tightly compacted together. It would take too long to dig through. He pulled some C-4 out of his backpack and inserted it between the rocks.

"What are you doing?" Ben asked warily. "Tell me you're not going to set off an explosion down here. This tomb has to be over two thousand years old."

"More like forty-five hundred years. And it will be just a tiny, baby explosion."

"What if it brings down the roof?"

"It won't. I've made the calculations. Back up. There may be a few shards." He lit the fuse and started moving back himself. "You might cover your eyes. Not that I think—"

The C-4 ignited. The explosion was loud, but it caused little reverberation.

Tavak lifted his head to see a jagged hole in the rocks of the wall. "That should do it." He started to crawl back. "Let's see if we've struck pay dirt."

"My God, you're crazy." Ben crawled after him. "I've suspected it for years, but this is proof positive."

Tavak was already tearing the stones away from the wall. "There's something . . ." He shined a beam from his flashlight into the darkness beyond. *"Yes."* He wriggled through the opening. "Come on. We've found her."

Dust.

Dank odors of centuries.

And, in the darkness, color gleaming on the wall across from him.

He rolled over as he reached the floor and pulled out his lantern from his backpack. He turned it on and lifted it to view the mural on the wall. "There she is."

"Wow," Ben murmured as he climbed through the broken wall into the chamber. He sat back on his heels. "Do you think it's really her?"

"Oh, yes." Tavak didn't have the slightest doubt that the woman in the mural was the legend that had brought him here.

Peseshet.

"Hell, it's no wonder the Pharaoh had her murdered," Tavak murmured as he stared at the mural on the tomb wall. "They didn't tolerate any usurping of power. She looks like a damn Pharaoh herself."

The woman in the mural was sitting on a throne

with arms crossed, and in her hands she was holding forceps and a long thin knife. She couldn't have looked more proud or royal.

"Take the picture," Ben said nervously. "This place is smothering me. And Ali said we could only have thirty minutes down here before the guards came back. The Egyptian government doesn't tolerate trespassers at new finds."

"Relax." Tavak was already taking photos of the mural from every angle. "A few more minutes . . ."

"It's weird that this mural is even down here. It's not her tomb. You said it belonged to one of the rich merchants in the town. Why would he have put in a secret room with a shrine to Peseshet?"

"I have no idea. With any luck we may find out . . ."

"How did you know it was here if the locals had no idea there was a chamber?"

"I had the help of another lady who may just be as smart as Peseshet. Thank you, Rachel Kirby." He took a close-up shot of the hieroglyphics on the side of the mural. He removed the camera's memory card and slid it into his computer. "But I don't want to leave until I let my program run a check on the text and see if there's anything else down here that we should be checking out."

"Will your laptop work underground?"

"It should. I set up a relay outside in the sand before we started down. It's connecting . . ." Not fast and not clean. But then deciphering hiero-glyphics was usually a slow, painstaking process

42

even with the power he'd harnessed from Rachel Kirby's supercomputer. Well, not harnessed, stolen. "I'm getting bits and pieces, but it's a jumble." He e-mailed the text to his computer in Cairo and closed down and returned the memory card to the camera. "You're right, this isn't going to be fast enough. We'd better get out of here." He took a few more shots of the mural, then of the other walls of the tomb to study later. "I think I've got enough."

"Good," Ben said, relieved. "I can't breathe down here. Next time you decide to go tomb raiding, I'm going to opt out."

"I'm not raiding the tomb, I'm just taking a few pictures." Tavak smiled. "And if I find what I need in this text, then we won't have to look further."

"If? I don't like ifs."

"Too bad. The world is composed of ifs."

"And you're obsessed to resolve every one that comes your way."

"Only the ones that offer a great deal of money."

Ben snorted. "Bullshit. If that was true, we wouldn't be crawling around down here when the chance of you finding the tablet is a million to one."

"You never know. There are always answers if you work at any problem hard enough."

"For you. Not for me." Ben backed away from the wall and stood looking at the mural. "She's no Nefertiti. Look at that big nose."

"She evidently had brains, not beauty. Though if she'd lived a little longer she might have invented plastic surgery. And I like her. She's going to make us billionaires." He took a final photo. "I think I've got everything. God knows if it will do us any good. We may have to go down another path. I can't see anything that even resembles a—"

The stone floor heaved upward!

"What the—" Tavak dove for the floor. "It's a cave-in. Down!"

Rocks falling. Walls collapsing.

He heard Ben cry out, but he couldn't see him through the veil of dust and falling rock. "Ben!"

The rocks had stopped falling. The lantern had been smashed, but he still had his flashlight. He turned it on and looked around. The entrance to the chamber was blocked with rocks, and the ceiling had collapsed. The only wall fully intact was the one on which the mural was depicted. Peseshet was still sitting serenely on her throne staring coolly out at the world that had called her a goddess, then destroyed her.

Tavak heard a choked gurgling sound behind him.

Ben.

He spun around to see Ben half-buried in the rubble, with a mixture of blood and dust caked over his mouth.

"Don't try to move," Tavak said. "I'm on my way."

"Like I have a choice?" Ben rasped.

Tavak lifted the larger stones from the right side of Ben's torso and shined his flashlight over him.

Blood.

Chunks of flesh protruding from his ripped shirt. Shit.

"That bad, huh?" Ben's voice was hollow.

Tavak grabbed the first-aid kit out of his backpack. "You'll be fine."

"That's not what your expression is telling me."

The blood was flowing, not gushing. He could probably stop it. He set to work. "Be still. Don't try to talk."

"Fat chance." Ben winced in pain. After the spasm subsided, he glanced around the chamber. "Looks like your brilliant calculations were wrong. You almost brought down the entire tomb."

He sliced through Ben's trousers to look at his legs. No open wounds. Maybe broken bones in his hips or back. Better not move him. "No way. I don't make that kind of mistake." Tavak sniffed the stale air. "Cyclotol."

"I thought you used C-4."

"I did. Someone else set another charge. One meant for us."

"Ali?"

"If not him, then someone he told about us."

Tavak nodded toward the still-intact south wall. "It's no coincidence that wall is still standing. Someone besides us knew the room was here."

"Then don't let the bastards get away with it. Find a way to get yourself out of here."

"I'm working on it. And it will be both of us, not just me."

Ben grimaced in pain. "I don't think so, Tavak."

"You're coming with me."

"I can't feel my legs, and my chest hurts like hell." His lips were thinned with pain. "Sorry to be . . . such a wimp."

The extent of Ben's injuries scared the hell out of him. They had to get out of here. Tavak began to go through the contents in his knapsack. There had to be something he could use . . . "You're not a wimp, or you wouldn't have come along for the ride."

"If Ali really set us up, no one even knows we're here."

Tavak shook his head. "Except the person who wants to kill us."

"Dawson?"

"Good chance." He looked at the mural on the wall. "You know, many of the priests in the Middle Kingdom hated Peseshet. I'd think they rigged something to make sure no one would ever resurrect anything she stood for, except that they had no explosives in 2500 B.C."

Ben closed his eyes. "Keep looking in that magic

bag of yours. I hope to hell you find something to use to get us away from here."

So do I, Tavak thought grimly. He wasn't claustrophobic like Ben, but he didn't like the idea of spending his final days being buried alive down here. "It's not magic. If it was, I'd be turning it into a flying carpet and buzzing out of here." He set out the contents of the knapsack on the ground. "But I might be able to find something."

"Have you ever been in a cave-in before?"

"Once. Australia. Opal mine outside Perth."

"And were you prepared then?"

"No, I almost died of thirst before I crawled out of there. Live and learn. I swore I'd never go more than six feet underground. And then only when they buried me."

"Yet here you are."

"What can I say? I got greedy."

"So did I, my friend."

Tavak stared at the stones and rubble separating him from the rest of the tomb. Even if they made it out, they might be met with lethal force. Whoever had set up this scenario hadn't wanted them to come out alive and wanted to preserve the information on that wall. "There's got to be a way to get out."

"Like Jonah in the whale? I wouldn't count on divine intervention."

"I never do. I've always believed God helps he who helps himself. If he feels in the mood. Let me think about this."

· · ·

Someone was holding her hand . . .

Rachel knew that touch. She had to open her eyes. Maybe Allie needed her.

"Allie . . ." She struggled to lift her lids. Lord, it was hard. The sedative had taken hold, and every effort was almost impossible. She finally managed to open her eyes.

Allie's face a blur beside her. Allie's hand on hers. "Go back to sleep, Rachel. I didn't mean to wake you."

"Are you . . . okay?"

Allie nodded. "I should have known that would be the first thing you'd say. You're the one who was shot."

"Who told you?"

"Not Simon. But he's not hard to read. I had Letty check and see what was really happening."

"Did she bring you?"

"Yes, she's in the waiting room. Now hush. I'll have to leave if I disturb you."

She was barely able to form the words. "Shouldn't be here. It's not good for you. Hospitals . . ."

"Don't bother me anymore. I've been in so many, it's like a second home. And where else should I be when my sister is sick?"

"Not sick. Some nut—"

"Tried to blow your head off." Her eyes were glistening with tears. "And you didn't even want

48

them to tell me. How worthless do you think that makes me feel?"

Don't cry, Allie. It hurts me. You never cry. "Sorry. I thought . . . Don't worry. It will be all right."

"I love you. I'm not well, but I'm still able to function as a human being. Why did you try to take that away from me? Listen to you. Even now you're trying to comfort me."

Didn't she understand? "It's not right. I'm . . . so strong. There should be some way I could give some of it to you."

"Yeah, real strong." Allie leaned forward and brushed a kiss on Rachel's cheek. "Go back to sleep."

"You shouldn't be here."

"I'll leave as soon as you drift off."

Rachel's lids closed. "Promise?"

"Yes. I'll let Letty take me home and tuck me into my safe little bed."

"I just want you to be . . ."

"I know. I know."

How is she?" Letty Clark asked, when Allie came into the waiting room. "I was talking to the nurses. They think she'll be fine."

"She's Rachel. What else can I say?" Allie took the jacket Letty handed her and slipped it on. "She wants you to drive me home and take care of me." She shook her head. "And she doesn't even realize how ridiculous she's being."

49

Letty smiled. "She's protective. But then so are you. You'd like to whisk her away from this place." She tilted her head. "And I can see you standing guard over her."

"As she hired you to stand guard over me?"

"It made her feel better since she couldn't always be with you." Letty handed her a cup of coffee in a Styrofoam cup. "And we've made a good thing of it, haven't we, Allie?"

"A very good thing." Allie smiled affectionately at Letty. When Letty Clark had appeared in her life eight years ago, she'd fiercely resented this new inroad on her independence. She'd known at once that the term "housekeeper" was really a misnomer. Letty had been a registered nurse for most of her career.

But Allie had been won over within two weeks. Letty was in her midfifties, with short red hair and hazel eyes that gleamed with humor. She had boundless energy only matched by her intelligence. That intelligence translated in letting Allie go her own way, but she was always there when she wanted to talk or had a problem. Now they were close friends.

Allie reached out and gave Letty's arm a quick squeeze. "Thanks for coming tonight. I knew Rachel would worry if someone wasn't with me."

"No problem," Letty said. "Finish your coffee. Your body temperature always goes down when you get tired."

"Stop sounding like a nurse." She took another sip of the coffee and started for the elevator. "My body temperature is plummeting because I'm scared to death. I almost lost her, Letty."

"But you didn't, and the police will find out who did it."

"They'd better. I'm not taking any bullshit. They've got to find that bastard." Her lips tightened. "If they don't, I'm going to be camped out in their squad room."

"That idea would be funny except I know you're fully capable of doing it." Letty punched the elevator button. "And making Rachel bail you out of jail."

"At least she'd be too busy to run around getting herself shot at." She held up her hand as Letty opened her lips. "Okay, okay. I won't do anything right away. Not until I see if the police are doing their job, and Rachel is on her way to recovery." She threw the empty cup into the trash. "I'll meekly play the part of Rachel's albatross. I'll finish that painting I'm working on. I'll give your SUV a tune-up." She added grimly, "Four days. Then I'll go after their asses."

"I'm sure they'll appreciate your forbearance." She hesitated. "There's something you should know. I ran into Dr. Lowen while I was waiting for you. He was called to take care of Norah Beldwick."

"Norah? She was admitted again?"

Letty nodded. "Seizures. She's grown resistant to the anticonvulsive medicines."

"Dear God." It was one of her worst nightmares. Years ago she'd been admitted three times for seizures herself, and they went on for hours if not controlled. The effects and ramifications of GLD were all over the board. Blindness, deafness, paralysis; it could attack any part of the nervous system, and the violent seizures were one of the worst symptoms. "Can't Lowen do anything? Find anything that will work for her? He did for me."

"He's trying," Letty said. "He knew that you'd gotten to know each other when you were at his clinic." She paused. "He said to tell you that he didn't want you visiting her."

"Why? Of course, I will."

Letty shook her head. "She's bad, Allie. You don't want to see it."

She braced herself. "What else?"

"Brain damage. She wouldn't recognize you."

"Oh, damn."

"I didn't want to tell you. Lowen was afraid that one of the nurses might mention it and let you see her. They know you here."

"I'm going to see her." She turned away from the elevator. "What room?"

"Are you a glutton for punishment? She won't even know you."

"I don't care. She has GLD. That could be me. I won't ignore her. What room?"

"Three twelve."

"It's okay, Letty." She moved down the hall. "I won't be long. I wouldn't be able to stand it. I'm not that brave. But I just have to let her know she's not alone."

It's almost eleven. Why are you so late?" Rachel said as soon as Simon appeared in her room. "Did you bring me anything to wear?"

"I was dealing with those police detectives at the lab. They were going through the client list and asking questions."

"What kind of questions?"

"About the people involved, the kinds of projects we're working on, that kind of stuff. They said to tell you that they needed to talk to you today." He dropped a tote on the bed. "Allie packed it for you last night. She wanted to come herself, but I stalled her."

"It didn't do any good. She paid me a visit in the middle of the night."

He shrugged. "Sorry. But you know how determined she can be."

"Yes." That determination had probably kept Allie alive. She tapped the tote. "Is my laptop in it?"

"Of course. I knew you'd want to start working while we were driving down to Galveston."

"I wish I'd had it this morning while I was waiting for you." She grabbed the tote and headed for the bathroom. "Check me out of here before Norton shows up. I don't want to deal with him right now."

"But he wants to deal with you." Wayne Norton stood in the doorway, his expression grim. "You seem to have recovered quickly, Dr. Kirby. I'm sure you won't mind sitting down and having a short discussion."

"I do mind." But she could tell by glancing at his face that he wasn't going to listen to anything he didn't want to hear. "Five minutes." She sat down in the visitor's chair. "It's okay, Simon, go and pay my bill. I'll meet you at the front entrance."

"I could stick around."

"Go." She gazed at Norton. "Talk."

"Who's taking potshots at you?"

"How do I know? It could be you. You were sputtering like Vesuvius the last time I talked to you. Maybe you decided that if I weren't around, you could get my replacement to give you what you want."

"What a pleasant thought," he murmured. "I'm sure almost anyone else would be more cooperative. However, I don't have time to negotiate, and you're the only one who knows how to provide me with what I need as quickly as I need it. You know your process is unique. I don't want someone to kill you and leave me in the lurch."

"Then find out who did it. I have no idea."

"I'm trying to do that. I've started to investigate

every charity and research facility that you accepted or refused. Ordinarily, I'd go for personal ties first but you seem to have practically no personal life." He paused. "Except for your relationship with your sister."

She could tell that pause was the deliberate crouch before the pounce. "I'm busy. Tell me, do you have a personal life, Norton?"

"We're not talking about me. We're talking about your sister, Allie Kirby." His lips tightened. "And the reason why you cut my computer time."

"That has nothing to do with Allie."

"I think you're lying. Do you believe I wouldn't have had you investigated before I chose you? By the time you were twenty-three, you'd managed to locate an obscure research facility in Ohio that was dedicated to finding a cure for Globoid Cell Leukodystrophy—your sister's illness. GLD is an extremely rare disease of the central nervous system. So rare, in fact, that research funds were almost nonexistent. The big pharmaceutical companies aren't interested in putting money into developing a medicine that wouldn't pay decent dividends. Did that make you angry?"

She didn't answer.

"It probably did, but you found a way to work your way around it. You talked three business tycoons into funding the facility and suddenly it became the GLD Hope Foundation. But they probably wanted a payback, so you had to offer them something. You went after the control of the supercomputer recently donated to the university by Alvin Jones. You talked Jones into getting behind you and influencing the university board to let you manage the projects. Pretty amazing." He paused. "And those three businessmen who are funding the research lab for your sister's illness are still listed on your client list."

"There's nothing illegal about that. I've been completely aboveboard in my records. Their businesses require only a small percentage of the computer time Jonesy distributes."

"But you pour a hell of a lot more into your research foundation, don't you?"

"Of course, I do." She stared him in the eye. "But I also give a tremendous amount of time to other research projects. I've never cheated any of them of computer time they might need. What's your point?"

"My point is that you cut my time. I want it back."

"I'm having a few technical problems. You'll get it back when I solve them."

"I think your technical problems are bullshit," he said bluntly. "I believe you're getting desperate. Most GLD victims don't even reach the age of two. Even with late-onset cases like your sister's, it's rare for victims to reach adulthood. You know your sister is running out of time. Are you giving my computing cycles to that damn medical foundation?"

"Heaven forbid I try to save lives instead of letting you have it," she said bitterly.

"How do you know I'm not doing something a thousand times more important than your foundation? The chances of your sister surviving are practically nil, but you won't admit it. You're a fanatic. Well, I deal with fanatics all the time. I'm not letting you get in my way. I need that processing power."

"Then steal it from the FBI's computers." She stood up. "But I don't think you want to do that. You found Jonesy and me because whatever you're doing is shady as hell. I don't know if it's agency business or personal, but you don't want anyone to be able to tap into it. Perhaps I should make inquiries in your Washington office exactly why you want this computer time to be off the radar."

"You'd find it labeled TOP SECRET and CONFIDENTIAL. Don't threaten me," Norton said. "I'll give you three days. After that, I'm coming after you. You don't want that. It could get nasty."

"I'll give you your time back when I iron out my problems. You guessed wrong, Norton. The problem is purely technical."

"I mean what I say."

"I'm sure you do." She headed for the bathroom. Lord, she didn't need this now. Norton was obviously dead serious and out for blood. "But I'm not cutting any medical research time for you."

"Three days," he said, as she closed the door behind her.

So much for his concern for her brush with death, she thought wryly. Norton had only hurried here to get her to reinstate his time with threats and possible blackmail. She felt a surge of anger but quickly suppressed it. She couldn't afford being pissed off at Norton. It would take effort, and she had to keep all her strength and effort focused on the goal. She would give Norton what he wanted just to keep him off her back as soon as she fixed the leak. She couldn't let a battle with him get in the way now. He was right, Allie was too close to the end.

Fear tightened the muscles of her stomach. Don't think of Allie right now. She had to concentrate on the leak Simon had found in the relay in Galveston.

For God's sake, Egypt.

THREE

'm going to die, aren't I?" Ben whispered.

"Hell, no. We still have air, and that means that we can survive. I managed to clear some of those rocks away, and it looks like the rest of the tomb may be fairly clear." Tavak stared down at

Ben's bruised and bloody torso. Damn. "I just don't want to move you just yet."

"I don't think there's—" Ben's words drifted off as he lost consciousness.

Shit.

Tavak checked his vital signs. Ben's heartbeat was fainter than it had been just a few minutes before. He had to get him out of here before long, or he could die. How? He'd have to go it alone and come back for Ben. But even if he made it through the rubble, he'd still be a sitting duck when he reached the entrance to the tomb.

He leaned back against the wall, his gaze resting on the woman in the mural on the far wall.

Peseshet.

She looked powerful, serene, and uncaring that she'd drawn him into this hellhole of a tomb. "You're right, it's not your fault," he murmured. "I got my ass into this, and it's up to me to get my ass out of it."

If he was careful, and lucky, he'd be able to make it to the surface. But once on the outside of the tomb, he'd need someone to run interference. Who could he trust that could get here fast enough?

No one.

All right, then who was clever and determined enough to jump over the obstacles and make it happen anyway? Think, dammit.

A name jumped into his mind. He rejected it instantly, then he stopped and began to think.

Possibly.

If he could furnish motivation, and he thought he could.

Yes.

He reached in his backpack for his computer and flipped it open. "Okay, Peseshet, let's go for it . . ."

Rachel and Simon were halfway to the lab in Galveston, and she had just begun to check the network links binding Jonesy to the relay in Galveston when she heard the tonal signal that she had e-mail.

Dammit. She didn't want to get out of the program now.

"Are you going to answer it?" Simon asked.

"Of course, I'll at least see who it is. Allie sometimes e-mails me." She saved the program and went into e-mail. Three old messages from Norton, one from Val, and the latest one from a John Tavak.

"Who the hell is—" She stiffened. "Holy smoke, this message didn't come directly to this laptop. It was transferred from Jonesy."

"What?"

"You heard me. It was transferred from Jonesy's closed network."

"How?"

"I don't know how. It should be impossible. But I'm going to find out, dammit." She clicked open the document.

Hello, Rachel Kirby, I do hope you don't blow this message away. I don't think you will since I took the precaution of sending it through your beloved computer. Curiosity alone should make you read it. I'm writing this from a Fourth Dynasty tomb in Saqqara, and I'm not in the best situation that—

"Saqqara . . ." Her shocked gaze flew to Simon's face. "Egypt. Simon, it's from Egypt."

"I'll be damned," Simon murmured.

"You're not the one who should be damned," Rachel said through set teeth. "This has to be the bastard who has been tapping Jonesy."

"Why would he decide to contact us now and let us know who he was?"

That was what Rachel was wondering. Her gaze shifted back to the monitor.

By now you're trying to guess why I'm blowing my cover. The reason is pure self-preservation. I'm in something of a fix and I had a talk with Peseshet and she suggested that you were the answer to saving my neck. Not that you'd probably want to do it. And since Peseshet has been dead for over four thousand years, she may be considerably out of touch. But since I've been thinking of the two of you as mirror images of each other, I thought I'd give it a shot.

There's not much time. I have a wounded friend and partner who may die if I don't get him out of this tomb. Unfortunately, once we reach the surface, there will probably be a few scumbags waiting who will want to kill us both. Not a good choice.

Good riddance, you're thinking. I can't blame you. So I thought I'd better throw something out that would pique your interest.

Peseshet.

Look her up. You won't find much but she'll intrigue you. She was the overseer of a staff of female physicians in the time of the pyramids. Her son's tomb is in the Louvre in Paris. She was totally brilliant, but not much was known about her.

But I know a good deal about her, and I'm going to know everything before I'm done. The tidbit that might interest you is that she claims to have found a way to regenerate damaged cells of the central nervous system. It wasn't high on her list. She seems to have been more interested in other cures. Cancer and heart disease were her main focus, but she had more opportunity to experiment on the injured laborers who were building the pyramids. After six years she stated that she'd had almost total success. Her cures were always inscribed on tablets, and presumably could still be in existence. In fact, I've enclosed a portion of the cure that Peseshet created at the end of this message. Only a portion because that was all she teased us with. But it may be enough to excite you. Check it out. But at supersonic speed, please, because I don't have much time.

Interested? Of course, you are. And your next reaction is going to be anger and disgust that I'd use such an obvious ploy to get what I want from you. Justified since I've already stolen a hell of a lot from your Jonesy. When I was researching the potential for total cellular regeneration of the nervous system, I came across your name and the foundation you'd set up. Since I needed massive amounts of cycles to do the research to help me locate those tablets, it appeared that fate had taken a hand. I could find your cure and snatch a billion or so for myself by selling her cures to the world. We'd both be happy.

But to do that, I have to stay alive. I know you're desperate, and I'm counting on it. You're looking for a miracle, and if you find a way to save my bacon, I promise I'll perform one for you. I've enclosed directions to the tomb where I'm waiting rather impatiently to be rescued by you. Peseshet thinks you can do it.

I agree with her.
John Tavak

"Who the hell is John Tavak?" Simon said. "Besides being an opportunist beyond the scope of imagination."

"I never heard of him." Rachel couldn't take her gaze from the message in front of her. "I should ignore this e-mail, shouldn't I?"

"He's trying to manipulate you."

"Yes. The chances are that it's all a bunch of crap."

Total cellular regeneration.

"He's a criminal. He's dangling that cure like a carrot before a donkey."

"But he's absolutely brilliant. We both agreed that he had to be a genius to be able to do what he did with Jonesy."

"He's a criminal," Simon repeated.

Total cellular regeneration.

"What if he's telling the truth?"

"Rachel, get a grip. He's trying to use you."

I know how desperate you are.

Oh, yes, she was desperate, and he was ruthlessly playing on that feeling of mounting panic.

"Rachel."

"Do you think I'm blind?" she asked fiercely. "I don't give a damn if he's trying to manipulate me. I'd let the devil himself use me if he could promise me a cure for Allie."

"Promises are cheap."

"But life isn't cheap. Allie's life isn't cheap. And it has to be bought and paid for any way I can do it."

64

"You're going to do it."

"Maybe." She cleared the screen. "Let's see if he told the truth about the only thing I can check. What was her name? Peseshet." The information about the woman physician was scanty, just as Tavak had said it would be. "Not much here. But she was an important physician, and part of her son's tomb is in the Louvre."

"That doesn't mean anything. You're crazy, Rachel."

"Probably." She looked at a photograph Tavak had embedded in his message. It featured a portion of a stone tablet, along with a translation of the carvings. "It says here that the principal ingredient of her treatment was the crushed bones of Horus."

"What's a horus?" Simon asked.

"Horus is the name of an Egyptian god, but it probably means something else in this context. I'll send this to Dr. Carson at Allie's foundation and ask him to look at it and report back immediately."

"You're actually going to try to save the bastard."

"If I can. 'If' is the key word." She activated the portable printer and punched a button that printed out the directions to the Saqqara tomb. "If he's in that tomb, if he's telling the truth, if he can deliver what he promised."

Simon's lips twisted. "A miracle."

"A miracle," she repeated. "*My* miracle." Her smile was tiger bright. "And if he doesn't produce it, I'll cut his nuts off."

I t was done.

Tavak shut down the computer. Rachel wouldn't reply to the e-mail. She would either act or she wouldn't. He would have to wait and see if she made her move. Or left him to rot down here.

His gaze went to Peseshet sitting on her throne, serene and confident and completely uncaring of whether he lived or died.

But Rachel Kirby would care if he'd convinced her that he could give her what she wanted.

"She's a hard nut to crack," he said softly. "Kind of like you, Peseshet. I think you would have liked her. Or maybe not. You were pretty damn arrogant with all those healers you oversaw. You and Rachel might have come to blows. It would have been something to see. I wish that I—"

Ben was coughing. Perspiration was filming his face. Fever? Dammit, Tavak could only give it a little more time, then he'd have to leave him, head for the surface, and make his play.

His gaze wandered back to the mosaic on the wall. "If you've got any influence with her, I wouldn't complain if you hurried Rachel along a bit. After all, we're trying to make a damn goddess of medicine of you."

But she already knew she was a goddess. Just as Rachel knew exactly what and who she was.

He closed his eyes and leaned his head back against the wall.

Come on, ladies, let's get the show on the road.

W hat are we waiting for?" Sorens asked Charles Dawson. "They've got to be dead. Let's go in."

"Don't be impatient." Dawson settled himself more comfortably outside the tomb, his hand grasping the stock of the M16. "Tavak is unpredictable and has as many lives as a cat. We'll wait and see if he surfaces. It's much safer staying out here and picking them off than having to worry about him ambushing us in the dark." He smiled. "Everything comes to he who waits. You've never learned that, Sorens."

Sorens shrugged and turned away.

Donald Sorens was clear as glass, Dawson thought with impatience. He believed he was an egotistical bastard and was salivating to find a way to take him down. It's not going to happen, Sorens. There are people who were meant to lead and people who were meant to serve. You're way down on the food chain.

He turned to Ali, who was hovering a few feet away, and said mockingly, "You've been shaking in your shoes since the explosives went off. I take it you're in no hurry to rush down into the depths?"

Ali shook his head. "I'm not going down there. It could collapse and I—" He stopped as he met Dawson's gaze. "It wouldn't be safe," he finished lamely.

"But it would be less safe if I had to go down there without a guide, wouldn't it?" he asked softly. "And if I were forced to do that, I really couldn't let you walk away from here. So I think that you should be content to keep me company."

Ali moistened his lips. "Of course. Whatever you say."

"I thought you'd have second thoughts." Dawson's gaze shifted back to the tomb opening. Ali was a complete asshole, and he was tempted to break the slimy toad's neck. But he knew Kontar's tomb, and Dawson might need him once he got down to Peseshet's chamber. He felt a flicker of excitement as he thought of that chamber and the bitch who ruled it.

If there was a chamber. Tavak had thought it existed and had Ali mark off the possible route to reach it. It had been amusing to have Tavak prepare the way for him, and he was beginning to feel eager and excited.

Are you dead, Tavak?

God, I hope not. There are so few men who can make me stretch and give me a challenge. Tavak was the leader Sorens could only dream of being. It was a pity Dawson couldn't let him survive.

Why was he lying to himself? There was no way

he'd let Tavak live. Dawson might enjoy that challenge on some level, but the hatred he felt toward Tavak was a constant burning and tearing that had driven him since he'd been hired to do this job. Sometimes he even dreamed about the son of a bitch and woke up in a rage.

But he would let him live for a little while.

Yes, live, Tavak. I want you alive and able to talk.

A few hours of "persuasion" and he'd know everything Tavak knew about Peseshet's tablet.

Then he could permit himself to toy with him and loose all the corroding fury inside him. He would no longer have to remember the humiliation Tavak had heaped on him. It would all be erased. He would be the superior one, as he should be.

And when Tavak was broken, then he could let him die . . . slowly.

Norton leaned forward in his desk chair and squinted at the caller ID screen on his phone. Rachel Kirby.

Bitch.

He'd just been told that she'd practically ripped the IV out of her arm and fled the hospital with one of her lab assistants. But at least now she was calling him. In the two years he'd known her, his only decent chance of an actual conversation with her was if he climbed into his car and schlepped to the university. The prima donna couldn't be bothered with returning his phone calls.

He punched the TALK button. "This better be good news, Kirby."

"It is. You'll have all the processing power you need within twenty-four hours."

Her voice sounded tense. Jangly. Not the icy-cool Rachel Kirby he knew and detested. Maybe their conversation had had more effect than he'd thought. "Is that a promise?"

"It's an offer."

"What do you mean?"

"You need to do something for me. There's no time for explanations or bargaining. And it has to be done immediately."

"There's always a catch, isn't there?"

"You haven't heard the catch yet. I'm talking about something that needs to be done seven thousand miles from here."

"What?"

"Outside Cairo. I know you have the capability. What happens when you get intel about a possible terrorist?"

"Is that what we're talking about here?"

"No. But you'll need to use whatever contacts you have in place."

"You're insane. You want the CIA, not me."

"Don't tell me you don't have a finger in every dirty mud puddle in or out of the U.S. If you can't help me, you can pull strings to make it happen."

"Why should I bother?"

"Whoever has been siphoning off our computing

cycles is in Egypt. He's gotten himself into a jam. He needs a bit of rescuing."

"This isn't what the NSA does, Kirby."

"What about when one of your own gets into trouble? You'd pull in all the help you could get. Tap some favors with the CIA. Besides, the NSA is very good at furthering its own interests. That's exactly what you'd be doing."

"But a rescue mission? It sounds like if we do nothing, it's a problem that will take care of itself."

"I don't want it to take care of itself. The man who's responsible is John Tavak, and I need to talk to him. He's responsible for Jonesy's brain drain, and he has some other information I need."

"Dammit, I thought your system was secure. If any of my projects have been compromised . . ."

"Your information is safe. I designed the entire network to go down if there was that kind of breach."

"But this Tavak person obviously managed to get past your other safeguards. Why should I trust that—"

"I know better than to believe you'd trust anyone or anything," she interrupted. "If you have concerns, you can talk to him yourself. But you'll need to hurry, or he'll be dead and not any use to either of us."

The bitch was cold as ice and trying to ram her agenda down his throat. He'd love to tell her to go to hell. But he wasn't going to do it. He needed her damn computer, and she was the keeper of that particular temple. "How quick would I have to move?"

"The sooner the better. Four hours tops."

Norton swore beneath his breath. "I can't put together a job that fast."

"You can if you want to do it."

"Just to get back what you owe me? Go screw yourself."

She was silent. "I think you're about to do that to me, Norton. Spit it out."

"I want my processing cycles back plus a reserve of a third more to be used at my direction."

"You son of a bitch."

"Take it or leave it."

She didn't answer for a moment. "I'll give you an additional fourth of power and only for the next three weeks."

"A third."

"Good-bye, Norton."

It was time to back away. He had satisfactorily taken her down a peg and gotten his own back. He might be able to squeeze some more after he got his hands on Tavak. "I won't be greedy. I don't want to take anything away from your medical research groups. I'll accept your offer."

"You're all heart," she said sarcastically. "I'll give you the GPS coordinates and all the other information Tavak gave me. Get moving, Norton."

CAIRO, EGYPT

Nuri settled back in his chair at the outdoor café and tapped the bowl of the hookah. He cast a glance around. It was almost 1 A.M. and the place was packed, just like most of the other cafés along al-Azhar Street. He closed his lips around the wooden mouthpiece and sucked a lungful of double-apple molasses tobacco smoke.

The café's owner had been a friend of his late father's, and he'd recently been victimized by a group of thugs offering "protection" for his café. Nuri offered to confront the hoodlums on their next visit and show them the error of their ways.

How did his father's friend know to come to *him?* Nuri wondered. They hadn't seen each other in years. Had his reputation really spread that far?

No matter. He would take care of those thugs.

There was a squealing of tires at the curb. Nuri turned to see a familiar pickup truck loaded with six men and three canvas-covered crates.

Nizam was behind the wheel. He called out the window. "Get in. We have a job."

"What's the pay?"

"Trust me. You'll want to do this one."

Nuri glanced at the men sitting in back. They were Nizam's best and most expensive, and he guessed that there was enough artillery under the canvas wraps to fight a small war.

Nuri walked over to Nizam. "CIA? MI6?"

"Does it really matter?"

"Of course not."

"Then get in."

SAQQARA, EGYPT

t was time to move.

Dawson motioned to Sorens. "No Tavak. We go after them. Has Kipler rigged the other charge on the other side of the tomb?"

Sorens nodded. "But why bother? Let's just use the entrance."

"No. There's no way we're going to go barreling down that main corridor. One blast to give us access and one final blast to destroy the tomb once and for all. It's cleaner this way."

Kipler finished setting his charge and gave the thumbs-up sign.

Dawson nodded. "Blow it."

Kipler turned his back to the tomb entrance and twirled his finger to indicate for the others to do the same. He raised a small black box, pressed a button on its top surface.

A muffled explosion opened up a hole in the sand.

Dawson smiled. "See? No major cave-in and we have our very own entrance. Flashlights, everybody. Johnson, you stay out here and keep watch."

Kipler joined them as Dawson, Sorens, and Ali turned on their high-powered flashlights and crawled through the hole. The rubble had formed a makeshift staircase for them to maneuver to the tomb's main level.

"Where's Peseshet's chamber located, Ali?" Dawson asked.

"I'm not sure. It should be right around the corner," Ali gasped. "I can't breathe. I knew we should have come in the main entrance."

"You're not sure? You'd better be right, Ali."

A few minutes later they rounded the corner and through the ruin of stone and debris he caught a glimpse of the gold-flaked mural on the far wall.

"Holy shit, it's actually here," Dawson murmured. "Tavak found her. I shouldn't have—" Kipler stepped forward, but Dawson blocked his path. "Wait a minute. Do you see Tavak?"

Kipler motioned toward the rubble. "No way he survived this."

"You think not? I once saw him survive a—"

Gunshots. Aboveground, outside the tomb.

"What the hell?" He whirled toward the entrance, where pounding footsteps echoed in the next chamber. He and Kipler raised their weapons.

Johnson appeared, running toward them. "Eight men in a truck," he said breathlessly. "Lots of artillery. They could be following me in here."

Dawson muttered a curse as fury tore through him. He had been so close. Close to Peseshet's secrets and close to killing that bastard, Tavak. "You're sure we're that outnumbered?"

Johnson nodded. "And they're too well equipped. I saw at least two AK-47s. They're not Egyptian police. They opened fire as soon as they saw me."

"It doesn't matter who they are. We have to get out of here now. Head for the front entrance of the tomb. They'll probably be following Johnson down the hole we blew." Dawson reached into his bag and pulled out a camera. "Don't stop for anything. Open fire if you see so much as a shadow."

"But our own men are—"

"It doesn't matter. If those bastards take positions inside, we're finished. Move!"

Johnson and Kipler ran through the chamber with their guns ready.

Dawson turned with his camera and squeezed off several photos of the mural wall behind him. He had come prepared to cart it away, but this would have to do. Maybe he could come back later and get a closer look. Dammit!

Are you here, Tavak? Did the bitch give up her secrets to you?

It didn't matter.

Dawson bolted for the entrance, jamming the camera back into his bag even as he checked the ammo cartridge of his semiautomatic. Now that he knew the mural was here, he wouldn't stop until he knew everything it had to reveal. And every instinct was telling him that Tavak was still alive. He wouldn't be cheated for long.

Just a postponement, Tavak.

· · ·

Gunfire. Automatic weapons. At least one was an AK-47, Tavak could tell and there was no mistaking the sharp reports from a pair of M9s. A battle was raging outside the tomb.

But why?

He had heard Charles Dawson's unmistakable voice in the adjacent chamber, then the sound of men running. Dawson wanted to kill him almost as much as he wanted Peseshet's priceless treasure. Why hadn't he tried to follow through?

More running footsteps coming down the corridor toward the chamber where he and Ben lay.

Dawson again?

He slumped to one side and closed his eyes.

"I've found him." Someone was kneeling beside him, turning him over.

In an instant Tavak snapped his arm around the man's neck and jumped to his feet. There were four other men in the chamber, he realized quickly. Before they could react, Tavak had the man's gun and was using him as shield. "Step back. Or I'll blow his head off."

"That's most uncordial of you," a tall, bearded man with an AK-47 cradled in his arm said. "But Abu probably deserves it for being so careless."

Tavak's gaze circled the men in the room. All bronze-skinned, all carrying weapons. "Where's Dawson?"

"If that was the man who was shooting at us outside, I assume he's on his way back to Cairo. He didn't seem eager to stay." He shrugged. "We let him go. Our job was just to see that you were safe."

"Who are you?"

"Nizam. I assume you are John Tavak." He added, "Would you please release Abu. He's looking a little pale. I don't believe he likes that gun at his head."

"Your job? Who sent you?"

Nizam ignored the question as his gaze fell on Ben. "He does not look well." He gestured. "Nuri."

Nuri quickly knelt beside Ben and opened a large medical kit. He prepped a hypodermic needle.

"Don't touch him," Tavak said. "Or your friend, Abu, will be on his way to paradise."

"It is only midiocane," Nuri said. "He's gone into shock. If I wanted to kill him, I'd do it with something less subtle." He looked at Tavak. "May I?"

Tavak hesitated. He wasn't sure what was going on, but he had to rely on instinct. He slowly nodded.

Nuri injected a clear substance into Ben's chest.

"Are you a medic?"

Nuri nodded. "By talent, not occupation. We need to get your friend to a hospital."

"Will he be okay?"

"Difficult to say. But we'll get him the very best help."

"We mean you no harm," Nizam said. "You have very strong allies, Mr. Tavak. We've been well paid to see that you come out of this tomb alive."

Tavak believed him. Take a chance. He released Abu and pushed him away from him. "You still haven't told me by whom."

"My employers prefer that I keep their names confidential," Nizam said. "Now it is time we left this place. We not only have to worry about the Egyptian police but the return of the man who was so eager to kill you."

Two of Nizam's men unfolded a stretcher made of canvas and long wooden dowels. Under Nuri's direction, they gently moved Ben onto it.

Tavak glanced at the mural of Peseshet. Nizam was right, Dawson might very well return. If he'd had time, he might have photographed the mural, but there was a chance he might think it necessary to get a closer look. He'd not gotten what he wanted, and the bastard would never give up. "Why don't you go on to the hospital with Ben? I'd like to stay here for a little while."

"You wish to confront your enemy." Nizam shook his head. "That was not my orders. You must come with us."

"Must? That doesn't sound very friendly."

"I am most friendly." He smiled and gestured with the AK-47. "Come along, my friend. Let me complete my mission with nothing but the happiest of endings."

FOUR

low down, Rachel. You'll make it."

Simon practically ran to keep up with Rachel's long, determined strides. He moved her garment bag from one shoulder to the other as they rounded a corner in the airport's main concourse.

Rachel shook her head. "You know how horrific the security lines can be here. My plane could be halfway to Cairo by the time I get past the metal detector."

"You're exaggerating."

"Only a little." She checked her phone. "Norton has already e-mailed me a preliminary dossier on this John Tavak guy. He must be on an NSA watch list."

"Either that, or they have dossiers on everybody. My money is on option number two." Simon stared at her for a moment. "Is this really a good idea? Just forty-eight hours ago you took a bullet. Now you're flying across the world to confront some hacker."

"Don't try to talk me out of it. He's not just 'some hacker.'"

"You don't know *who* he is."

"I know that few people in the world could have pulled off what he did. You know more about Jonesy than almost anyone on the planet. Could *you* have tapped in from the outside?"

"Look, I have questions for this guy, too. And obviously so does Norton. But we both know it's more than that for you. He's stolen from you, and now he's trying to use you."

"Don't you think I know that?"

"Then let Norton handle him. There's no reason why you have to go."

"I need to talk to Tavak. If there's even a possibility he was telling the truth in his message to me, I would—"

"I know. I know. I just don't want you to get hurt."

She made a face. "Funny thing to say to a woman after she's just been picked off by a high-powered rifle."

"You know what I mean."

"I do know, Simon. And I appreciate it. But I have to do this, and I need you to finish plugging the data leaks in our system and find any back-doors Tavak set up. I promised to bring Norton back up to a hundred percent immediately."

"How are you going to pull that off?"

"Beats me. But I have a long plane ride to think about it."

"What can I do to help?"

"I don't trust the info Norton is feeding me about

81

John Tavak. I want you to tap into the CIA and Interpol and see what you can find out."

"That's not going to be easy. It would take an Einstein to get past the firewalls they've put up against security breaches." He added slyly, "Who do you think I am? John Tavak?"

"I hope not. I don't need another Tavak to deal with. Just do your best."

"And my best will be superb," Simon said. "Anything else?"

"I still haven't heard from Dr. Carson at Allie's foundation about his opinion on the information regarding the cell regeneration that Tavak sent me. I told him to contact you while I was in flight."

He shook his head. "And you're going without even knowing if that cure has even the slightest possibility of being legitimate?"

"I'm not going to have regrets about not moving fast enough. There's no time." Not for Tavak. Not for Allie. "One last favor. Allie. Watch over her. Try to keep her from worrying about me."

"Did you tell her you were leaving?"

She shook her head. "I'll call her from Cairo. I thought maybe you could—"

"Coward."

"Yes." Her pace quickened. "What could I say? Raise her hopes about a cure when Tavak may be playing me for a sucker? Tell her I'm going to throw in with a criminal on the faint chance that he can help her?"

"No, she'd feel guilty as hell." He paused. "Because we both know you're doing something crazy."

"Crazy or not, I'm doing it." She stopped and turned to face him. She had to steady her voice. "Allie's showing signs of fading. I won't let her go. I don't care if it's a wild-goose chase. There's nothing I won't do to keep her alive."

"Rachel."

"And don't look at me like that. I don't want pity. I want help. Give it to me, Simon."

"You've got it." He cleared his throat. "I'll take care of her as much as she'll let me. But in that gentle way, she's as tough as you. I don't know which one I'd dread most being up against."

"Me," Rachel said. "E-mail me anything you can find out about Tavak." She took her garment bag from him, turned away, and headed for the security gates. "Or I'll call you from Cairo."

ARDMORE UNIVERSITY
11:20 A.M.

The news was blaring on the radio when Detective Finley drove onto the campus.

Dammit, the local media was playing the event like any other campus shooting, the work of a random psychopath. Hundreds of parents had converged on the campus to take their children home, and although the school was still open, classes were running at only a 70 percent attendance level.

Finley didn't think there was anything random about the shooting. There had been only one shot. One target. When the shooter thought he'd put Kirby down, he'd gotten the hell away without anyone seeing him.

Definitely not your typical blow-the-hell-out-of-everybody-and-everything-and-finish-with-the-gun-in-your-mouth campus attack. When had schools replaced postal-sorting facilities as the rampaging psychopath's venue of choice?

Finley parked in front of the large white trailer that served as the Ardmore University campus police headquarters. He hopped up the three short steps and opened the door into a sterile reception area. Before he could speak to the receptionist, Gonzalez appeared in a doorway.

"I just came from the hospital," Finley said. "Rachel Kirby checked herself out."

"What?"

"Against doctor's orders. No one seems to know where she is."

Gonzalez sighed. "Great. I'm not doing any better. Come back and take a look."

Finley followed him down a narrow hallway to a dim A/V center, where two security officers watched a bank of a dozen monitors. Every few moments, each monitor changed to a different view of the campus.

Gonzalez motioned to one of the officers, a petite

young woman with round wire-rimmed spectacles. "This is Tricia Denton. She was here when Rachel Kirby was shot. And, no, she's not a witness."

Finley shook her hand. "You didn't see anything?"

"Not until Dr. Kirby fell." Tricia gestured to her control panel. "I was able to pan and zoom every camera in the area, but I couldn't find the shooter."

"He probably blended in with the students coming and going. We'll need to comb through each one of your feeds. You do record them, don't you?"

"Each video-camera feed goes to an array of hard drives. It's automatically kept for forty-eight hours, but within that time we can preserve any recordings indefinitely."

"Tell me you did that."

"Of course. The minute we realized what had happened, we locked all the recordings down." The woman and Detective Gonzalez shared a quick look.

Trouble. "So what's the problem?"

Gonzalez grimaced. "The recordings are gone."

"What?"

"They're gone. Wiped clean."

Finley turned back to Tricia. "How?"

"I don't know. We lost six camera feeds from three different hard drives. Only in the area where your shooter was."

"The recorders were sabotaged?"

Tricia bit her lip. "If they were, someone sure knew how to cover their tracks. The machines are in a locked closet at the end of the hall. The closet door and the recorders don't appear to have been tampered with. And the recorders work fine—it's just that we're missing everything from a few hours before and after the shooting. Whoever did it had to know just what machines to target."

Finley cursed under his breath. "Who has access to that closet?"

Gonzalez answered. "Only the head of campus security. I've already talked to one of our tech guys, and he's clueless as the rest of us. He's familiar with this system, and he says no one could have done this without some high-level know-how. He says that even the company that designed it might have a problem pulling this off."

Finley pulled out his phone. "Okay. Then let's have somebody take a closer look at those machines. If it really takes high-level know-how, there can't be that many people capable of it. Let's figure out who could have done it and where they could have learned."

"Gotcha."

"And let's look at the camera feeds that were knocked out. If nothing else, it tells us where the shooter didn't want us to see. We'll focus our canvass on those areas and see if anybody saw something."

"Anything else?"

"Not unless we can locate Rachel Kirby," Finley said grimly. "I have an idea that she's in more trouble than she realizes."

CAIRO, EGYPT

'm not saying anything more, Polk," Tavak said. "I've told you I didn't breach any U.S. security. That wasn't my agenda. I'm no terrorist." He looked the CIA agent directly in the eye. "And you know it. This interrogation has been bullshit." He glanced at Nuri sitting on a chair across from him. "If you'd really believed I was a threat, you wouldn't be letting these mercenaries hold me. My ass would be on the way to Langley."

"You're in no position to refuse anything," James Polk said sourly. "You're in deep trouble. Blowing up a tomb, destroying precious artifacts."

"My, my. And yet all you can ask about is my hacking expertise. I find that interesting." He shook his head. "But not interesting enough to make me answer any more questions. Go back to whoever sent you and tell them to do whatever they want. I never give something for nothing, particularly information." He turned his back on the agent. "Nuri, will you show this gentleman out?"

Nuri chuckled. "It's only one room. I think he can find his way."

Tavak heard a muttered curse from Polk, then the slam of the door.

"You made him angry," Nuri said. "Better you than me. The CIA makes me nervous. I like everything straight and clear. I never know what the CIA's going to do."

"Neither do I. Then I take it that you're not working for the CIA?"

"I work for Nizam. That way, he's the one who has to worry."

"Sounds like a good arrangement." Tavak restlessly paced the length of the windowless ten-foot-by-twelve-foot room. He had been blindfolded before they even left the tomb site and taken to what appeared to be a single-family home. As in much of Cairo, there were sounds of heavy traffic outside. He smelled strong citrus and cabbage odors wafting from the other side of the room's only door.

He turned to Nuri, who was leaning back in a small chair. "How much longer do I have to stay here?"

Nuri took a bite from a large, juicy date. "Difficult to say. We have our instructions."

"Instructions from whom?"

"I assumed you would know, Mr. Tavak. Do you have so many friends who would go to such trouble for you? Would you like some dates? They're quite tasty."

"No, thanks. I want to see Ben Leonard."

"He's in a hospital five minutes from here. The last I heard, he was doing quite well. As soon as we have clearance, I will take you there myself."

"Clearance? Great. Dammit, you've kept me here for the last eight hours. Why? What are we waiting for?"

Nuri smiled. "I realize that you were hoping to get back to the tomb. You thought this Dawson might return, and you wanted to do painful and lethal harm to your enemy. I understand revenge. I approve of it. But you must understand that we must do what we must to make a living."

"I only understand that Dawson and his men are free and had all the time in the world to go back and examine that mural. While I'm still under lock and key."

"Very sad." Nuri patted his shoulder-holstered firearm. "And with an armed guard. Quite ironic. That's the word, isn't it? 'Ironic'?"

"That's the word, all right."

"You're lucky the CIA didn't turn over the interrogations to our local officials. They are not bound by your human-rights laws."

"The CIA always has its own agenda, and evidently having me tortured or beheaded wasn't on the current one."

Nuri beamed. "That's very good news."

"Better news if you'd let me go."

"It would be my pleasure. But unfortunately, you'll be here until at least tomorrow."

"Tomorrow?"

"You are to have another visitor. A young

woman. She's on her way from the U.S." He tilted his head. "You're smiling. Is this pleasing to you?"

"It could be. Intriguing anyway."

"I think her name is Kirby."

Tavak started to laugh.

"Is something funny?"

"No. Not at all." It was what he had expected. Through the anger and frustration he had felt at not being able to go after Dawson, there had also been the underlying impatience to confront Rachel Kirby. He realized that he had been almost disappointed that Rachel had not put in an appearance yet. Now he could feel a tingle of eagerness and exhilaration surge through him. "There's nothing funny about Rachel Kirby. The interrogation I got at the hands of that CIA agent will be child's play compared to the treatment I'll get from her."

Nuri's gaze narrowed on his face. "But you look forward to it." He smiled. "I think you're a very strange man, John Tavak."

He won't talk," Polk said, when Norton picked up the phone. "And I'm not about to pressure him any more than I have already. Have your own agency do your dirty work. I've done a cover-up on the explosion at the tomb, and that's going to be dicey enough for us to manage. The Egyptian government isn't fond of people destroying their treasures. They need those tombs for tourist revenue."

"I didn't have anyone on-site," Norton said.

"And I promise you'll get a return favor when you need it."

"You'd better. We're too busy to run around and plug your damn security leaks." Polk paused, then said maliciously, "What a pity the NSA data files are so unsecured that a hacker can breeze right in and screw you."

Norton wanted to hang up on the bastard. If there had been any other way to tap Tavak for information before Rachel Kirby got there, he would have done it in a heartbeat. And it had been for nothing. Now he owed this CIA bastard, and he would probably take it out of Norton's blood. "It wasn't our computer, and evidently Tavak is fairly remarkable."

"I don't know about that, but the son of a bitch is cold as an iceberg," Polk said. "And he told me to go back to whoever sent me and tell them he never gives something for nothing. So I'm telling you. Go after him yourself." He hung up.

Norton muttered a curse beneath his breath. Polk didn't realize how much he wanted to go after Tavak. Tavak had been able to break into that computer, and that was a prize beyond belief. If he had Tavak's information, he'd be able to control Rachel Kirby. God, he hated the idea of that bitch being able to call the shots.

But he would have to put up with it for a little longer. He could be patient. Let Rachel Kirby handle Tavak and dig the information out of him.

Polk had called him an iceberg and Kirby had all the force of a *Titanic* waiting to happen. He'd just give them a chance to collide and destroy each other.

Rachel's phone rang as she was leaving Cairo customs.

Simon.

"What have you got for me, Simon?" she asked when she picked up.

"John Tavak, age thirty-eight, unmarried, no children. Born to an affluent upper-class family; father Randolph Tavak, stockbroker, mother Nancy Carter Tavak, socialite, jet-setter. Only child."

"And this is the son of a bitch who stole my processing cycles?"

"Almost certainly. Because it turns out Tavak is something of a phenomenon. He was a child prodigy whose IQ couldn't even be measured. He was taking classes at Harvard by the age of ten. His teachers said with proper guidance and encouragement, he could be another Einstein. His problem-solving ability was astonishing." He paused. "Infiltrating Jonesy and stealing our cycles must have been a piece of cake for him."

"It was *not,*" Rachel said. "I don't care if he was a second Einstein, I made sure that it was almost impossible to do what he did. He would have had to work damn hard at it. And why would he want to do it anyway? If he had a background like that, why steal anything? He could make any amount of money he wanted."

"Sometimes money doesn't matter. Evidently it didn't to him. According to the report, his parents treated him like some kind of prize showpiece to display to friends and business clients. He got tired of it and walked away from the good life when he was eighteen and never looked back. He disappeared from the think tank where he was the star attraction and set out to taste the world. Or maybe I should say gobble it up. In the next five years he did everything from fighting as a mercenary in Africa to smuggling artifacts out of China."

"He has a criminal record?"

"No, only under suspicion. But the report from Interpol was pretty damn conclusive."

"Is he still smuggling?"

"Not for a long time." Simon hesitated. "Considering his later activities, I'd guess he got very bored during those first years. It might have been different experiences but not much challenge. Even as a kid he needed constant stimulation and was something of an adrenaline junkie. He was a mountain climber, into powerboat racing, a pilot. At one time he made his living repossessing airplanes."

"What?"

"He was paid to repossess fighter planes for manufacturers that didn't receive payment from the third-world countries which had purchased them. Extremely risky since he had to sneak into military bases and literally steal the planes back."

"Crazy."

"And profitable. It pays upward of a million dollars a plane. But he only does that occasionally these days. Lately he's been working at solving archaeological and technical problems. He can read hieroglyphics and several other ancient scripts and has become something of an expert on antiquities. His focus is recovering lost or stolen objects, kind of a high-tech repo man."

"Like stealing those planes?"

"Not exactly. If a company buys a defense network and refuses to pay for it, Tavak finds a way to shut it down until the money is paid. He also tracks down priceless objects that may have been pilfered from museums and private owners during time of civil unrest and steals them back. Very lucrative, very dangerous."

"My God, he really is an adrenaline junkie."

"Without a doubt. Maybe you can use that. He's going to be difficult to handle. You're going to need all the firepower you can find."

"I'll handle him. I'll stick his ass in jail if he doesn't cooperate."

"Good luck. After I hang up, I'll send you a photo of Tavak."

"I'll be seeing him in person within the hour."

She paused. "Have you heard from Dr. Carson at Allie's foundation?"

"Yes, but I probably shouldn't tell you what he said about that excerpt you sent him."

She tensed. "He thought it was bullshit?"

"No, he was thrilled. Off-the-charts excited. Remember that crushed 'bone of Horus' that was listed as a primary ingredient in the cure? Turns out that's what ancient Egyptians called magnetic lodestone. Just in the past couple of years, the University of Miami has come out with some research that suggests that magnetic nanoparticles, or MNPs, can stimulate growth in damaged central nervous system axons."

Rachel almost had to remind herself to breathe. "If this pans out, Peseshet may have been almost five thousand years ahead of her time."

"Maybe. But there's a lot more to her cure that we don't have. As you know, the body sends chemical signals to inhibit growth of damaged neurons in the central nervous system. But if her cure delivers what this tablet promises, she may have discovered a way to stop those chemical signals. It could be a combination of plant extracts, sediments, or who knows what. In any case, Carson wants more."

"I don't have more."

"That's what I told him. But I knew after you got Carson's input that you wouldn't stop until you did."

"You're damn right I won't." Hope. For the first time in years, a glimmer of hope in the distance. "Tell Carson to get back to me if he thinks he's got anything. Have you been in touch with Allie?"

"Yes, she said for you to call her so that she can tear you apart." He added, "And since I did the dirty deed and broke the news, you'd better do it. Someone else besides me needs to get it in the neck."

"I'll call her. Thanks, Simon."

"Call me if you need me." He hung up.

She stood there for a moment while the news Simon had given her sank in. Hope. Carson was brilliant and not prone to jumping on the bandwagon if there wasn't some basis for doing it. There was a possibility that what she was doing here wasn't completely irrational.

He wants more.

So did Rachel, and that need was a deep and terrible hunger.

All right, then start moving. Reach out and take what Allie needed.

She pressed the button to access the photo Simon had sent her. It was a snapshot of Tavak standing beside an airplane, dressed casually, dark hair ruffled by the wind. He looked younger than thirty-eight, she thought. He was tall and deeply tanned, with sun wrinkles at the corner of his eyes. His nose was too long, his lips too full, but his blue eyes glittered with life. He was not a handsome man, but the vitality and intelligence in his expression were almost mesmerizing.

High impact, she thought.

Everything about Tavak had been high impact since that first moment she had opened that e-mail.

Ignore it. She closed her phone and headed for the exit. It didn't matter if Tavak was a power house. She had met strong men before and stood toe-to-toe with them. Tavak would be no different.

FIVE

Rachel hesitated as she stood before the small house to which Norton's instructions had sent her.

Knock or just go inside and face the bastard?

Knock. Norton had said Tavak was guarded, and she didn't want to surprise them and possibly get shot.

The small, dark man who opened the door beamed at her. "You are Miss Kirby, yes? I am Nuri. That is John Tavak at the table. We have been waiting for you." He flung the door wide. "He has been very impatient. Such ingratitude. I give him food, I play chess with him, I tell him interesting stories about my family, and still he wants to leave me."

"Your family obviously numbers more than a small city," Tavak said. "After you went to the second generation you lost me." He stood up and inclined his head. "I couldn't be happier to see you, Rachel Kirby."

High impact, she had thought when she had seen his photo. But seeing Tavak in person, she realized that description had been an understatement. His eyes were electric blue in his tanned face, and the aura that surrounded him was also electric. He was dressed in a white shirt, dusty brown boots, and jeans, and that tall, muscular body possessed a sort of tough elegance.

"Don't be happy." She slammed the door behind her. "Because I'm not in the least happy to see you, Tavak. You're a thief and a sneak and the worst kind of criminal. I'd like to cut your throat."

He smiled. "But then I wouldn't be any use to you at all." He drew out a chair for her. "Won't you sit down? Nuri, could we get a glass of wine for the lady?"

"Certainly." Nuri got another glass from the cabinet. "My uncle grew the grapes for this wine. Did I tell you that, Tavak?"

He made a face. "Many times." He took the chessboard from the table and set it on the bed. "And about his wife who divorced him and his daughter he sent to the Sorbonne and is going to change the world."

"She will, you know." Nuri poured wine into the glass and set it on the table. "She's very smart. She only needs a chance. Sit down. Sit down. Would you like some fruit?"

"No," Rachel said impatiently. "I don't want wine. I don't want fruit. I want to talk to Tavak alone. Will you wait outside?"

"That's discourteous," Tavak said. "Nuri is our host."

Nuri chuckled. "That is true." He patted the gun in his holster. "I must protect you from her. She seems very fierce."

"Get out," she said through bared teeth.

Nuri's smile didn't waver, but he started for the door. "As you wish. I have orders to obey you without question. Be gentle with him. He owes me money from that last chess game."

She watched the door shut behind him before she turned back to Tavak. "Talk to me."

"Where shall I start? Oh yes, I'm eternally grateful for you being so prompt in meeting my need. It was close. Very close."

"I don't want your gratitude. You know why I came. I had to find out if you were telling the truth about that tablet or just making up a story to manipulate my emotions." She paused. "I don't like being manipulated, Tavak. It makes me want to be ugly. And I can be very ugly."

He chuckled. "So I've heard. The stories about you are definitely scary."

"They didn't intimidate you enough to keep you from hacking into Jonesy."

"No one else had the power I needed so I decided to brave the dragon."

"Were you telling the truth about this Peseshet and the cure she discovered? Regeneration of the central nervous system?"

"Absolutely. As far as I know. I won't know for certain until I actually find the tablet." He paused. "Or tablets. I'll be satisfied with one cure, but it would be a bonanza if we found others. As I told you, her prime focus wasn't cellular regeneration."

"But that's my prime focus, my only focus."

"I realize that," he said quietly. "But this is something that could have a profound impact for millions of people across the entire spectrum of nervous system diseases. I'm talking Alzheimer's, Lou Gehrig's Disease, Huntington's . . . not to mention the fact that it might enable paraplegics to walk again."

"Pardon me if I don't get too excited, but over the years I've learned to adopt a wait-and-see attitude toward any kind of miracle cure."

"I'm sure you've already transmitted that little teaser I sent you to your Dr. Carson for an opinion. What did he say?"

"You can guess what he said."

He nodded. "Otherwise, you'd be much too practical to go off on a wild-goose chase like this. And how is your sister?"

"None of your business." Her hands clenched at her sides. "Now how can I get my hands on that tablet so that I can see for myself whether or not it's a piece of crap?"

"That's the question." He sat down at the table and gestured to the chair across from him. "And it's not one I can answer to your satisfaction in a few sentences. You can stand there and glare at me, but it's not going to make explanations go any faster. Why don't you sit down and have a glass of Nuri's wine? It's not bad."

She didn't move.

He lifted his glass to his lips. "I know that standing over me is supposed to give you a psychological advantage, but it won't work. Because you don't need an advantage. I pay my debts."

"You couldn't pay for all the cycles you've stolen from my projects."

"You never know. I told you that from the beginning I was planning on sharing information if I found the tablet."

"And I'm supposed to believe that?"

"Probably not." He leaned back and stretched his legs before him. "Just thought I'd put it on the record."

"Give me answers. I could have you thrown in jail. Norton with the NSA didn't like having you infiltrate Jonesy. All it would take is a word from me, and they'd—"

"NSA? I was wondering who you used to spring me. The CIA was amazingly lackluster in their questioning. Norton asked a favor, and they sent in the cavalry." He tilted his head, thinking about it.

"He moved fast. Does he always jump when you snap your fingers?"

"You'll know if I don't find out what you know about that tablet."

"You're tense." He pushed the glass Nuri had poured for her a few inches. "The wine will relax you. I promise that I won't think it's a victory that we're drinking together."

She stared at him in frustration. He was totally relaxed, totally casual in his confidence. Threats had not fazed him at all. Go at it from another direction. She sat down, her back arrow straight in the chair. "What do you want? What can I give you?"

He studied her. "You'd give me anything, the whole damn world, wouldn't you? You shouldn't be so transparent, Rachel."

"There comes a time when putting up barriers doesn't matter any longer." She stared him in the eye. "And yes, name it. If I don't have it, I'll get it for you."

"You do like to pamper a man, don't you?" His gaze wandered to the bandage on her temple. "You're hurt. What happened?"

"That doesn't matter. What can I pay you? If you don't have the tablet, you must have an idea where it is. Dammit, you've used up enough of Jonesy's cycles to remap the human genome about five times over."

"Information can only take you so far. After that,

it's analysis and working out the puzzle." He sipped his wine. "You know that, Rachel."

"Yes. Give me the information, and I'll do the rest."

"That's just what I'd expect from you." He added, "And from Peseshet. Did I tell you how much you're alike? I've been working so close to both of you in the last months that I feel as if I know you."

"You don't know me."

"You're wrong. I think I know the basics, and I'm looking forward to finding out the rest." He held up his hand as she started to speak. "I know. Information. Okay, here goes. I told you that Peseshet was the overseer of an institute of female doctors at about 2500 B.C. All knowledge of her existence was lost until her son's tomb was unearthed in 1929. Even that gave us only her name and profession. Nothing else was known about her until recently."

"I couldn't find anything more, period."

"Because the other info was discovered only a few months ago by Arthur Jamerson, the curator of a small museum in Brighton, England. Jamerson was more ambitious for himself than for either history or the benefits to mankind. The museum's Egyptian displays were totally unimportant. They had been in that tiny museum in Brighton for over a hundred years. Among the artifacts was a false door from a tomb that had been virtually forgotten for over a hundred years."

"A false door?"

"A wall that looked like a door. These tombs, or mastabas, almost always featured false doors with elaborate carved reliefs. The Egyptians believed that this representation of a door would allow the deceased to pass to the afterlife. They're fairly common, and the Egyptian government sold them by the hundreds in the early twentieth century. There was nothing special about this one until technology finally caught up to that Brighton museum. Jamerson had the wall X-rayed and discovered that it encased another wall. Carved on the secreted wall was Peseshet's story recounted by one of her physician disciples, Natifah." He paused. "And a portion of a cure of some sort. Something to do with healing nerves that had thought to have been destroyed. Cellular regeneration. Remember, Peseshet practiced while the pyramids were being built. There were undoubtedly many construction accidents, so she had a steady stream of patients on whom to try out her treatments. And, most likely, many opportunities for autopsies to observe how her treatments did or didn't work."

"But it's only a portion of a cure. Dammit, that's *nothing*."

"No, that's a start," he said. "And enough that Jamerson copied down the procedure and sent it to an associate, Ted Mills, who was head of a pharmaceutical company in the U.S. Mills was cautiously excited. He wanted to know where the rest of the formula could be found. That was enough for Jamerson. He knew how much money medical breakthroughs could bring a man. He decided to go after the big prize. He falsified his X-ray results so that, as far as anyone at his museum knew, their Egyptian exhibit remained just as unremarkable as everyone always assumed it was. Jamerson searched until he found someone who he thought might possibly be able to find out more about the rest of the formula."

"You?"

"Me." He inclined his head. "I'm sure you have a dossier on me by now and know my credentials are unique. I met with Jamerson, and he handed over the transcription on the Natifah mastaba wall to me."

"What did he pay you to take the job?"

"Less than I'm worth. But the possibilities intrigued me."

"I want to see that transcript of the message on the mastaba wall."

"Of course."

"Now."

He shook his head. "Eventually."

"I'll go to Jamerson and get it."

"It would be a long trip. I imagine he resides in hell these days. Greed and corruption aren't looked upon kindly at the pearly gates."

She stiffened. "He's dead? You?"

"No, I took his job. I never kill the goose that lays the platinum egg. He was killed by Charles Dawson, the bastard you were so kind to save me from last night." He scowled. "But they wouldn't let me go back after him. I'm not pleased about that. Dammit, there's too good a chance that he probably went back to that tomb."

"I don't give a damn what you're pleased about. Norton was supposed to save your life and pen you up for me. That's all."

"I'll bet you'll give a damn before very long. You'll probably feel as pissed off that Dawson is still walking around as I do before this is over."

"Why? Just who is this Charles Dawson?"

"Dr. Charles Ansel Dawson. He has several degrees, one of which is medical. He's very bright, has all the ethics and conscience of a cobra, and is completely egotistical."

"Sounds like you."

"No. We differ on a number of fronts. I do have a few grains of conscience."

"So you say. Is Dawson after the Peseshet cure, too?"

Tavak nodded. "He's the hired gun for Ted Mills. That's what he does for a living. He's principally a cleanup man. When pharmaceutical companies get into hot water abroad for illegal practices, they hire Dawson to come in and make sure that their names and reputations aren't compromised. He does anything he has to do to clean up their dirty laundry."

He shrugged. "And sometimes his cleanup is worse than the filth the pharmaceutical companies spread."

"And why did Dawson kill Jamerson?"

"As I said, he was hired by Jamerson's buddy, that pharmaceutical executive, Ted Mills, to uncover the same information Jamerson hired me to dig out. Dawson's first stop was Jamerson, and he wasn't gentle in his questioning. Jamerson died of a heart attack, but he'd obviously been beaten and had two ribs broken. Since Dawson has been on my trail since his death, it's logical to assume Jamerson told him everything he told me." He grimaced. "But Dawson didn't have the advantage of having Jonesy to help him, so he had to rely on my doing the work. That bloodsucking vampire would like that better anyway."

"You know him?"

"Oh yes, we had a run-in a few years ago. It wasn't a pleasant encounter for either of us, but I came out better than he did."

"What kind of run-in?"

"Nasty business. A British drug company had a manufacturing plant in Bolivia. It contaminated the groundwater and soil in several villages. Hundreds died. Dawson and his team descended on the area with a checkbook and enough firepower to change people's perceptions about what really happened. Suddenly it was announced that an abandoned pre–World War II cleaning-products factory was the culprit, and that long-forgotten underground waste-disposal tanks had ruptured."

"Long forgotten?"

"It's difficult to remember something that never existed in the first place. Local officials backed up the story. Anyone who didn't take the bribes was murdered."

Rachel shook her head. "And how did you get involved?"

"The United Nations was offering multimillion-dollar rewards for evidence of just this kind of corporate abuse. I got wind of it and decided it would be an interesting challenge."

"Naturally," she said sarcastically.

"I went down there and stayed alive long enough to get the evidence I needed. It cost the company billions. And for a long time it damaged Dawson's reputation as a corporate fix-it man. He was totally humiliated, and he's still having repercussions from it. He'd like nothing better than to see me dead."

"He can take a number." Rachel thought for a moment. "Mills Pharmaceuticals has never shown any interest in regenerative central nervous system research. It's just not their focus."

"Of course not. If Peseshet's cure works as well as I think it could, it will earn billions for the company that brings it to market. But Mills makes tens of billions every year with the medicines they sell now. Look at their portfolio: you'll find a range of analgesics and anticonvulsants, all designed to treat symptoms of nervous system damage. And their patients are customers for life, not just the few months it might take to administer a cure."

"You think Mills Pharmaceuticals wants the cure so they can bury it?"

"Yes, and to keep it out of anyone else's hands who could bury *them*. But don't take my word for it. Do the research. I think you'll come to the same conclusion." Tavak tossed back the rest of his wine. "And now I think I've given you enough to keep you content for a while. It's time you started making me happy."

"Are you crazy? I am *not* contented. You've told me practically zilch."

"It's all relative. You know more than you did when you came in here." He pushed back his chair and stood up. "And you did say you'd give me anything I want. Right now, I want you to call Norton and tell Nuri to go away and let me go back to my hotel. I was able to take photos of the mosaic of Peseshet and the hieroglyphics beside it. I sent it to my computer here in Cairo to be translated and possibly decoded if there was anything hidden in the script."

"That's a hell of a complicated program."

"That's what Jonesy thought when I asked him to develop it for me. I thought he'd never get the hang of it. But give him enough cycles . . ."

"You son of a bitch."

"Anyway. I'll let you come with me. I'm sure you'll be interested to see if Jonesy did what he was supposed to do."

"'Let'?" He knew she wouldn't let him go and check that program without her. "Yes, I'm going." She stood up. "And I'm not telling Nuri to go away. He's going to follow us to the hotel and make sure that you don't try to slip away."

He nodded. "Smart move. I'm not above trying to regain my independence, but it won't be before I see that readout." He grabbed his backpack and headed for the door. "And actually we've been together so long I'm becoming attached to Nuri. Not that he wouldn't blow me away with that fire-power he's carrying, but I believe he'd regret it for at least an hour or two."

will stay here." Nuri leaned against the wall across from the hotel-room door Tavak was unlocking. "Unless I'm needed, Ms. Kirby? You have only to call and I will charge in and take care of disposing of him. After he pays me what he owes me, of course."

"Of course." Tavak opened the door and stood aside to let Rachel enter first. "That goes without saying." He turned on the overhead light and dropped his backpack on the floor before he shut the door. "Stay where you are. I need to check the room out."

"Why?"

"Because Dawson has had almost twenty-four hours to do any damn thing he wanted to do." Tavak took out a small device and moved carefully around the room. "And one of the first things would be to hit this room if he hadn't already done it before he went to the tomb."

She watched him run the device over the windows and closet door. "What kind of hit?" Then she realized what he was talking about. "An explosive?"

"It's what he used in the tomb. I'm sure he still had cyclotol enough for a little job like this."

Fear surged through her as she realized this ordinary hotel room could be a death trap. "Wouldn't it have gone off when you unlocked the door?"

"No, it wasn't the door. I set up a signal device that would have gone off if the lock mechanism had been tampered with." He glanced at her. "Would you like to wait outside with Nuri?"

"No, I would not." She moistened her lips. "Just do what you have to do, and let's check that readout."

"I didn't think you'd let me out of your sight."

"What's that detector you're using?"

"It's a sensor that reads particulates in the air—the same way bomb-sniffing dogs do." He ran the device over the lamp on the bedside table, then turned it on and checked the area behind the table. "There are about nineteen thousand odors associated with explosives. This detector works very well, and it isn't affected by distractions and fatigue as dogs are."

"Do you always prepare your hotel rooms to be bombproof?"

"I try."

"That's pretty drastic. There must be a lot of people who dislike you."

"Only one would be enough." He checked the bathroom door, then opened it. "One like you, Rachel."

"I wouldn't plant an explosive . . . unless you tried to set me up. Unless you kept me from finding help for my sister."

"Unless." He came out of the bathroom. "That word makes me uneasy."

"It should."

"Well, I can't find anything that seems suspicious." He grinned. "Which makes me suspicious." He moved toward the desk occupied by the laptop and a small six-inch-square external hard drive. "Let's see if Natifah sent us anything we can use." He ran the small detector over the desk area and flipped open the computer. "Better still, let's see if Jonesy was able to decode anything."

"What's the external hard drive for?"

"It's Jonesy's decoding program. It was using too much memory, so I put it on a separate hard drive." He pulled up the transmission that revealed his photo of Peseshet in the tomb. "Here she is.

Your first glimpse of Peseshet. Looks arrogant as hell, doesn't she?"

"Yes, but I doubt if she posed for it. It's just the way she was perceived."

"Perception is everything. Whoever created that image thought she was either a goddess or a Pharaoh." He zoomed in on her face. "And if she saved the life of Kontar, the man who occupied that tomb, he probably worshipped her as if she were both. And you're right, she didn't pose for it. She was dead by the time this tomb was built. Natifah was undoubtedly the one who told the man who built it how Peseshet should be portrayed and what should be written on the wall."

"Natifah?"

"Remember? She was the physician who carved the story of Peseshet on that mastaba wall in Brighton. She was one of her disciples and evidently was chosen by Peseshet to hide her formulas from the Pharaoh. Pretty difficult since she was on the run herself."

"Why? I thought you said the Pharaoh appointed Peseshet the head of his institute of female doctors."

"He did and was elated at her success. She was a jewel in his crown. He sent her and the other doctors to all the countries in the civilized world to show them the power and brilliance of his court. Peseshet became famous and a very valuable resource since the Pharaoh could barter their services to foreign leaders in exchange for goods, access to trade routes, or whatever else he could hold them up for. As she continued to make medical discoveries, his prices skyrocketed." Tavak zoomed in on the hieroglyphics on the wall beside Peseshet's mosaic. "At some point Peseshet rebelled and told him she wanted to give away her formulas and procedures to whoever needed them."

Rachel shook her head. "That wasn't very smart of your 'brilliant' doctor."

"No, but he thought he had the solution. He'd forced her to give him copies of all her research work. Now all he had to do was rid himself of a troublesome insurgent before she gave away his precious secrets. He ordered his soldiers to hunt down and kill Peseshet and all the other women doctors, which they did with great efficiency. As far as we know, only Natifah survived the bloodbath."

"It's sickening."

"In his eyes, he was a god, and they had tried to take something from him. So he let loose his lightning. Only later did he discover that Peseshet hadn't given him and his personal physicians the entirety of her cures. She had left out some vital ingredients and processes in all of them."

"Good for her." She frowned. "But maybe if the Pharaoh had gotten the right formulas, we wouldn't have to be searching for them now."

"Or maybe he would have kept the secrets and

had them buried with him. After all, he considered them as belonging to him to take to the next world if he pleased." He frowned. "I can't see anything that could be encoded here. Let me check and see if Jonesy found anything . . ." He typed in an access code and waited. "It's not responding. This is damn slow going."

Rachel waited for a couple minutes, staring at the blank monitor screen before she asked, "So before Peseshet died, she told Natifah to hide her secrets from the Pharaoh?"

"Yes, but she also told her that the knowledge must not be lost. That she had to find a way to cheat him, yet give her legacy to those who needed it. So Natifah set out to do what she'd been commanded to do. She couldn't risk just hiding the tablets in a single place. Their location had to be a puzzle so complicated that no one in Pharaoh's court would be able to put the pieces together. So, like Hansel and Gretel she started scattering bread crumbs of information that would eventually bring someone to the tablets."

"If I remember correctly, Hansel and Gretel were almost eaten by the witch before they had the opportunity to make a try at getting home," Rachel said dryly.

"Yes." He smiled. "That comparison must have been a Freudian slip. Ben and I were almost devoured by Dawson because we followed Natifah's bread crumbs."

"And the first crumb told you to go to that tomb and find the chamber of Peseshet? She wrote that on the mastaba wall?"

"It wasn't that simple. But in the story she casually listed Kontar as a friend to Peseshet along with many others. And after Natifah said that about scattering information and setting her puzzle, I set Jonesy to work on developing my decoder. Translation of hieroglyphics and decoding combined was a monumental task. He finally picked up Kontar as a possibility and came up with this tomb."

"Do you think that the text you sent to this computer will point the way to the tablet?"

"She used the term 'scatter' and the word 'five.' I'd bet the most we can hope for will be another bread crumb." He pressed the access button again. "Why the hell aren't we getting anything?"

Rachel was wondering the same thing. "Maybe your decoding program isn't as good as you thought."

"I have more trust in Jonesy than you do. It led me to Kontar's tomb."

"This may be more difficult than—"

The words suddenly popped up on the screen.

No information available. External drive has failed.

"Son of a bitch." Tavak frowned. "It couldn't have failed. I built in so many safeguards that—" He stopped his gaze going to the lamp on the bedside table. He tensed. "That bulb is flickering."

"Why would—"

"Oh, shit!" Tavak jumped to his feet and grabbed Rachel's arm. "Out!" He was dragging her across the room. "Fast!"

"What are you—"

"Don't argue. Move!" He tore open the hall door. "He got fancy. He substituted the lamp. I didn't—"

The lamp exploded.

The force of the blast blew them into the hall.

Tavak covered her body as a storm of debris hurled on top of them.

She heard Nuri cursing and saw him pick himself up off the floor.

"Are you all right?" Tavak was looking down at her.

"I—think so." She drew a deep breath. She was dazed and shook her head to clear it. "It was a bomb?"

"What else?" He got off her and turned to Nuri. "Okay?"

"Yes, no thanks to you." Nuri straightened his shirt. "Why do people keep trying to blow you up? It's most unsettling."

"I'd say that was an understatement." Rachel got to her feet. Lord, her legs were shaking. She stared at the ruin of the hotel room. "What happened? I thought you said that detector would sniff out any explosives."

"Most of them. But lately there are a few explosives that have been formulated that don't have a common odor. They've been used in Iraq." He was brushing flakes of drywall from his hair and shoulder. "Dawson must have configured the computer as a triggering device that wirelessly set the bomb off in the lamp with a Bluetooth signal when the computer came online. Crafty son of a bitch. The computer had no explosive properties, and the lamp had no complex electronic triggering device to be detected."

"Bluetooth." She was trying to remember the details of those last confusing minutes. "The light was flickering."

"The compound was heating up in the lamp," he said absently, his gaze on the flames erupting in the room. "I have to get back in there before—" He started for the room, then stopped. Doors were opening, and people were streaming out into the hall. "Get her out of here, Nuri. Quick. Take the stairs. The hotel is going to be a little upset about this, and security should be up here any minute. I'll meet you down at that coffee shop two blocks away."

"Right." Nuri took Rachel's arm and led her toward the exit door. "Come along. I will take care of you."

Rachel looked back over her shoulder to see Tavak going into the room. "What are you doing?"

"I have to get something. If it didn't get blown to hell. I'll be right behind you."

• • •

It wasn't until Rachel and Nuri were walking down the street that it hit home what an idiot she had been. She stopped in her tracks. "I'm going back."

Nuri shook his head. "Not wise. The hotel will call the police, and they will not be kind to you. Better just to disappear."

"That's what Tavak is going to do. He'll just disappear and leave me without a hope of finding him again. I'm going back."

"It's too late. If what you say is true, he'll already be gone, and you'll be left to deal with the police." Nuri took her elbow. "Come, we will go to the café and wait. Maybe you are wrong."

"Not likely." But Nuri's reasoning was correct. Tavak would have had enough time to make his escape. She had no choice but to wait, on the chance that he might come. Dammit to hell.

She started toward the café a few doors down. "Let's go."

"He may come," Nuri said. "If it pleases him. It's hard to say. I find Tavak puzzling."

So did Rachel. Puzzling and infuriating . . . and intriguing. Dear God, the lightning speed of the way his mind had worked in that hotel room was astonishing. It had been only seconds from the time that he had caught a glimpse of that flickering light that he had put everything together and was pulling her out of the room.

Events had moved so fast since she had met him that she had barely been able to catch her breath. Her head was whirling with all the information he had thrown at her, and hope, confusion, and anger were fighting for dominance. She had come here on what she had thought was probably a wild-goose chase, and that chase was proving wilder than she had dreamed.

Yet, dammit, she believed what Tavak had been telling her. He was mocking, unscrupulous, reckless, and completely self-absorbed. But the confidence and intelligence that were present in his every move and word were fascinating. Intelligence always fascinated her, and Tavak had already proved that he was brilliant. She just had to control that brilliance until she got what she needed from him.

If she got the chance of controlling him.

How was she going to find him in this huge maze of a foreign city if he'd decided to run out on her?

SIX

Rachel and Nuri had been sitting in the café for over thirty minutes when Tavak walked in the door. He was wearing a white linen jacket that was too small and pulled taut over his broad shoulders.

Rachel tried to hide the relief that she felt.

Evidently she wasn't successful. Tavak made a tsk-tsking sound as he dropped into the chair. "You thought I'd done a flit? I keep my word, Rachel."

"I don't know that. All I know is that you're a tomb raider and a thief." She took a sip of her black coffee. "And people want to blow you up."

"It does seem incriminating." He motioned for the waiter. "But you usually look deeper than the surface."

"She was worried," Nuri said. "I told her you were an honorable man—maybe."

"Your endorsement touches me," Tavak said. "And I'm sure that it comforted Rachel."

"What are you doing in that jacket?" Rachel asked. "You look like a waiter."

"It is a waiter's jacket. I stole it from the linen closet on the second floor of the hotel. The back of my shirt was ripped from the blast, and I would have attracted too much attention. I would have been here sooner, but I had to slip out the back way and down the alley to avoid the firemen and police."

Rachel hadn't noticed his torn shirt. It wasn't surprising considering the shape she'd been in after that blast. And he didn't really look like a waiter, she realized. He wore the jacket with a casual elegance that reminded her of the movie heroes of the thirties. That was the only thing casual about him. His blue eyes were glittering in his tan face, and his every muscle seemed ready to go into action at any second. He was so alive that she felt as if she'd get a shock if she touched him.

The disaster that had almost killed them had only served to energize him, she thought incredulously. "Why did you go back in the room?"

"To get my backpack. It was by the door, so it had a chance of not being totally destroyed." He nodded at the bag at his feet. "It's pretty torn and ripped, but my computer survived. The case of the computer is dented, but it still booted up."

"Why did you need it?"

"I have the original photos from the tomb still in it."

"But the external hard drive blew up. You don't have Jonesy to decode those hieroglyphics."

"Well, that's not exactly true."

She stared at him in surprise. "You had a backup?"

He nodded. "I'm a very careful man about some things. I made a copy of Jonesy's most recent decoding program on another hard drive and stashed it in a safe."

"Where?"

"Paris. But I'll have to activate the software package and start it working on the coded message we found here in Egypt."

"How long before it will be ready to give us answers?"

He shrugged. "It's fairly complicated. Four or five days maybe."

"That's too long."

"She is becoming angry," Nuri said. "I think I will let you deal with it, Tavak." He stood up and looked at Rachel. "It has been a great pleasure to meet you, Ms. Kirby. I will stay as long as you need me, but I believe he is no real threat to you. With your permission, I will go now."

"Yes, you don't need to stay. Good-bye, Nuri. And thank you."

Nuri turned to Tavak. "You were very interesting. It was pleasant protecting you."

" 'Protecting'? I thought I was a prisoner."

" 'Prisoner' is an ugly word. Did I not feed you and keep you entertained? I'm not even asking you to give me the money you owe me." He grinned. "It's a small world. We may meet again."

Tavak nodded. "Good-bye, Nuri."

Rachel watched him walk away before she turned back to Tavak. "Four or five days is too long to get answers. Can't you hurry it?"

"I might." He paused. "If you can give me more cycles, I can cut that time in half."

"Damn you."

"More power, quicker answers. Isn't that the principle on which you've based your operation?"

"Yes." She looked down in her cup. "Okay, you'll get them. I suppose I don't have to ask if you're able to siphon them off yourself."

He nodded. "I'll manage. Just tell your assistant, Simon, to ignore the loss."

"You know about Simon?"

"I know about Simon and Val and Allie and everything else that I could find out about you."

"Do you always research your victims so thoroughly?"

"No." He sipped his coffee. "You interested me. You're unique."

"Everyone is unique."

He shook his head. "I don't agree. I'm bored with most people after a while. It's my own fault. I have an analytical mind that can be a curse. I find myself studying everyone around me, trying to take them apart. Eventually, I can predict what they'll say, what they'll do." He gazed at her over the rim of the cup. "It's only occasionally you run across someone who has that spark of originality that never goes out. I don't think I'd ever find you boring, Rachel."

"Is that supposed to mean something to me?" Yet she could see how boredom might be a problem for Tavak. With an IQ soaring off the genius scale, he would find few people who would be able to meet him at even half his level. "And you sound egotistical as hell."

"I probably am." He smiled. "You'll have to slap me down every now and then. Now I suggest we leave for Paris right away and take a flat there so that I can get to work."

"We're not going anywhere until we come to an agreement." She held his gaze. "If I help you, if I don't call in the police to arrest you, will you turn over the information on that tablet to me immediately? You won't hold out for the highest bidder?"

He didn't speak for a moment. "I get the rights to any medical finds, but I'll let your foundation have the formula or procedure first to develop it. Good enough?"

"Yes. But you also have to agree to show me every backdoor you created to get into Jonesy."

"Deal." He smiled. "Then let's head for Paris."

She thought about it, then shook her head. "We'll go to Paris to pick up that external drive, but we're not going to stay there."

His brows rose. "No? Then where are we going?"

"Las Vegas."

"What?"

"I have a job to do there. You said it would take you a few days to program the computer and get that information. I have to use that time. I promised Norton I'd give him back the cycles I took from him when you were bleeding me dry. It was the only way I could persuade him to get you out of that tomb." Her lips tightened. "And now you tell me you're going to take more computing power from Jonesy. I have to make it up somehow."

"In Las Vegas?"

"It's my best chance."

"Then you can go to Las Vegas and leave me in Paris."

"No way."

He smiled faintly. "You don't trust me? What a surprise."

"Until we find that tablet, we're joined at the hip."

"What an interesting picture that brings to mind." He nodded. "But I like it."

"I don't, but that's the way it has to be." She stood up. "Let's get to that airport."

"Not so fast." He got to his feet. "I have to stop at the hospital and check on Ben."

"Ben?" Then she made the connection. "The man who was with you in the tomb. Was he badly hurt?"

"Not critical, but it could have been. He's doing well." He smiled. "Thanks to you, he'll live to curse me for getting him into that spot."

"Sounds like an intelligent man." She turned and moved toward the door. "Okay, we'll stop on the way to the airport."

It's about time you showed up," Ben said. "I've been lying here wondering if you'd gone after Dawson."

"I won't have to," Tavak said. "I'll only have to look behind me." He gestured to Rachel. "This is Dr. Rachel Kirby. I thought you'd like to meet the woman who got us out of that particular mess. Ben Leonard."

Ben made a face. "Hi. I won't ask how he got a nice lady like you involved with all those tombs and stuff. He usually manages to do what he wants to do. But I do thank you for saving my neck. I thought this time I'd bought it."

"You're welcome. I hope you recover quickly, Mr. Leonard."

"The doctor says I'll be out of here in a week or so." He glanced at Tavak. "Will you need me sooner?"

"No, I have some data to retrieve, and that will take some time." He smiled. "I believe we can afford to let you take a little time to heal."

Ben gave him a wary look. "What then? Tell me there won't be any more tombs."

"I can't tell you that. But I'll handle it myself if we run into any."

"Good." Ben gave a sigh of relief. "I don't want to have anything to do with underground burials. I think I'm going to be cremated when I buy it. Until then, I'll stay up top and guard your back."

"That will probably work just as well. Do you need anything?"

Ben shook his head. "Just a pass to get out of here. But maybe I'll enjoy the rest. You're not a very relaxing person, Tavak."

"You'll get bored."

Ben shook his head. "No, you're the one who can't be still for more than a couple hours. I have a lazy nature. I just don't get to pander to it when I'm around you." He glanced at Rachel. "Watch yourself, he's not like other people. He gets restless, then all of a sudden you're tiptoeing through a minefield."

"Then why are you still going to work with him?"

He shrugged. "Damned if I know. I guess I have a death wish." He grinned. "Or it might be that he promised to make me a rich man. That could have something to do with it."

"A lot to do with it," Tavak said. "You have to be able to pay for that fancy cremation." He reached out and shook Ben's hand. "They'll take good care of you here. If they give you any trouble, call me, and I'll be back."

"I will," Ben said. "You owe me." He paused, gazing at Tavak. "Don't you go getting yourself into trouble until I get out of here."

"No, just a little research as I said." Tavak turned toward the door. "Get well, Ben. I need you."

Ben's face lit up. "Yeah, I know you do. I'll be in touch as soon as I get my discharge papers."

"Do that." Tavak waved from the door. "I'll be waiting."

Rachel was silent as they walked down the corridor to the elevator. "You care about him."

"Yes, why are you surprised?"

"I just—you can't have much in common."

"I admire him. He's no hero. But when he's frightened, he faces it and keeps going." He grimaced. "He doesn't have the best character judgment, but that's in my favor. Sometimes people find I'm a difficult dose to swallow. He relies on his instinct. He doesn't know why, but he likes me. I'll take that."

"Do you really need him?"

"No, but it makes him feel good to hear it. What's the harm?"

"No harm." But Rachel didn't know if she would have thought to say those words. She had the reputation of being a bulldozer, and most of the time she deserved it. She was totally focused and didn't stop to see or analyze anything but the goal ahead. "It just surprised me."

Tavak glanced at her as he pressed the elevator button. "You'll get over it. Surprises are natural when you're getting to know someone. I'm looking forward to the first time you surprise me, Rachel."

She looked away from him. "From what you tell me, I have no secrets from you."

"Not true. We all have secrets." He gestured for her to precede him into the elevator. "In the mind, in the heart, in the body. I'd like to explore every one of yours."

She felt a ripple of shock. The words had been spoken almost casually, but they still had an intimacy she had never expected. "Then be prepared to be disappointed."

"I'm always prepared. That makes it so much better when I'm wrong."

Rachel didn't speak for a moment. "I've already discovered that you're an expert manipulator. Never try to manipulate me in that way, Tavak."

"Is that what I'm doing?" He smiled. "It's possible. I don't think so, but sometimes I find I do it unconsciously. You'll have to keep your eye on me."

Her eyes on him and her wits about her, Rachel thought. "Don't worry, I never intended anything else."

They're still alive," Sorens told Dawson, when he answered the phone.

Dawson muttered a curse. "Why? Didn't the bomb go off?"

"It went off and blew the room to pieces. Tavak and Rachel Kirby must have been out of the blast range. They scooted out of the hotel and met at a café a few blocks from the hotel. Then they went to the hospital and visited Ben Leonard. Forty minutes later they headed for the airport and booked tickets for Paris."

"Son of a bitch. Why the hell would they go to Paris?" But Tavak must have a reason. He had thought he'd erase that particular problem for good, but Tavak had slipped away again. Oh well, he had the information he'd copied from Tavak's external hard drive, and he'd had experts working on determining exactly its capabilities. It appeared to be a decoder, but they had been astonished by the power and complexity of the program. It was no wonder that Tavak had been able to do what Dawson could not.

And Dawson wasn't surprised at the power of

the program. Not since he'd been told that the woman with Tavak was Rachel Kirby. It appeared that Tavak had taken a partner who could tap into that gigantic brain trust. The knowledge filled Dawson with rage and frustration.

Calm down. Soon they'd also be able to process the information Tavak had gotten from the wall of the tomb. He mustn't be impatient. He'd been assured the safeguards Tavak had put on the program would be broken. Then he'd be able to process Natifah's leads himself instead of following Tavak around like a trained dog.

"Should I have a man follow him to Paris?" Sorens asked.

That was a stupid question. Tavak was a threat wherever he was, and this sudden trip to Paris made Dawson uneasy. He'd thought by stealing the information on Tavak's hard drive, then erasing it, that he'd finally left him in the dust; but you could never tell. "Hell yes, I want to know what he's doing there. Get someone out to the airport right away. Make sure you don't use anyone he might recognize from that tomb."

"I'll send Medelin. He's a very good man. And he might be able to get on the same plane."

"Good." Dawson paused. "And tell him if he gets an opportunity to correct that bungle in Tavak's hotel room, by all means do it. I'm not that curious about what he's doing. I'd rather have him dead."

T he flight for Paris won't leave for another two hours," Tavak said. "Do you want to find a restaurant and grab some dinner?"

"No. Not now." Rachel reached in her bag and pulled out her phone. "I have a phone call to make." The call she'd been dreading since she'd reached Cairo. "I promised to call my sister."

"And you're not happy about it," Tavak said as he moved closer to the check-in counter. "I'll give you some privacy. I have some work to do anyway."

"Tavak."

He glanced back over his shoulder.

"I want to read the transcription of Natifah's words on that mastaba wall. Don't try to put me off again."

He nodded. "I'll pull up the transcription on my computer and send it to yours. You can read it on the plane. Good enough?"

"Yes." She watched him settle down with his computer before she punched in Allie's number. She braced herself as Allie picked up the phone. "Don't start arguing with me, Allie. You're not going to change my mind."

"Oh, no. You never change your mind, do you?" Allie's voice was hard and tense. "You just go your own way and let me worry. Don't you do it, Rachel."

"Simon told you why I'm here? Of course, he

did. Then you must realize that I have to do this."

"I don't realize any such thing. It's crazy. You're clutching at straws and wasting your time. Our time. Stop this and come home, dammit."

"There's a chance. It's a long shot, but I have to take it. I'll come home as soon as I can. Understand, Allie."

"I don't understand. You were almost killed a few days ago, and now you're traipsing all over the Middle East. It's not safe there. What if someone decides to take another potshot at you?"

"There's no reason for anyone to try to shoot me. That was just a random screwball incident."

"You don't know that."

Rachel couldn't argue. "I don't believe there was a connection."

"And I suppose someone blowing up this tomb was a random incident, too."

"If someone is willing to commit a crime to get their hands on that cure, there must be some value to it. That's only logical."

"The hell it is. And what about this Tavak? What kind of man is he?"

Rachel's gaze moved to Tavak across the gate area. His expression was focused, absorbed as he studied his computer screen. She was once again aware of the intelligence and intensity that radiated from him. "He's . . . different."

"That's a nice side step." Allie paused and Rachel could practically feel her frustration in that silence. "I'm not getting through to you, am I?"

"I have to do this, Allie. If I get to a point that I don't see any hope of finding that tablet, or if I discover the whole thing is bogus, I'll stop. You may have given up, but I can't."

"I can see that you won't. And I can't talk to you any more right now, Rachel. Good-bye."

"Please. I didn't mean to upset you, Allie."

"That's pretty lame. Of course, I'm upset. But I shouldn't worry, I shouldn't let anything real touch me. I should go to bed and let you ward off the whole damn world for me." Allie's voice was shaking. "Now you listen to me. All this risk taking can't go on. I can't take it. You be careful. Nothing is going to happen to you because you have the bad luck to be my sister." She hung up.

Shit. Shit. Shit.

Rachel hung up the phone and stared out the huge windows at the planes on the runways. The conversation hadn't been any worse than she had thought it would be, but it still hurt. Even more because she could understand where Allie was coming from. Well, she had made her decision, and she wasn't about to change it. Try to forget Allie for the time being.

No way. Allie was always with Rachel, and she wouldn't have it any differently. She was the only person in Rachel's life whom she loved, and she wasn't going to let her go. She'd let her sister cool down for a few days, then call her again and try to smooth things over. Maybe she'd have good news by that time.

She got to her feet and moved quickly toward Tavak. She needed Tavak to help her, and she'd run him ragged until she got every bit of information and assistance she could wring out of him.

"Tavak."

He looked up, and it took him a few seconds to clear his mind from the problem in front of him. "Done? Dinner?"

"Yes. I'm hungry."

He studied her and then smiled. "Yes, you are. In more ways than one. I've already sent Natifah's transcription to you, and that should fill one need." He stood up. "But let's feed this urgent and particular appetite at once."

She won't listen." Allie turned to Letty after hanging up the phone. "She's going to get herself killed. What the hell have I done to her?"

"You haven't done anything," Letty said quietly. "And I won't have you blaming yourself because Rachel is world-class stubborn. She can't help how she feels, and you've just got to cope."

"If I get the chance." Her lips tightened. "No, I *will* get the chance. I'll see to it." She went over to the portrait of Rachel she'd been working on before the call. She'd done it from a sketch because Rachel never had time to pose. She'd caught her in the garden, and her expression was thoughtful, not smiling, but all the intelligence and intensity and emotion that was Rachel was in that painting.

I love you, dammit. Listen to me.

She drew a deep breath and picked up the brush. Patience.

She'd gotten through a hell of a lot in her life. She could get through this and come out on top.

Work. Plan. Get ready.

Rachel opened the Natifah file as soon as they were airborne for Paris.

I greet you. I am Natifah, chief aide to the great physician Peseshet, and I write as commanded by my honorable lady. A terrible crime has been done against Peseshet and all my sister physicians. They died at the hands of Pharaoh's soldiers, and I only escaped because I was still in Babylonia doing my lady's bidding. She knew that Pharaoh might act against her and sent me word to stay out of the kingdom and hide from his wrath. But she also ordered me to preserve her story and all the work she had spent her life creating.

She knew there would be no tomb to shelter her body and no earthly goods to take with her on her soul's journey to the afterlife. Her image was struck off every wall in the kingdom, and I burn with anger when I think of it. No one deserved an honorable burial and the respect and glory in life more than my lady. Who else could save the dying that no one else could save? Who else could make the lame walk? The gods sent her to shine her light upon the kingdom, and she became the sunrise of the world.

She told me to hide her cures and medicines only until it was safe to release them to the people. When will that be in a kingdom that strikes down one such as Peseshet? So I have hidden them well so that no one will find them without great labor and greater wisdom. The gods know that there is not a quantity of either in this kingdom. I have spent six years setting the puzzle of five in place so that if I am also killed, Peseshet's command has a chance of being fulfilled. Her work may be lost, but only until wisdom and sanity return to the kingdom.

And, by the gods, I will find a way to honor her and let all know her glory.

Below I have told in detail my lady's story and shown a little of her great wisdom of healing. Seek the rest yourself. Peseshet told me that all that was worthwhile in life came from within.

Believe her.

Honor her.

Rachel scanned the rest of the transcript. It was basically the story of Peseshet that Tavak had already told her but with many more details. Following it was a list of ailments and her cures for them and her accomplishments in healing. She had outlined treatment options for tumors, chest pains, breathing problems, and sleeplessness, among a multitude of other things.

She glanced at Tavak sitting next to her. "My God, some of these cures Natifah listed are astonishing. They could refer to cancer, heart disease, diabetes . . ."

He nodded. "I told you that I was hoping for more than that single tablet that you're interested in. What do you think of Natifah?"

She glanced back at the transcript. "I like her. Loyalty. Power. Decision making. She did what Peseshet wanted, but she did it her way." She smiled faintly. "And she managed to honor her 'lady' by browbeating Kontar and heaven knows who else into making those shrines. Two birds with one stone."

"And I have a hunch that she didn't give a damn whether those tablets were found or not. She just wanted to keep them from the ruler who had killed Peseshet." He tilted his head. "Or maybe she just wanted to make sure whoever found them had the intelligence and drive to use them well. Whatever her motive, she made a conscious decision to set up obstacles."

Her gaze was still narrowed on the transcript. "I don't see any reference to Kontar's tomb in this. There's only a huge list of all Peseshet's friends and clients."

"I didn't pick out Kontar either until Jonesy's decode. She refers to a puzzle on which she worked six years. Natifah was a very smart woman, and I couldn't see any obvious puzzle. But a code could be a puzzle, so I decided it was worthwhile raiding Jonesy and putting him to work on it."

"Breaking into *my* computer on this slim a chance?"

"Wouldn't you?"

"I have a motive."

He smiled. "So do I." He changed the subject. "I've been having the flight attendant check schedules. There's no flight to Las Vegas or New York out of Paris until tomorrow morning. It will take me an hour or so to retrieve the hard drive from the safe. Do you want to check into a hotel close to the airport?"

"If we can't get out any sooner."

"You're welcome to try if you don't believe me."

She didn't speak for a moment. "I believe you."

"Within limits."

"Definitely within limits."

He chuckled. "And I suppose you want to go with me to retrieve the hard drive?"

"You know it." She paused. "All you said was a safe. Where is this safe?"

"In my own private bank. It's about thirty minutes from Charles de Gaulle Airport, where we'll be landing."

"You have your own bank?"

"Of a sort. I suppose it's more like a safety-deposit box. I don't like banks run by the financial community. I know how easy their accounts are to access and move around."

"Only by someone like you."

"If I could do it, someone else might manage. No, I prefer my own bank. Much safer."

"And where is your bank located?"

"Gare du Nord railway station. We board a train at the airport and get off at Gare du Nord. We should be in and out of that station with the hard drive in hand in fifteen minutes. Then we'll take the train back to the airport and go to the Hyatt Hotel. Okay?"

"It will have to be. We need that hard drive."

SEVEN

ood Lord, this place is busy." Rachel's gaze wandered over the huge station, teeming with people. They had just gotten off the high-speed train at Gare du Nord, and Tavak had his hand beneath her elbow, urging her forward and keeping her with him as they tried to negotiate their way through the crowds.

"It should be busy. It's the third largest station in the world."

"Now, where the hell is your bank? Should I be—What are you looking at?"

Tavak was staring over his shoulder at the passengers getting off the train. "Nothing. At least, I hope it's nothing." He quickened his pace. "Let's get moving."

"We're practically running now."

"So we are." He slowed a little. "As much as we can in this mob. You're right, it's damn crowded here. I don't like people this close."

"Claustrophobic?"

"No." He was glancing over his shoulder again. "Wary." He was suddenly guiding her toward a row of shops and food stands. "It's right ahead. Keep moving."

"What's right ahead? I don't see anything resembling a bank."

"We're right on top of it." He'd stopped at a colorful booth selling magazines and newspapers and spoke to the tall, thin man behind the counter. "Bonjour, Raoul. How's business?"

"Well enough." The man Tavak had addressed as Raoul gave him a toothy smile. "It's a slow time. Weekdays are better."

"It doesn't seem slow to me." Tavak gestured to Rachel. "Raoul Joubert. Rachel Kirby."

Raoul nodded. "Delighted." His gaze shifted back to Tavak. "Have you come to make a withdrawal?"

"Yes."

"Good." He made a face. "You pay well, but holding your merchandise always makes me uneasy."

"It shouldn't. It's nothing illegal. Not even weapons this time."

"Maybe it's you who make me uneasy." He lifted the wooden gate. "Come and take it off my hands."

Tavak glanced at Rachel. "Wait here."

"I'm not going anywhere." She watched him go behind the gate, squat down, and move a pile of magazines. "This is your bank?"

"Why not?" He had opened a trapdoor to reveal a lockbox with a combination. "I trust Raoul. He's been my banker for the past twelve years." He quickly punched the buttons that opened he box. "And my deposits always stay where I leave them." He drew out a gray plastic bag and shut the lockbox. "Come on. It's past time to get out of here." He stood up and turned to Raoul. "Thanks. I'll be in touch."

"Yes," Raoul said absently, his gaze on the crowd. "You do know there is someone following you?"

"Medium height. Brown hair. Black jacket, gray pants." Tavak lifted the gate. "He came on the same train from the airport. I also saw him at Customs. He was probably on the same plane we took from Cairo."

"Be careful," Raoul murmured. "And stay away

from me for at least six months. I wish to be careful, too."

Rachel's gaze had flown to the spot where Raoul was looking, but she was too late to catch anything but a fleeting glimpse as the man faded into the crowd. "You didn't tell me we were being followed."

"I wasn't sure for a little while." He grabbed her arm. "I'm sure now. We need to get you out of here."

"The train back to the airport?"

"No." He was heading in the opposite direction and moving in and out of the crowds with snake-like speed. "The street."

"Why?" She was running to keep up with him. "You said the train—"

"I want out of these crowds. Anyone could slip a knife between my ribs, and no one around me would know it."

"You think he wants to kill us?"

"Not us. I'm the target. But I don't want you getting in his way. I think we've lost him for the moment, but he'll see us as soon as we climb the stairs to the street." He was pulling her up those stairs now. "He could either have orders to steal the hard drive or to take me out." He opened the door and glanced outside before pushing her out on the walk. "Don't wait in that queue to get a taxi." He put the bag containing the hard drive in her hands. "Hurry. Go at least two blocks. Catch a taxi from there to the airport hotel. I'll meet you later."

"You'll meet me? Come with me now."

He shook his head. "I'll play the decoy and go back and draw him away. Get going."

"You're overreacting. Maybe he's not following us."

"I'm not overreacting. Move."

"The hell I will."

"Don't argue." He turned and headed back toward the door to the station. "Get out of here now."

She still hesitated.

He glanced back over his shoulder, and she stiffened with shock at his expression of cold ferocity. "Listen. Dawson's man doesn't want the hard drive," he said softly. "I doubt if anyone even knows there's a copy. That would only be a bonus. He wants me." He opened the door. "So he's going to get me. I'm tired of running from Dawson and his slimeballs. Let them see what happens when I decide to stop."

Rachel stood frozen for a moment staring after him. She had never seen that deadly side of John Tavak. There had been a savage recklessness that had sent a chill through her.

Get out of here.

Yes, move. Get away from here. Let Tavak go on the hunt if that was what he wanted. He could have come with her and been safe, but he had chosen to walk the tightrope of violence that he had chosen when he had walked out of the think tanks and into the real world. It mustn't matter to her. She had the hard drive in her hands, and she had to keep it secure.

Secure for Allie.

She turned and strode quickly down the street and away from the station.

Tavak paused before going down the steps, his gaze searching the crowds below.

There he was, plowing his way toward the door through the mob of people. But when he caught sight of Tavak, he stopped by a booth and pretended to look at umbrellas.

The game was starting.

Tavak felt a familiar rush of adrenaline.

Come on, let's move it, bastard. Come and get me.

Who are you? He didn't recognize him as any of the men in Kontar's tomb. It would be better if he knew who he was dealing with.

He reached for his phone and shot a quick photo before he started slowly down the stairs. He punched in a number and Ben answered before Tavak even knew it was ringing.

"It's Tavak. Is your laptop on?"

"No 'Hi, how are you feeling?'"

"No time. I just e-mailed you a picture. Compare it with the file of Dawson's known associates that

I gave you to research. You still have it, don't you?"

"Sure, what have you gotten yourself into?"

He started striding quickly through the crowds. "Just look, will you?"

"I already am. I see your photo. Oh, kind of a scary-looking son of a bitch, isn't he?"

"He's about twenty feet behind me now."

"I guess that's why you're in a hurry."

"Are you opening the Dawson file?"

"As we speak. I'm scrolling through it now. Not all of these names have photos attached, though. I'm still looking . . . You didn't send me the best photo, you know."

"Maybe I can ask him to strike a pose. He's about ten feet closer now."

"Okay. Okay. I think I've found him. David Medelin. Dawson picked him up in Croatia. He's good with firearms, but his specialty is knives. He was detained in London Heathrow for trying to board a plane with a ceramic blade in his boot. Need anything else?"

Knives. Okay, Medelin. The rules of the game are set. "No, thanks."

"What are you going to do?"

"Take care of it." Tavak cut the connection. He glanced over his shoulder and saw that Medelin had dropped back a few yards.

Tavak glanced at the electronic schedule board that hung over the terminal's large atrium. A

Thalya train from Amsterdam had arrived a few minutes before and was probably still on platform eight. That would fit the bill.

He made his way down the stairs that would take him to the open-air platform. A silver-and-red TGV high-speed train was waiting. Perfect.

Tavak walked the length of the train, glancing through the long windows and noting that a cleaning crew was aboard. The first and last cars were power cars, with sleek, angled heads that reminded him of a snake. The door of the last car was propped open.

Come on, Medelin. Your coach is waiting.

Tavak stepped inside the train and surveyed the interior, which was similar to an airline cockpit with its two bucket seats situated before an instrument panel and a large window.

You like knives, Medelin? Too boring. I kind of like the idea of using the train itself.

He picked up a metal clipboard and used it to pry open a door behind the seats. He shimmied through the narrow engineering section and stopped.

He heard something.

Medelin had entered the car.

Tavak slid into a recessed area between engineering panels.

Medelin's footsteps echoed in the forward compartment, then moved into the engineering section. Silence. The man had stopped, probably gauging his next step.

Then there was a deep breath, a rustle of fabric, and a tentative step forward.

Tavak couldn't see him yet. Okay, picture him. If Medelin was holding a blade, it was probably level with his waist. Men typically held handguns closer to their chests.

He was betting on the blade. Thanks, Ben.

Now!

Tavak lunged out of the recess, grabbed Medelin's wrist, and struck the back of his hand hard against the metal panel. A brown ceramic knife flew from his hand and stuck upright in the tiled floor.

Tavak threw open a door labeled TRANSFORMA-TEUR and jammed Medelin's head against the mechanism. With one hand around the man's throat, Tavak reached up and placed his thumb on a red button. "Twenty-five thousand volts, friend. Don't move."

Medelin froze. "You're crazy. You'll fry us both."

"No, I won't. I'll shove you deep into that transformer the same time I push the button. The electricity will come off those lines outside, down the pantograph, and into your body. Trust me, I know a thing or two about trains. I've been in and out of this station for years, and my friend, Raoul, is very proud of all these supertrains. Now let's talk. Why are you following me, Medelin?"

"I wasn't following you."

Tavak's hand moved closer to the red button.

"Okay," Medelin said. "I was paid to do it."

Why was he even bothering to ask these questions? Tavak thought impatiently. He knew the answers. It wasn't going to change anything.

It was because he had this stupid horror of making mistakes. He always had to be sure. "Dawson?"

"Since you know my name, I'm sure you already know that. I'm not here to hurt you."

"No?"

"He just wants to know where you're going."

"I'm sure he does. But what happens when I— Shit!"

Medelin had snapped a blade from his wrist and stabbed Tavak in his right side. When Tavak's grip loosened, Medelin pulled away from the transformer.

Tavak shoved him back and grabbed the arm with the blade.

Medelin's lips were curled back in an ugly sneer. "Why, you're bleeding, Mr. Tavak."

Tavak twisted Medelin's wrist and buried the blade in the man's stomach.

"Why, so are you, Mr. Medelin."

He pressed the red button.

It has been over three hours, Rachel thought. Where the hell is Tavak?

Maybe he wasn't coming. Maybe that bizarre episode at the train station was just a trick to cover

Tavak's attempt to disappear. After all, Rachel hadn't checked out that hard drive. She'd probably been stupid to trust what Tavak had said was really on it. Here she'd been sitting here worrying about the son of a bitch, and he could be playing her for a fool.

But the expression on Tavak's face when he'd gone back into that station had not been an act for her benefit. It had shocked her and brought home what kind of man she was dealing with. She should take the hard drive and run.

And she should certainly not be worrying that Tavak might be hurt or—

A knock on her door. "Tavak."

She was across the room in seconds and throwing it open. "You could have called me. Where have you—"

"Do you mind if I come in?" Tavak didn't wait for an answer. He entered the room and shut the door. "I need a little help." He shrugged out of the leather jacket. "I stopped at a pharmacy and picked up a first-aid kit, but it will be quicker if someone else does the bandage."

"First-aid kit. What—" She stopped as she saw that the right side of his chambray shirt was soaked with blood. "My God."

"It looks worse than it is. Flesh wound in the side." He handed her the plastic bag. "Please."

She gazed at him, stunned. "What kind of wound?"

"Knife."

"You should go to a doctor. Report it to the police."

"No. And no. Too many complications." He sat down in the chair at the desk. "Will you do it or shall I?"

Rachel didn't move for a moment, but then she opened the bag and took out the first-aid kit. "I'll do it." She turned and went into the bathroom and got a clean cloth and water. "What kind of complications?"

"Delays. Explanations." He took off his shirt. "See? Not too bad."

A jagged, bloody, three-inch laceration. "Not too good." She washed the blood away. "This didn't have to happen. You should have come with me."

He didn't answer.

"Are you going to tell me what happened?"

"I took care of business."

"That's all? This is business?"

"It was Medelin's business." He gazed into her eyes. "His name was David Medelin, and he was a vicious son of a bitch. And that knife wasn't meant to just wound, Rachel."

She put tape to hold the wound together. "His name *was* David Medelin?"

"I don't make mistakes. There won't be repercussions. It's over. Past history."

"What did you do to him?"

"What I said I'd do. I stopped running and let him catch up with me."

"That's no answer."

"It's all you'll get from me." He smiled faintly. "Admit it, that's all you really want. I'm making you a little uncomfortable. I told you that we all had our inner secrets, and you just uncovered one of mine."

She placed the large bandage over the wound. "You liked it. You wanted to go after him."

"Yes."

"And you're probably as violent as he was."

"It appears I'm more."

"And you're a damn adrenaline junkie."

"Yes, among other things." He put on his shirt. "We're all many things, aren't we, Rachel?" He stood up. "For instance, you're deeply emotional and yet tough as nails. I'd bet you were probably torn between worrying about me and wondering if I'd set you up to run out on you. Did you try to check the hard drive?"

God, he was sharp. She wouldn't deny it. In this situation, suspicion was intelligent. "Not yet. It would have been my next move if you hadn't gotten here when you did."

He smiled. "You would have found I hadn't lied to you. Not about the hard drive and not about that bastard who stuck his dagger in me. You can keep the hard drive and take a look at it, if you like."

And in some cases suspicion was *not* intelligent.

"No, that would waste time. I want you to start working on it right away."

He nodded. "Tonight. I should be able to make some progress by the time we get on that plane in the morning."

"Are you sure that I'm not going to be arrested for fleeing the scene of a crime?"

"Crime? What crime? I told you that I don't make mistakes."

"You made one at that hotel in Cairo and nearly got us blown up."

He chuckled. "Well, I don't make them often." He took the hard drive from the desk and headed for the door. "I'm two doors down if you need me. I promise I won't run out on you."

"No? I'm not going to sleep well tonight."

"That's your problem. I'm going to have problems enough of my own with your alter ego, Jonesy, tonight. I'm going to try to siphon off some cycles to help me out."

She shook her head. "And now I know I won't sleep at all."

The next morning Rachel and Tavak boarded the Delta flight for Los Angeles, with connections to Las Vegas.

"We're not sitting together?" Tavak asked as they walked down the first-class aisle. "I was looking forward to togetherness."

"And I'm looking forward to your finishing the

work on that program on the external drive that you started last night. Besides, I have work to finish myself, and I don't want to be distracted."

"I got a lot accomplished last night. Jonesy was very cooperative . . . and generous."

She flinched. "Then it's a good thing that I'm going to Las Vegas and replenish those cycles you took. You'll probably get even more done on this long flight." She frowned. "Why are you arguing about a seat?"

"I want to watch you work."

"What?"

"Your work is your passion. I'm curious about the intensity you bring to it. I always find that aspect of a person interesting."

"Well then, you'll have to contain your curiosity." She sat down in her seat and unzipped her computer case. "Or observe me from a distance. Your seat is on the other side and two rows back."

Tavak nodded and moved toward his seat. "I'll see you in Los Angeles." He settled, opened his computer, and set up the external hard drive also on the tray. Then he leaned back, his gaze on Rachel across the aisle.

She had already forgotten him and was absorbed in the screen in front of her. Occasionally, he'd see a flicker of expression, a flare of excitement or annoyance. He supposed he should start his own work, but it was well on the way to completion. He had a little time to watch Rachel and enjoy the play of expressions, even try to predict them, as he learned this crucial part of her.

It was an opportunity he hadn't been able to explore before. When they were together, he was too aware of other aspects that made Rachel who she was. When he'd done his research on her, he hadn't thought sheer physical attraction would get in the way. Wrong. Almost from the first he'd had a megasexual response whenever he looked at her. Now for a little while he could distance himself from her and just appreciate the qualities that had led him to her in the beginning.

Work Rachel, let that fine brain shine. I'll study you, and by the time we reach L.A., you'll have given up one of your most important secrets to me.

FEDERAL BUILDING
HOUSTON, TEXAS

Mr. Norton!" Detective Finley yelled across the plaza as lunch-time office workers poured from the twenty-two-story building on Smith Street.

Wayne Norton didn't break stride at the sight of Detectives Finley and Gonzalez moving toward him. "Sorry, I'm in a hurry. Call my office."

Finley reached into his breast pocket and flashed his police badge as he and Gonzalez stepped in front of Norton, blocking his path.

"We *have* called your office," Gonzalez said. "Several times. You're a difficult man to reach."

"I told you I was in a hurry," Norton said coldly.

Finley nodded. "Good. So are we. Let's get this over with fast. We're investigating the Rachel Kirby shooting."

"And?"

"If we can just have a moment of your time."

Norton stared at them for a moment and shrugged. "I'm always willing to cooperate, but I'm really not sure what help I can be."

"We're looking at all of the projects that Rachel Kirby's computer network was involved with. Yours is probably the most interesting."

"I'd say it's the *least* interesting."

"Why do you say that?"

Norton smiled. "Ninety-nine percent of what the NSA does is sift information. Receipts, tax returns, various forms of boring communication . . ."

"E-mail? Private telephone conversations?" Gonzalez asked.

"I can't discuss that, but we do nothing illegal. One way to keep this country safe is to analyze the information flying around. We caught a terrorist last year only because he was picked up on a DUI in Phoenix. Our computers logged the arrest and matched it to a raft of suspicious activities. If we had been a few minutes slower, he would have posted bail and been on his way. And the Golden Gate Bridge might not be standing today."

"I heard about that," Finley said. "But what specifically are you using Rachel Kirby's network for?"

"It's not one thing. Or even five or a hundred things. It's bits and pieces of everything. It's no secret that the NSA already has a massive computer system. But the amount of information available to us is increasing exponentially—I'm talking traffic cams, newsgroup postings, you name it. We're struggling to keep up. We invest in systems like Ms. Kirby's to help shoulder some of the load while we get our internal systems up to speed."

Finley nodded. "Is there anything in your projects that might make Ms. Kirby a target?"

"Absolutely not."

"Are you sure?"

"Yes." He paused. "Why are you being so persistent, Detective?"

"It's suddenly become apparent that we're dealing with a very sophisticated attacker. Our shooter managed to squeeze off a shot in the middle of a busy college campus and get away without anyone seeing him. Plus, he managed to cover his tracks by erasing data only from the cameras that might have caught him."

"What?"

"That's not the kind of thing that just any nutjob campus shooter could pull off. Seems like a pretty sophisticated trick. Are you sure you can't help us?"

"No. Sorry. Are we finished?"

"For now. Have a nice day, Mr. Norton. We'll be in touch."

Norton walked out of the plaza.

Gonzalez turned to Finley. "Why did you tell him about the camera feeds?"

"I had a hunch. I wanted to see his reaction."

"There wasn't much of a reaction. He's a stoneface."

"There was enough," Finley murmured, his gaze on Norton's retreating figure. "Yes, there was enough."

"Tavak and Rachel Kirby boarded a flight for Las Vegas this morning." Sorens told Dawson when he answered the phone. "They picked up a package at a train station last night, but Medelin didn't know what was in it."

"Tell him to find out."

"I can't do that." Sorens paused. "I haven't heard from Medelin since he called me from Gare du Nord station last night. I haven't been able to reach him. I flew to Paris myself to keep an eye on Tavak."

Dawson muttered a curse. "I thought you said Medelin was good."

"He is good. You said you wanted Tavak dead. Medelin probably tried to obey orders. Tavak is no pushover."

No, Dawson had seen Tavak in action, and he was a lethal son of a bitch.

"Do you want me to stay here?" Sorens asked.

"Why would you stay there? Get a flight to Las Vegas. Someone has to keep an eye on Tavak."

"Right. I just thought—"

"Don't think. Obey orders. I have to go to Kentucky myself."

"Mills?"

"He wants to see me." And Mills had issued a royal command to come to Mills Pharmaceutical, and the bastard expected him to jump. "Keep me informed." He hung up.

LAS VEGAS MCCARRAN AIRPORT
LAS VEGAS, NEVADA

So what's your plan?" Tavak asked, as he and Rachel side-stepped a group of tourists at the airline terminal. "Or am I permitted to ask? You've noticed I've contained my curiosity with admirable restraint."

She shrugged. "Same as it's always been. To get Demanski to give up a major chunk of his company's computing power willingly. The NSA is going to start pressuring me soon to be back up to full capacity, and I'm not taking cycles away from any of my research projects."

"And you're working all out to be able to do a little pressuring yourself. Fascinating."

"I'm glad you're enjoying yourself."

"Oh, I am. What I want to know is *how* are you

going to get Demanski to give you access to his system? I've heard he's not exactly a charitable man."

"You're right. But he can be, if he knows his generosity will benefit him directly."

"But unless you've become an elected official since we left Paris, you're not in a position to grant him gaming licenses or tax breaks."

"I'll give him something better."

"Like what?"

Rachel didn't answer as they walked past a row of jangling slot machines.

"No answer?"

"This has nothing to do with that tablet. You're on a need-to-know basis right now."

"What if I suddenly decided to put *you* on a need-to-know basis? Now that we're back in the United States, what if I just walked away?"

His tone was mocking, but there was also curiosity in his expression. She had become aware that both that mockery and curiosity were dominant characteristics. He was always going one step further to see how she would react. "That wouldn't be smart. The only reason you're a free man right now is that I provided the NSA data analysts with info they needed to know you weren't cracking into their classified files. If I hadn't, you'd either still be in an interrogation room in Egypt or in a federal penitentiary."

"Go on. I like it when you show your teeth. It's

one of the most interesting sides to you, Rachel."

"You want teeth? Just know that it would take me about ten minutes to write a few lines of code that would convince the NSA that you were fishing for classified information relating to their counter-terrorism activities."

He studied her expression. "You'd do it."

"I have to keep you close. You'd find it difficult to get anywhere with that kind of heat on you."

Tavak shook his head. "My, my. You're one tough customer. Okay, I'll let you keep me as close as you want. I guess I need to stay on your good side."

"Join the club." Simon smiled as he approached them and extended his hand. "I'm Simon Monteith. You're the famous John Tavak?"

Tavak shook his hand. "I try very hard not to be famous."

"So I've learned from reading your dossier. You've failed miserably."

Rachel motioned for them to keep walking. "Did you round up our team, Simon?"

"Yes. I have six of the university's best and brightest students holed up in a suite at Bally's."

"How much did you have to tell them?"

"Surprisingly little. When I told them it was a special project of yours, they were all pretty much on board. I guess your name looks good on a résumé."

Rachel shrugged. "It also didn't hurt they were

getting a free, all-expenses-paid weekend in Vegas."

"Well, there's that, too."

"Would either of you care to tell me what's going on?" Tavak asked.

"Later." Rachel turned back to Simon. "Have you been running the drills I e-mailed for them?"

"Almost nonstop. They can do everything you're looking for. Val really wanted to be part of this, but you said you wanted them to be inconspicuous. I had to explain to her that she's way too hot."

"I'm sure she loved that."

"She didn't. Not coming from me anyway."

"I worked out my system on the plane," Rachel said. "I'll need about four hours with our team this afternoon. Did you get the money?"

"Sixty thousand dollars in cash. Your sister *really* didn't want to hand it over. I'm pretty sure she thought we had you tied up someplace, making you ask her for the money at gunpoint."

"I need to interject something here," Tavak said. "Are we really staying at Bally's?"

Rachel nodded. "Yes. Is that a problem?"

"Not the Bellagio? Not the Venetian?"

"Mr. Tavak, we're just a poor, underfunded university research project," Rachel said sarcastically. "Bally's will be fine."

"Okay, it's probably best that you keep a low profile anyway." He paused. "Since you're going to try and break the bank at Demanski's casino."

Rachel stiffened. "Who says I'm trying to do that?"

"You didn't have to say it. I saw you on the plane with your charts and graphs, juggling Hans Felder's papers on rules theory." He tilted his head. "Do you really think you've cracked Demanski's software packages?"

"Only one way to find out."

Tavak shook his head. "There's another way, a better way. And if it blows up in your face, I'm the only one who gets hurt."

Rachel interchanged a look with Simon. "Oh, I do like the sound of that."

Tavak smiled. "I knew you would."

"So what do you have in mind, Tavak?"

"I'll lay it out for you. But I need you to trust me." He saw her expression and chuckled. "I didn't say this was going to be painless. Live with it, Rachel."

EIGHT

LEXINGTON, KENTUCKY

Charles Dawson sipped his mint julep as he gazed around the tree-lined courtyard of Mills Pharmaceuticals. He savored the irony of a health-care corporation plying its guests with alcohol. His host, CEO Theodore Mills, had insisted that he join him in sipping a mint julep in the afternoon sun.

Mills smiled. "Tasty, ain't it?"

"Refreshing." Dawson tried to hide his impatience with the forced Southern charm. Between the ridiculous drink, the Princeton-educated Mills using the word "ain't," and the receptionist's calling Dawson "honey," he was about to gag.

"This really hits the spot," Mills said in an accent that seemed to be getting thicker by the moment. "I might have to get me another one."

Dawson wondered if this bullshit came naturally or if some high-priced image consultant had crafted it for the company. Either way, it appeared to be working. To the general public, Mills Pharmaceuticals had protected its reputation as The Company That Cares.

He knew better.

"I shouldn't be here," Dawson said. "I've already given you my Egypt report. That should be enough."

"Tavak appears to be troublesome."

"Nothing I can't handle."

"Where is he now?"

"He's left Egypt. He's on his way to Las Vegas."

"Really? Why on earth?"

"I have no idea. But I have a man watching his every move."

Mills nodded. "You seem to be moving forward. I appreciate that you don't put this stuff in writing. Plausible deniability and all that."

"Understood. In any case, the operation was a success."

"I'd say it was a *partial* success. I don't have the tablet. But you got what you needed from the tomb?"

"Yes. We're not quite sure what it means yet, but we're working on it. Once we crack it, we can move on to the next step."

"The question being, is there really a pot of gold at the end of this rainbow?"

"Difficult to say. I guess we won't really know until you get Peseshet's cure into your labs."

"True." He looked down into his mint julep. "When my old friend Jamerson sent me that partial formula, I was very excited. I was even more excited when my lab chief came back with the report. Missing pieces but the possibilities were incredible. I knew then that I was the only one meant to have this discovery. I was the one who could handle it with the care it deserved."

"And if it takes you a few decades to evaluate the cure and keep its existence hidden from the world, that's all the better, isn't it?"

Mills flinched. "That wasn't necessary."

"Of all the pharmaceutical companies in the world, yours is the one that stands to lose most if this cure comes to light. But you've set up a research lab devoted solely to the mere possibility of this cure being genuine. You expect me to believe that you're devoting all these resources to bring out a product that could actually ruin you?"

"That's none of your concern, Dawson."

"Of course it's not. But don't try to play the part of the great philanthropist with me. I know better." It had felt good to pierce the bastard's grandiose vision of himself, but it was time to back off. "Besides, don't you think you're jumping the gun? Natifah's information is scanty at best."

"But you're going to get me more information, aren't you? All the information I'll need." Mills sipped his julep. "I know you're going to come through for me. I regard my judgment as excellent, and the moment I met you I realized I could put this project in your hands." He paused. "And I forgive you for killing my old friend Jamerson. I'm sure it was an accident. You wouldn't have killed him just to make sure he wouldn't spread word of our mastaba wall to anyone else."

"He'd already hired Tavak." Dawson stared down into his drink. "You told me to persuade Jamerson to fire him. He wouldn't be persuaded. So share the guilt, Mills."

"No, I hired you to shoulder the guilt. It's the nature of our agreement. You do the dirty work. I remain clean as snow."

"Snow isn't clean anymore. It's tainted by the environment."

"I'll *not* be implicated." The Southern accent was suddenly gone, and clipped steel appeared.

"You're very clever, and I can see you trying to insinuate yourself into this project at a high level. But you're a hired man, and that's all you'll ever be."

Dawson kept any hint of anger from his face. The son of a bitch was trying to humiliate him, treating him as if he was an inferior, like he was a yapping hound at his heels. "I know better than to take more than I'm given. Particularly when you've given so generously." He sipped the julep. "Is that why you asked me to come here?"

"I have good instincts, and I sensed a troubling aggressiveness beginning to manifest itself in you."

"You'll need that aggression if we're going to find that tablet before Tavak does."

"I have no problem with you being aggressive toward Tavak as long as it's handled discreetly. Just don't think you can turn that aggression loose on me."

"I wouldn't be that foolish." Dawson smiled. "But I do expect a bonus if I manage to escalate the recovery of that tablet. Is that too aggressive for you?"

Mills chuckled. "I never mind paying for good work. I'm glad you understand I'm the one in control."

Dawson stood up. "The person who was going to hold the reins was never in question. I'll call you when I have more to report."

"Soon," Mills said quietly. "Very soon." He looked down into his drink. "I have the means to help you, but that would be very expensive for me. Since I've already paid you a great deal of money, I see no reason why I should have to do that. Do your job, Dawson."

"That's what I'm doing."

"A little more efficiency, please." He smiled. "Or I might have to deal with Tavak."

Rage tore through Dawson at the thought. Don't let him see it. "That won't be necessary. You've got the best man working on it now. It wouldn't be smart to change in midstream."

"That's why I haven't made that move." He lifted his mint julep in a toast. "To a mutually profitable relationship. And to Peseshet's tablet, which I earnestly hope lives up to its hype."

Dawson lifted his glass. "Well, a Pharaoh and his entire kingdom believed that formula was the real McCoy."

"Aw, hell, that's no comfort. Those same people thought crocodiles were gods."

"It's no more ridiculous than many of the things in your Bible."

Mills frowned and suddenly slid back into all the Southern phoniness with which he had first confronted Dawson. "Hey, hey, hey. No reason to get all blasphemous."

"Sorry. No offense intended."

"Don't apologize to *me*."

Surely this fat hypocrite couldn't be serious. Dawson smiled. "Mills, if you really believe in a Christian god, you know we're both going to hell." He inclined his head. "I'll call you."

He could feel Mills's gaze on him as he walked away. Mills had shown a perceptiveness he hadn't expected and had caught him off guard. But Dawson had handled the bastard very well considering the burning anger he was feeling. No one humiliated him as Mills had done. No one treated him as an underling.

In spite of Mills's so-called instincts, he'd bet the man hadn't even realized that he'd just signed his own death warrant.

Rachel left her suite and walked down the hall to Tavak's room. She felt tension tighten her stomach as she rapped on the door. What if he had taken off?

She shook her head. If she couldn't even trust him to stick around, why in hell was she crazy enough to trust him to do what he had proposed?

Tavak answered the door. He had shaven and now wore khakis and a white undershirt. He gestured for her to come in. "How are your graduate students?"

"Smart as hell. Simon did a good job rounding them up. He's still running drills with them now."

"Good."

Rachel stared at the room's king-size bed, now

cluttered with a laptop, cabling, and several peripheral devices. "I see you've been busy."

Tavak smiled. "It was actually easy, thanks to you." He held up four silver keycards.

"Are those what I think they are?"

"Yes."

Excitement flared through her. "Are you absolutely sure?"

"I'll know in about an hour."

The computer beeped. Tavak leaned over the device, pressed a few keys, and pulled a fifth card from an attached EPROM writer. Tavak held up the card, his eyes dancing. "Want one?"

"No. I'm not sure this is a good idea anymore. You're enjoying it too much."

"It's a great idea. Not only do we get to test your algorithm, but it makes the kind of statement Demanski will respond to."

"You're acting as if you know him."

"I know men like him. Hell, *I'm* like him."

He could be right. Demanski was a high-stakes gambler, and so was Tavak. Only the stakes they played for differed.

Tavak was staring at her. "Let yourself go," he said softly. "Stop worrying. Remember the Rachel who got banned from this strip when she was only a kid. Wasn't that a hell of a kick?"

"I wasn't playing for the same thing. This is serious."

"Then pretend it isn't. Let's have fun with it." He

turned back to the computer. "Trust me. And whatever you do, don't send your team in until you get my call."

Three hours later Rachel walked across the bridge that traversed the huge reflecting pond of the Demanski Hotel and Casino. It was almost midnight, and thousands of tourists were gathering for the elaborate laser light-and-water show that had become a Demanski trademark. She had been to conferences in which even the most jaded attendees had practically knocked each other over in their rush to see one of the several nightly shows.

"Miss Kirby?" A tall, blue-blazered security officer opened one of the casino's massive front doors for her. "Mr. Demanski is expecting you. Please follow me."

She was surprised. There were hundreds of people pouring into the casino, yet this young man had immediately zeroed in on her.

"This way, ma'am." He motioned for her to follow him through the main walkway.

She looked at the hotel's stately décor and beautifully appointed fixtures, seeing that Demanski had upgraded his taste since the days he had pioneered family-friendly-themed casinos. She turned back to her escort. "What if I told you that I wanted to play a few hands of blackjack?"

"We both know that can't happen."

"Really? Why is that?"

The security officer cast a sideways glance at her. "We all got your file before we came onto the floor tonight. I think you'd have a difficult time playing blackjack in any casino in town."

"Still?"

"When Mr. Demanski says 'banned for life,' he means it. I'm surprised he's actually meeting with you."

Rachel glanced at the multitude of security cameras scattered around the casino's main floor, knowing that there were dozens more above the one-way mirrors lining the ceiling. Somewhere in the hotel, she knew there was a control-room monitor bank that rivaled NASA Mission Control.

She smiled at one of the cameras. "What facial-recognition technology are you using here? FaceIt? Betaface?"

"You know I can't discuss that."

"Everyone knows you have them. Anybody who's ever been accused of card counting or a casino robbery has a visual record in your database, which is then shared with almost every other gaming establishment in the world. Whenever I walk through a casino to a restaurant or my hotel room, it usually only takes about forty seconds before a small army of security guys appear around me."

He smiled. "Maybe they just find you attractive."

"Even Angelina Jolie doesn't get that much attention."

The security officer motioned for her to enter an open elevator. He slid a gold card into a slot on the panel, then stepped out. "Have a nice evening, Miss Kirby."

The doors slid closed before Rachel could respond.

After what seemed like only seconds, the doors opened on the sixty-fifth floor. She stepped onto the marble tile of a spacious atrium lined with floor-to-ceiling Dutch paintings. There was no one in sight.

"Hello?" she said tentatively.

No reply.

"Mr. Demanski?"

There were angry shouts coming from the end of the corridor.

"Hello?" She walked toward the sounds.

"You stupid asshole!" A booming male voice shouted. "Shit!"

Rachel moved quietly down the corridor as the shouting continued. She heard a series of low blasts.

"What are you thinking, dumb-ass? I'm wide open here! Fall back! Regroup, regroup!"

Rachel rounded the corner to see Hal Demanski, dressed to the nines in a tailored black tux, standing in front of a wall-sized plasma television screen. He wore a wireless headset and gripped a futuristic laser rifle. A computer game was on the screen, and Demanski appeared to be shooting acid-spewing aliens. "Dammit, guys! Get your asses over here!"

Four soldiers appeared on the screen and joined him in the alien assault.

"About damn time!" Demanski spotted Rachel in the corridor. "Okay, guys. I gotta run. Clean this up before I get back, will you?" He muted the sound and pulled off his headset. "Rachel Kirby."

"Am I interrupting something important?"

He gestured toward the screen. "Believe it or not, the four men on my team are all Fortune 500 CEOs. Tech guys, mostly. Seeing how much time they spend on this game, I wouldn't invest in *any* of their companies."

Rachel stepped closer. "It must be quite a team."

"Not really. We're getting our asses handed to us by five fifteen-year-olds in Prague." He flashed the smile she had seen on *60 Minutes*, countless magazine covers, and numerous ski-lift chairs alongside supermodels. Demanski was in his late forties and he possessed the athletic, square-jawed charm of a retired football player. But there was an undeniable wit and intelligence behind those brown eyes. He threw down the headset and strode down the corridor. "So why in the hell are you here?"

She kept pace with him. "So why in the hell did you agree to meet with me?"

"Curiosity. I wondered what a woman who stole half a million dollars from me could possibly have to say."

"I did nothing illegal. You have teams of statisticians calculating odds for you. But because I was able to do it for myself, I'm a thief?"

"Spare me. I've heard all the arguments."

"If I was really a thief, why didn't you call the police? Why wasn't I arrested?"

"You know that the law-enforcement community doesn't share our opinion of the situation."

"Because card counting is not stealing. No more than it's stealing when you instruct your blackjack dealers when to hit or stay."

"Makes no difference. We now have systems in place that keep that from happening. Your scheme may have worked ten years ago, but it would never work today."

As they rounded another corner, they came into sight of Demanski's office. It was cavernous, at least as large as the foyers of most big-city office buildings. The ceiling was thirty feet high, and the entire back and sides of the room were made up of floor-to-ceiling windows that offered stunning views of the city. Demanski plopped into the large chair behind his ten-foot mahogany desk. "This desk used to belong to the Romanoff family. What do you think? Too much?"

"Only if you had to cut it in half to get it up here."

"I'd never do that. It's priceless. We took out two of these windows and had a helicopter bring it up."

"Incredible."

"I never do anything halfway."

"That's nice to see. It makes me think you'll like my proposal."

He tilted his head. "That remains to be seen. I'm listening."

"How would you like to help form one of the most powerful computer systems in the history of the world?"

He stared at her for a moment. "For what purpose?"

"Several purposes. Most of the resources are directed toward disease cures. We can save millions of lives."

"Not millions. Thousands, maybe."

She frowned. "What are you talking about?"

"Late-onset Globoid Cell Leukodystrophy. It's an extremely rare disease. Your work benefits a very small group of people."

"You're familiar with my project, then?"

"I do my homework. Very impressive, but your real interest is helping your sister, isn't it?"

She ignored the question. "First, I currently have nine projects that have nothing to do with GLD, including weather-systems modeling and earthquake simulations. And this is only the tip of the iceberg. One day, disease research labs all over the country will use my software for their projects."

"You're very sure of yourself."

"Yes, I am." She stared him in the eye. "Aren't you?"

He chuckled. "Hell, yes. Give me another ten years, and I'll own this state."

"And I won't own much in ten years. But instead of donation boxes, foundations will put cartons of USB memory sticks on store countertops that people can take, insert in their computers, and help cure cancer. It won't cost donors a penny, and it won't interfere with their computer usage one bit."

"So what do you want from me?"

"Computing power. You purchased an enormous networked system eighteen months ago, and most of it is underutilized."

"So my tech people keep telling me. They want me to buy a payroll and billing services company to make use of it."

"I have a better idea. Let me have those processing cycles to make the world a better place. Promote it any way you want. I know you're trying to expand your casinos into new markets. You'll have an easier time of it if you can convince the local politicians that you're an upstanding citizen."

Demanski laughed. "Thanks, but a private jet stocked with food, alcohol, and beautiful women usually does the trick."

"You're not going to buy a payroll company, Mr. Demanski."

"Call me Hal. And what makes you so sure?"

"You can't even say the words 'payroll company' without your eyes glazing over. You like the big ideas. Ideas like your casinos, your race-car teams, and your commercial space shuttle everyone is sure will fail."

He leaned back in his chair. "It *could* fail."

"But if it does, it won't be because you didn't try."

Demanski nodded. "Nice pitch, but you forgot something. All those things have some risk attached, but they have a tremendous upside. I see no real upside in helping you and your project."

"Even for causes as worthy as mine?"

"They still don't benefit me or my business."

Rachel shrugged. "I thought you might react that way. You see, I also do my homework."

"Good."

She walked over to the tall windows overlooking the strip, which was practically on fire with neon. "You said that you now have systems in place to catch card counters."

"Of course. You're not the first superbrain to try and break the bank. And you certainly weren't the last."

"But no system is infallible."

"Oh, we may lose a few thousand here and there before we catch on. But we *do* catch on."

"I'm guessing there's no way you would give me a tour of your surveillance center."

"No way. Especially not with your history."

"But if I were to get a tour, I'm sure I'd see analysts at keyboards entering the cards and bets of all your big winners. The software would tell you pretty quickly if you have a card counter at the table."

"That's fairly common knowledge. The trick is to develop the right software."

"And I'm sure you've committed a lot of resources to that."

"I have. I've employed some of the world's finest mathematical minds, including a Nobel laureate."

"Impressive."

"Like I said, I don't do anything halfway."

"I happen to know that your Nobel laureate is Dr. Hans Felder. You mentioned him in your *Wired* magazine profile. He's brilliant."

Demanski's eyes narrowed. "You've met him?"

"No, but I saw him read a paper at a conference once. And of course I've read every other paper he's ever written."

"Of course." A sudden wariness had entered Demanski's voice.

"He has some interesting ideas about rules theory. I have a pretty good idea how he thinks."

"Maybe you should have a Nobel prize of your own."

"All in good time." Rachel pulled a portable DVD player from her satchel and lifted the screen. She placed the unit on Demanski's desk.

"What's this?"

"It's a video taken in my conference room at Bally's." She angled the player in Demanski's direction. Rachel herself was on camera, handing stacks of money to four young women and two men. "I spent many hours of research deciding how Hans Felder would catch card counters. I then spent another two hours devising a system in which he might *not* catch one. Today I taught my system to these six young people and gave them ten thousand dollars apiece to turn loose on your tables."

Demanski stared at the video, then looked back up at her. "There's no way. We'd know if they hit us."

"Unless you've heard from your security chief this evening, I'd say you *wouldn't* know. It's really a simple system, once you get the hang of it. Each player assigns points to the cards as they appear on the table. We alternate between variations of the Revere Advanced Point Count system and the Red Seven Count system, mostly. Bets are dictated by however many points have been accumulated."

"I guarantee you, half the muumuu-wearing, blue-haired ladies in the casinos downtown know those systems. We would have caught on in under five minutes."

"Not if we changed systems every fifth, ninth, and thirteenth hands."

Demanski's brow wrinkled. "Fifth, ninth, and thirteenth . . ."

"Each prime number plus two. There's more to it than that of course, but that will do for a start."

Demanski gazed at her face for a long moment. "Holy shit," he murmured. He grabbed a red phone on his desk. "Gower, get up here. Now!"

Rachel leaned closer. "Tell him to bring up my team. I told them to wait by the main elevators."

He grimaced, then spoke into the phone. "Did you hear that? Yeah, two men and four women. They look like they're in their early twenties. Bring them up."

Demanski let the phone receiver fall back into the cradle. "How much?"

"We'll have to ask them."

"Shit."

In less than two minutes, a short, dark man who looked like a bar bouncer entered the office with Rachel's team.

Demanski stood up. "Rachel Kirby, this is my director of security, Larry Gower."

Despite his brutish appearance, Gower spoke with a gentlemanly air of sophistication. "Good evening, ma'am. A pleasure."

Demanski crossed his arms. "How are things downstairs tonight?"

"Pretty calm. We had to eject a few rowdies at the table slots. The bank was hit hard by some high rollers." He gestured to the six young people behind him. "Who all happen to be right here."

Rachel nodded to her team. In almost perfect synchronization, they unzipped their identical knapsacks and dumped the contents on the desk.

Demanski stared at the mountain of cash. The bills were collected in hundreds of identical stacks, neatly held together by his casino's white paper bands.

A young woman with close-cropped blond hair stepped forward. "That's 2.7 million dollars. We could have gotten more if Dr. Kirby had let us play longer than seventy-eight minutes."

Demanski was still staring at the cash. "Seventy-eight minutes?"

Rachel picked up a stack of hundred-dollar bills and rifled though it. "That's as long as they could play without being in danger of getting caught." She tossed the stack back down on his desk. "I've been in touch with colleagues near your casinos in Reno, Monte Carlo, and Macao. I estimate I can take you for almost 200 million before your statisticians catch on."

"Really?" Demanski said without expression. "*Unless* I give you the computer cycles you want."

"Let's just say I'd be very appreciative."

"That's extortion."

"Damn right it is," Gower said. His face was red with anger. "What do you want me to do with them?"

Rachel raised her eyebrows. "Are you going to take us to one of your back rooms?" She turned to Demanski. "If you lay a hand on any of these kids, I'll break you. And if you don't think I know how—"

"Easy, easy." Demanski held up his palms. "What exactly do you want?"

"Just computer cycles that aren't being used anyway. I'll run it by your IT guys, and you'll see it won't impact your business at all."

"It's a good deal, Demanski," Tavak said from the doorway. "Take it." He was wearing a tuxedo and looking completely different from the Tavak to whom Rachel had become accustomed.

Demanski stared at him. "Who in the hell are you? How did you get up here?"

Tavak came toward them. "Tavak. I'm a friend of Rachel's. I thought I should be here." He smiled. "Actually, I just wanted to be in on the fun."

Gower was obviously stunned. "Mr. Demanski, I swear I didn't let him up here."

"He's telling the truth," Tavak said. "I let myself in a couple of hours ago. I've been enjoying a private behind-the-scenes tour. Quite a place you have here."

"I'm glad you approve," Demanski said. "Am I to be told what the hell is going on here?"

Tavak produced his five silver keycards and tossed them onto the desk. "I knew that Hans Felder was behind all of your software security systems here. The trouble with a world-renowned mathematical genius for hire is that it's pretty easy to find documentation on how he thinks. I applied Dr. Kirby's algorithm to defeating his security encryption packages. After that, it was fairly simple to strike new security keycards that let me go pretty much anywhere I wanted. The one on top is a copy of yours, Demanski."

"Indeed." Demanski leaned back. "Is that supposed to make me feel threatened?"

"Maybe." He met Demanski's eyes. "Or maybe you can take it as a wake-up call."

"Yes, but it's my choice how I decide to take it."

Tavak shrugged. "Anyway, it also let me test Rachel's algorithm before she sent the students in here. I'd say it worked on both counts."

"Oh, it worked all right. Believe me, I'll be calling Dr. Felder to tell him just what he can do with his Nobel prize."

Rachel stepped forward. "It's a win-win. You help us, we help you."

Demanski pointed to the cash on his desk. "And what about this?"

"Keep it. If you go back on your word, I can always come for more. A *lot* more."

Demanski stared down at the cash. "If I agree to this, I'll also need to know how you did it."

"Of course. This will *save* you money. It was only a matter of time before someone figured out how your system worked, especially with the way you like to brag in interviews. Lucky for you, I figured it out first."

"Yeah, I'm a lucky guy."

"After you're up and running on my network, I'll tell your software experts everything they need to know to plug the hole. It's an easy fix."

Demanski sat on the edge of his desk, looking between Rachel, Tavak, and the stack of money. He finally nodded. "Part of being a good poker player is knowing when to fold. Okay, Dr. Kirby. You've got yourself a deal."

Rachel felt a wild surge of triumph. They'd *done* it!

Then, as she saw Demanski's expression, some of her elation ebbed away. She was suddenly aware of the immense power and intelligence that Demanski radiated. Backing Demanski into a corner was like going into a tiger's cage without a weapon.

Demanski's glance shifted to Tavak. "You took a big chance, Tavak. I don't like intruders in my space."

"So I've heard."

Demanski studied him for a moment. "And that made it better for you."

"Just more interesting."

Demanski shook his head and turned away. "Crazy as a loon. Get them all out of here, Gower."

They had barely reached the front door of the casino when Tavak told Simon, "Take everyone over to Bally's and give them all the liquor they can drink. My treat. Great job, guys."

"We'd do better to get them out of town," Rachel

said. "Demanski's not going to take kindly to us celebrating his defeat on his turf."

"He doesn't own Bally's."

"He might next week. He says he's going to own all of Nevada."

"Well, we'll worry about that next week." He took her elbow as they started across the street. "We did good. I want to pat ourselves on the back." He glanced at her. "And so do you. You had a hell of a good time up there. Your cheeks are flushed, your eyes are bright, and you're walking tall."

"I did what was necess—" She broke off. "Okay, I loved it. And I *was* ten feet tall."

He chuckled. "Then let's go sit at a bar and let those kids tell you that you were."

NINE

Come on." Tavak took Rachel's arm. "We're all going to back to Demanski's to watch the fountains."

Rachel shook her head. "For God's sake, it's almost four in the morning. And why risk going back there and pissing Demanski off?"

"Because Demanski's fountains are the only ones that have light shows all night long."

"That's a hell of a reason."

Tavak grinned. "I thought so. So did the kids."

"We've got to get a flight to Houston in a few hours. Don't you ever stop?"

"Occasionally." He nudged her toward the entrance, following Simon and the students out into the street. "But not if I have good company, and the music is playing."

"There's no music playing."

"Then we make our own music." He tapped his temple. "Up here. Listen. Don't you hear it?"

"No."

"You will. Maybe you haven't had enough wine."

"Alcohol-induced hallucinations?"

He shook his head. "Magic. It just sometimes has to have a little help."

"Alcohol-induced magic." She smiled. "Demanski was right. Crazy as a loon."

He nodded. "Sometimes. A little madness makes the ugliness easier to take." His smile faded. "Simon told me about that sniper. He said another inch, and you would have died. Why didn't you tell me?"

"It was my problem. It wasn't your concern."

"The hell it isn't. Quite a coincidence. I start stealing from Jonesy, and all of a sudden you're a target."

"Simon must have told you that a lot of people resent me, even hate me. It probably had nothing to do with you or Peseshet. If I didn't know what you were doing, why would anyone else? And if they did, why would they want to shoot me?"

"I don't know. To shut down Jonesy at least temporarily? Without you, everything goes bust." His lips tightened. "Anyway, you should have told me. I thought I was the only target, or I wouldn't have let you go back alone to the hotel from that train station in Paris. Going at anything blind is stupid. Don't do that to me again."

"No." She repeated, "It's not your concern."

He shook his head. "Stubborn." He suddenly smiled. "No matter. I'm on the scene now, and I'll know everything you'll know." He pulled her the last few yards to the wrought-iron fence that enclosed Demanski's fountains. "We have five minutes to go. We'll stand here and I'll shut up and you'll hear the music."

The hell he'd know everything she knew. Things weren't going as she wanted them to go. Tavak had managed to insinuate himself into her life when she'd only meant to use him. It was time to distance herself.

"No music in my head. That's the Demanski light-show sound track." She started toward Simon standing several yards away. "And for your information, everything would not go bust. I'm not that irresponsible. I've made provisions. Simon would take over until a new head was appointed. No one is irreplaceable."

"You're wrong." She heard Tavak chuckle behind her. "You'd be pretty near impossible to replace, Rachel."

She glanced over her shoulder to see that he

wasn't following her but had turned and was staring at the fountains. No, he was too clever to push when he knew that he had irritated her.

"You look pissed," Simon said, as she reached him. "I knew it couldn't last. You were having too good a time. I can't remember the last time you had enough to drink to mellow you."

"Well, I'm not mellow now."

He glanced at Tavak. "What did he do to you?"

"He tried to tell me what to do."

"Oh, that would do it." He smiled. "I thought he was smarter than that."

"He was smart enough to get you to tell him about that sniper."

"I didn't think it was top secret."

"It's not. I just didn't think it was his business." She shrugged. "But he seems to be good at inveigling information."

Simon clapped his hand to his head in mock horror. "God, I've been inveigled."

"Oh, shut up."

Simon glanced at Tavak. "You're right. He's something of a Pied Piper. All the students are nuts about him."

"So I saw tonight." She had watched Tavak become one with that group of students, telling jokes and stories and turning on that vitality like flashing neon. "That only makes him more dangerous."

Simon was silent. "I like him, Rachel."

"You were the one who warned me against being manipulated."

"I like him," he repeated. "And he got you to party. He can't be all bad." The fountain sprays suddenly exploded, leaping high in the air. "Here we go. What a blast."

Tavak and the Kirby woman are outside looking at the light show," Gower said sourly as he came into Demanski's office. "Of all the bitchin' nerve. Do you want me to go down and toss them into the fountain? Maybe we'd get lucky and they'd drown."

"It's not likely." Demanski hung up the phone. "There's supposed to be a special providence that protects the fools and the madmen of the world."

"And which one is Tavak?"

"Well, he's not a fool. I'm not sure what else he is yet." He leaned back in his chair. "But I intend to find out. I don't like not being able to gauge an enemy. Rachel Kirby is no problem. I know what she wants and what she'll do to get it."

"She's already got it." Gower's eyes narrowed. "Or has she? Are you actually going to let her hold you up like that?"

"Have you ever known me to break my word?"

"No. So let me break it for you," Gower said. "Along with both their heads."

Demanski chuckled. A loyalty like Gower's was rare, but it often escalated into mayhem if

190

Demanski didn't rein him in. "No, it's a done deal. I won't back out. I've just been on the phone making sure that Kirby gets her precious cycles."

"You don't seem upset about it."

Upset? Demanski had been mad as hell earlier, but now that he'd calmed down he was feeling something entirely different. It had something to do with the excitement and exhilaration he had seen in the faces of Kirby and Tavak and those kids they had used to bilk him. How long had it been since he had felt that same zing in anything he did? The thrill of the chase, the pleasure of being the best, of being able to pull the rug out from under an opponent at incalculable risk. His battles were much more civilized these days.

But Tavak was still experiencing that intoxicating jolt. Demanski had seen it in his expression in those last few minutes before he had thrown them out of his office.

It had made him jealous as hell.

"No, I'm not upset. The first battle seldom decides a war. They took something away from me. Now let's see what we can take away from them."

"Yes."

"Kirby and Tavak impress me as being an odd duo. I believe we need to know why they're working together. To do that, I need to know everything I can about Tavak."

"No problem." Gower's smile lit his rough features. "Consider it done. But I still think you should let me break their heads."

ARDMORE UNIVERSITY

Nice campus," Tavak said, gazing out the window of Simon's Toyota. "I generally don't like anything connected to university life, but this is very unprepossessing."

"Why don't you like universities?" Rachel asked.

"I grew up in one." One side of his lips lifted in a sardonic smile. "I was a freak, and Harvard might have been a high-class carnival, but I was a sideshow nonetheless."

"I imagine you were," Simon said. "But you seem to have survived pretty well."

"When I was able to shrug off the brainwashing and set off to do my own thing."

Rachel tried to recall all the details of his dossier. "And your own thing was being a mercenary, a thief, and God knows what else."

He smiled. "God knows. He also knows I usually have a hell of a good time, and I never look back." He gazed at the building they were approaching. "Is that Jonesy's domain? I'm eager to come face-to-face with him."

"Well, you're not going to do it yet. We're just here because I want to pick up my car. I left it here before I went to Cairo. Simon is going to take you to the Galveston lab so that you can show him all your backdoors into Jonesy. You used that branch of the network to tap into us, didn't you?"

"Yes, but I can just as easily show you what I did from here."

"Not anymore. Until we get your hooks out, we've isolated that branch from the rest of the system."

Tavak nodded. "Of course. Very wise. You're not going to escort me personally?"

"Simon can do it. He's the one who found the break. I'm going to see my sister."

Tavak was silent a moment. "I'd like to meet her."

"And I don't want you to meet her." Rachel got out of the car. "I'll be back here at the lab by six tonight. That should give you enough time to show Simon what we need to know."

"Probably," Tavak said. "Why don't you want me to meet her?"

"You're something of Pied Piper. She thinks I'm nuts to believe you can find a cure for her. But after I started thinking about it, I decided it's better if she does think that. You have a way of making black look like pure gold. I don't want her hopes raised, then dashed." She opened her car door. "So you stay away from her."

"Whatever you say." His brows rose. "Pied Piper? I never thought of myself like that. Didn't he lead the rats into the river? That's almost a heroic role."

"You're no hero." She glanced at Simon. "Make sure we close every backdoor in Jonesy, Simon."

Simon nodded. "Every single one. I remember what a headache it was looking for them." He backed the car out of the parking area. "See you at six, Rachel."

She watched them drive away before she got into her car. It was noon, and that gave her at least five hours to spend with Allie. Lord, she wasn't looking forward to it. It was going to be difficult as hell trying to handle Allie.

Dammit, she *would* look forward to it. Forget the problems. Every moment she spent with Allie was precious.

Allie! I'm home," Rachel called as she opened the front door. "Where are you?"

"Here." Allie came down the hall from the direction of the kitchen. "I've been cooking lunch. I've found a new Paula Deen recipe for crab cakes that's terrific."

Rachel gazed at her warily. "Paula Deen?"

"Yes, Southern cooking is better than anyone else's. Don't you think so?"

"Your cooking is always wonderful."

"Yes, it is." She smiled serenely. "I'm quite the chef. It's one of the few skills I could learn that you gave your full approval. Probably because I could do it within the safe confines of home and hearth. That's also why you approved of my becoming an artist."

"For heaven's sake, you have an incredible talent."

"Yes, I do. But wasn't it convenient that I could exercise that talent here with no stress? I could enjoy the creativity and have a limited fan base. No risks. No challenges I couldn't handle." She turned away. "Lunch is almost ready. Go wash your hands and we'll eat and you can tell me what a fantastic cook I am."

"How do you feel? You look great."

"I'm good. I'm on the upswing again." She was moving down the hallway. "Lots of energy."

"Wait. What's happened? You were upset as hell when I last talked to you."

"You bet I was." She turned around to face her again. "And then I thought about it and realized I wasn't being fair. You were desperate and you wanted to do something. You grabbed for the brass ring again." She smiled faintly. "Do you remember when we were kids and used to ride the carousel in the park? I could never stand up and reach for that brass ring, so you'd do it for me. You were pretty small, but you'd stand up on the horse's back and try and try until you got it for me."

"It wasn't worth it. Just a cheap little trinket."

"I still have one of those brass rings in my jewelry box. It wasn't cheap to me. Whatever you do has value for me." She wrinkled her nose. "Even going on crazy quests for the biggest, brightest brass ring of all. It was hard to swallow that particular sacrifice. It choked me."

"It's no sacrifice. That's bull. Nothing I do for you is a sacrifice."

"The hell it's not. You never even thought about getting that brass ring for yourself." Her lips tightened. "And I wasn't generous enough to think of it for you. I just accepted everything when I was a kid. After I grew up I tried to stop, but the habit was firmly in place for both of us." She looked her in the eye. "It's time to put an end to it, Rachel."

Rachel shook her head. "I have to do this, Allie."

"I know you do." She paused. "But this time I'm not going to let you be in it alone. If you think there's a brass ring to be had, then I'll help you reach for it. I'll give you a little time to get used to the idea, but I'm not going to be left behind. I'm not helpless. I'm on the upswing and feeling much better now. I may not be as smart as you, but I'm intelligent, and I have skills that you don't."

"Allie, no."

"Rachel, yes," Allie said softly. "You're not going to leave me home and take this challenge away from me because I'm sick and you want to protect me. It's too late for that now. I won't have it."

"Allie, there's nothing for you to do."

"We'll see." Once again Allie gave her that serene smile. "Now come and eat my crab cakes. They're better when they're hot."

ARDMORE UNIVERSITY

Six sharp," Simon said as he pulled into the parking spot beside where Rachel was standing. "As you commanded. But I didn't get all the work done in Galveston."

She gazed at Tavak. "You didn't cooperate?"

He shrugged. "I gave him what he wanted."

"Simon?"

"He gave it to me, but it's so damn complicated it's taking me a hell of a long time. So I thought I'd drop Tavak off and go back. Okay?"

"Okay." She watched Tavak get out the car. "Phone me if you have trouble, and I'll come."

"I know how to do it. I've already closed one backdoor. It's just that I don't think the way Tavak does. Hell, nobody thinks like Tavak." He grimaced. "It's like being in a maze with no exit."

"You did pretty well," Tavak said. "In fact, you did damn well."

Simon grinned. "Are you patronizing me?"

"I wouldn't think of it." Tavak got out of the car. "I never intended to make closing those doors easy."

"Then you succeeded." He waved his hand. "I'll call you if I need rescuing, Rachel."

Rachel turned to Tavak as Simon drove away. "Could you have made it easier for him?"

"Well, I could have done it myself. But then he wouldn't have had the satisfaction of working through it. Simon needs a challenge." He smiled. "That's why he works for you."

She had seen that quality in Simon before she had hired him. Tavak was very perceptive. And that perceptiveness made him even more dangerous. "Just so you didn't hold anything back."

"I didn't." He grinned. "But that doesn't mean I haven't an idea or two about getting back into Jonesy by another method and route. It would be much more difficult now, and Simon isn't the only one who needs a challenge."

"Don't you dare." Lord, that was feeble, she thought wearily. He'd dare whatever he chose, and she'd have to find a way to cope with him. At the moment, that prospect seemed insurmountable.

Evidently Tavak must have sensed that weariness because his eyes narrowed on her face. "Not such a good visit with your sister? She's not well?"

"Well? She's *dying,* dammit." She turned and strode toward the security entrance of the building. "And she wants to help. She wants to catch the brass ring for me. She wants me to stop protecting her."

"Help?"

"Peseshet's cure. She doesn't believe in it, but she wants to help me try to find it." She leaned back against the brick wall beside the door. "Do you know how many times she's been in a hospital in her life? I would have crumbled away at all the things those doctors did to her. She just kept on. She always just takes the pain and doesn't complain. I won't let her spend what might be her last days searching for something that might not exist. I told her that, but she just smiled at me." She could feel the tears sting her eyes. "And she kept talking about that damn brass ring."

Tavak reached out a hand, then let it drop before he touched her. "I'd like to help you, but I know you aren't going to listen to anything I say. Besides, I'm not good at comforting people. I'm awkward as hell."

"I don't need you to comfort me." She straightened away from the wall. She didn't know why all that emotion had erupted. Maybe because he was a stranger, and she felt less vulnerable venting with someone who didn't know her. She cleared her throat. "I'm sorry. You don't care about any of this. As you said, it wasn't a good visit." She turned and unlocked the door. "Let's have you meet Jonesy. The main computer is much more complex than that Galveston branch."

"I'm looking forward to it." He paused. "You know, your sister may be like Simon and me . . . and you. She may need a challenge in her life."

"Staying alive is her challenge. She couldn't have a bigger one."

"She may be ready for another one."

"Then she's not going to get it." Rachel opened the door and made an effort to smother the emotion that was tearing her apart. "The subject is closed, Tavak."

He nodded. "But I don't think it's any more firmly shut than those backdoors I showed Simon." He didn't wait for an answer as he surveyed the computer lab they'd entered. "This is your supercomputer? I expected it to be—"

"Bigger?" Val turned from a bank of three monitors. "That's what everyone says. But you don't need a building full of processors when you're using power from machines all over the world." She stood up and walked toward Rachel. "I don't know how you did it, but Demanski's computer network has already been integrated with Jonesy. It's an incredibly powerful system."

Rachel leaned over Val's desk and checked the readings. "That's why I wanted it so much. By the way, Val, this is John Tavak."

Val glanced at him. "I've spent two days figuring out how you tapped into our network. It was ingenious."

Rachel shook her head. "Don't encourage him."

Val shrugged. "Give credit where it's due. Every time one of your security protocols did a system sweep, his spyware mimicked the behavior of one of our thousands of processing donors. That's why we couldn't catch him. His software was constantly adapting and learning new ways to stay hidden. I'm impressed."

"Coming from an expert such as you, Val, I take that as a great compliment."

Rachel was surprised to see the color flush Val's cheeks. The young woman had always received a lot of attention from her male colleagues, but Tavak was obviously having as potent effect on her as he'd had on the students last night. She pointed to the allocation tables. "So Norton is back up to his full power?"

Val took off her wire-rimmed spectacles and wiped them on her shirt. "Yes. Maybe he'll finally get off our back. Whatever projects he's working on, they're using every ounce of his computing power."

"Aren't you curious about what the NSA is doing with your system?" Tavak asked.

Rachel smiled. "Me? No. But Val and Simon have wasted countless hours speculating on what he's doing."

"You're exaggerating," Val said.

"Only slightly. As the NSA gets more and more interested in the personal lives of U.S. citizens, there are millions and millions of pieces of information to be analyzed and sorted out. If one person buys airline tickets for himself and a couple of buddies, and one of said buddies happens to buy materials that could be used to make bombs, the NSA wants to know about it. And they want to know about it now, not in a few days or weeks. It takes a lot of computing power to sort through all those billions of transactions. Jonesy can do in minutes what might otherwise take them hours or days."

"Can't they build their own supercomputers?"

"They already have. But we're on the cutting edge here, and they're still playing catch-up. And Norton may be doing something with Jonesy that he doesn't want anyone to be able to tap or subpoena. The truth is, I don't care what they're doing. It's all encrypted anyway, and the information could be parsed out among hundreds of other systems. Even if we wanted to crack the NSA encryption—not a smart thing to try, by the way—our tiny piece would probably still be meaningless."

Tavak nodded. "If you say so. But the NSA project could be the reason that sniper was using you for target practice. Did that occur to you?"

"It occurred to me." Rachel crossed her arms and leaned against Val's desk. "Make up your mind. You were telling me your hacking into Jonesy could have gotten me shot."

"I find that even more reasonable. Less than seventy-two hours ago, Dawson tried to kill me for Peseshet's secrets. He wouldn't hesitate to do the same to you." He glanced at the monitor. "But what would Dawson have to gain from your death?"

"I'll give you the same answer you gave me. He could have been trying to slow you down."

He shook his head. "If you were out of the picture, it would only be easier for me to commandeer more of your computer network's resources." Tavak turned to Val. "No offense."

"None taken," Val said. "And you're right. Nobody knows this system better than Rachel."

"Okay, then," Rachel said. "Let's explore the possibility that perhaps I was shot by someone who wanted you to *succeed.*" She stared him in the eye. "Perhaps you or someone you've been working with."

"Not my style."

Rachel laughed. "That's all you've got? 'Not my style'?"

Tavak nodded.

It was enough, Rachel realized. Tavak's calm, offhand manner inspired trust, no matter how cavalier he'd been about hacking into her network. She actually *believed* him.

Dammit.

Tavak leaned toward the monitors. "Now that I don't have to waste processing power hiding from you and Ms. Cho, your system should make faster headway processing my code." He produced a USB memory stick and handed it to Rachel.

"What's this?"

"The next piece of the puzzle. I managed to

retrieve the first part of the message from the hard drive this afternoon. I worked on it in Galveston while Simon was laboring over all those back-doors."

Rachel muttered a curse. "And you didn't tell me?"

"I'm telling you now. If we can insert this into the code that I already have your system working on, retrieving the rest should be a slam dunk."

Rachel gazed at the stick for a moment. "Val, pull up Mr. Tavak's problem. Let's give it priority." She turned back to Tavak. "But what now? Even if we increase the processing cycles devoted to this code, it could still take days."

"True," Tavak said. "But as we confirm that your supercomputer is on the right track, it should get easier. That is, if Peseshet's disciple, Natifah, didn't change the code in each place. And we're also counting on her former patients—and the tradesmen who crafted these markers—to have correctly transcribed the symbols she gave them."

Rachel nodded. "I'll take a look at the decoding software you wrote. I've gotten pretty good at har-nessing Jonesy's brute force in solving problems."

Tavak smiled. "I have a feeling that's like saying Tiger Woods is 'pretty good' at golf."

Val didn't look up from the keyboard. "You got *that* right."

"Part of the message is easy to read. It alludes to another former patient of Peseshet's who would protect her legacy. But I discovered that the scope of this puzzle may be larger than I first thought."

"What do you mean?"

"We already knew that Natifah had persuaded Peseshet's former patients to honor the doctor by erecting hidden monuments in their tombs. I assumed all of these patients were in Egypt, but that may not have been the case."

"You mean Natifah may have gone to other countries to hide the clues?"

"It makes sense. She was on the run, and it would have been smart to leave Egypt. She was in Babylonia when Peseshet was killed. She had to return to Egypt to retrieve Peseshet's tablets, but she wouldn't have had to stay there. In their travels, Peseshet and Natifah would have encountered any number of rulers or noblemen who would have been grateful enough to honor Peseshet as she requested. And since they weren't subjects of the Pharaoh, there would be less danger to them and their families for erecting these hidden monuments to her."

"So where does that leave us?"

Tavak showed her the pages. "The inscription on the wall of Kontar's tomb mentions a 'soaring bird of twilight' who protects the next piece of Peseshet's legacy. It says that this piece is written with the fire of the sun on his tomb. I couldn't find anyone in Old Kingdom Egypt who might match that description, but when I had Jonesy broaden the search, I found something interesting."

Tavak pointed to a photo that depicted a stone-chiseled representation of a man wearing ornamental robes. "This was a holy man in Babylon. We don't really know his name, although modern archaeologists call him Nemop. He's thought to have gained his powers only late in life, so he was well-known as the Eagle Who Soars at Sundown."

"The soaring bird of twilight . . ."

"Yes. Babylonia was an important trading partner to Egypt during Peseshet's time, so it's entirely possible that she was sent to minister to the country's VIPs in exchange for goods or access to trade routes."

Rachel looked at Tavak's handwritten notes, which included a list of half a dozen items. "What's this?"

"Things that were probably buried with him to take to the afterlife. Clothing, work animals, dried fruits, twenty-two ounces of oil from a silli-cyprium tree, among other things."

"I don't like where this is going. Does this mean we're about to raid another tomb?"

"I don't think so. Nemop did have a temple that he used in life and became a sort of shrine to him after his death. It was discovered in 1937 by an archaeologist named Danielle Hutton."

Tavak raised a downloaded black-and-white photo of a woman wearing tall boots, broad-pleated pants, white blouse, and a pith helmet. She appeared to be at a dig site.

Rachel glanced at the picture and smiled. "Are you sure this isn't a movie lobby card? She looks like Katharine Hepburn."

"Danielle Hutton was the real deal. But I can't find any information about where Nemop's shrine went. We know it was moved shortly after the discovery, but the trail goes cold after that. An occasional stray artifact from the site can be found in online museum catalogues, but I haven't been able to find anything else."

"It could have been lost or destroyed during World War II."

"Possibly. But there is someone we can talk to."

"Surely not Danielle Hutton."

"Afraid not. She died in 1995. But look at this." Tavak raised the picture and pointed to a little girl in a khaki outfit standing in the background alongside several men. "This is her daughter, Emily. She took up the family business and became a great archaeologist in her own right. She teaches at Berkeley."

"So we're headed to California?"

Tavak smiled. "Not exactly."

TEN

QUANTO VALLEY RIDGE
ARIZONA

Rachel folded her map and looked at the expanse of desert before her. She and Tavak sat in an open Jeep driving toward the unobstructed horizon.

She wiped her forehead with her handkerchief and leaned forward in the passenger seat. "It must be a hundred degrees."

Tavak smiled. "Try a hundred and fourteen."

"And this woman is *camping* out here."

"That's what I was told."

"Is that really a good idea for an eighty-year-old?"

"From what I understand, it's her graduate students on the expedition who are having the problems. She's been doing this her whole life."

"Amazing."

"I just hope she can give us something we can use. It's a long way to go for nothing."

Two hours later, Tavak slowed as they approached a small village of tents situated in the shadow of a craggy rock formation. A dozen students worked with shovels, pickaxes, and wire brushes at various spots around the encampment.

They pulled alongside a young man with mirrored sunglasses. Tavak called out to him. "Where can I find Dr. Hutton?"

"Find her yourself." The young man plopped onto the ground cross-legged. "That lady's gonna kill me."

"So she's here?"

"Oh, yeah. She's here." He squinted at them. "Think maybe I can hitch a ride back with you guys? Maybe it's not too late to switch my major. I've got a pretty good—"

"Stop your whining, Benjamin!" A strong, sharp voice cut through his sentence.

Rachel and Tavak turned to see a woman who could only be Dr. Emily Hutton. Her tanned, weather-beaten face was creased with deep lines, but otherwise she looked astonishingly like the photo of her mother. She possessed the same angular features, and her gray hair was pulled back in a ponytail.

Emily took off her hat and struck the young man about the head and shoulders. "Drink some water and get back in your hole. Now!"

"I can't. Not yet."

"Sure you can. And you will. How would you like Cassie Davis to see an eighty-year-old woman taking your place because you're too much of a wuss to finish what you've started?"

The student glared at her. "You hit me. That's abuse. I could write you up, and—"

"For God's sake, you're twenty years old. You'd

get laughed off the campus if you filed a report. Now get back to work."

Benjamin muttered something beneath his breath. Then he picked himself up and trudged back toward one of the dig sites.

Emily turned back toward Rachel and Tavak. "I take it you're not here to give me the extra supplies I need."

"Afraid not," Tavak said. "We want to talk to you about a discovery your mother made."

"Ah, shit. Which one?"

"Nemop, in Babylonia."

"You couldn't have called or sent me an e-mail?"

"Your graduate assistant wouldn't give us the number of your satellite phone, and she refused to pass along a message. She said it was for emergencies only."

Emily chuckled. "Good girl. I'm very busy out here. See me in my office in ten days." She turned away.

Rachel jumped out of the Jeep. "Wait!"

Emily stopped, but she didn't turn around.

Rachel ran around to face her. "Dr. Hutton, please. I'm Dr. Rachel Kirby. I'm a university professor, too. I know how important this project is to you, but if you could just give us a few minutes of your time."

Emily glanced between Rachel and Tavak. "Young lady, if you're a college professor, you know how precious my time is out here. I have to fight like hell to get the grants I need to mount these shindigs."

"I understand."

"And still you want to take some of my valuable time."

"Yes. It's important."

"Of course it is." Emily sighed. "Just a few minutes, huh?"

"Absolutely."

"Uh-huh. Okay. Come see me at the end of the day. We'll talk."

Tavak shook his head. "We need to get back right away."

Emily shrugged. "Then go. I'm not stopping you."

"Okay, okay." Rachel put a hand on her arm. "We'll stay. Thank you."

Emily's face lit with a broad grin that was definitely elfish. "Don't thank me, Rachel Kirby." She bent over, picked up a pair of shovels, and handed them to Rachel and Tavak.

Tavak looked at his shovel. "I'm afraid to ask what this is for."

"Last time I checked, it was for digging. Which is what you're going to be doing for oh, the next seven hours or so. It so happens we can use a couple grunt laborers here today."

"Are you serious?"

Emily turned and walked away. "Talk to the tall blond girl over there. She'll tell you where to dig."

. . .

As the last rays of sunlight dipped below the horizon, the excavation site's atmosphere changed from that of a slave-labor camp to a block party. Torches were lit and folk-rock music suddenly blared from an array of speakers. Two of the students erected a long table, while another uncovered a grill pit and started a fire.

On the hill where Rachel and Tavak had worked in relative isolation, Tavak threw down his shovel. "I guess the whistle has blown."

Rachel glanced at her throbbing hands. "I hope we were really accomplishing something. I have a feeling they just put us up here so everyone could look up whenever they needed a laugh."

Tavak smiled. "I wouldn't put it past the old girl. Come on, let's find her."

They worked their way down into the heart of the camp, where they finally found Emily seated on a canvas folding chair, holding court for a half dozen of her students. She held a shot glass in one hand and a bottle of tequila in the other, which she used to frequently refill her students' cups.

Rachel ventured into circle. "Dr. Hutton?"

"Welcome, welcome!" Emily now appeared much looser than she had earlier in the afternoon, and her eyes appeared as two tiny slits. She smiled. "Don't worry, I'm not drunk. At least not yet. But a couple of hours from now, that'll be a different story."

The students laughed and clinked their glasses.

Emily poured herself another shot. "So tell me, why in hell would you want to know about Nemop?"

"It was a major archeological find," Tavak said. "But little seems to survive."

"Oh, it survives. Just not anyplace where people can easily study it."

"Why not?"

"It was the deal my mother struck with the government. She could dig, study, and catalog, but none of her finds could be taken from the country. They went into storage. There was some talk of a national museum, but it never happened. Eventually, everything was either sold off or pilfered. As you know, ancient Babylon is modern-day Iraq. Some of those Babylonian archaeological sites have been paved over and have military helipads on them. Nice, huh?"

Rachel knelt next to her. "Do you know where the artifacts ended up?"

"My mother kept track of that stuff. She was hoping to interest a foundation in gathering it for a permanent collection, but she never got very far. What are you interested in?"

"The temple itself. The walls, anything with inscriptions on it."

Emily laughed so hard that the student next to her had to grab her wrist to keep her from spilling her drink.

"Did I say something funny?" Tavak asked.

Emily wiped her eyes. "Do you like monkeys?"

"Monkeys?"

"Yes. You see, that temple went on the auction block in 1939 to line the pocket of some corrupt government official. I think a few museums were in the running for it, but an American with far too much money was also there. His checkbook was bigger, so he went home with it."

"*What* American?"

"William Randolph Hearst. Heard of him?"

Tavak nodded. "Of course."

"He was buying art treasures all over the world for a little place he was building on the California coast."

Rachel's brows lifted. "Hearst Castle? It's there?"

"In a matter of speaking. You see, Hearst never bothered reassembling the temple. I guess he just didn't know what to do with it. The walls, floor, ceiling—the whole thing—became a sidewalk."

"You're joking," Rachel said.

"Wish I was. My sense of humor isn't this good. Those priceless temple walls became an inlaid out-door walkway in Hearst's zoo on the property. It was the largest private zoo in the world."

"Incredible," Rachel said. "And it's still there?"

Emily nodded. "Near the monkey cages. There are no animals anymore, of course. I don't think the tours even go up there nowadays. And the whole estate now belongs to the California Park Service."

Rachel and Tavak exchanged glances.

"You never answered my question," Emily said. "Why does this matter to you?"

Rachel turned back toward her. "We think Nemop may have had an association with someone else we're studying. Peseshet."

"The lady doctor? It's possible. Timing would be about right."

"But there were no inscriptions on those temple walls that mentioned her?" Tavak asked.

"No. And my mother photographed everything. If you hunt around, I think you can find the pictures online."

"Yes, I've found quite a few of them," Tavak said.

Rachel stood up. "Thank you for your help, Dr. Hutton."

"You're welcome." Emily stood, steadying herself by gripping the back of her chair. "Do something for me, will you? When you find what you're looking for, let me know. My mom carried the memory of Nemop around with her most of her life, and she would have been happy that people are still talking about the guy."

HEARST CASTLE
SAN SIMEON, CALIFORNIA

For heaven's sake, why use a boat?" Rachel asked as she helped Tavak pull the blue-and-white motorboat onto the narrow strip of white sand below the castle. "It would have been quicker to drive here."

"But not as serene or beautiful." He drew a deep breath. "Sea air, golden sunlight . . . It's good for the soul." He took her arm. "Come on, it's a little hike to the main gate."

Before long they were within the gates and had taken the tram from the visitor center to the main house. They stood next to the Neptune pool facing the remnants of the zoo over a quarter mile away. Rachel handed Tavak the binoculars. "The cages are to the right."

Tavak peered through the lenses. "All I can see is concrete. Our inlaid walkway must be in front of the cages, hidden by those trees."

"That's what I think." Rachel stepped back and took in the estate's massive, Spanish-style structures, clay tennis courts, and the long, winding road that led down to the Pacific Coast Highway. They had just seen the exotic gardens on the other side of the main house, and their odors blended with the ocean air in a combination she could only describe as intoxicating.

Tavak smiled. "It's easy to imagine Charlie Chaplin, Cary Grant, and Carole Lombard going for a midnight swim here, isn't it? Or maybe playing tennis with some foreign head of state?"

"Or going for a stroll on a priceless four-thousand-year-old temple wall?"

216

"That, too."

She motioned toward the long-abandoned zoo cages. "So how are we going to get over there?"

"I'm working on it."

"I guess it would be too much to suggest that we go through official channels. You know, write a few letters, contact an administrator . . ."

Tavak shook his head. "That's a good way to drown in red tape. Dawson isn't waiting for anyone. He won't be writing letters."

"So what's your master plan?"

"We hitch a ride. Tonight."

HEARST CASTLE
9:20 P.M.

You okay back there?" Tavak called back to Rachel over his shoulder. He was in the passenger seat of a white-paneled van, sitting next to Paul Deakins, a stocky fifteen-year veteran of Marsh Food Supply. Deakins was making his nightly delivery to the Hearst Castle food-service kitchen, and he'd been persuaded to risk his job for a generous cash bribe from Tavak.

Rachel clung to the metal racks in the back of the van. The vehicle lurched on a steep incline as it neared the visitors' center. "Oh, I'm just great. Tell me again, why aren't *you* back here instead?"

"This company has never had a female delivery person. You'd stick out."

"That sounds as flimsy now as it did the first time."

Deakins laughed. "Hang on, we're almost there."

Within a minute, they were at a small loading dock at the visitors' center, a building that contained the ticket windows, souvenir shops, and restaurants. It was a waiting area between the parking lots and trams that took guests to the main houses and gardens of the estate.

Deakins backed the van into place and cut the engine. He sat in silence for a moment.

"What is it?" Tavak asked.

Deakins glanced at them. "I'm just—You guys aren't terrorists or anything, are you?"

Tavak smiled. "It's a little late for a guilty conscience, isn't it?"

"You said you just want to look around."

"It's the truth. We're not going to take or harm anything."

Deakins glanced back at Rachel, who gave him a reassuring nod. "Okay. If you get caught, remember your promise. You snuck in over the fence somewhere. Let 'em wonder why their sensors didn't pick it up." He grimaced. "And be careful. These grounds have as many security alarms as Fort Knox. Anyone thinks there's something funny going on, and that hill will be lit up like a Christmas tree."

Tavak handed him a thick envelope of cash. "We'll be careful. Thanks."

He nodded. "Okay. Each of you grab a case of hot dog buns and follow me."

Rachel and Tavak each picked up a white carton, climbed out of the van, and followed Deakins to a door on the other side of the loading dock. Deakins glanced around, but there didn't appear to be anyone around. He whispered, "There's a Lakers game on, so the guards will probably be pretty scarce for the next hour or so." He motioned for them to put down the boxes. "If you walk through that path, the trees will give you some good cover."

"Right." Tavak and Rachel sprinted toward the path and moved through the dense foliage.

In less than ten minutes they found themselves standing among the curved white structures that once housed Hearst's collection of monkeys, cougars, and even grizzly bears.

Tavak shined his flashlight toward the walkway in front of the cages. "Check it out."

Even from a distance of thirty yards, Rachel could see the ornamental carvings that reminded her of other Babylonian artifacts she'd seen. They ran toward the cages and stepped onto the walk made from the former temple of Nemop.

Rachel felt a twinge of guilt. Oh, what the hell. She wasn't the first and wouldn't be the last to violate this ancient Babylonian treasure.

Tavak reached into his knapsack and produced a metal box attached to a silver sensor wand.

"What's that?" Rachel asked.

"It's a sonar reader. Short of X-raying these slabs, it's the best way of seeing if there's anything else hidden inside."

Tavak waved the sensor over each section of walkway. After he reached the end, he switched off the device and shook his head. "Nope. These slabs are solid. Nothing hidden inside."

Rachel stared at the inlaid walls. "You told me that Kontar's tomb in Egypt said that the message was written in fire in this temple."

"I took that to mean the passion and conviction of the person passing the message along."

"That's what I thought, too." She studied it for a moment longer. "Which of these stones was the floor of the tomb?"

Tavak aimed the flashlight down the walkway. "That large one over there."

She and Tavak stood over it. "Notice how all the carvings are etched in varying depths. They're carved almost an inch deep in some places, maybe less than an eighth of an inch in other spots. Even sometimes within the same figures."

Tavak studied them. "You're right. That's not something we could see in the photos."

"But on the wall slabs, the depths of all the lines and flourishes are perfectly uniform." Rachel squatted next to the stone floor slab. "And look at this figure holding the torch. The flame is indented, with carved-out channels that connect to adjacent areas." She looked up at him. "In the carvings back in Egypt, how much sillicyprium oil did it say was Nemop to take with him to the here-after?"

"The equivalent of about twenty-two ounces."

"What was it used for?"

"It's basically castor oil."

"Was it used for lamps?"

Tavak nodded as he followed her train of thought. "I'm pretty sure it was."

Rachel stared at the torch etching. "If we were to pour that amount into the torch, the oil would run to the surrounding lines. It would pool in the deeper cut areas, and drain away from the shallower lines . . ."

Tavak gazed at her and then nodded slowly. "A message written in fire."

"Exactly." Rachel's heart was pounding with excitement. "If we lit the oil, those pooled areas might form our message . . ."

Tavak smiled. "It might. Aren't I lucky to have you here to supply the brainpower in our little enterprise?"

"And you'd probably figured out this possibility yourself. So stop being sarcastic."

"I'm not being sarcastic. I feel very lucky tonight . . . and very proud."

There was something in his tone that made her eyes fly to his face. No, there was no mockery in his expression, but there was something else there that disturbed her. She glanced away from him back at the walk. "It's a possibility, but it doesn't mean I'm right. We need to see if it actually works."

He nodded. "Yeah. Trouble is, there's never twenty-two ounces of sillicyprium oil around when you need it."

"How about a substitute?"

Tavak thought for a moment. He unzipped his knapsack, pulled out a bottle of water, and emptied it on the ground. "Wait here. I'll be right back."

"Where are you going?"

He was already moving through the trees. "Wait here!"

Less than ten minutes later, Tavak returned with the bottle and a paper cup.

Rachel sniffed the air. "Gasoline. Where did you get it?"

"I used a garden hose to siphon it out of a land-scaping truck. This water bottle holds twenty ounces, and I can pour another two ounces from this paper cup I found in the trash."

"Two ounces? Are you sure? If we're even a little off, the wrong etchings might fill up and totally throw off the message."

"I've mixed enough drinks to know what I'm doing. Trust me, I know what two ounces looks like." Tavak leaned over and poured a small amount from the cup into the carved-out flame on the walk. "There." He handed the bottle to Rachel. "Would you like to do the honors?"

"Yes." Rachel took the bottle and poured the gasoline into the same place. The liquid ran through the adjacent channels and settled in the deeper-set lines and carvings.

Tavak produced a lighter and a Hearst brochure, lit it, and dropped it on the slab. The gasoline ignited and raced through the lines. The shallower parts quickly burned off, but deeper lines held the flame.

Several recognizably Egyptian characters suddenly appeared, etched in fire.

"Holy shit!" Rachel gasped.

"I see it, I see it." Tavak was already snapping photos with his digital camera.

"Can you read those characters?"

Tavak shook his head. "Not immediately. And if it's in code, it may be a job for your Jonesy."

What had she been thinking? Of course it wouldn't be that simple. Nothing had been easy or simple since the moment she had received that first e-mail from Tavak.

"I'll transmit these pictures to Val at the lab as soon as we get back to the car."

Tavak leaned over for a closer look.

A bullet whistled past the place where his head had been. A tree branch splintered behind him.

Rachel's head lifted. "What's hap—"

Two black-garbed figures were running toward them.

Another gunshot.

"Down!"

Whoosh! The sidewalk exploded into flame.

Before she could register what was happening, she was thrown to the ground only inches from the wall of flame.

Tavak. He'd tackled her, she realized. And even as he'd brought her down, he'd tossed the rest of the gasoline onto the flame, erasing the message.

"Get the camera!" one of the men shouted.

Tavak rolled across the walkway with her, then pulled her to her feet. "Come on!"

Another bullet whistled past them.

They ran through trees, down a steep incline.

"Faster!" Tavak said.

"Dammit, I'm going as fast as I can. I can't see where I'm going."

"Neither can they."

Branches cracked behind her. They were gaining on them.

Tavak yanked her to the left. "This way."

How did he know where to go? He hadn't seen any more of the place than she—

"Get down!" He pushed her to the ground, half beneath an outcropping of earth on the hillside.

She twisted to see Tavak kneeling, lifting something long and snakelike from the ground. Was that a—

"Aughhh!" A scream issued from the throat of one of the men as they both tripped, appeared to take flight over the embankment, then disappeared into the darkness far below. The next moment Rachel heard cursing and the crunch of foliage coming from the area where they'd fallen.

"A water hose." Rachel gazed at Tavak still holding the end of the water hose two feet above the ground. "You led them here to make sure they tripped on that water hose. How did you—"

"It was the landscape hose I used to siphon the gasoline." His gaze was on the hillside to the west. "Oh shit."

Blinding white lights were dotting the darkness. Suddenly shrill, earsplitting alarms sounded from the trees.

"Those gunshots screwed us. It's a security alert. We have to get out of the park, or we'll be sitting ducks."

"Then stop talking and move." Rachel was on her feet. "The main entrance. And we'll have to steer clear of the trails."

They worked their way down the hillside, dodging the glaring security lights shining down from the trees. Security vehicles were driving slowly down the roads. Tinny voices blared from radios and walkie-talkies.

"We have to be close to the main gate," Rachel said. "I hear the sound of cars on the highway."

"We are." Tavak was peering through the brush. "Wait."

A white security pickup truck was parked at the main entrance. Two officers were standing by the truck surveying the hillside with their high-powered flashlights.

"We have to go for it," Tavak said. "The local police could be here any minute. Are you ready?"

"Hell, no." But she was already slipping through the brush and sprinting across a dark stretch of the highway. She heard Tavak right behind her.

Had the guards seen them?

No, she realized with relief. No shouts. No blaring horns.

They ran past the hotel, the restaurant, and finally to the narrow beach. The blue-and-white motorboat rested on the sand where they had left it.

Rachel and Tavak pushed the small boat into the water and climbed in. Tavak started the engine, then motored quietly away under cover of darkness. "I think we're okay. We should be back to our car within the hour."

Rachel looked back at the hillside, where the lights indicated that even more security vehicles had joined the search. "This is why you insisted on taking the boat to the estate. What are you? Psychic or something?"

"Just an eternal pessimist. I always operate on the theory that what could go wrong, will go wrong."

"And it did. Were those Dawson's men?"

"Who else? One of them may have been Dawson himself. He's a smart man with a lot of resources. Since he already had my original info in the hard drive, he had a head start. But if we're lucky,

Dawson is still stymied about the decoder, and we were just followed."

"I don't think that's lucky. Do you think they saw the message?"

"Hard to say. I threw the rest of the gasoline on it as soon as I saw them, but they could have been watching from the trees."

"They wanted the camera."

"And they wanted us dead. But barring that, they may have wanted the camera to keep us from having the message. Get the camera out of my knapsack and take a look. Unless you'd rather take time to get your breath. We could wait until we get back to the motel."

"No way." Rachel had the camera out of his bag and was flipping through the pictures on the tiny screen. "You can read hieroglyphics. I know the cure portion is probably in code, but can you see anything else that would give us any lead about Natifah's next piece of the puzzle?"

"It's actually fairly easy to read, but I don't know what the hell it means. That will take time and research." Tavak ran his finger over the top edge of the fiery message. "This refers to a stoneworker of some kind, and this indicates that he built great cities."

"That doesn't narrow it down much."

"No, but there's something else there." Tavak tapped the screen with his forefinger. "What does that hieroglyph look like to you?"

Rachel squinted at the image. "I'm not sure. Maybe a dog?"

"It looks a little too squat to be a dog. The Egyptians usually made their dogs tall and thin. Perhaps a pig?"

"A pig that built cities?"

He shrugged. "As I said, we'll need to research."

She was suddenly panicked. "Dammit, what happens if we can't figure out who it is? Or if it's a monument or tomb that hasn't been discovered yet?"

"Then maybe we'll have to discover it ourselves."

She wanted to hit him. "Just like that."

"Just like that. If that's the only way."

"You're nuts. I don't have *time* to go exploring. Allie doesn't have time."

"Look, you're jumping the gun. I guess I'm not the only one who's a pessimist. I can't promise anything else, but I *will* manage to figure it out. I have Jonesy on my side." He stared out at the water. "And I have Rachel Kirby. That's a double whammy."

She stared at him for a moment, then looked away. "Don't try to con me, Tavak."

"I wouldn't presume. But I believe it's time that you started to trust me. Think about it. Have I given you reason to doubt me since we came together?"

She shook her head. "Other than being what you are."

"And being what and who I am, do you think I couldn't have slipped away from you and disappeared? It wouldn't have been that much of a challenge."

"I had Norton to use as a threat."

"And?"

She was silent. "You're deranged. You'd probably have enjoyed trying to wriggle out of the noose Norton would tighten around you."

"Perhaps. Then we're back to square one. Haven't I kept my word to you?"

She didn't speak for a moment. "Yes."

"Then trust me. It will be easier for both of us."

He was right. It was difficult to give up the anger and suspicion that she'd felt from the moment she'd realized he was the one who had stolen those cycles. Added to that known criminal act, she had come to realize just what a multi-faceted and dangerous man he could be. One moment she was put on guard by some act of violence, and the next she was being swept along by the sheer power of his personality. Yet he had kept his word so far, and it would be easier to trust him, at least tentatively. She felt an unexpected rush of relief at the decision. She slowly nodded. "On one condition."

He gazed at her inquiringly.

"You find me the pig that can build cities."

ELEVEN

Dawson hurled the stack of photos at Sorens. "What the hell is this supposed to be?"

Sorens leaned over and picked up the photos from the floor of Dawson's hotel suite. The pictures were all the same: smears of light against dark backgrounds. "I told you they were difficult to make out."

"Difficult? Try impossible."

"We didn't know what Tavak and the Kirby woman were doing. We assumed they were going to take something with them." He made a face. "We weren't prepared for a message written in fire."

"It's your job to be prepared for everything. Why else do I pay you?"

Sorens held up one of the prints. "We can make out a few Egyptian characters on this one. I ran them by your expert, and he thinks it may refer to someone who may have been brought back from the brink of death."

"Brought by the great doctor, Peseshet?"

"That's not clear."

"Not clear to us. I'm sure it's clear to Tavak and Kirby, by now though. I need to know who this is. I have to get a step ahead of Tavak."

Sorens frowned. "It would be risky, but I could take the team back to San Simeon tonight. We can pour the oil into the walkway and light it just as easily as Tavak and Kirby did."

"No, not just as easily. The guards will be on alert now."

"They work for the park service. Most of them are unarmed. If any of them get in our way, we can take them out."

"By all means," Dawson said sarcastically. "Why use a scalpel when a chain saw will do the job?"

"I thought you said we had to beat Tavak to the punch."

"I did. But nothing will slow us down faster than focusing even more attention on that temple. All we need is more people joining the chase." Dawson grabbed the photos back. "We may need to take another approach."

"Like what?"

"Mills presented me with an option that might keep us on the fast track. But that means going to him and begging for his help. Dammit, I hate like hell letting him call the shots."

Sorens was relieved to be off the hook. "Here's every picture we took." He handed him a flash drive. "Oh, and I suppose you heard about Medelin."

"Yes. I heard that they had a hard time making the ID. I guess a few thousand volts from a passenger train can do that do to a man."

What an icy son of a bitch. "Then I take it that you're not concerned that he bought it?"

"There might have been a slight possibility that I would have been concerned"—his gaze meeting Sorens's was as cold as his words—"if he hadn't failed me."

Detective Gonzalez pointed to the computer on his desk in the squad room of police headquarters. "Have you ever seen this?"

Finley looked at the screen. "College Confidential?"

Gonzalez nodded. "It's a social networking Web site for college kids. My niece is on it all the time. Kind of like MySpace or Facebook. There are discussion boards, e-mail directories . . . and webcam feeds."

Gonzalez clicked on a link which displayed a list of colleges and universities all over the world. He clicked on ARDMORE UNIVERSITY, which revealed another list of locales around campus: PRACTICE FIELD, PHI KAPPA THETA, STUDENT UNION, DIEHL QUADRANGLE, APPALOOSA GRILL. He clicked one of the buttons and revealed a flat, grassy expanse backed by several buildings.

"What's this?"

"It's the Diehl Quadrangle on the Ardmore campus. It's a live feed. Those kids playing Frisbee are there right now."

"So these are security cameras?"

"No. All these feeds come from the kids. In

most cases, it's just a fifty-dollar webcam propped onto a dorm windowsill."

Finley looked up. "You don't think—?"

"Rachel Kirby's shooter got to the campus security cameras, but he might not have thought of these. I talked to our tech guys, and it's doubtful that any of these feeds was intentionally recorded. But if the computer connected to this webcam has been on the entire time, footage may be cached in RAM or on the hard drive."

"Even from the day of the shooting?"

Gonzalez shrugged. "One way to find out."

An hour later, Detective Gonzalez was walking across the campus quadrangle, his brow furrowed, holding his laptop computer in front of him like a high-tech divining rod.

Finley smiled. "I wish I'd brought my camera. This would make an amazing picture." He glanced at Sergeant Michael Tunison, a self-described ubergeek who was obviously uncomfortable outside the small windowless computer lab he ran on the police headquarters' third floor. "He's definitely not in your league, Tunison."

"Few people are," Tunison said. "That's why you called me in. Do you think Rachel Kirby is here on campus today? I'd like to meet her."

"Afraid not," Finley said. "She's traveling this week."

Tunison shrugged. "That's okay. I'd probably

start stuttering and stammering and just make a fool out of myself."

"You?" Finley gazed at him in surprise. "Really?"

"Oh, yeah. In my field, she's like a rock star."

"Whatever starts your engine."

Gonzalez stopped short, still staring at the laptop. "Here! Is this what we're looking for?"

Finley and Tunison huddled around and shielded the screen from the sun's glare. There were over half a dozen Wi-Fi devices listed. Gonzalez put his finger on one named WEBCAM1. "This one."

Tunison nodded. "Most webcams are connected by a USB cable, but a lot of them are wireless. If this is the one we've seen on the College Confidential site, that will make our jobs easier."

Tunison pulled out a small gray box with a bright LCD screen on its face. He spent a few seconds looking at it, then motioned toward the detectives. "This way."

Gonzalez and Finley followed him into the Donner Hall dormitory, then climbed the stairs to the fourth floor. They finally ended up in front of a dorm room at the end of the hallway.

Tunison studied his device a moment longer, then looked up. "It's here."

Finley rapped on the door.

"Who is it?" a male voice called.

"Houston Police Department. May we have a word with you?"

Silence.

Then there were hurried footsteps, the sound of a drawer being opened, then running water.

"What's happening?" Tunison whispered. "Should we go in?"

Finley smiled. "Naah, give him a minute."

Gonzalez turned to Tunison. "We're on a college campus, remember? The guy is most likely dumping a baggie of pot down the drain. Let him finish."

Tunison frowned. "Shouldn't we bust him?"

"Which would you rather do? Get cooperation on an attempted murder case or bust a kid for possession?"

The voice finally called out again. "I'll be right there!"

"Take your time," Finley replied.

After another thirty seconds, the water was shut off and the door was answered by a small, wiry young man with frizzy hair. His face was shiny with sweat.

"Bad time?" Gonzalez asked.

"No. I was just . . . studying."

"Good. I'm Detective Gonzalez, this is Detective Finley and Sergeant Tunison. You are . . . ?"

"Dana Moreshead. Is everything okay?"

"May we come in?"

"Uh, sure." He opened the door wide for them to enter. The room was small even by college-dorm standards, with posters that revealed a fondness for beer, pot, and Natalie Portman.

The kid caught Finley eyeing a poster that featured a U.S. flag with a marijuana leaf on it. He moistened his lips. "That's my roommate's."

Tunison stood at the desk, where the webcam was angled toward the window. As if empowered by the presence of tech gear, Tunison's entire demeanor changed, from nebbish kid to a born leader. He pointed to the camera. "Yours?"

Dana nodded. "Yeah."

"You stream video to the College Confidential site, right?"

"A lot of people do it," he said.

"I know," Tunison said. "Calm down. You're not in trouble. We're hoping you can help us out. How long has this computer been on?"

Dana shrugged. "I don't know. A couple months?"

"You're not recording this feed by any chance, are you?"

"No."

"Okay, I'm going to need to take this computer."

"What?"

"There may be some important evidence on your hard drive."

The kid glanced between Tunison and the two detectives. "Don't you need a court order or something?"

"Not if you give us permission," Gonzalez said. "If you choose to withhold permission, I'll wait here while my partner goes and gets a warrant."

Tunison moved the desk chair to get a look at the computer tower beneath the desk. "If there are any files on this you need, I can transfer them to a flash drive for you."

"Do we have your permission to take the computer, Mr. Moreshead?" Gonzalez strolled to the sink and gazed pointedly down the drain. "We'd truly appreciate your cooperation."

Dana froze. "Yes. Take it." He managed an uneasy smile. "No problem."

The Madonna Inn.

Rachel frowned as they pulled into the parking lot of the large hotel that was located approximately forty-five miles from Hearst Castle.

"A theme hotel?"

"Why not?"

"An odd choice. A Marriott would have been fine."

"But not as much fun. I thought you might need a complete change of pace."

"Whatever." She got out of the car and headed for the front entrance. "Just so it has a bed."

"Oh, they do. Of all descriptions. The theme rooms will amuse you."

"I can hardly wait. Next time you'll probably take me to Disney World."

"I'll work on it. But you'll find this a little more outrageous."

Outrageous was right, she thought, when the bellman escorted her to her room.

Hot pink walls and fur-lined mirrors.

"Good God."

Tavak chuckled. "I told you. Actually, you look very sexy surrounded by mirrors. It has a certain sensuality, doesn't it?"

"If you want to be hit over the head with it." She looked at him and realized he was right. The mirrors reflected the hot color and made Tavak appear in dramatic relief. He looked very lean, very muscular, and very, very male.

And she was experiencing a response to that maleness.

She tore her eyes away from him. "I can hardly wait to see what room they gave you."

"I can wait. I'm enjoying looking at you here." He turned away. "But I'm across the hall. Let's go and see what fantasy they chose for me. It's called Rock Bottom."

Very appropriate, Rachel thought when she saw the rock walls of his room.

"Not nearly as interesting. Though that waterfall on the wall is a little unusual," Tavak said as he propped his laptop on the small table. "I like to see you when you're out of your element. You looked great in hot pink. Why don't we set this up in your room?"

"This is fine." She watched Tavak set up the encrypted Internet connection with her lab. "But you're right, this hotel is definitely a change of pace from anything within the known universe."

"But memorable. If life is the sum total of our experiences, we should always seek the most memorable experiences we can." He grinned. "You're sure you don't want to go back to your room and bask in those fur-trimmed mirrors?"

"That's exactly where I'm going. But I'm going to turn out the lights and go to bed." She turned toward the door. "I can do without any more bizarre experiences tonight. Good night, Tavak."

Rachel was up at seven and knocking on Tavak's door by seven forty-five.

"Good morning." Tavak opened the door. "Did you sleep well?"

"As well as could be expected," Rachel said. "Those pink walls seemed to pulsate even in the dark."

"I could have changed with you, but the water-fall on my wall might have been more distracting." He nodded at the laptop on the table. "I've set up the connection. Val should be on the—"

"Tavak?" Val Cho's voice suddenly blared over Tavak's laptop speakers.

"Yes, Val." Tavak angled the laptop to include Rachel in the video feed they were sending to Houston.

Rachel leaned forward. "Hi, Val. Did you get the new symbols we sent you?"

Tavak pushed a key to enlarge the tiny desktop

window to show Val full screen on his laptop. She was sitting at her desk in the computer lab.

"Yep. Simon has been entering them in. We've been wondering how many laws you had to break to get those."

Tavak smiled. "We won't go into that."

"The grad students you took to Vegas are talking about the party you had on the strip the other night. I'm still bitter I wasn't invited, you know."

"We needed people who could blend in. That's not Val Cho. If we ever need someone men can't look away from, we'll call you."

Even through the fuzzy laptop window, Rachel could see the faint flush on Val's cheeks.

"Simon tried to lay that line of bull on me," Val said. "I could have dressed down."

"Maybe next time," Rachel said. "I need you there to babysit Jonesy and make sure it's scaling to all the cycles we added last week."

"So far, so good. Norton didn't waste time hogging every bit of computing power we doled out to him."

"He hasn't called for a couple of days. I think we've finally managed to shut him up. How has Jonesy been doing on the code?"

"Nothing yet. It's difficult enough to translate ancient languages that are *meant* to be understood. For this code, Peseshet's disciple could have been using a language that's now lost."

"That's why we need Jonesy to figure it out for us," Tavak said. "With your help, of course."

"I'm on it. But I don't need to tell you that the more pieces you can give me, the easier it will be to crack this."

"We're working on it, Val," Rachel said. "Thanks for all of your help." She leaned forward and cut the connection.

Tavak turned to her. "Val is a good person to have on your team. It's obvious she'd do anything for you."

"Not only is she willing, she's able. That's a rare combination."

He studied her for a moment. "You demand the best from her, just like you demanded it from those students in Las Vegas. People come alive when they suddenly find themselves capable of things they never imagined."

"Yet you're the one those kids are talking about," she said dryly.

"I know how to reward good work and how to align my needs with those of others, but that's not the same. I envy you."

"Why would you—"

"I may have some potentially good news," he interrupted. "We may not have to go digging for the next piece of the puzzle."

He obviously wanted to change the subject from the personal, she realized. Tavak had come too close to soberness and sincerity, and he was quickly backing away.

"When did you decide that?"

"Last night." Tavak picked up several sheets next to his portable printer. "I couldn't sleep, so I started looking into our pig who builds cities."

"You actually found him?"

"I believe so. But it would be more accurate to say that he's a pig *farmer* who built cities. Although a good deal of his wealth came from construction, he may have been even more successful raising pigs."

Rachel took the pages and glanced through them noticing that they featured photos and text relating to an excavation site. "Who was he?"

"A nobleman named Nimaatra. He lived during Peseshet's time, in the area where she lived. The upper classes didn't eat pork, but some, like Nimaatra, did make a fortune *selling* pork. And he was also a renowned builder."

"That's a unique combination," Rachel said. "There probably weren't that many people with those two specialties."

"My thought exactly. He was known for constructing large homes and institutions. He may have even built the headquarters for female doctors that Peseshet headed. He could have been another one of her grateful patients."

"Do we know where his tomb is?"

Tavak double-clicked an icon on his laptop screen, and a window opened up with video of a museum exhibit behind Plexiglas barriers.

"Most of the tomb is still in Egypt, but the most

distinctive part is now thousands of miles away. This is probably what we need to look at."

Rachel leaned closer to the screen. The video was small, and the exhibit was occasionally obscured by museum visitors wandering in and out of frame. But she could clearly see a large, stone wall adorned with Egyptian characters.

"Where did you get this?"

Tavak smiled. "YouTube, believe it or not. We're looking at someone's vacation video. I haven't been able to find any photos of it online yet, but I sent requests out to a few friends. I'm sure I'll have a scan e-mailed to me in the next few hours."

"Where is this?"

"St. Petersburg."

"I'm guessing we're not going to be lucky enough that it's St. Petersburg, Florida."

"Afraid not. The Russian one. This is the Hermitage Museum."

"The Winter Palace?"

"One and the same. This tomb relief is a center-piece. It depicts a feast as an offering to the gods."

"I think this may be a bit more difficult to break into than Hearst Castle was."

"A tad. Although a few thousand revolutionaries were able to storm those gates once."

"Maybe we can come up with a plan that involves a few less executions."

He smiled faintly. "If you insist."

"So what now?"

"We wait to see if the photographs tell us what we need to know, but I doubt we'll be that lucky. We'll probably need to be hands-on with that tomb wall."

"And how are we going to do that?"

"We show up and assess the situation. After that . . ."

"Yes?"

He shrugged. "Why, we'll find a way to get exactly what we want."

Again, that damnable calmness and confidence that had at first so annoyed her. But that was what she needed right now, Rachel realized. What Allie needed.

Allie.

"If we need to go to St. Petersburg, we can catch a flight out of Houston."

Tavak shook his head. "I'm sure we can get a direct flight out of L.A."

"I don't care. I need to see Allie before we go. It's important to me."

Rachel expected Tavak to argue with her, but he only gazed at her for a long moment before nodding. "Fine."

NSA HEADQUARTERS
WASHINGTON, D.C.

This should be my office, Norton thought.

He was seated in the outer office of Deputy Director Robert Pierce, trying not to let his annoyance show. Annoyance at being kept waiting. Annoyance at the pissant assistant who treated him like an outsider. Annoyance at the fact that he still wasn't working here at headquarters.

Shit.

Pierce appeared in his doorway. "Norton, good to see you. Come in."

Norton stepped into Pierce's sparsely decorated office, ignoring the obligatory posed photos of Pierce with the president and other VIPs.

Pierce motioned him toward a small seating area. "I was disturbed when I got your call. What's the latest on your situation down there?"

Norton sat down. "We're still not sure why Rachel Kirby was targeted by the campus shooter. Our first thought is that it may have been a random act or maybe someone she had angered, either personally or professionally."

"What makes you think it isn't?"

"The level of sophistication in the attack and the shooter's escape."

"Except for the fact that he couldn't hit the bull's-eye."

"Another inch, and he would have killed her. Considering the distance that the shot was fired from, it was still impressive targeting."

"And I imagine it wouldn't have been too difficult to slip out of a busy college campus."

"Not only did he slip out, but he managed to erase any record of ever having been there."

"What are we talking about?"

Norton filled him in about the tampered security-camera feeds, despite the fact that he had spent considerable time outlining it in a memo. Didn't anybody read anymore?

"Have you been working with the local police?" Pierce asked.

"No, but we've been monitoring their progress through sources in the department. We thought it would be best not to make our interest known."

"Good."

"But I've already been contacted by two detectives on the case." He paused. "They do suspect that our project may have something to do with the shooting."

"Do we have a file on these officers?"

"It's in progress. I'll send something to you by the end of the day."

"I'd rather not get involved there unless we have to. We'll see how persistent they are. And you're absolutely sure this Tavak hasn't compromised our data in any way?"

"Our IT guys have gone over his intrusions into Kirby's system with a magnifying glass. He couldn't have been less interested in *any* of the projects her system is working on. His only concern was using her system for his own project."

"What project? Did we take a look at it?"

"Of course. Tavak is trying to decipher a code of some kind. A code written in Egyptian hieroglyphics."

"For what purpose?"

"At his interview in Cairo, he claimed not to know. He indicated that it was more for scholarly interest."

"And you believed that?"

"No. John Tavak is a fortune hunter, not an academic. Some of our intel suggests that Mills Pharmaceuticals may also be on the trail."

"Interesting."

"In any case, once it was determined that Tavak posed no threat to our project, we dropped it."

Pierce tapped his forefingers together. "Let's take a closer look at Tavak's code. Put our cryptography guys on it."

"Tavak already has one of the world's most powerful computer systems trying to decipher it."

"Are you arguing with me, Norton?"

"No, sir. Merely commenting. May I go now?"

Wrong move. He should have been more patient, but Pierce had pissed him off.

Pierce nodded. "By all means." He leaned back in his chair. "Run along, Norton."

That condescending dismissal annoyed him even more than the questioning that had gone before. Norton got to his feet and moved toward the door.

"Excellent work," Pierce said quietly. "I knew you were the one to handle Rachel Kirby's project.

But this is a team effort; I'd be very unhappy if I found out you were doing anything that would prove awkward for the NSA."

There it was in a nutshell, Norton thought. Who had tipped Pierce off? Or maybe it was a bluff. He forced a smile. "I don't know what you mean. I've always been loyal to the agency."

Pierce nodded and gazed down at the papers on his desk. "As you said, just commenting."

ussia?" Allie dropped down in a chair and watched Rachel toss her duffel onto the bed and unzip it.

Rachel pulled out the clothes she had just taken to Egypt and threw them in the hamper. "Yes. St. Petersburg. Our flight leaves at eight thirty tonight."

"You just got back here."

"Pit stop. I wanted to see you before I left."

"Why?"

"I need a reason?"

"I sometimes go days without seeing you when you're cooped up in that lab or at a conference. What makes you think I needed you to rush back here?"

Rachel stopped packing. "Has it occurred to you that *I* may have needed to see *you*?"

"We have time, Rachel. The peripheral vision is back, and I'm feeling pretty good right now. You don't need to do this."

"I told you, I just wanted to see you."

Allie studied her for a long moment. "What's wrong?"

"Nothing." Rachel pulled four shirts from the drawer and pressed them into her suitcase.

"Don't tell me that."

"It's the truth. Why would anything be wrong? This is the best hope we've had so far."

"Except that it all might be for nothing. Is that what's bothering you? You think this is my last chance?"

"Of course not."

She smiled. "Liar."

"It's just . . ." Rachel sat on the edge of the bed. "I think it's your *best* chance. At least right now. And I don't want to screw it up."

"You won't. You're incapable of that. You're like one of your supercomputers."

"You wouldn't say that if you knew how buggy some of them have been."

"It's not like you to doubt yourself. What's going on here?"

"It's sort of like a treasure hunt. With the biggest treasure of all just around the corner."

"Not quite around the corner," Allie said. "Russia."

Rachel chuckled. "Point taken. But it's a small world, after all."

"If that's supposed to remind me of that comforting Disney World song, you're failing big-time. There's nothing comforting about you getting shot and ending up in the hospital." Her lips tightened. "And, since you won't tell me the truth about what's happened since then, I can't be sure that you're not walking a tightrope whenever you walk out that door."

"I wouldn't do that." She didn't look at her. "I'm much too practical."

"But you admit you've been sugarcoating everything you've been telling me."

Allie was being as tenacious as a bulldog, Rachel thought. She couldn't lie to her. "I suppose I didn't want to worry you with no cause."

"I think there may be cause." Allie stood up and crossed the room to the bed where Rachel was sitting. "And before you leave here, I'm going to know the truth." She sat down on the bed beside her and took Rachel's hands. "You're not going to sugarcoat, you're not going to avoid the truth. You're going to tell me everything that's been going on." She looked Rachel in the eye. "Everything. If you love me, you won't cheat me by treating me like a child. It's not fair."

Dammit, she was cornered. Lie or risk worrying Allie. She should never have told Tavak she wanted to stop to see Allie.

"Allie, I don't want to discuss this."

"Tough. Talk to me."

It was Allie who was tough, she thought. Fragile in body but strong in spirit. She wasn't going to back down. She'd keep battering in that gentle way of hers until Rachel caved. "Damn, you're stubborn."

"It's a family characteristic. Talk."

Rachel sighed. "Where do you want me to start?"

"Egypt, then go on from there. Every detail."

Do it quickly. Just facts, no emotion. She began to talk.

After she finished, Allie sat in silence. Finally she got to her feet, opened the closet, and pulled out a suitcase.

"What are you doing?" Rachel asked.

"I'm borrowing your rolling bag."

"Why?"

"I'm coming with you."

"Like hell you are."

"You don't have a choice. I can't let you fly to the ends of the earth, risking your life for me, when I'm stuck doing nothing back here."

"You need to take care of yourself."

"I will. But I also need to take care of you. We need to take care of each other. Like we did before I got sick and you started treating me as if I was made of glass. Remember the Dennison sisters?"

How could Rachel forget? Yet that memory had faded, obscured by an Allie haunted by illness. Before the onset of the disease Allie had been a tough little kid. She had never shied from a fight when neighborhood brats picked on her nerdy sister. Allie's finest hour came in their elementary-school lunchroom, when she once used a cafeteria tray to beat the hell out of three girls who had been punching and otherwise tormenting her. "This is different than the Dennison sisters," she said.

"Of course it is. I might need *two* cafeteria trays."

Lord, all those childhood episodes were coming back to Rachel. They had been so close in those days that they could almost finish each other's sentences. That camping trip in the Rockies when they'd both fallen in a creek and nearly frozen. The piñata Rachel had made for Allie's eighth birthday party that had been so strong they couldn't break it open. All the love remained, but that untroubled innocence had been taken away from them.

"I can do it, Rachel," Allie said softly. "Let me help."

"This isn't a good idea. I promise to call you every day."

"You won't need to. Because I'll be right next to you."

"Allie . . ."

"I *need* to do this. Don't you understand? All these years, there hasn't been anything I could do to help you. I couldn't direct the resources of a supercomputer to help cure my disease. I couldn't grab a microscope and investigate treatment options. But this . . . this is something I can do. When I'm feeling good, like I do now, I'm as strong as I ever was. Use this time. Use *me*."

Rachel stared at her sister, overwhelmed at the passion in her voice. Allie had never seemed so strong, so *alive,* as she did at this moment.

"I need this," Allie repeated.

"I can see that."

"So I'm coming with you. My passport is current after that trip Letty and I took to Italy two years ago. If you don't take me along, I'll follow you. I was going to do it anyway. There's no way you could lose me. It would drive you crazy having me wandering around by myself trying to tag along. You'll feel much more comfortable having me under your wing."

"You have it all thought out."

"I'm going to do this. I had to find a way to make you agree."

Rachel slowly nodded. "There appears to be nothing I can say to talk you out of it."

"You know me better than that."

"Yes, I do." Once Allie was set on a course, there was no way to keep her from following it.

"And what will this Tavak say?" Allie asked.

"I don't know." Rachel shrugged. "Not that I really give a damn. I can't let him run everything. He'll be here in a couple of hours to take me to the airport. We'll tell him then."

TWELVE

Tavak's gaze shifted from Rachel to Allie. "I don't even get a vote in this?"

Allie smiled. "Sure you do. Two of us against one of you. I'm going."

Tavak glanced at Rachel. "Is that really the way you'd vote?"

Rachel nodded. "She has more at stake in this than any of us."

"I can't argue with that. But does she have any idea what we're up against?"

Allie stepped forward. "Yes, Rachel didn't hold anything back from me."

"She wouldn't let me," Rachel said ruefully. "She knows what she's doing. Allie is coming with us to St. Petersburg."

"Fine," Tavak said. "But she should know I'm a hazardous person to be around. The last person to help me is now recovering in a Cairo hospital."

"Is that supposed to frighten me, Mr. Tavak?" Allie asked.

"Not at all. It's just in the interest of full disclosure."

"Good, because I don't frighten easily," she said quietly. "I've had doctors telling me I was at death's door since I was thirteen years old. You want to know real fear? Try dealing with a death sentence when you're in the eighth grade."

"I can't even imagine," he said soberly.

"But when you come out the other side of something like that, it's liberating. You realize what's important in life, and what you and Rachel are doing is important."

"Unless it turns out to be nothing."

"You don't want to get my hopes up. It doesn't matter. It's the *attempt* that's important. And even if it is the real deal, I know it may never help me. Medical breakthroughs can take years to get from the labs to our neighborhood clinics."

"Don't say that," Rachel said.

"It's the truth, isn't it? And believe me, if we find a cure, I'll do everything I can to hang on. I've made it this long. But in any case, this could help a lot of other people." She turned back to Tavak. "This is too important for me not to be a part of it."

"As long as you're aware of the risks."

Allie pulled up the handle of her rolling bag. "Believe me, it would be a bigger risk for me to stay here and do nothing."

It was past 2 A.M. when Allie looked up from reading her magazine to see only one overhead light in the entire first-class section of the jet. Tavak's seat, she realized. He was three rows ahead and on the other side of the cabin from her and Rachel. She glanced at her sister. Rachel was dead asleep, her head resting against the window.

Allie quietly unbuckled her seat belt and moved toward Tavak.

As she drew closer, she could see that he was scribbling furiously in a notebook, occasionally consulting some kind of spreadsheet on his laptop.

Tavak looked up. "Hello."

"Hi." She motioned toward the empty seat next to him. "May I?"

Tavak moved some papers off the seat. "Of course. I thought you were sleeping."

"I tried, but I can never sleep on planes." Allie sat down and buckled herself in. "And I suppose you're one of those people who never sleeps."

"It's a curse. Every time I close my eyes, I'm afraid I'm sleeping my life away. Or that I'm missing out on something."

"Maybe that's why we have dreams."

"I don't have dreams. At least, none that I can remember. I guess that's why it's important for me to live mine when I'm awake."

"Rachel hardly sleeps, either. But with her, it's because she can't shut her mind off. She's always working on fifty problems at once, and she's afraid that if she shuts down for a while, she won't be able to get back on track."

Tavak glanced back. "She's having no problem right now."

"It's unusual for her. She must be exhausted."

"It's been a hectic few days." Tavak smiled. "Your sister is going to change the world. And what's more, she knows it. When you have that kind of purpose, it's hard to just shut down."

"If it was just her work, that would be okay. But sometimes I think that the work she's doing for my illness is pushing her over the edge. It's affecting her *own* health."

Tavak shook his head. "I don't believe that. She's found a way to focus her work in a way that may benefit you. Do you really think she would push any less hard if your situation suddenly resolved itself?"

"Suddenly resolved itself? That sounds ominous."

"Resolved in the best sense, of course. Your sister would find something else to focus her projects on. But you give her a sense of urgency, of impetus. Back at your house, you mentioned the clarity your disease has given you. I think it's given your sister the same clarity."

"I'll try to tell myself that."

"It's the truth."

"Whatever." She looked straight ahead. "I came up here to give you a warning."

"A warning? Now *that* does sound ominous."

"In a very short period of time, you've recruited one of the world's most brilliant women and one of the world's most powerful computer systems for your own purposes. The only reason you were able to do that is because you convinced her that it might help me."

"You're right."

Allie lowered her voice as a flight attendant passed. "Mr. Tavak, if I find you're using me and my illness to deceive my sister in any way, I'll take you down. I'll destroy you. You may not think I can, but I promise I'll find a way."

Tavak studied her for a long moment. He finally nodded. "I understand. And I assure you that I've been completely aboveboard with Rachel. I know how important this is to her—and you."

"For your sake, I hope you're telling the truth."

"I am. You're a good sister, Allie."

"Yes, I am." Allie unfastened her belt, stood up, and started back toward her seat.

"Allie . . ."

She turned. "Yes?"

His smile lit his face with sudden warmth. "I believe I may be glad you came along."

PULKOVO II INTERNATIONAL AIRPORT ST. PETERSBURG, RUSSIA

As Rachel, Allie, and Tavak entered the busy arrivals terminal, Tavak gestured toward the customs sign. "That's our first stop."

"What then?" Rachel asked.

"Someone will meet us after we get through Customs. From there, we'll go—"

"John Tavak?" The tall, bald young man who had interrupted him was dressed in a Russian

258

military uniform and spoke with a thick Russian accent.

"Yes?" Tavak answered warily.

"Come with me, please. All of you."

"Is there a problem?" Rachel asked.

The soldier adjusted the automatic rifle hanging from his shoulder. "Not if you follow me. This way."

Rachel and Allie looked at Tavak.

"It's not the time or place to ask questions. That gun appears to be an excellent argument." Tavak motioned toward the soldier. "This way . . ."

They followed the soldier through the terminal to a secured door, where he entered a numeric code into the keypad. He opened the door and gestured them through. They walked down a long hallway with a concrete floor and several closed doors.

Rachel turned to Tavak. "Tell me you're not on some kind of a watch list."

"I'm sure that's all been sorted out by now," he murmured.

"What?"

"I'm joking. I have no idea what this is about."

"Bastard."

The soldier pushed open another door that led outside, where they stepped out onto a narrow sidewalk. It was deserted save for a large, rotund man with a thick gray beard and a canvas bag slung over his left shoulder.

The man's eyes lit up. "John Tavak! Welcome to

St. Petersburg. I see that your taste in traveling companions has vastly improved."

Tavak smiled and shook hands with him. "And I see that you still look like Santa Claus."

"I *am* your Santa Claus. No awful customs lines, no muss, no fuss." He shrugged. "Christmas has come early for you."

"Lev, meet the sisters Kirby. This is Rachel and that's Allie."

Lev bowed. "Enchanted and delighted. I hope you weren't alarmed by the escort I arranged. After your long journey, I wanted to spare you any more discomfort." Lev opened the canvas bag and produced a new-in-the-box Nintendo Wii game console, which he handed to the young soldier. "Here you are, my friend. Many thanks for a job well done."

The soldier looked at the box in his hands. "Our original deal was for two people. I didn't know there would be three."

"Last-minute addition," Allie said.

Lev reached back into his bag. "Right you are. What's a game system without the latest and greatest games? Here's an amazing new Indiana Jones game, plus a water-skiing challenge, and a couple of others. You'll have a good time with these."

The soldier nodded and stacked the boxes on top of the console system. "This will be fine. Thank you."

"Thank *you*, my friend. I'll be in touch."

The soldier walked back through the doorway and locked the door behind him.

Tavak turned back to Lev. "Since when did video games become the currency of choice around here?"

Lev shrugged. "Depends on who I'm dealing with. For men under thirty, few things are more valuable."

Rachel thought of Hal Demanski playing the alien shoot-'em-up with his fellow multibillionaires. Boys and their toys.

Lev motioned toward the Mercedes parked at the curb. "Come. We have places to go."

In less than an hour, they found themselves walking through the wide, ornate corridors of the Hermitage Museum, once the Winter Palace for the Russian royals. Lev opened his arms at the majesty of it all. "Breathtaking, yes?"

Rachel looked at the massive chandeliers and gold leafing on the ceilings. Each room they had seen had featured intricately carved columns with more gold leafing on the base. "Yes. It's almost enough to make me understand why the starving citizens wanted the Romanov family's blood."

"That's no way to look at such things of beauty. If I didn't know better, I'd say you were a cynic."

Allie smiled. "You *don't* know better. But spend a few hours with my sister, and you will."

Rachel shook her head. "It's not cynicism to think about what things cost. And I'm not just talking about dollars and cents."

Lev turned to Tavak. "I think your friend is going to launch another revolution."

Tavak smiled. "It's a distinct possibility."

"The Egyptian collection is up ahead. It's fairly unremarkable, but the piece you're looking for is featured prominently."

They entered a large room, and Rachel immediately recognized the large display case from the video Tavak had shown her. They stepped closer to the limestone wall, which featured a carved relief of a great feast and an assortment of animals.

Tavak opened his notebook and compared the reliefs with drawings he had made.

"What are you doing?" Rachel asked.

"This depicts an offering to the gods. I just want to make sure there's nothing here that wouldn't normally be found in an Old Kingdom banquet."

"Kind of like, one of these things doesn't belong?" Allie said.

"Yes, but I'm sure we can't be that lucky. The code is probably something more complicated than that."

Allie shook her head. "How could this disciple, Natifah, have come up with these codes? I mean, the 'etched in fire' message was ingenious."

"It was," Rachel said. "And I'm guessing Natifah was ingenious. She was a doctor at a time when it was a rare thing for a woman to be. And she may have had help."

"From another patient of Peseshet's?"

Tavak looked up from his notebook. "It's possible. But whatever information this wall holds, it's nothing I can crack by just glancing at it. It's going to take time."

"I've already made arrangements with a guard," Lev said. "We can come back at ten o'clock tonight and get a much more in-depth look."

Rachel smiled. "Another video-game bribe?"

"No, he's much older. Two cases of vodka should do the trick."

"And if that doesn't work?"

Lev shrugged. "*Three* cases of vodka."

inley leaned back as three color-photo printouts suddenly landed on the desk in front of him. He glanced up to see Gonzalez and Tunison smiling as if they'd won the Powerball lottery.

Finley looked back down at the printouts. "Okay. I'd appreciate it if you could wipe those shit-eating grins off your faces long enough to tell me what I'm looking at here."

Tunison pointed to a tall man in a dark blue Windbreaker. "We think this could be our shooter."

"I'm listening."

"This came off the kid's webcam. Ballistics tells us that the gunshot came from this hill. The only route not covered by campus security cameras is down this path." Gonzalez traced the route with his finger. "And look at this guy."

Finley's eyes narrowed on the grainy printout. While the frame grab didn't offer enough resolution to get a clear look at the man's face, Finley could see the jeans, black T-shirt, close-cropped hair, and a large backpack. He glanced up. "Looks like a typical college kid."

"Of course he does. Why would he want to appear any differently? But notice how long that backpack is? And does it look like he has any books in there?"

Finley studied it. "No. But there is something poking at the top and bottom."

"Something like a disassembled SKS rifle, maybe?"

"Possibly."

"There's a digital time stamp," Tunison said. "The timing fits perfectly with Rachel Kirby's shooting."

Gonzalez pointed to the other two printouts. "We can trace him all the way up to the other side of this building, where the path curves around."

"Where does it lead?"

"Lots of places. A performing-arts auditorium, the law library"—Gonzalez raised another photograph printout—"and an off-campus parking lot."

"You're shitting me."

"Our guy didn't park there, but his car was on the

street close enough for the lot's security cameras to catch him. Either he didn't know about it, or he thought he was far enough away from the shooting that he wouldn't be connected to it. He obviously didn't count on a student webcam catching him in the quadrangle."

Finley took the fourth printout and looked at the backpack-toting man climbing into a black Mercedes-Benz automobile. "Okay, now he suddenly doesn't look so much like a student."

"It's a 2009 Mercedes 550 SL, and we have a partial on the plate."

"Let me guess. It's stolen."

"Nope. It was towed off the shoulder of a Katy Freeway exit ramp a couple days ago. It's now sitting in one of our impound lots. Wanna go take a look?"

Less than an hour later, Finley and Gonzalez were walking across the gravel impound lot with the facility manager, a sunburned man with a bright orange clipboard.

"Your forensics guys got here about ten minutes ago," the lot manager said. "I showed them where the car is, but they said they'd wait for you before goin' inside."

Gonzalez nodded. "Did you attempt to contact the vehicle's owner?"

The lot manager spit before consulting his clipboard. "We couldn't match the plate to anybody.

It's either a DMV screwup, or the plate's a counterfeit."

They turned down an aisle that bordered a long chain-link fence. Two white-shirted forensics specialists waved from the rear of the black Mercedes. But, as Gonzalez and Finley neared, they could see the grim expressions on the specialists' faces.

"What is it?" Finley asked.

In the next instant a gust of wind sent a sharp, pungent odor to them.

Gonzalez covered his nose and mouth. "Oh, shit." He and Finley exchanged glances. They were both too familiar with that smell.

One of the forensics guys handed them white face masks. "Here, these will help a little."

As they put on the masks, Gonzalez motioned toward the trunk. "If that's the owner we're smelling, it explains why the car wasn't reported stolen. Open it up."

A forensics specialist opened the driver-side door and popped the trunk. Finley pulled on a pair of evidence gloves, gripped the trunk lid, and lifted.

The men gathered around the car and stared inside the open trunk.

Gonzalez asked, "What do you think, Finley? Is it our shooter?"

"Maybe. Good chance."

Although they had been unable to get a clear picture of his face, the rotting corpse could very well be the man they'd seen on the webcam frame grabs. It was the same jacket, the same close-cropped hair, the same awkwardly filled knapsack.

Finley unzipped the knapsack and pulled the main compartment open enough to reveal the parts of a disassembled rifle. "An even better chance than I thought."

"I'll say." Gonzalez looked at the forensic specialists. "Any idea what killed him?"

"Hell, no. You want a guess?" One of the forensics guys shined a flashlight at the corpse's torso. "Maybe a knife wound to the chest?"

Gonzalez backed away. The smell was overpowering even through the mask. "Any ID?"

Finley shook his head. "Not that I can see. I'll leave it to our friends here to paw around that rotting carcass. I can wait." He turned to the specialists. "But not long. We need a positive ID on this fella right away."

ST. PETERSBURG, RUSSIA

Lev pulled his minivan to a stop along the bank of the Neva River. He smiled. "Here at last. Sorry about the traffic, but that's the price of progress. This city has changed a lot in the past twenty years."

"It's a beautiful city," Rachel said. She had never been to St. Petersburg, but she was impressed by the clean, wide streets and Dutch-inspired architecture. Most of the pedestrians she had seen were young and well dressed, and the city literally gleamed in the late-afternoon sun.

"Here we are," Lev said.

She stared in puzzlement at what appeared to be a large party barge docked on the riverfront. The boat was packed with revelers holding drinks, some talking, some swaying to the repetitious dance music. "I thought you were taking us to your house."

Lev smiled. "I said I was taking you to my *home*. Which I have. You're looking at it, my dear. It's actually quite spacious belowdecks."

"Are those people your friends?" Allie asked from the backseat.

"Oh, no. I've haven't met many of them."

"But why—?"

Lev climbed out of the van and motioned for Rachel, Allie, and Tavak to do the same. "It's like this every night of the week. The people I do business with always know where to come for a good time. And, in their gratitude, they will do almost anything for me. The soldier from the airport may be here later if he's not too wrapped up in his new Wii."

Tavak nodded. "Lev's parties are legendary. And he employs a bartender who can make any drink ever invented. I've tried to stump him, but it just can't be done."

Rachel shot Tavak an impatient glance. "Is this really the best use of our time?"

"Absolutely. We can't go back to the museum until after ten. I'd say this is exactly what we need."

"I agree." Allie smiled as she took the lead crossing a narrow gangway to board the boat. "*Exactly* what we need. Lighten up, Rachel."

"Allie—"

"Listen to that music." But Allie was already swaying to the beat and moving through the throngs of partygoers. "Wonderful . . ."

Rachel had a sudden memory of Tavak telling her that at the fountains in Las Vegas. Strange that two such diverse people would share that common joyous whimsy.

"Let her go," Tavak said. "She'll have fun."

Rachel wanted to follow her. To protect her. Exactly what Allie didn't want her to do. And maybe she was right. She had seen Allie like this before and had always admired her ability to dive into any situation and make it sing. She finally shrugged. "Fine."

"Good girl. Now can I get you one of those drinks I was telling you about?"

"Just one. I'm working."

"So am I." He smiled. "But I'm like Allie. You have to take the opportunity to dance if the music is playing."

Less than five minutes later, Rachel was staring at the golden spire of the Peter and Paul Cathedral and sipping one of the best lemon drops she'd ever tasted. She and Tavak leaned against a railing at the relatively secluded stern section.

"What did I tell you?" Tavak said. "The best bartender in Europe."

"You may be right. A good bartender is an often-overlooked secret to making people happy. Lev knows what he's doing."

"You bet he does."

"Do you have people like him in every city in the world?"

"Not *every* city. But there's always a need for people who know how to get things done, who know how to cut through the red tape. I've spent years cultivating my contacts. Some are hard to find." Tavak smiled as the revelers on the deck stomped to the music. "Others are not so hard to find."

She studied him. "You sound almost affectionate."

"Why not? They're as close to family as I'll probably ever get. I move around too much to form any more-lasting relationships."

"And heaven forbid you settle down."

"I can't do it. I've tried once or twice." He made a face. "The boredom nearly killed me."

She could see how it might drive him crazy. She had seen how that intelligence was always prodding him, opening new doors and ways of doing things. He would always have to look for new things, new ideas to stimulate him. "I'd think it would be lonely."

"Sometimes." He smiled. "But lest you think that I'm a total commitment-phobe, I was actually engaged once."

"Why did you break it off?"

"I didn't. She did. Nell was a photojournalist, and we had a lot in common. She found me exciting for a while but she had the good sense to realize that she couldn't change me. For the long haul, exciting wasn't what she wanted. She didn't even ask me to change. She just . . . left."

"Would you have changed if she had asked?"

"No, she was right to leave. Right for her and ultimately right for me. It taught me a valuable lesson. In the end you have to decide who you are and what you have to give up to be that person." He lifted his glass to Lev across the deck. "And then you go out and make friends, like Lev, who don't care a damn when you walk away."

"But will Lev be willing to stand by and watch you destroy one of his museum's priceless treasures?"

"It may not come to that."

"But it may. I understand you did quite a bit of damage getting to that secret chamber in Egypt."

"In all fairness, Dawson and his men did most of the damage there."

"But you would have done the same thing if that had been what it took to get what you wanted."

He sipped his drink. "You're right. I would have."

"And if the only way you can unlock that museum piece's secrets is to destroy it, what then?"

"I'll destroy it," he said simply.

"Ask a direct question . . ."

"I could always find a way to make it up to the museum later. There are thousands of ancient mastabas all over the world, and thousands more in the sand that haven't even been discovered yet. But what we're looking for could be more valuable than all of them put together. And it would bring more honor and respect to that society than anything the world has ever seen. So yes, I'd gladly sacrifice the wall of a minor nobleman to do that. Wouldn't you?"

Rachel smiled and took another sip from her drink. "We're talking about Allie. Just put a chisel in my hand."

"Good to know we're both on the same page." Tavak pointed toward the crowd. "By the way, your sister appears to have made friends."

Rachel turned to see Allie on a small flag platform. A burly, shirtless man had hoisted her onto his shoulders, where she sat swaying to the music. As Rachel and Tavak watched, two other women, also astride their partner's shoulders, approached and high-fived Allie.

Rachel shook her head. "She doesn't play the part of an invalid very well, does she?"

"She looks happy."

"When she's feeling well, she's the happiest person I know. She doesn't take anything for granted and cherishes every new experience. I could learn a lot from her."

"And when she's not feeling well?"

"She's changed over the years. For a little while there was nothing but anger, especially when she was a teenager. She lashed out at everyone."

"It must have been difficult for you."

"It was. For my mom and dad, too. But you have to consider how much worse it was for her."

"You had a close family?"

"The best. But my mom had a heart attack and died when I was sixteen. That was a real blow to all of us. She was very special. My dad took over and tried to be everything to both of us. Pretty difficult when one daughter has a fatal illness and the other is a self-absorbed nerd. He was amazing. He died in an automobile accident when I was in Japan, and I came home to do my best to take care of Allie."

"You've done a good job."

"I love her," she said simply.

"Total devotion? All the research I've done about you . . . there was almost never mention of a man in your life. I saw pictures of you at banquets when you were receiving awards, but you were usually with your sister. Occasionally, I'd see you with a date, but you were rarely with the same man twice."

"I knew better than to subject the men in my life to those boring ceremonies."

"I see."

She made a face. "And, I guess, I never kept them around for very long."

"Jonesy was your main focus?"

"Jonesy is only the latest in a long line of projects that have consumed my time and energy. But that's not the only reason. I tend to be attracted to men who are just as passionate about their work as I am about mine."

"Computer guys?"

"Not usually. One was a financial analyst, one was a musician, and another was a college football coach. Their devotion to their work made each of them terribly interesting and exciting, but it possibly wasn't the best thing for our relationships." She smiled. "It was probably just as well. I had Allie to worry about. She absorbed most of my attention."

"You're not even a little resentful?"

She shook her head. "As I said, she had a little while when she was bitter against everything. But when she came out the other side, she was one of the best people I'd ever known. It was as if I'd suddenly gotten my sister back, but even better. She wanted to learn everything, be everything. She was always taking classes. You may have seen some of her paintings. She's fantastic. She was crazy about cars and got her mechanic's license when she was fifteen. She and Letty went to the Indianapolis speed races a few years ago, and she persuaded one of the drivers to let her help in the pit."

"You didn't go along?"

She shook her head. "I wanted to go. I was busy." She made a face. "I'm always busy."

"Trying to save her life."

"She's made it a wonderful life. And we all have our places in it." She looked down into her drink. "There's so much love in her, and every day she sees things that you and I just take for granted." She smiled. "Like tonight, when she took one look at this Russian party barge and knew it was just one more experience to be savored."

Tavak chuckled as they watched Allie try to communicate with her new Russian friends with an assortment of hand signals. "She loves you very much. She threatened to take me down if I crossed you."

Rachel frowned. "Take you down?"

"Her exact words. And elaborated it with a promise to destroy me. She's watching your back." He glanced down at her. "I'll just have to convince her that I'm watching it, too."

"As long as I don't step on your toes while you're running toward Peseshet's treasure."

"How do you know I wouldn't step aside for you?"

His tone was quizzical, but there was a curious note that made her gaze fly to his face. What she saw there made her eyes drop quickly to her drink.

She was suddenly acutely aware of everything about him. The smell of a spicy aftershave, his long fingers on the glass holding the drink, the strength of his shoulders, the tightness of his stomach and buttocks. The desire to reach out and touch him was dizzying in intensity. What was happening to her? Stupid, she knew what was happening. Sex. Just try not to let him see he was disturbing her. "Because that's not your modus operandi. If I've found out one thing from being with you, it's that you don't meekly step aside for anyone."

"You never know," he murmured. "Maybe Peseshet is casting out her serene influence and trying to change me."

"Not likely."

He was silent a moment. "You're probably right." He was suddenly smiling recklessly. "So I've just got to go with what I am." He grabbed her hand. "Come on. I'll hoist you on my shoulders, and we'll give Allie a run for her money."

THIRTEEN

STATE HERMITAGE MUSEUM
10:02 P.M.

What the hell!" Tavak whirled on Lev. "Dammit, what did you do?"

"Nothing." Lev was gazing in bewilderment around the exhibition hall. "I swear, my friend."

Rachel, Tavak, Allie, and Lev stood in the exhibition hall where, just hours before, they had seen the large relief from the tomb of Nimaatra.

Now there was nothing.

The other exhibits appeared just as they were before, but the mastaba wall and its wood and glass display case had vanished.

"I don't believe this," Rachel whispered.

"What in the hell happened to it?" Tavak's harsh voice echoed in the large, dimly lit room. He walked around the empty space where the display had been.

Rachel turned to Lev. "Ask the guard where it is."

Lev spoke in Russian to the elderly guard, who seemed more surprised than anyone at the exhibit's sudden disappearance.

The guard's only response was to hold out his hands and give a vague shrug.

"Could it actually have been stolen?" Allie asked incredulously.

The stunned guard mumbled something to Lev, who translated. "The guard says he knows it was here when the museum closed at 6 P.M. He's been in one of the other buildings since then, but he's going to try and find a guard who was working here this evening."

The guard hurried away, obviously eager to get away.

"Dawson?" Rachel asked.

"I don't know." Tavak was staring at the floor, which was mildly discolored where the display case stood. "Maybe."

"Looking for something, Tavak?"

"Oh, shit," Tavak said.

Hal Demanski was leaning against the archway of the entrance, wearing another one of his impeccably tailored suits. He crossed his arms across his chest and smiled. "Perhaps I can help."

Rachel glared at him. "You son of a bitch."

"Aw, come on, Rachel. And here I was getting all warm and fuzzy at the thought of us being together again."

Tavak stepped toward him. "What did you do?"

Demanski shrugged. "I took the exhibit, if that's what you're asking."

"Dammit, you don't know what you're doing."

"I know you need that exhibit. You were less than discreet in your inquiries about it."

"I didn't have time to be discreet," Tavak said. "And what does it matter to you?"

"You made it matter when you broke into my casino's private floors. Just as Ms. Kirby made it matter when she extorted computer time from me."

Rachel and Tavak were on the verge of erupting, but Allie quickly stepped forward. "Stop baiting them. Just tell us what this is all about, asshole. And I seem to have been left out of the loop. You are Demanski, right? I'm Allie Kirby."

"Ah, yes." Demanski took her hand and raised it

to look her up and down. "You look healthier than I might have imagined, Ms. Kirby. Much healthier and quite . . . interesting. Aren't you supposed to be wasting away somewhere?"

Allie shrugged and jerked her hand away. "I figure I can do that as easily in Russia as I can back home."

"Excellent point. A pleasure to meet you, Allie Kirby. Yes, I'm Hal Demanski."

Lev's eyes widened. "*The* Hal Demanski?"

"Oh, my Lord, be quiet," Rachel said. "His ego is big enough already."

Demanski smiled, still staring at Allie. "Sorry to disappoint you, but I didn't steal that exhibit."

"Then what happened to it?" Tavak said.

"I borrowed it. Legally." Demanski tilted his head. "At least I think it was legal. Oh well. In any case, the museum director signed off on it."

Rachel shook her head. "Just like that."

"Yes." Demanski strolled across the room toward them. "I decided that my casinos should feature a 'Treasures of the Hermitage' traveling exhibit. We had success with a Louvre exhibit a few years ago, and it didn't take much to convince the Hermitage director that this could be a mutually beneficial arrangement."

Rachel stared at him incredulously. "You convinced him of this in the space of twenty-four hours?"

"Well, I agreed to loan them some artwork of

mine that they've inquired about in the past. One painting is from the corridor outside my office. I'll miss it."

"My heart bleeds," Rachel said.

"Of course, I also made an extremely generous contribution toward the museum's improvements program. I assume that's what it was for, anyway. I paid it to the director in cash. Think I should have gotten a receipt?"

Tavak turned to Lev. "We bribed the wrong man."

"Don't blame yourselves. How could you have known I'd come along? Of course, all this was contingent on my taking possession of the exhibits immediately." Demanski pointed to a tapestry on the wall. "Damn. I should have asked for that, too. It's exquisite."

"Why?" Tavak asked. "Do you even know what we're doing here?"

"Since we met the other night, I've made it my business to know everything about you, Tavak. You'd be surprised what a man in my position can find out if he's willing to commit the necessary resources."

"I can imagine," Tavak said dryly.

"I know you've been following a trail that begins and ends with the great Egyptian physician Peseshet. And the fact that Rachel Kirby has taken such a keen personal interest indicates that a treatment option for GLD must be involved. But any such treatment almost certainly goes hand in hand with regenerating the cells of the central nervous system. That's quite an endgame."

"It would be, if any of it were true."

"Don't insult me, Tavak. The only question now is, where do we go from here?"

Rachel exchanged looks with Tavak and her sister before turning back to Demanski. "What do you want?"

"I want to be your partner."

Tavak laughed. "Go to hell."

"If my computer cycles are feeding the system that's generating the answers you need, I'm already a partner. And, since I possess a piece in which you obviously place great importance, that should make me even more indispensable. I want to share in the hunt . . . and the spoils."

"What kind of share are we talking about?" Tavak said.

"Half."

"No way."

"I have the exhibit."

Tavak smiled. "For now."

"Is that a threat? You think you can take it from me?"

"Did you think Rachel Kirby could take your casino for over two million dollars the other night?" Tavak shrugged. "If she and I put our heads together, I'm sure we could come up with something."

"Debatable. In the meantime, maybe I should cast my lot with another team. Mills Pharmaceuticals, perhaps? I'm sure they'd love to take a look at the mastaba wall." He smiled at the surprise on Rachel's and Tavak's faces. "Why are you so startled? I told you I do my homework."

Rachel was once more aware of the intelligence and driving force that was Demanski. He had executed this extraordinary coup, and he was not going to stop until he had what he wanted. It would be better to negotiate than have him constantly in their way.

"One-third," Rachel said. "If this is as big as we think it could be, that would make your casino empire look like chump change."

"You're overstating things a bit."

"You don't believe that," Rachel said. "You like the big ideas. Whatever the financial rewards, this idea is one of the biggest. And this is the team you want to be on. You wouldn't be wasting your time here with us if you didn't."

"A third is quite generous," Tavak said. He shot Rachel a look. "More generous than I would have been if my partner had bothered to consult me."

Demanski shook his head. "I've already invested a lot of money in this venture."

"A lot of money?" Allie snorted. "My sister was almost killed not too long ago. Stop bellyaching about your damn checkbook."

"I thought it was worth a shot." Demanski smiled at her. "One-third, huh?"

"Mr. Demanski?" A thin, white-haired man in a black suit stepped into the room, followed closely by the guard to whom Lev had spoken. The white-haired man was gazing warily at Tavak, Rachel, and Allie. "Is there some problem?"

"Not at all." Demanski clasped his hand on the man's shoulder and turned to the others. "I'd like you to meet Dennis Chernov, director of this fine institution."

Chernov's brow creased. "May I ask, who are these people?"

The guard held his breath, gazing in panic at Lev.

Demanski didn't answer immediately, obviously savoring the moment. Then a smile lit his face. "Only business associates of mine. We just closed a deal to work together on a very exciting project. I invited them to join me here. Hope you don't mind."

After Demanski settled a few final details with the director, he exited with the others down the short stairway to the street.

"I assume we have a deal?" Rachel asked.

"Yes," Demanski said. "Why not?"

"So where's the mastaba wall?" Tavak asked.

Demanski looked down the dark street and raised his hand. Headlights lit up the night and a truck and two police cars roared to life. "Crated up

283

inside that truck. Do you know what you're looking for on it?"

"Not in the slightest."

"I have a cargo plane waiting on an airstrip outside the city. I suggest we get off Russian soil before anyone realizes what just happened here. Agreed?"

Tavak nodded. "Agreed. Where is the plane going?"

"Wherever I want it to go." He lifted his hand and gestured. "Need a lift back home?"

A black limousine raced up the street and skidded to a stop in front of them. The vehicle's automated rear doors slowly swung open.

Rachel shot Demanski a sideways glance. "Tempting, if I wasn't so afraid of being thrown out over the Atlantic."

"The idea has its charms, but I'm quite sure you'll be calling and texting people to let them know you were with me. Besides, the cargo plane is a charter. Do you have any idea how much I'd have to pay to keep that crew's mouths shut?"

Allie shook her head. "This is going to be some partnership."

Tavak turned toward Lev. "It appears that we have another way home. Our paths diverge here, old friend."

"I can see that. I hope you find everything you're looking for."

"Me too."

Lev turned toward Rachel and Allie. "And it was a pleasure to meet two such charming sisters. Remember, you're always welcome at my place. You must promise you'll return."

Rachel clasped his hand. "I can't thank you enough, Lev."

Allie playfully pushed her sister aside. "And I'll *definitely* be back. *Do svidaniya*, Lev." She gave him a hug.

Lev was practically beaming, Rachel noticed in amusement. Allie had won another fan.

Demanski gestured toward the open limo doors. "Please."

Rachel, Allie, Tavak, and Demanski piled into the limo. The doors automatically closed, and the limo pulled away from the curb.

After a block, one of the police cars passed them and took the lead. The other squad car, Rachel noticed, dropped behind the truck. Within a few minutes, the caravan was on the ring road that circled the city.

Demanski leaned forward and faced the others on the limo's long, U-shaped seat. "So how close are you to cracking this?"

"We don't know," Rachel said. "Each of these pieces contains a bit more of Peseshet's cure, plus a clue to the location of the next piece. My system has decoded some, but not all, of the pieces we've gathered."

"How do you know the cure even works? Our

craziest new age treatments look absolutely sane and reasonable compared to a lot of the stuff that passed for medicine in those days."

"Yes, but some were right on target. Did you know that the pyramid workers were prescribed large quantities of garlic, onions, and radishes? For centuries no one knew why. Only in the early 1900s did we realize that an antibiotic, raphanin, could be extracted from radishes. And allicin and allistatin are now derived from onions and garlic. The Egyptians knew things that took over a millennium for us to rediscover."

Demanski nodded. "I can see that I'll have to play catch-up. Who wants to bring me up to speed?"

"Rachel and I will fill you in," Tavak said. "On the plane. We have a long flight ahead of us."

"Can't wait." He smiled at Allie. "Though I might prefer to have you do it. I haven't been called an asshole in a long time. It was an interesting experience. I'm already intrigued by our new association. This may prove to be better than an in-flight movie."

"What's that?" Rachel was staring out the window at a tall, white suspension bridge of stark, modernist design. Brilliantly illuminated, it featured a tall center span with cables splaying outward to each riverbank in a pattern that reminded her of a spiderweb.

"It's the Big Obukhovsky Bridge," Tavak said. "Beautiful, isn't it?"

"I don't know. I haven't made up my mind yet."

"It's the only nondrawbridge on the river," Demanski said. "Most cargo-boat traffic is scheduled for evenings, and I didn't want to get stuck waiting for one of the other bridges to open. We'll be on the plane in fifteen minutes."

Their caravan drove onto the bridge, which Rachel realized was actually two parallel structures, one for each direction of traffic.

They had traveled more than halfway across when a municipal T-bus suddenly pulled in front of the lead police car and slowed.

Tavak turned to peer out the front windshield. "What's the holdup?"

"Just a city bus," Demanski said.

Tavak studied it and then shook his head. "I don't like this."

Demanski took a second look at the bus. "What's the big deal?"

"All of its interior lights are turned off. The lights have been on in every other bus we've seen."

"You're right," Rachel said. "We can't see inside."

The bus slowed down even more.

Demanski called out to the driver. "Go around the bus. Now!"

The limo immediately changed lanes. Demanski opened the sun roof, stood, and motioned for the truck to do the same. The truck and the rear police escort moved to the left lane behind the limo.

"Flash your brights at the police car up ahead," Demanski instructed the driver. "We need to get away from this bus. And once we get past—"

The limo lurched to a stop, throwing them all from their seats. Rachel struggled to her knees and looked out the window. The bus had swerved and stopped, blocking all lanes of traffic.

"Shit!" Tavak pulled himself up and turned to Demanski. "I only have my Magnum. Do you have any other weapons?"

"No. Why should I? We have a police escort."

Tavak began to curse.

The bus's rear window shattered, and a long, dark barrel suddenly appeared through the hole in the glass.

"I think we're going to get your answer. They've got us beat," Tavak said.

The barrel flashed, and the lead police car exploded and flipped over. Fiery debris rained down on and around them.

"A rocket launcher," Demanski said in disbelief.

Rachel felt as if she couldn't breathe. "Dear God . . ."

Tavak threw open the passenger door. "Everybody get out! And hit the bridge running."

They scrambled out of the limo, leaping over piles of burning debris as they ran back past the other stopped cars.

Some of the drivers of those cars were screaming, but most merely stared ahead in shock.

They were numb, Rachel realized. Just like she was. They couldn't believe this was happening.

Another low, sickening blast sounded behind her, and she turned just in time to see the limo explode. A burning tire rim flew from the wreckage and rolled past as if trying to race them from the carnage.

"Don't stop!" Tavak yelled. "Keep running!"

Rachel turned to Allie. Her sister's breathing was labored. "You okay?"

Allie nodded, not wasting breath to speak.

"We've got company," Demanski said grimly.

Rachel turned. About a dozen black-uniformed men charged from the bus, outfitted with Kevlar vests and automatic rifles.

Tavak rapped on the windshield of the other police car. The shaken officer was on his radio, but upon seeing the approaching gunmen, he dropped the microphone and drew his revolver. Tavak shook his head "no" and motioned for the officer to climb out and follow them behind the stopped cars. The policeman scrambled from the squad car.

They took cover behind a white panel van. "They're not interested in us," Tavak said. "They want what's in the truck."

He leaned toward the police officer and spoke in Russian. The officer nodded, and he and Tavak took aim with their handguns and fired several shots toward the truck.

"You didn't hit anyone!" Allie said.

"We didn't mean to. We blew out the tires on the truck and the bus."

As they watched, six of the gunmen climbed on top of the truck while six others swung out their rifles and covered them with a perimeter around it. The men on the truck quickly affixed a series of silver discs down the length of the roof and down the rear side.

"What are they doing?" Rachel asked. "Are they trying to destroy it?"

"No," Tavak said.

The men jumped off the truck, ran back fifteen feet, and the discs detonated. When the smoke cleared, Rachel saw that the rear compartment had been cleaved lengthwise in two. The gunmen were already throwing wire cabling over the jagged edges and peeling back the compartment shell. The metal siding groaned as it pulled away, revealing dozens of crated objects.

"Priceless," Demanski muttered. "Every last one of them."

"They only want one thing." Tavak tilted his head, listening. "What's that?"

A chopping, throbbing sound cut the air. Rachel looked up. At first there was nothing to see, but a spotlight suddenly appeared from a helicopter approaching the bridge.

Taking cover behind a car, Tavak and the officer opened fire. Rachel turned away as blood sprayed from two of the gunmen's foreheads. The others returned fire and took positions behind the truck and the limo's burning wreckage.

One of the wounded gunmen dropped a canvas bag. Several explosive discs rolled across the pavement, narrowly missing a pool of burning fuel from the limo explosion.

"Stay here," Tavak told Rachel. He, the police officer, and Demanski weaved through the burning wreckage to take positions closer to the truck.

Rachel felt the helicopter rotor pounding in her chest as it came closer. The engine noise overwhelmed her as the blades kicked up a fierce, howling wind.

The helicopter moved directly over the truck and dropped several lines. As the gunmen moved toward them, Tavak and the police officer pushed them back with a barrage of gunfire.

"We should *do* something," Allie said.

Rachel pulled her behind the van. "Got any ideas?"

"Anything's better than—Rachel!"

She whirled and saw that one of the gunmen had crept around the stopped cars and pounced, snapping his arm around Allie's neck. He held a handgun to her head.

"Call them off!" the gunman shouted over the wind and engine noise. "Tell them to lay down their weapons."

"Don't hurt her!" Rachel said.

"Tell your friends to back off. Now!" He pushed the gun barrel hard against Allie's temple.

Rachel backed away. "I will. Just . . . don't shoot."

She looked into Allie's eyes. Never comfortable in the role as a victim, Allie was now pissed as hell.

Save it, Allie. Please, baby. Don't do anything that will make him pull that trigger.

"Call them off." His arm tightened around Allie's throat. "Now."

"I'm going to do it. I have to—"

Demanski.

He had suddenly stood up next to the car behind her sister.

Thank God.

He was holding one of the silver explosive discs. He moved closer to the gunman as he carefully turned a dial on the disc's side.

Distract the bastard. Keep him from noticing Demanski.

She yelled to the gunman. "They can't hear me from over here. I need to go to them!"

The gunman hesitated, then nodded. He started to motion for her to move forward. "Go. Keep close to—"

In the next instant Demanski slammed his elbow down over the gunman's wrist. The gun flew out of his hands!

Before the gunman could turn around, Demanski jammed the silver disc down the back of his bullet-proof vest.

He yelled to Rachel and Allie. "Move! Move!" He picked up the gun and pushed them forward. "Get away from him."

Rachel turned to see the gunman twisting and turning, desperately contorting himself to reach the disc.

Boom!

Rachel took one look at the carnage that was left of the man blown apart by the blast before glancing quickly away.

"I was afraid we'd get blown off the bridge." Demanski stared at the gunman. "I guess Kevlar works both ways."

Gunfire erupted from the open doors of the helicopter. Rachel and Allie took cover, and Demanski glanced over to the truck. "They've pinned down Tavak and the cop."

As the helicopter cut loose with more suppressing fire, the gunmen swarmed over the now-open truck. With military precision, the gunmen gripped the lines and clipped them to hooks on their uniforms. They dragged four lines into the truck, and after one of the gunmen gave a thumbs-up sign, the copter rose, lifting the men and a large crate into the air.

Demanski looked up in amazement. "Holy shit." He raised the gun and squeezed off several shots before a volley of gunfire from the copter pushed him back down.

The helicopter roared away, and as the sound and

wind subsided, it seemed to Rachel as if a vicious, terrible storm had come and gone.

She glanced dazedly around her. Small fires burned, and pockets of debris were strewn across the bridge. Drivers had begun to emerge from their cars, and there was screaming and crying issuing from every direction.

Tavak ran toward them. "Is everybody okay?"

Rachel nodded. "Who the hell was that?"

"I have my suspicions. There are only a few mercenary teams who are that skilled and high-tech. I'd bet on Kilcher." Tavak turned to Demanski. "You saw the crate. Is that what I think it is?"

Demanski nodded. "It was the mastaba wall. They knew what they wanted, and they went right for it."

"Better than an in-flight movie, huh?" Allie said through her teeth. "What the hell do we do now?"

Tavak looked in the direction of the helicopter, which had by now disappeared in the night sky. "Now we get it back."

OIL TANKER *PHOENIX*
BALTIC SEA
1:14 A.M.

Dawson adjusted his earplugs as the helicopter touched down on the oil tanker's helipad.

Before the door even slid open, he spied the crate behind the tempered glass.

Success!

Kilcher and his team climbed from the copter and strode across the deck, pulling off their helmets and flak jackets.

Dawson chuckled. Testosterone practically dripped from the men. Even from the one woman in the team. Hell, maybe *especially* from the woman. He'd chosen Kilcher because he was experienced but still had the intelligence to pick young and agile subordinates who'd try anything. Kilcher was in his midfifties, his face lined and weather-beaten. The rest of his team were in their twenties or thirties.

Kilcher was glaring at Dawson as he stopped before him. "I lost three men tonight."

"Then your team isn't as efficient as you told me it was."

Kilcher looked as if he wanted to rip Dawson's throat out. "They were good men. It's gonna set me back."

"Then it's a good thing I'm paying you so well, isn't it? Did you get the item?"

"Yeah, it's in there. But I did a bit of research today, and it's not even worth half what you're paying us." He gestured around the oil tanker's massive top deck. "Never mind what all this has to be costing you."

"When my employer wants something, no cost is too great."

Kilcher said sourly, "So he's one of those billion-aire nutjobs with a roomful of stolen artwork only he can look at."

"That's no concern of yours." Dawson gestured toward the waiting crew members he had hired for the occasion. They pulled the crate from the helicopter and moved it onto the loading platform.

Dawson picked up a crowbar and pried off one of the wood panels. He pulled out several handfuls of packing straw, then peeled away a thick rubbery membrane to reveal a corner of the limestone mastaba wall. He backed away and turned to an operator with a large remote box in his hand. "Okay, take it down."

The platform lowered and took the crate belowdecks.

Exhilaration soared through Dawson as he turned back to Kilcher. "Good job. I may have other uses for your services. I'm sure we'll be speaking again soon."

"As long as the money is good enough. That attack turned out to be a little high-profile. I may need some downtime."

Dawson glanced back at the mastaba wall. Oh, yes the money would definitely be good. "But now get your helicopter as far away from here as you possibly can. The commanders of this tanker have been gracious hosts, but I'm afraid there's a limit to their indulgence."

The Feds are taking the body."

Finley was still half-asleep when he picked up his phone. "Gonzalez?"

"Who in the hell else?"

"So what about the Feds?"

"I told you. The Feds are taking the shooter's corpse. Peterson down at the morgue got the call, and he just tipped me off."

Finley sat up in bed. He'd been living in a one-bedroom apartment since he'd split with his wife a year earlier, and he still felt as if he was in a strange hotel room whenever he woke up. "*Which* Feds?"

"I'm not sure Peterson even knows. The agent on the phone told Peterson that this case has suddenly become a national security issue."

"Our case? Shouldn't somebody have told us?"

"Somebody did. The morgue guy."

"Nice."

"Anyway, I'm already on my way down there. I don't want them to cart away our biggest piece of evidence without answering a few questions. You want in on this?"

"Yeah, I'll see you there."

Twenty-five minutes later, in the corridor outside the crime lab's morgue, Wayne Norton jammed a sheaf of papers at Finley. "There's all the authority I need, Detective. Now if you'll excuse us . . ."

Norton motioned to the two young men behind him. They had the shooter's bagged body on a gurney, ready to be rolled out to the adjacent parking garage. Finley and Gonzalez had arrived just in time to catch them leaving.

The detectives blocked Norton's path. "We're not done with him," Gonzalez said.

"Those papers say you are."

Finley cursed under his breath. "Come on, Norton. Who is this guy?"

"I can't discuss that."

"Why the hell not? You wouldn't even have him if it wasn't for us."

"Then let me express my deepest gratitude on behalf of the United States government."

Finley glared at him. "Screw that. Give us something to go on. The corpse's prints don't show up on any database, and there was no match on a facial scan. What are you not telling us?"

"Who says there's anything to tell? You're the ones who have had the corpse for the past couple days. Maybe we just want a crack at it."

"In the name of national security."

"Yes."

"Security from campus shootings?"

"Possibly."

"Uh-huh. Strange that your agency showed zero

interest in this case until we started sending around this guy's prints and scans."

Norton shrugged. "I know you guys have been busting your hump on this case, and I'm sorry. But I can't say any more. When I can, I promise I'll get in touch."

Gonzalez leaned closer to him. "We both know what's going on here. Our inquiries tripped something on one of your databases, didn't it? One of the databases that you don't share with anybody else. And it must have been something really good for you guys to schlep out here at two thirty in the morning and drive off with a corpse from our crime lab."

"We're a twenty-four/seven operation, Detective. Just like your department."

"Uh-huh. You know, of course, ballistics matched the weapon we found with him. We know it's the same gun used to shoot Rachel Kirby."

"I do know that. Excellent work. As a matter of fact, the rifle is already in our truck."

Gonzalez laughed bitterly. "Great. Just great."

"We picked it up before we came down here. The authorization is in the paperwork I gave you."

"Of course it is."

"We're through here, gentlemen. Good luck with your investigation." Norton moved past them.

The other two men followed him, pushing the gurney down the corridor and through the red exit doors at the far end.

After the doors clanged shut, Finley turned to Gonzalez. "Dammit to hell."

"Yeah."

Finley scowled. "We could take the easy way out. We could just file the paperwork and close our eyes."

Gonzalez looked at him. "That's not going to happen."

"Are you thinking what I'm thinking?"

Gonzalez nodded. "We need to talk to Carlos."

The white-paneled van had just pulled onto the Katy Freeway when Norton's phone buzzed. He checked the caller ID screen. Deputy Director Robert Pierce.

He answered the call. "Good morning, Mr. Pierce. Are you up late or early?"

Pierce ignored the question. "Do you have the corpse?"

"Yeah, we just left the morgue. Someone tipped off the local cops and they gave us a little flack. No big deal. We're heading for Ellington Airport per instructions. Anything else?"

"No. You've done very well, Norton." Pierce cut the connection.

Better than you could dream, you arrogant bastard, Norton thought. He was walking a tightrope, but the delivering of this body should rid Pierce of a few of his suspicions.

Yes, he'd done very well.

FOURTEEN

Tavak pocketed his phone and joined Rachel and Allie in the small aircraft hangar where Demanski's jet was warming up.

Rachel moved toward him. "Okay, tell us how we're going to find that mastaba wall."

His brows lifted. "You're assuming I know."

"You didn't know an hour ago, but now you do. At least you think you do."

Tavak's gaze narrowed on her. "How do you figure that?"

"You're walking straighter now, your stride is longer, and your jaw is clenched. All signs of a man with a plan. Am I right?"

"A tentative plan. And here I thought you were only proficient at reading that computer of yours."

"And are you going to share this brilliant plan with us?" Allie asked.

"I said tentative, not brilliant."

"Either way, you'd better tell us, dammit." Demanski walked up from the other side of his jet. "Remember, I'm on the hook for that thing. Or at least my insurance company is."

Tavak shrugged. "It just occurred to me that whatever information that mastaba wall holds,

301

photographic images alone aren't enough to unlock them. Dawson needs to get an expert in front of it. That's the key."

"For him or us?" Rachel said.

"Us. Because as far as I've been informed, Dawson has consulted only two Egyptologists since he's been on this trail—Dr. Scott Collier from Cambridge and Dr. James Wiley from the University of Chicago. I'm pretty sure he will either take the wall to one of them or bring one of them to it."

"Unless he's found someone new and brighter," Demanski said.

"It's possible, but Dawson probably wouldn't risk forging a new relationship over such a high-profile stolen piece. Every major newspaper in the world will be printing a picture of that mastaba wall tomorrow. Dawson will go to someone he can trust."

Rachel nodded. "So we get to them first."

"If it's not too late," Demanski said.

"I really don't think it is. Dawson had to move fast once he found out you were taking the mastaba wall away."

Allie glanced thoughtfully at Demanski. "That's one thing I can't figure out. How did Dawson find out Demanski was taking it away tonight? We sure as hell didn't know."

Tavak shrugged. "A lot of people could have tipped him off. Dawson may have been making his own inquiries at the museum, and someone there could have told him. And you mentioned your insurance company, Demanski. If they were covering the trip, they would have had your entire itinerary. To value the objects, they might have consulted some antiquities experts. The same experts Dawson may have on his payroll." Tavak grimly smiled at Demanski. "I'm not the only one who needs to cover my tracks better."

"So do we tail these Egyptologists and wait for them to make contact with Dawson?" Rachel said.

"That's what I'm thinking. But I need to find out a bit more about them. I just got off the phone with their places of employment, and neither has left town."

Demanski jerked his thumb toward the jet. "So where do I tell him to take us? London or Chicago?"

"Chicago. I think Dawson would be much more likely to consult Dr. Wiley in this instance. Wiley has done much more work in Old Kingdom linguistic studies."

"Okay," Demanski said. "But what are we going to do about hedging our bets with this other expert?"

"We should keep tabs on him, too."

Demanski pulled out his phone. "I know a good P.I. in London."

"Not necessary. I've already made arrangements for a very efficient man to keep an eye on him."

"And you trust him?"

"Completely."

Rachel frowned. "Ben?"

Tavak shook his head. "Nuri. He'll arrive in London from Cairo this afternoon."

AS SALAM INTERNATIONAL HOSPITAL CAIRO, EGYPT

Ben Leonard gingerly pulled on his shirt as he tried to avoid the nurse's withering stare. "Stop arguing with me, Nuri. I'm going with you."

"Tavak did not invite you." Nuri sat in the hospital-room visitor's chair, his legs extended in front of him and crossed at the ankles. "I only told you I was being sent out of the country so that you would not be concerned when I didn't show up for our daily game of chess."

"I don't give a damn. Tavak would have given the job to me if I hadn't been laid up here in this blasted third-world pig—"

Nuri was holding up his hand. "Do not insult my homeland, or I will be forced to punish you for it." He sighed. "Perhaps you should listen to your nurse. She says you are not ready to leave."

The nurse, a heavyset woman in her sixties, frowned. "Your doctor says it, too. He is on his way to tell you himself."

"Then we'd better get out of here quick, Nuri." Ben opened a cabinet and pulled his belongings down from a high shelf. When Nuri had told him that Tavak had sent for him, Ben had jumped at the chance to get out of this hospital and back to the real world. He felt totally rejuvenated. In the past few days, lying in pain and boredom in that hospital bed, he had even flirted with the idea of partnering with his brother in a Florida car dealership. What the hell had he been thinking? He was no kid, but he wasn't ready to retire in some suburban hellhole.

The nurse grew even more insistent. "You cannot leave until the doctor signs you out!"

"When will he be here?"

"Thirty minutes. Get back into bed!"

"In thirty minutes, I'll be gone. Have you seen my belt?"

The nurse threw up her hands in frustration and stalked out of the room.

"Good," Ben said. "I hate bossy women. She reminds me of my second wife. Now can you get me a ticket on your flight?"

Nuri held up two folded color printouts.

"What's that?" Ben asked.

"Our airline tickets. Cairo to London."

Ben grinned. "Nuri, I could kiss you."

"Don't you dare. I would really punish you then. I couldn't stand the thought of leaving you here at the mercy of that extremely efficient and totally intimidating dragon. I could see how restless you were becoming. I prefer to have control of the situation." He grimaced. "But Mr. Tavak is not going to be pleased with my decision."

"Probably not. But he'll get over it." Ben glanced at him as he closed his suitcase. "Then why are you doing it?"

"I've grown accustomed to beating you at chess. It's excellent for my ego. Also you would probably follow me anyway." His smile faded. "Finally, perhaps because I sympathize with your boredom and frustration. It's difficult to sit and watch a friend be unhappy."

"Are we friends, Nuri? You're not just Tavak's idea of a babysitter?"

"Perhaps it was like that in the beginning," Nuri said quietly. "But that changed, didn't it, Ben?"

"Yes." Nuri had been with him through pain and frustration, and his humor had made both bearable. "Yes, we're friends, Nuri." He paused. "And partners?"

Nuri nodded. "And partners." He picked up the suitcase on the bed. "Come on, we have a flight to catch."

ARDMORE UNIVERSITY
HOUSTON, TEXAS

Val Cho swiped her ID card across the scanner, waited for the reassuring *ping,* then pushed open the door that led to the computer lab. She had planned to work from her apartment tonight, but it was just too frustrating to deal with the sluggish remote connection with Jonesy. It was easier to drive to the lab in her sweats and grab a few winks on the folding cot she kept in her office. Just like she did almost every other night of the week.

No wonder she couldn't keep a boyfriend. Ah, no biggie. She was young, and there would be plenty of time later to—

She stopped.

There was a single desk lamp on, and she saw movement near the consoles on the far wall.

Who in the hell . . . ?

She held her breath. Had they heard her?

She crouched low and tried to get a better look between the steel racks. The desk light abruptly switched off, plunging the room in near darkness.

Shit.

Still crouching, Val moved between the server racks. She couldn't see or hear anyone. Where the hell had they gone? The only way out of the lab was down the main corridor. Unless . . .

A strong pair of hands gripped her shoulders.

She screamed, and the hands violently spun her around to reveal . . .

"Simon!"

He was laughing as his hands raked her sides, tickling her.

"You asshole!" She hit him in the stomach.

He held his hands up. "Hey, *you* scared the hell

out of *me!* You told me you needed to get away from this place."

"I did. But you know how it is." She glanced around the darkened lab. "Why didn't you turn on the lights?"

"I guess I didn't want to announce my presence here. After what happened to Rachel, I've been a little spooked."

Val walked over to the wall panel and switched on the overhead lights. "Don't worry. I'm here to protect you now."

"Thanks," he said dryly. "I'm actually glad you're here. I was about to call you."

"About what?"

He motioned for her to follow him back toward his desk. "The project that Rachel and your boyfriend are working on."

"My boyfriend?"

"John Tavak. You have a thing for him, don't you?"

"Don't be ridiculous."

"If you say so." Simon pointed to his desktop monitor. "Rachel and Tavak have Jonesy searching for patterns based on the symbols on those tombs. They're looking for a code based on geography, mathematical theorems, religious signs, and various languages, among other things."

"I know. I've already taken Tavak's program apart and put it back together to figure out how he's doing it. It's brilliant. It's probably one of the most elegant—"

"Enough of the hero worship. The point is, I think Jonesy is onto something."

"What?"

Simon pointed to the screen.

Val leaned over and peered at the scrolling rows of symbols. A text box offered a few lines of explanation:

PATTERN MATCH:
  DIAMICUS (LANGUAGE)
87% PROBABILITY
DECRYPTING RUN SEQUENCE IN
  PROGRESS

She turned back to Simon. "Diamicus?"

"It's a dead language. It was probably dead even in Peseshet's time. I just did a quick search on it, and it's not totally understood. There's no Rosetta stone that completely translates it for us. But Jonesy picked up some patterns that suggest it may have been the basis of the code that Peseshet's disciple, Natifah, used."

"This is huge."

"I agree. Should we call Rachel?"

Val checked her watch. "No, she's still in the air. Bundle the output screens and send them to her as an e-mail attachment. She and Tavak will know what to do with them."

• • •

Tavak and Rachel studied the computer readouts that had just come in from Val and Simon on the large LCD screen in the main cabin of Demanski's jet.

"It seems I'm going to have to become fluent in Diamicus," Tavak said. "With all possible speed."

"It's not like taking a Berlitz course." Rachel surveyed several more pages of Jonesy's progress on her laptop, which was connected to the wall screen via a cable port on her armrest. "But if it's any consolation, Jonesy is directing more computing power toward cracking it than there has ever been."

"Brute force computational power is one thing, but instinct and experience also counts for a lot. It might help to have an expert guiding Jonesy's progress."

"I thought *you* were the expert." Rachel smiled slyly. "In *everything.*"

"I wish that was case. Hard as it may be to believe, I occasionally have to rely on outside expertise."

"Expertise like mine, for example?"

"Don't remind me."

"Didn't you say that James Wiley is an expert in Old Kingdom linguistical studies? Since we're on our way to him right now, is there some way we can use him?"

Tavak shook his head. "I wouldn't even want to try. He's in Dawson's pocket."

"Then whom do you propose?"

"I need to think about it." He smiled. "In the meantime, I'm glad Jonesy is making progress. That's quite a tool you've developed."

She made a face. "You make it sound like a screwdriver."

"No offense. I know that insulting Jonesy would be like calling a woman's child fat or ugly."

"Jonesy's not my child. Don't lump me in with the crazies who think that way. And you're right. It *is* a tool, but it's one with almost limitless uses. We're only scratching the surface with what's possible for it and other systems like it. Just last week we started an amazing new project."

"What is it?"

"You probably know that most laptops these days have an accelerometer chip inside."

Tavak nodded. "It detects movements to allow the hard drive to protect itself when the laptop is dropped or hit."

"Exactly. One of our software packages configures these chips as makeshift earthquake sensors. Laptops collect seismic data from these thousands of locations and, using models from earlier events, determine in seconds where the quake will spread from the epicenter. We might be able to send alarms minutes before a quake hits a major city. Can you imagine the lives we can save?"

"You're doing this now?"

"Yes. Seismic-monitoring stations in any given area once only numbered in the dozens. Now there are thousands. In a few years, with all those laptops running our software, it could be millions."

Tavak smiled. "When I was researching you, I was wondering if you'd be like this."

"A total geek?"

"An idealist."

"I've never been accused of being *that*."

"But you are. These projects aren't just a proof of concept for your computer system. You're trying to save the world."

She'd thought Tavak was teasing her, but now she realized that he was dead serious. There was genuine admiration in his face and voice. Good God, she could feel the heat flush her face. Great. Next she and Val would be comparing notes about Tavak at a sleepover.

"I'm not trying to save the entire world. Maybe a few million people. Plus my sister."

"Fair enough. Your system controls an amazing amount of computing power. You designed it to do all these amazing things for the good of mankind, but have you taken a moment to think of the harm it can do?"

"You've been watching too many *Terminator* movies."

"It's not the machines I'm afraid of. It's the humans controlling the machines. Instead of trying to break an ancient code, what if I had tasked your system to crack nuclear launch sequences? Or instead of synthesizing protein strings, someone used it to synthesize an incurable disease? For every wonderful thing of which Jonesy is capable, it's also capable of a horrific act we can't even imagine. I'm sure you've considered that there are people out there who will make it their business to imagine these things."

"Of course, I have. It goes with the territory," Rachel said. "This conversation has taken a grim turn."

"Sorry, but it's been something I've been thinking about even before I met you. It's a tremendous responsibility. I sure wouldn't want it."

"Point taken. Neither do I. But I made the commitment, and I have to ride with it."

"And you do it well."

Why did those words mean so much? So he might be one of the most brilliant and ingenious men she had ever met. She wasn't even sure she could trust him.

It didn't seem to matter. When she was with him, it was like being swept away to a place where anything was possible. It might only be that she was drawn to him physically. Oh, yes, there was definitely that factor to figure into that equation. That moment back at the barge had been too revealing to ignore. She had to ignore it. She had to think clearly and weigh everything that was happening. There could be no more disturbing moments like the one earlier this evening.

Tavak glanced toward the back of the plane. "How is your sister doing?"

She eagerly seized at the change of subject. "Tired. Even though she's been feeling better, she's not used to this kind of activity. Demanski is setting her up in one of the staterooms."

"Staterooms? I'll say this, the man knows how to live."

"We could have a worse partner."

"You mean this jet? Yes, it's nice."

"No, not only the money. He's a dynamo. He may be a rough diamond, but he cuts deep." She smiled. "You once told me that you were like him. You're right, I can see you hijacking that mastaba wall. I think that's why you're so angry with him."

"Maybe. But if he hadn't bribed that mastaba wall out of the museum, it probably never would have been taken. And now not only do we not have it, Dawson almost certainly does. I'm not at all pleased about that. Demanski gets a lot of credit for weakening the power of the Las Vegas crime syndicates, but I'd make a bet he's never dealt with a man like Dawson."

"A criminal is a criminal."

Tavak shook his head. "No, Dawson is a special breed. Ugly. Very ugly. I've learned what drives him, how he thinks. It all comes down to pride. As long as we keep that in mind, it will give us an edge. I know what buttons to push."

"Aren't you afraid of him pushing your buttons?"

"I'd be a fool if I wasn't."

D emanski switched on a light in the rear of the plane, and Allie's eyes widened at the sight of the elegant, well-appointed bedroom that wouldn't have been out of place in a luxury hotel suite.

She burst out laughing. "When I said I wanted to take a nap, I thought we might just push two chairs together."

"That can be arranged, but I think you'll be more comfortable here."

She collapsed on the king-size bed. Lord, it felt good. She had held up pretty well through that nightmare on the bridge. She didn't think that even Rachel had noticed the tremors that had attacked her afterward. Thank heaven everyone had been too frustrated and upset to pay any attention to her. "Uh, yeah. This bed might be a little more comfortable than those chairs."

"Starlight ceiling on or off?" Demanski flipped another switch to demonstrate the hundreds of pinpoints of fiber-optic lights on the room's dark blue ceiling.

She gave him a cool glance. "Definitely off. I

don't like being reminded that I'm sleeping in your make-out chamber."

He turned the starlight ceiling off. "No, you're thinking of my stateroom down the hall."

She laughed. "Oh, the one with the heart-shaped bed, the disco lights, and the mirrors everywhere?"

His lips indented. "Don't forget the champagne-glass bathtub."

"You're kidding, right?"

"Of course. I can only take the billionaire playboy thing so far. My room is actually very tasteful."

"I'm glad to hear it."

"I'll leave you now. I don't want to disturb you. I know that you're not exactly pleased at my interference in this project."

"Anything that puts Rachel in more danger pisses me off. But it appears we're stuck with you." She was silent a moment. "And I suppose I should be grateful that you saved my neck back there on the bridge."

"That's very generous of you considering that it was my fault your neck was in jeopardy to begin with."

She nodded. "That's true. But you took a chance that you didn't need to take. Life is precious. No one knows that better than I do."

He nodded slowly. "I imagine you're pretty much of an expert."

"At any rate, it would be counterproductive not

to cooperate with you." She paused. "As long as you behave in a reasonable manner."

"Oh hell, that blows it. These days I tend to act on instinct instead of reason."

She smiled. "Like stealing that mastaba wall? That wasn't at all reasonable."

"But it got me what I wanted, didn't it?"

"For about an hour."

He made a face. "Okay, rub it in."

"I have. I will." She gazed up at him. "But I have to admit it was a ballsy move."

"What a compliment. I feel as if I've been given the keys to the White House."

"You'd probably install all the historic bedrooms with slot machines."

"Probably. But I'm keeping you from getting your rest." He nodded at the windows. "The window shades will close automatically just before the sun rises, so the light won't bother you. And there's a shower in your bathroom. Do you need anything else?"

"Can I call the U.S. with that phone on the night-stand?"

He nodded. "It's satellite. But I thought you needed to rest."

"I have to call Letty and tell her we're all right."

"Letty?"

"Letty Clark." He was still gazing at her inquir-ingly, and she said, "My housekeeper, my friend." She added deliberately, "She's also a registered nurse who keeps me company while I'm wasting away."

"Ouch. You know I'd never have said that if I'd thought you were really doing that. I've never seen anyone who looked less ill."

"I didn't mind. I can accept rudeness more easily than cloying pity."

"I'll have to remember that." He smiled. "But I promise I'll make up for my rudeness. Ask anything, and it's yours. Put me to the test."

"Really? You sure know how to spoil a girl."

"I like to make my guests comfortable."

"Even at thirty-seven thousand feet."

"Especially at thirty-seven thousand feet. Flying can be such a hassle."

Allie sat up on one elbow, staring at him. Demanski possessed the same charm and confidence she had seen in television interviews, but in person, his bravado was tempered a bit. A definite improvement, she thought.

"I still haven't figured something out," she said.

"What's that?"

"Why are you bothering with this treasure hunt of ours?"

"You don't think it's worthwhile?"

"Of course I do. But you don't need this. Flying around the world in your luxury jet, checking in on your billion-dollar casinos with Oscar-winning actresses on your arm."

He held up his hands. "Nominees only, I'm

afraid. Get your facts straight. I've never dated an Oscar winner."

"My mistake."

"And I'm always on the lookout for a good business opportunity."

"I'm sure you have many opportunities that are far less risky than this."

"True. But as your sister pointed out, I'm a fan of the big idea. The game changer. There aren't many things out there that can rewrite the rule book. But if this works out, we'll be part of something incredible."

"I can't think that big. For me, it's just about staying alive."

"You've been doing a good job of it so far."

"I have. I've been beating the odds since I was thirteen years old. But there are things I can't do."

"Like what?"

"Like having a family."

"You can have children, can't you?"

"I think so. But every time I think about it, I get another reminder that I might not be around to see them grow up. Just last week, I started losing my peripheral vision. I think it's stopped, but you never know. On top of that, GLD is a genetic disease. I had adult-onset GLD, but when it hits infants, it's almost always fatal by the age of two. I just can't risk it."

"Too bad. Is there a man in your life?"

"No one special. You wouldn't believe how many guys out there try to cast themselves as my rescuer. It's the Galahad complex. Needless to say, I don't keep them around long."

"Needless to say." He crossed his arms and leaned against the dresser. "Meeting you on this trip was actually a pleasant surprise. My intel didn't tell me you were a part of this expedition."

"Last-minute addition."

"I spoke with Rachel about you in Las Vegas, but I didn't tell her how taken I was with your paintings."

She gazed at him in surprise. "You've seen my work?"

Demanski nodded. "I'd never seen your paintings in person, but I've recently spent a lot of time looking at them online. They're very powerful."

"Thank you."

He raised his index finger. "Don't go away."

"Where would I go?"

Demanski disappeared through the doorway. In less than a minute, he returned with a large, framed painting. He turned it around to show Allie a landscape with a tiny lone figure on a hilltop dwarfed by a massive evening sky.

Allie's eyes widened. "That's one of mine!"

"I know."

"Where did you get it?"

"The Tauck Gallery in Denver. I saw it on their online catalog and couldn't get it out of my mind.

I had them bring it to the airport, and I stopped and picked it up on my way out of the country."

Allie scrambled to the edge of the bed to get a closer look at the painting. "It's called *Biography*. I sold it to a collector in New Mexico a few years ago. I didn't know it was back on the market."

"Lucky for me it was." Demanski placed the painting on the dresser and gently leaned it against the wall.

Allie stared at it for a long moment. "It's always hard for me to part with my work. They're pieces of me, you know?"

"That's why there's such passion there." Demanski crouched to look at the painting head-on. "The gallery owner gave me her interpretation of it. In her opinion, you're showing how overwhelming the universe is. How it can overpower you and make you feel insignificant."

"Really?" Allie studied the painting, as if trying to see it with different eyes. "Do you agree with that?"

"Not at all."

She turned from the painting to look at his face. Demanski suddenly looked older now that he wasn't trying to be glib. His eyebrows were no longer raised as impish arches, and his jaw wasn't set as firmly.

Not older, she decided. More mature. Grounded. And yes, dammit, fascinating.

"What do *you* think I'm saying?" she asked.

"This figure on the landscape isn't overwhelmed by anything. It's taking in the majesty of it all, enjoying the infinite possibilities. It's a big world out there, but that's what makes it so wonderful. There's a feeling of excitement, not dread. I see hope."

Allie smiled.

He turned toward her. "So who's right? Me or the gallery owner?"

"Artists shouldn't impose their thoughts on the people who experience their work."

"Don't give me that. What is this about? Hope or dread?"

"It doesn't matter what I think."

"It matters to me."

She looked away for a moment. "It's exactly as you said. Hope."

"I knew it. But I'm glad to hear you say it."

"I only get afraid when options are taken away. In my mind, there's nothing overwhelming about a world of possibilities. This is a celebration, not a requiem. I'm surprised at that gallery owner."

"It says more about her outlook on life than yours. Or mine."

He picked up the painting, but Allie raised her hands to stop him. "Would you mind . . . leaving it here for a while?"

He looked at her for a moment, then nodded. "Sure. I'll prop it up down here on the floor. I'd hate for it to get knocked around by turbulence."

"Thank you."

He carefully positioned the painting. "There. But don't get used to having it around. I'm very fond of this piece, and it's *not* for sale."

FIFTEEN

RIVER OAKS COUNTRY CLUB
HOUSTON, TEXAS

Gentlemen. How nice to see you. I didn't know you played golf." Carlos Dobal smiled at Finley and Gonzalez as they approached him on the fairway. He was a tall, good-looking man who spoke with only a trace of a Spanish accent.

"We *don't* play golf," Finley said.

"You should. Did you know that your police chief's promotion was decided somewhere between here and that hill over there?"

"Damn," Gonzalez said. "And here I thought it was because he was a decent cop."

Dobal shrugged. "What can I do for you, gentlemen?"

"We're investigating the campus shooting. You've heard about it?"

"Of course. Your suspect was found dead, wasn't he?"

"Yes," Finley said. "But we still don't know who he is or who he was working for."

"Fingerprints?"

"We have a complete set, but no match. No match on the facial scans, either. But we have reason to believe that the NSA knows who he is. They seized the corpse and the weapon just a few hours ago."

"Interesting. Did they offer an explanation?"

"No. And we're still trying to work this case. Can you help us?"

"What help do you think I can be?"

"I believe we both know what you can do for us." Finley paused. "If you'd be so kind, Mr. Dobal."

Dobal looked down and away from them.

Finley studied him as he waited for his answer. Dobal looked remarkably the same as he had when they first met four years before. The man's wife and child had been kidnapped by an old enemy from his days as a Spanish intelligence agent, and Finley and his then-partner had succeeded in bringing them back unharmed.

But at a terrible cost.

"How is Detective Pace's family?" Dobal asked.

"Her husband got remarried last year, and they moved to Oregon. I think her two girls are doing well."

Dobal nodded. "Such a tragedy. I think of her often."

"Me too."

"Whatever happiness I have in my life, I owe to her." He looked up at Finley. "And to you, Detective. What do you need?"

"Since our own intelligence agencies seem to be stonewalling us, I wondered if you might go to your own sources. Maybe some of your old colleagues will be more forthcoming."

"What do you have?"

Gonzalez handed him a large manila envelope. "This is everything we have on the corpse. Prints, photographs, dental X-rays, body scans, the works. Something in here triggered the NSA to swing into action. We'd like to know what it is."

Dobal placed the envelope on the seat of his golf cart. "You know, of course, I'm now just a dull, ordinary investment counselor. I don't have direct access to any of the databases you probably require."

"But you know people who do, right?"

"Possibly." Dobal reached into his golf bag and selected an iron. "But I know from personal experience that the NSA agents may have a good reason for keeping you in the dark."

"Even if it means that we can't do our jobs?"

"Yes. This may not be only for the sake of their interests, but for your sakes as well."

"We'll take our chances," Gonzalez said.

"Once you start down this path, there may be no going back. I daresay those NSA agents have a much better idea what awaits you than you do. Are you sure you want to venture into this territory?"

Finley nodded. "We wouldn't be here if we weren't. Rachel Kirby is an innocent victim of whatever is going on. She deserves to be protected. I don't want this case buried in a NSA TOP SECRET box somewhere."

"Very well." Dobal walked toward his ball on the green. "And do consider taking up golf, gentlemen. It's a very relaxing game."

CHICAGO-WAUKEGAN REGIONAL AIRPORT WAUKEGAN, ILLINOIS

Rachel frowned as she watched the fire red Maserati speed away from the aircraft hangar. Demanski and Allie never looked back as they roared through the complex's main gate.

"I wish she'd stayed with us," Rachel said.

"Splitting up the dual surveillance on Wiley made sense. Demanski said he needed to pick up a report on Wiley in person."

"He didn't have to take Allie."

"As I recall, she volunteered."

Rachel grimaced. "Yeah. That Maserati may have had something to do with it. Allie loves fine cars." For the major part of the journey, she had watched Allie and Demanski talking and joking together like old friends. "But I think she likes him."

"I understand he has a certain appeal to some people." Tavak slung his travel bag over his shoulder. "To tell the truth, I'm glad your sister is there to keep an eye on Demanski."

"You don't trust him?"

"I do. Sort of. But he's an opportunist, and I feel better knowing that Allie can report back on what he's doing."

"Do you think they'll come up with anything?"

"Demanski says he already has someone monitoring Dr. Wiley's telephone and e-mail communications, just in case Dawson tries to make contact."

"I'm going to pretend I didn't hear that part."

Tavak laughed. "Dawson tried to kill me, and I do believe those were real bullets whizzing by your head at Hearst Castle the other night. You're upset by somebody reading his e-mail?"

"Sounds ridiculous, I know. Somehow, a bullet in Dawson's brain seems less objectionable to me than invading his privacy. I guess that's something I need to get over."

"Immediately."

They walked toward a black Escalade SUV parked just outside the hangar. Tavak opened the rear hatch and tossed his and Rachel's bags inside. "Funny how Demanski rented that hot little Maserati for himself and this behemoth for us."

"Well, I feel better in this."

"I do too, actually. It's more inconspicuous if we're going to be tailing someone around the streets of Chicago. Too bad Demanski didn't show a bit more restraint with his own car."

"The words 'Demanski' and 'restraint' should never appear together in the same sentence."

Rachel suddenly realized something. "I think that's why Allie is drawn to him. She's been restrained by her illness and fighting those strictures for most of her life. Demanski's recklessness and flouting the rules must be very appealing."

"You're not worried that she might be unduly influenced?"

"Allie's no fool. She might enjoy him, but she's too strong to let him change anything about her."

"Then there's no problem. You know her better than I—" Tavak's cell phone rang, and he picked up. "Tavak."

"You tried to shut me out, dammit. Okay, so I told you no more tombs, but I can handle—"

"Ben?"

"Yes. You should have come to me first. You've known me a hell of a lot longer than Nuri."

"You're still in the hospital, dammit."

"No, I'm in London."

"Oh, for God's sake."

"I'm fine. A little wonky, but at least I'm not bored. That hospital was driving me nuts."

"Ben, go back to the hospital."

"Nope. I'm on the job. Nuri and I will get back to you as soon as we find out something."

"Is Nuri there? Let me talk to him."

A moment later Nuri was on the line. "I'm sorry, it was necessary that I either bring him or have him follow me."

"How bad is he?"

"Not too bad. The hospital would have released him within a few days anyway."

Tavak muttered a curse. "Listen to me. Take care of him. Sometimes he's—Don't let him do too much."

"Trust me. I know he's your friend." He paused. "But now he's my friend, too. I will watch over him. And now I must go because Ben is looking at me with extreme indignation. Good-bye."

"Your friend, Ben?" Rachel asked, as Tavak hung up.

Tavak nodded jerkily. "He checked himself out of the hospital and tagged along to London with Nuri."

"Nuri seemed to be very capable." She studied him. "But you're not with Ben, guiding, watching him yourself. You don't like that. You're very protective."

"Yeah, that's why I almost got him killed in that tomb. Well, there's nothing I can do about it now." Tavak checked his watch. "Ready to go to school?"

It took less than an hour for Rachel and Tavak to drive to the University of Chicago, park, and make their way to the five-hundred-seat auditorium where Dr. James Wiley was lecturing.

As they entered the hall and allowed their eyes to adjust to the darkness, Rachel realized that Wiley was speaking on the subject of Babylonian customs. He spoke in a painful monotone, and to illustrate his lecture, he used a large projection screen and a particularly unimaginative PowerPoint slide presentation.

Rachel glanced around the auditorium. "These poor kids," she whispered.

"Half of them are asleep," Tavak said. "Can you blame them?"

Wiley pulled up another slide of a colorful painting. "For the next hour, we'll take a look at some of the headpieces of this era . . ."

Rachel was sure she heard about two hundred anguished sighs in the room.

"That's our cue," Tavak said. "Let's go."

Tavak was already out of his seat and heading for the door. Rachel ran to follow him.

Outside, in the bright sunlight, Tavak briefly consulted a campus map on his phone before pointing to another building. "His office is over there in Haskell Hall. He just told us the coast will be clear for the next hour."

"What are you going to do?"

"Remember that thing we decided you needed to get over?"

"Invading people's privacy?"

"Yes. Over it yet?"

"Guess I'd better be," she said, as they walked into the building and climbed the stairs to the second floor. Tavak consulted a scrap of paper as they walked past a row of faculty offices. They finally stopped at a door with a typewritten card affixed to it that read DR. JAMES WILEY and listed office hours. Before Rachel even realized what was happening, Tavak had jimmied the door and was ushering her inside.

"You did that way too fast," she said.

"I admit I've done this once or twice before." He pulled her into the office and closed the door behind them.

Rachel flipped on the lights to reveal a small, windowless room with a desk, a set of floor-to-ceiling bookshelves, and a long table covered with what appeared to be ancient stone cookware.

Tavak leaned over the desk and looked at Wiley's computer monitor. "His e-mail application is open."

"Is there anything there?"

"You mean a subject heading that says 'come look at our stolen Egyptian artifact'?"

"Yeah, something like that."

Tavak scrolled though Wiley's e-mails for the previous week. "Afraid not. And nothing about plane reservations or travel plans of any kind. Too bad."

Tavak reached into his jacket pocket and pulled out a black box the size of a pack of cigarettes. He pulled off an adhesive backing and affixed the box to the underside of Wiley's desk.

"What's that?"

"A listening device."

"A bug? I thought those things were smaller."

"This is a special one. It records all conversations from here and e-mails them to me as audio files."

She nodded. "Interesting. You know, if you set up a relay with a simple voice-recognition software package, you could have a written transcript created and e-mailed to you at the same time."

"I hadn't thought of that."

She shrugged. "I can set that up in fifteen minutes. I'll work on it tonight."

He smiled. "You're a natural."

"A natural what? Criminal?"

"Spy. I'm glad you're on my side." Tavak pulled a small plastic disc from his pocket and walked over to the door, where an overcoat hung from a hook. He unzipped a corner of the lining, placed the disc inside, then closed it.

"Let me guess," Rachel said. "GPS transmitter?"

"You catch on fast. I don't know what Demanski's source has, but Dr. James Wiley won't be able to make a move without us knowing about it." Tavak pulled out another GPS transmitter and again consulted his scrap of paper. "Now let's go to the faculty parking lot and find his car. According to the Illinois Department of Motor Vehicles, it's a gold Toyota Camry."

W hy did your contact want to meet down here?" Allie asked as she walked with Demanski down the busy stretch of Michigan Avenue known as the Magnificent Mile. Allie watched as the high-end shoppers jostled with businessmen, tourists, and a large group of children who had obviously come from a *Star Wars*–themed birthday party.

Demanski stepped around a small child wearing a Yoda mask. "It was my idea, actually."

"*Your* idea?"

"I thought it would be fun. Have you ever been here on the Magnificent Mile?"

"No. My first time in Chicago."

"Good. Then I made the right choice by bringing you here. I guess we could have arranged a handoff at night on a dark side street, but that would have been so . . . depressing."

Her lips curved in a slight smile. "You're more like John Tavak than you care to admit."

"Perish the thought. I didn't think you knew him that well."

"I don't, but Rachel has told me a bit about him. He's a focused and driven person, but like you, he wants to enjoy the ride."

"There's one big difference between us."

"What's that?"

He looked out at the lake. "From what I understand, Tavak never hesitates to go all the way. Before last night, I had never killed a man."

Allie looked at him. "The man on the bridge?"

Demanski nodded. "I've led a rough life, but

that was one transgression I'd never committed. It felt very . . . strange. I've been in some pretty intense situations before, and I've never had to resort to that. I've had a price on my head on three different continents. My own casino manager once came to work one night with the intent to kill me. There have been many times I could have taken care of my problems—and ended someone's life—with a simple phone call. But I chose not to do it. It's been one of the rules I wouldn't break. Until last night."

She was silent for a moment, then impulsively put a hand on his arm. "Then I'm sorry you had to do it for me."

He smiled. "I'm not sorry. I'd do it again. I've never met a woman more worth breaking all the rules for."

Allie couldn't look away from him. The words were said very simply. It wasn't bullshit. It wasn't Demanski trying to make a score. She finally managed to tear her gaze away. "Why did you decide to hijack that mastaba wall?"

"You don't believe it was revenge?"

She shook her head. "And it wasn't the prospect of another potload of money on the horizon."

"I'd be interested to hear your take on it."

"Boredom. You've seen everything, done everything. You wanted to see if you'd missed something along the way."

"That makes me sound somewhat shallow."

"No, there's nothing shallow about you. You're smart, and you're always thinking. You're just not sure that where you're going will be enough for you."

"Then you're not condemning me for not being totally devoted to the great quest?" he asked mockingly.

"Why should I? I can understand your motivation perfectly. I haven't seen everything, and I certainly haven't done everything. I wish I had."

Demanski didn't speak for a moment. "I wish you had, too."

She glanced at him and sighed. "Oh, Lord. I've seen that expression before. You're revving up for a major pity party. I thought better of you, Demanski."

He looked away from her. "Sorry. I'll work at regaining my respect in your eyes. It was just a temporary failing. How could I forget what a tough nut you are, Allie?"

That moment had been too emotional and come out of nowhere. Time to veer away. "Where are we supposed to meet your contact?"

"He's already here." Demanski nodded ahead to a plaza in front of the Wrigley Building, located on the north bank of the Chicago River. A gray-haired man in a sports coat was watching two teenagers on their skateboards.

"He's very good," Demanski said. "I once used

him to get some information on a Chicago business consortium that was trying to muscle me out of a real-estate project I had put together. He has great connections at the phone companies, and a lot of the private detectives in town use him."

One of the kids, a ruddy-faced young man with long blond hair, picked up his board and waved to the other. "Later, dude." He walked toward Demanski and Allie.

"His name is Tyler K.," Demanski said. "He's a good kid."

Her eyes widened. "You're joking, right?"

"No. Why do you ask?"

Allie watched in amazement as Demanski playfully bumped fists with Tyler K. "Good moves on your board," Demanski said. "You can still bring the magic."

Tyler K. laughed. "Aah, I was just screwing around. I haven't been worth shit since I busted up my leg."

Demanski turned to Allie. "Allie, meet Tyler K. He'll be an Olympic skateboarding champion one day."

Tyler K. shook his head. "Doubtful. I was ninth in the U.S. one year, but they'll never give medals for that." He nodded to Allie. "Pleased to meet you, ma'am."

She smiled. "The pleasure's mine."

"What do you have for me, Tyler K.?"

Tyler K. reached behind him and pulled a large white envelope out from underneath his shirt. "Here it is."

"What did you find out?"

"I got phone records for his home, his cell, and his office. My source at the local phone company jacked me around on the price, so I'm gonna have to ask for an extra thousand. Cool?"

"That's fine. Did you cross-reference the numbers as I asked?"

"Dude, you just called a few hours ago."

"I know. I guess I thought you were a miracle worker."

"Aw, you're playin' me, man." Tyler K. lit up with a broad smile that revealed two missing teeth. "You wanted to know about cell-phone calls from out of the country. There are quite a few cell-phone calls in the past couple of days, but I don't know yet if they went through overseas providers. I'll work on it, but you may have other people who might be able to get you that information faster."

"Thanks. Keep on it, and I'll see what I can do on my end."

Demanski produced a small envelope that Allie assumed contained money. He then pulled out his wallet, counted out ten one-hundred-dollar bills for the extra thousand, and handed the cash and envelope to the kid.

Tyler K. jammed them into the front pocket of

his shorts. "So when are you gonna set me up in one of your Las Vegas high-roller suites?"

"Anytime, my man. Anytime." Demanski bumped fists with him again.

"You'll hear from me." Tyler K. dropped his skateboard to the sidewalk and rolled away.

Allie shook her head. "Where on earth did you ever find him?"

"My director of security recommended him. As I said, Tyler K. does this kind of thing for several of the private investigators in town."

"So what do we do now?"

"We wait to see if Dawson makes contact with our professor." Demanski pulled out his iPhone, launched the e-mail application, and showed Allie a map on the screen. "Tavak and your sister have been successful."

"What's that?"

"The GPS tracking device they're using sends out an e-mail that plots the current location on a map. Tavak can also track it in real time. This tells us that Professor Wiley is still on campus."

"Do you think Dawson will really contact this Wiley?"

Demanski motioned for her to continue up the street with him. "Tavak thinks so, and he seems to have a pretty good insight into Dawson."

"But Tavak thinks he could also be in England."

"That's true. I just hope Tavak's man there is as good as he says he is."

• • •

MUSEUM OF ARCHAEOLOGY AND ANTHROPOLOGY CAMBRIDGE, ENGLAND

Ben walked through the Maudslay Gallery on the museum's first floor, looking at several displays of Native American sculptures. The gallery was relatively empty except for a few college students who sat cross-legged on the floor, sketching on large pads.

Ben stopped to examine a particularly oblique object, wondering what the sculptor's contemporaries thought of it. Hell, they probably couldn't make any more sense of it than he could. He turned and was startled to see Nuri standing beside him.

"Jeez, Nuri. You about gave me a heart attack. How were you able to sneak up on me like that?"

Nuri shrugged. "I only use the movements I require, no more."

"Is that an invisibility trick?"

"To the unobservant, perhaps."

Ben cocked his head. "You have a sneaky way of insulting me, you know that?"

Nuri gazed at him blandly. "I am sure I do not know what you're talking about."

"Well, you just called me unobservant, and on the plane you pleasantly insinuated that it was my waistline, not the narrow seats, that was responsible for my discomfort. Add that to the fact that you told the bellman to fetch the bags for your 'elderly friend,' and I'm starting to get a complex." Ben wrinkled his brow. "Apparently, I'm old, fat, and unobservant."

"It was not my intention to slight you in any way."

"It may not have been your *intention* . . ."

Nuri nodded. "I see. In early stages of dementia, social situations are very often misinterpreted."

"Early stages of . . ." Ben laughed. "You son of a bitch."

Nuri smiled. "I will be mindful of your exceedingly sensitive nature as we move forward."

"Why do I feel more insulted than ever?"

"That I cannot say."

Ben glanced behind Nuri at the man approaching them. "Okay, we're on. Ready?"

Nuri nodded and suddenly took on a regal air. "Of course."

A bearded man in khakis and a brown sports jacket approached them. "Mr. Mubarek, sorry to have kept you waiting."

Nuri smiled. "No worries. I took the opportunity to admire your fine collection."

Ben shook hands with Dr. Collier. "I'm Ralph Conners. We spoke on the phone."

"Yes, of course. We're very excited that you're considering us for such a generous donation."

Ben gestured to Nuri. "The decision, of course, is Mr. Mubarek's. I'm just assisting him in this process."

Nuri stepped forward. "My late father was a man of considerable means, and his collection of ancient Egyptian artifacts was immense. Alas, his interests are not mine, and I have no desire to keep his collection. But I wish to keep it intact in a place where it will be presented with respect."

"Of course."

Ben handed Collier a thick binder filled with pages and photographs encased in sheet protectors. "This will give you an idea what we're talking about."

Collier thumbed through a few of the pages. "This is extraordinary. This was your father's private collection?"

Nuri nodded. "He was very proud of it."

"I can see why. But you realize there may be a problem transporting these objects out of Egypt. Your country isn't fond of its treasures being taken away."

"My father never liked being told what he could do with his personal property." Nuri smiled. "And almost all of it is in a warehouse in Holland. I've been assured there will be no problems."

Collier looked through the book a moment longer. "Very impressive. Not that I'm not grateful, but why us? As you can see, our Egyptian collection is rather modest."

"You have Mr. Conners to thank for that. He suggested your institution."

Ben shrugged. "For one thing, we're confident

your museum will properly showcase the collection. The Egyptian Museum in Cairo would gladly accept it, but you and I both know that most of it would always remain in storage."

Collier nodded. "I'm afraid you're right."

"Second, you have a terrific reputation for your expertise in Old Kingdom Egyptian studies. But for some reason, you have found yourself at a university museum without a notable Egyptian collection. We think this could be a good fit, don't you?"

"I do indeed." Collier closed the book. "Well, I'm definitely interested, and I believe we can give your father's collection the showcase you're looking for. What more can I tell you?"

Nuri looked at Ben, who turned to Dr. Collier. "Before making his decision, Mr. Mubarek would like to spend some time here at the museum and with you. He has a good feeling here, but he wants to make sure. You understand, don't you?"

"Of course."

"We'll be here for the next ten days or so, and Mr. Mubarek's schedule is quite uncertain. He may call you anytime during the day or night with questions or a request for a meeting at a moment's notice. Would this be acceptable to you?"

Dr. Collier thought about this. "I'll give you my cell-phone number. I do have obligations, but I can make myself available almost anytime you need me."

Nuri smiled. "Thank you. How is your schedule today and tomorrow?"

"Days I'm fairly flexible, but tomorrow night I have a professional commitment."

Nuri raised his eyebrows. "Really? I would welcome the opportunity to meet some of your colleagues."

"Oh, it's nothing like that. I occasionally do some consulting work, and an outside project has suddenly fallen into my lap. But it's nothing we can't work around." Collier reached into his pocket and produced a card. "Here. My home and cell numbers. Feel free to call anytime."

Ben took the card. "Thank you, Dr. Collier. On the phone, you promised us a personal tour. Is this a good time?"

Collier smiled. "Of course."

Twenty-five minutes later, Ben and Nuri walked along the tree-lined path outside the museum, each holding piles of pamphlets that Collier had given them during their brief tour.

"Okay," Ben said. "First, we need to know more about the special project that has suddenly come up for Collier."

"I could have pressed him further," Nuri said, "but I didn't want to arouse suspicion. I could only take this act so far. I'm not comfortable in the role."

"No, you were right to hold back." Ben thought

for a moment. "We'll keep an eye on him for the next couple of days, especially tomorrow night."

"An eye? I'm pleading with you, Ben. Join the twenty-first century."

"We've been through this. I'm not a fan of tracking devices, bugs, and all that James Bond gear."

Nuri sighed. "But it works."

"*Sometimes* it works. If you're someone like Tavak. And sometimes it doesn't, usually just when you need it most. How often do you drop a call on your cell phone? Every day? Four or five times a week? That's no big deal. But when a tracking device drops out, you're royally screwed. I know, because it's happened to me."

"They're now much more dependable than they were back in the sixties."

"Very funny. You sound just like Tavak, trying to drag me into the future."

"The present, Ben. It's happening now all around you."

"Do whatever you want to do, Nuri. But as far as I'm concerned, all that stuff is just backup for good old-fashioned legwork."

SIXTEEN

CHICAGO, ILLINOIS

S hould we meet for dinner after we get settled?"
Tavak punched the button at the elevator of the
Millennium Knickerbocker Hotel. "Providing we
can hook up with Demanski. He disappeared right
after we checked in."

"He knows the owner. He wanted to touch base,"
Allie said.

"Of course he did. Who doesn't he know?" He
looked at Rachel. "Dinner?"

"I don't see why not."

"I do," Allie said. "We'll meet you for drinks
later, Tavak. I want to have dinner alone with my
sister. Things have been topsy-turvy, and I want to
make sure we're on the same page." She glanced at
Rachel. "If that's all right?"

Rachel felt warmth surge though her. "More than
all right."

Tavak smiled. "Heaven forbid I interfere with a
family get-together. I'll call you later."

Thirty minutes later Allie was knocking on
Rachel's door.

"Gorgeous hotel," she said as she came into the
suite. "Demanski chose well." She went to the
phone. "I'll call room service. What would you
like?"

345

"You choose. I don't care." She went to the window. "This is a good idea. I've been feeling as if we've been running at full speed."

Allie chuckled. "Because we have. Jet speed. Why don't you sit down and put your feet up?" She picked up the receiver. "I'll order something high protein and lots of coffee."

Rachel watched lazily as Allie placed the order. Allie was bright, alert, and seemed to be thriving. Lord, it was good to see her so well.

"You look very mellow. What are you thinking?" Allie asked as she hung up the phone.

Rachel grinned. "That you seem in better shape than I do. I'm not used to being coddled like this."

"And you'll bounce back any minute now and try to run things." Allie plopped down beside her on the couch. "But you've been very good about restraining yourself." She added quietly, "I know it's been difficult for you."

Rachel nodded. "Because I love you."

"And you have the instincts of a healer. Demanski has been telling me a little of the details concerning our Peseshet. You're a lot alike."

Rachel shook her head. "Tavak said something like that once. But you're both wrong."

"Are we? You're both geniuses at building and fixing things."

"Computers and the human body aren't the same."

"But Peseshet was ahead of her time. I've been wondering if she lived today if she might not have had a Jonesy of her own."

Rachel laughed. "Then she would probably be in competition, and neither one of us would like that."

Allie was silent, thinking about it. "I don't believe it would be like that. I think she would consider you her sister."

"Like Natifah?"

"No, Natifah was really a disciple. Peseshet would realize you were her equal."

"But I already have a sister." Rachel reached over and took Allie's hand. "You're all I need."

"Am I?" Allie laced her fingers through Rachel's as she leaned back on the couch. "What about Tavak?" Her grip tightened as she felt Rachel stiffen. "Don't get on guard. I wasn't sure that Tavak was going to be good for you. I was feeling very protective."

"So he told me."

"But then I realized I was behaving exactly the way you did with me. Not many men turn you on, but I've watched you with him. You have a yen for Tavak. You should reach out for the experience."

"Whether he's bad for me or not?"

"I don't think he is." Allie smiled. "But if he proves to be a problem for you, then I'll go after him. After you've had your fun."

Rachel gazed at her in surprise and started to

laugh. "I never realized how ruthless you could be."

"Only for you," Allie said. "You're my sister, and I've got to step up to the plate since you don't have a Peseshet here to protect you."

"Thank you." She squeezed Allie's hand. "But I don't need either you or Peseshet to protect me from Tavak. We're not heading down that road."

"The hell you're not. I'm not blind. I can see the sparks fly."

Lord, had she been that obvious? Rachel wondered.

"It's not surprising," Allie said. "He's Indiana Jones with a brain that's almost as powerful as Jonesy's. I can see how you'd be drawn to him. You want this particular brass ring? I'll do everything I can to help you get it." She held up her hand as Rachel started to protest. "Okay, I just wanted you to know that I'm here for you." She met Rachel's eyes and smiled luminously. "Always."

Rachel's throat was so tight she couldn't speak for a moment. "Me too," she said unevenly. "Always."

Rachel watched Tavak stride through the open-air bar on the rooftop of the Millennium Hotel and make his way toward the table where she, Allie, and Demanski were sitting near the railing.

I can see the sparks fly.

She wished she could get Allie's words out of her mind. It had been difficult before to ignore the disturbance she always felt when she was with Tavak. Now it was almost impossible. She was suddenly acutely aware of everything about him. The lithe way he moved, the eyes that glittered with vitality, the expressions that were always full of intelligence and humor. Little things that shouldn't have had this physical effect on her. Good God, she could feel the pulse pound in her wrists and the heat rising—she tore her gaze away from him and encountered Allie's amused stare.

As he reached them, Tavak glanced over the railing. "That's a spectacular view of Grant Park."

"Yes," Allie murmured. "I was wondering if they had carousels in Grant Park."

"I have no idea," Tavak said. "Why?"

"No reason. Just a thought."

Thank heavens, even though Allie was definitely in teasing mode, at least she hadn't seen fit to mention that damn brass ring, Rachel thought.

Tavak's gaze was narrowed on Allie, then shifted to Rachel. Rachel could almost see that formidable mind going into high gear.

But he evidently decided not to pursue it. "Nice hotel," Tavak said to Demanski. "I'm surprised it's not one of yours."

"Not for lack of trying," Demanski said. "I know

the owner, and he's very attached to this place. Your rooms should be spacious and comfortable, and I have a two-thousand-square-foot suite just one floor down. I figure we can base our operation there."

"Are you trying to impress us?" Allie asked. "That stateroom on the plane wasn't enough?"

"Not at all," Demanski said. "I wouldn't be such a fool. Particularly not you, Allie. You don't impress easily."

Rachel laughed. "You've got *that* right."

"I just talked to Ben," Tavak said. "He says Dr. Collier in Cambridge has some kind of consulting project that has suddenly come up."

"Any more details?" Rachel asked.

"Apparently, Collier wasn't very forthcoming about the nature of the project. But whatever it is, he'll be busy with it tomorrow night."

"Then maybe we should be there," Demanski said.

Tavak shook his head. "Nuri said they have a good handle on things. They won't make a move until they know for sure the mastaba wall is there. As for this special project, it could be nothing more than Collier appraising a few items for an auction house. Ben will keep us posted."

Demanski frowned as he gestured at a nearby table, where there was a pile of newspapers with news of the St. Petersburg bridge assault. "You were right, Tavak. The story is in newspapers all over the world. And, dammit, they're trying to tar and feather me with a blasted scandal."

Allie smiled. "Another irate husband?"

Demanski gave her a look. "No, it appears that the Hermitage's director approved of my traveling art exhibit without the proper clearances. So the Russian government is holding the rest of the pieces pending an official inquiry."

"That's too bad," Rachel said. "I guess you might have to bribe some more people." She turned to Tavak. "Do we know where our fascinating college professor is right now?"

Tavak reached for his phone and checked the screen for the pulsing yellow dots that showed the location of the GPS tracking devices he had planted.

"He's at school," Tavak said. "Wiley is teaching an evening class tonight. He should be there until at least nine or so."

"Dammit, I don't like all this waiting around," Demanski said.

"It's part of the game," Tavak added, "since you let Dawson heist our artifact."

"Touché," Allie murmured.

"Rub it in," Demanski said sourly.

"You deserve it," Allie said. "You're spoiled. You need to learn to be patient."

Demanski grimaced. "I've never been good at that."

"Neither have I, Demanski," Allie said quietly. "But sometimes we have no choice."

The frown left Demanski's face as he gazed at her. "I could use a teacher."

Allie shook her head. "I'm not applying for the job. It's too long-term. You're on your own."

"And I'm on my own," Rachel said as she stood up. She didn't have the patience to watch Demanski and Allie play off each other. She was restless, and she needed to get away from here. Away from Tavak. "I'm going to bed. Good night."

"I'll walk you to the elevator." Tavak rose to his feet. "I might as well have an early night, too."

She didn't want him to go with her. She knew damn well he was sensing her disturbance. "You never have early nights," Rachel said. "You don't give in to sleep any more than you give in to anything else. I've watched you."

"I'm flattered," Tavak murmured as he took her elbow and headed for the bank of elevators. "But it's always the exception that proves the rule."

His touch on her elbow was light, but heat was spreading through her arm and down to the sensitive flesh of her wrist. She pulled her arm away, then wished she hadn't as his gaze went to her face.

"I believe in exceptions, don't you?" he asked softly. "I think you might be ready to make one tonight."

She didn't answer.

"Shall I define exception?" Tavak asked. "Pleasure, pure and simple. No ties. No responsibility. No demands for commitment or a repeat performance."

Pleasure, pure and simple. And intense, Rachel thought. Sex with Tavak would be beyond the scope in intensity. The mere thought of his touching her was causing her body to ready.

"I'm not into ships that pass in the night."

"Maybe not in the usual run of things, but I don't think you'd accept anything else with me." His thumb pressed the elevator button. "And I'll take anything you'll give me."

He stood near, without touching her, but she could still feel the heat of his body. It seemed to surround her, encompass her. She couldn't breathe. "It would get in the way."

"No, it wouldn't. Not of Peseshet's cure. I wouldn't let it," he said. "Afterward, I don't make any promises."

"That doesn't sound like an exception."

He turned to look at her. "I'm doing the best I can. I want you, and that's messing up my thinking. Do you want to know how much I want you?"

"No." The heavy ornate door opened and she got in the elevator. "Good night, Tavak."

"You want to know. Give me the chance, and I'll show you."

She punched the button, and the door began to close.

She could see him standing there, hands clenched, his face slightly flushed and totally sensual.

I want you to have the brass ring.

She wanted it, too. She couldn't remember ever wanting anything as much.

What the hell. Why not take it?

She quickly pressed the button, and the door slid open again.

"Show me, Tavak." She tried to steady her voice. "And I'll show you."

"Deal." He was in the elevator in a heartbeat and pressing the button for her floor. "But not now. Don't even touch me, or we'll never get out of this elevator with our clothes on."

She reached out and touched his arm. "I've never done it in an elevator."

He shuddered. "I wouldn't object to being a first, but you might regret it later. I can't afford the chance." The elevator doors opened, and he took her arm and pushed her out into the hall and down the corridor. "Give me your key. Quick. Very, very quick."

Would you really have done it in the elevator?" Rachel cuddled closer to him in bed. She was still trying to catch her breath. "You'll never know. You never gave me the chance."

"We could do a replay."

She shook her head. "It wouldn't be the same.

You have to seize the moment. Like Allie does."

"I like Allie, but I really don't want you thinking about her right now."

"Why not? She'd approve." She rubbed her cheek catlike against his shoulder. "Brass rings. No, more like skyrockets, Tavak."

"What are you talking about?"

"Sex and pleasure and seizing the moment."

He was silent a moment. "I had no idea you'd be this . . . joyous."

"I may not always hear the music, but I've no trouble with the dance."

"No, you don't. Thank God." He kissed her lingeringly. "And thank you."

"Thank you," Rachel said. "The pleasure was definitely mutual." Mutual and heady and completely mind-blowing. "But I find I have a slight argument with your definition of exceptional."

He stiffened. "What? No ties. No commitment. I'm not going to push you, Rachel. That's what you want, right?"

She didn't know what she wanted at the moment. Yes, she did. She wanted to stay in bed for a month and do nothing but screw Tavak. But that wasn't what she should do. Distance herself until she could think clearly. Accept this night for what it was and let it go.

Why did that thought bring such a pang?

"That's what I want. But you put in a clause that I don't find acceptable." She moved over him. "No demands for a repeat performance? No way, Tavak. We have all night . . ."

HOUSTON, TEXAS
2:30 A.M.

Wayne Norton stared at the buzzing, tweeting disposable phone, thinking that it had the most ridiculous ring tone he had ever heard. He had paid cash for it at the 7-Eleven, so there would be no way calls could be traced back to him.

He couldn't be too careful.

He picked up the call. "Are you in a secured location?"

"I'm not an amateur, Norton," Paul Simmons said sarcastically. "I've worked for the agency longer than you have. Believe me, I know how to keep my tracks covered."

No, he wouldn't have called Simmons if he wasn't as sharp as he was malleable. "Just checking." He paused. "I need an answer."

"I'm thinking about it."

He'd like to tell Simmons to take a hike. But he needed the bastard. "Stop thinking and commit, dammit."

He hesitated. "You're asking a lot. This could blow up in our faces."

"I'm not denying that. No risk, no reward. But that's why I want you. You're the best. And if I'm going to pull this off, I need the best." Simmons had an ego as big as the Grand Canyon. It was the best way to manipulate him.

Simmons finally spoke. "If this goes south, you'd better not hang me out to dry."

"I gave you my guarantee. Are you in?"

Simmons didn't answer for another moment. "I'm in."

Tavak was gone when Rachel woke the next morning.

Disappointment. Loneliness.

Get a grip. He was only keeping to the letter of his promise.

It was to be an exception, no commitment. No ties that would interfere.

Then why did she feel that the bonds were there? All the stronger and more enduring for the denial of their existence. Ignore it. Tavak had given her an extraordinary night that was off the charts on the sensuality scale. But he had also thrown in freedom, and that was a priceless gift.

Accept it. Don't ask for anything more.

She threw back the covers, got out of bed, and headed for the bathroom. The night was over, fading into the past. Shower and start the new day.

Forget about anything but that blasted mastaba wall.

Wiley's on the move!" Tavak strode into Demanski's suite four hours later. Rachel,

Allie, and Demanski were already gathered in the large living room.

Allie pointed to the wall. "We know. We're watching it on TV."

Tavak turned to see a wall-mounted plasma television connected to Demanski's laptop. A Chicago street map was displayed on the screen with a pulsing yellow dot indicating Professor Wiley's position.

Demanski picked up his phone and jacket. "I've already called down. They're bringing the Escalade up to the main entrance. I figure we can set up somewhere on campus and keep an eye on him there. He only has one class today, right?"

Tavak nodded. "A morning lecture class, then he has office hours until one. After that, it's anybody's guess."

Demanski turned to Rachel and Allie. "If you two would like to stay here, we can call you once he begins to move again."

Rachel clucked her tongue. "Oh, I see. The boys will take care of the cloak-and-dagger stuff, and the girls will eat breakfast on the terrace, hang out at the spa."

"Have a facial, then a massage," Allie added. "And then, if we're not too exhausted, maybe some shopping."

"Forget I suggested it," Demanski said.

"I'm already trying to forget it," Allie said. "Because I'd hate to have to—"

"Wait a minute." Tavak suddenly moved closer to the television screen. "Are you seeing this?"

"What?" Rachel said.

"Wiley." Tavak studied the screen for a moment longer. "He just turned onto I-90 heading east."

Rachel nodded. "He's heading away from the college."

"And away from the city," Tavak added. "Now where are you going, Professor?"

Demanski was already heading for the door. "Let's move!"

Two minutes later they were buckling up in the rented Escalade and seven minutes after that they were on the Chicago Skyway heading out of town. "How close are we to Wiley?" Rachel asked.

Tavak checked his GPS. "Probably another seven or eight miles. Keep an eye out for that gold Toyota."

Ten minutes later, Demanski suddenly pointed ahead. "That's Wiley's car, isn't it?"

Rachel could see little more than a speck of gold in the distance.

Tavak eased off the accelerator. "Yes."

She turned toward him. "Why are you slowing down?"

"We're in farmland now. It's practically deserted out here. We can't let him know he's being followed."

Allie leaned forward. "You have a file on him,

Tavak. Does he have family out this way? A girlfriend? A lake house or something?"

"Not according to any information I have on him."

Demanski checked the map screen on his phone again. "Tavak, we need to talk about what's going to happen if he leads us to the pot of gold."

"What's there to talk about? If we see the mastaba wall, we figure out a way to take it back."

"I already have a way."

Tavak's gaze narrowed on his face. "I can hardly wait to hear what it is."

"I set up a private security force on standby back in Chicago."

"You what?"

"One phone call, and they're on the road. They'll secure the location until the police can get here."

"We'll see."

"*We'll see?* Dammit, Dawson took that mastaba wall away from me. I want to take it back. Do you have any better plan?"

"It depends on where we end up."

"Tavak, there's no way we could pull off a military operation like that one on the bridge in St. Petersburg. We don't have any razzle-dazzle weaponry, and in case you haven't noticed, none of us are exactly Green Beret material. We need help."

"We'll see."

"Will you stop saying that?"

"Okay. I'm just telling you that this game doesn't always go to the one who plans every move. Try going into a third-world military base with no weapons and making off with an eighty-million-dollar fighter jet without getting captured or shot out of the sky. It helps to go in with an idea how you're going to pull it off, but mostly it's about instinct and thinking on your feet."

Demanski threw up his hands. "I wouldn't need to sneak into that base because I'd hire qualified people to take care of it."

"People like me. So relax."

"You're making that very difficult."

Tavak sped up to keep Wiley's car in view. "I'm not going to do anything stupid. I just want to see where Wiley is going and reconnoiter the area to see the possibilities. I'm leery of involving the police until we get some quality time alone with that wall. The Russian government has made it clear that you're no longer the official custodian of anything you were given from their museum. Once the police are involved, we may not be able to get near it."

"He's right," Rachel said. "We don't know how much time we're going to need."

Demanski looked at her in surprise. "You, too?"

"I'm just saying we should keep an open mind. And I agree we have to know what Wiley is up to." She shrugged. "Anyway, this could all be moot if

Professor Wiley is just skipping work to spend the day at his favorite fishing hole."

Demanski nodded. "Okay, we'll play it your way for a while, Tavak."

But they'd only driven another few minutes when Demanski began to curse.

"What is it?" Allie asked.

"I've lost his signal."

"The GPS tracker transmits through the cell phone towers," Tavak said. "The coverage may have just dropped out."

"Do you still see him?" Rachel asked.

"Possibly." Tavak grimaced. "Look."

Up ahead, a beige-and-cream Gulfstream jet lifted into view and soared into the sky.

"I don't believe it," Rachel said.

"You'd better start." Tavak pointed to a road sign that read MCCOY AIRFIELD 1 MI. "It's a private airport. Wiley may have had a plane waiting for him."

"Shit!" Demanski cursed. "Shit shit shit!"

"That would explain why his signal dropped out of range," Tavak said. "It's a damn bad break."

"A bad break?" Demanski said. "That's all you have to say?"

Tavak nodded. "Yes. If he's on that plane, it's a bump in the road, nothing more."

"Will the tracking signal start up again once he lands?" Rachel said.

"It should, but I'd rather not count on that. I'll

talk to the people at the airstrip. The pilot of that jet would have filed an itinerary, but that's no guarantee of where the plane is really heading. Still, it's a good place to start." He glanced at Rachel. "Let me go in alone."

She shook her head.

"There's no reason for any of you to tag along. I'm not used to having to work by committee."

She shook her head again. "Together."

Tavak muttered a curse as he pulled off at the tiny airstrip, which was no more than a single runway, an open hangar, and a small tower. There were no planes in the hangar; only an eighteen-wheel tractor-trailer stood inside.

Tavak pulled next to the tractor-trailer, stopped, and climbed out. There was no sound except for the wind blowing against the hangar's corrugated tin roof and walls.

"Where is everybody?" Rachel said.

Demanski pointed outside the hangar to four parked cars, one of which was the gold Camry they had been following. "Unless you think the drivers of all those cars are now in the air, there's someone still around."

Tavak stiffened, his head lifting. "It's too damn quiet." He whirled back toward the Escalade. "Everyone get back in the car."

"I'm afraid I can't allow you to do that, Tavak."

They spun around to see a lean, fiftyish man

step out from behind the tractor-trailer. He was pointing an AK-47 at them. "Dawson said that you'd track Wiley down. You work quickly. We just managed to whisk him away in time."

"You were waiting for us. You knew we were tailing Wiley. Who are you?"

"Les Kilcher. We're not strangers." He smiled. "We ran into each other recently on Big Obukhovsky Bridge."

"You're the one who heisted my exhibit?" Demanski asked.

"I certainly did. I did a bang-up job. Literally. I'd do the same here, but I have my orders. Dawson wants to handle it himself." Kilcher spoke over his shoulder to one of the two men who had just come from behind the trailer. "Weitz, keep an eye on them while I dial Dawson. He said we had to exercise extreme care with Tavak."

"Yes, sir," Weitz said, raising his automatic weapon. "No problem."

"Dawson?" Kilcher spoke into the phone. "I have Tavak, Demanski, and the Kirby sisters. Yes, all secure." He put the phone on speaker. "He wants to have a few words with you before turning you over to me."

"Actually, I'm sorry not to be there," Dawson's voice came loud, clear, and full of malice from the phone. "But I'm on my way to meet Wiley and, in the end, money is always more important than revenge."

"This whole thing was just to draw us out?" Tavak asked.

"Not quite. I've just learned to make the most of my opportunities. Each time I've confronted you in the past, Tavak, I made the mistake of not giving you enough credit. You're quite a clever man, so I merely asked myself what *I* would do if I were in your position, watching that precious artifact airlifted out of your grasp."

"And?"

"I knew you were aware of the only two men I would be likely to consult in this matter. My first thought was to find someone else, but then I realized it was a great opportunity."

"Because you knew we would be watching Dr. Wiley," Rachel said.

"And Scott Collier in Cambridge, where I know your friends have already made contact." Dawson paused. "Poor Ben Leonard. Out of the kettle into the fire. He should really have learned his lesson in that tomb. He must be very loyal to you, Tavak. In another fifteen minutes I'll make a call and tell my men that he's to give you final proof of that loyalty."

Tavak tensed. "Why? You already have us. It's stupid to act without reason. It's the sign of an amateur."

"But I have the discretion to act however I please." He added maliciously, "Don't I? You guessed that I'd choose Dr. Wiley. His linguistic specialty tipped the scales for you, yes?"

Tavak didn't answer.

"I'll take that as an affirmative response. And you would be quite right. Dr. Wiley is on his way to the mastaba wall now, enjoying what I've been told is his first trip ever aboard a private jet."

"Then Dr. Collier in Cambridge has nothing to do with it. Whatever you have planned there, call it off. There's no reason for it."

"You keep harping on logic and reason. Yes, there's no reason for it. Like there was no reason for you to humiliate me in Bolivia?"

"You humiliated yourself the day you signed on to do the pharmaceutical companies' dirty work. And you've been humiliating yourself ever since." Tavak stopped and tried to control himself. "I'm the one you want, Dawson. Let them go. Take their phones, disable the car. By the time they could get help, you'd be long gone."

"And so would you, Tavak."

"Yes."

"That's all very noble, but you know there's no way I could do that. Three witnesses, and your blood on my hands?" He chuckled. "It would be ironic if you were the one to put me away for the rest of my life . . . by dying."

"Then what's with the monologue?" Tavak said. "Why not just shoot us?"

"My employer is rather squeamish. He's a fan of the convenient accident, but that's rather diffi-cult to pull off with four victims. Particularly such well-known people as your friends. So were going to have to strive to give him what he wants. Good-bye, Tavak. I'm only sorry I couldn't see you buy it. Kilcher, go ahead with it." Dawson hung up.

Kilcher nodded to Weitz, who ran to the Escalade, climbed in, and started it up. He backed the vehicle up a steel loading ramp and into the bed of the tractor-trailer.

Kilcher gestured with his gun. "Take their weapons and phones, Hannigan."

The man, Hannigan, to whom Kilcher had spoken couldn't be over twenty but was wearing a holstered knife and also carrying an AK-47. Hannigan patted down each of the captives. He took phones from each, plus a knife and handgun from Tavak.

"Don't worry," Kilcher said. "You'll be reunited with your items soon enough. Now into the trailer. All of you."

Tavak didn't move. "What's the plan, Kilcher?"

"It will be apparent soon enough," Kilcher said. "Climb in. Of course, if you don't follow Dawson's instructions, I'd be just as happy to shoot you. I'm a professional. I don't run risks when I can just move on to another job that doesn't have all those damn restrictions. Your choice."

What the hell could they do, Rachel thought. She glanced at Tavak, instinctively trying to tap into that confidence and ingenuity to which she had become accustomed.

She didn't like what she saw.

Tavak appeared resigned. Defeated.

"Tavak?"

He started toward the truck. He said curtly, "Just do what Kilcher says."

They walked up the loading ramp and stood in front of the Escalade. The last thing they saw as the trailer doors swung shut was Kilcher's unsmiling face.

Large chains rattled outside as the doors were secured.

Rachel glanced around. Light spilled from the ventilated sides of the trailer. "What is this?"

"It was made to transport cattle," Demanski said. "Which, at the moment, happens to be us."

The truck started up. It rolled out of the hangar and pulled onto the highway.

"You know Dawson," Rachel said to Tavak. "What is he doing with us?"

"No idea. All I know is that we couldn't do anything back there under Kilcher's guns. We need to find a way out of here right now. Before Dawson makes that call to Cambridge. Fifteen minutes. Shit." Tavak jumped on top of the Escalade and pounded his fists on the roof of the trailer. He glanced down to Demanski and pointed to the trailer's side vents. "Help me with this."

The two men slid their fingers through the

vents and pulled, but the steel framework didn't budge.

"Dammit!" Demanski struck the trailer's side with the heel of his hand.

After a few minutes more of struggling with the vents, Tavak went still. "We're slowing down."

Everyone listened as the tractor-trailer downshifted. Gravel kicked from the tires.

Rachel peered through the thin vent slits. "We're off the highway. It's a gravel road. Whatever they're going to do, it's going to happen soon."

Tavak threw open the door of the driver's side door of the Escalade.

"Keys in the ignition?" Allie said.

"No." Tavak ran around to the rear door, opened it, and burrowed into the spare tire compartment. He came up with a tire iron. "I don't know what use this is going to be against those AK-47s." His gaze became suddenly speculative. "But maybe I can find a use for it in another way."

The truck stopped. Then they were almost thrown from their feet when it lurched into reverse.

"What's happening?" Tavak yelled at Rachel.

She peered through the vent and fear tightened her chest.

Water.

Water everywhere.

"It's a lake, a pond, or something." She whirled

back toward Tavak. "They're going to drown us."

Tavak nodded. "They'll submerge the trailer, drown us like rats, pull us out, and set up their accident scene. They'll roll the SUV off a bridge or something."

"With us inside," Allie said. "And the autopsies will show that we drowned just like we would from that staged accident."

Demanski shook his head in disbelief. "Can that tractor really pull out a trailer full of water?"

"It's a beefy rig," Tavak said. "It's possible, especially if they pull it out slowly enough for the water to drain from these vents."

The tractor-trailer slowed.

The crunching of gravel gave way to a sloshing sound, and water poured in through the lowest row of vents as the trailer entered the water.

"Shit." Tavak's grip tightened on the tire iron, then turned to the driver's side of the Escalade.

But Allie was ahead of him. She was already slipping underneath the wheel. "Give me that tire iron."

Tavak frowned. "What?"

"We don't have time for arguments. You were going to try to hot-wire this baby. I can do it faster. You and Demanski try to get those doors open. Give me that iron. Now!"

He thrust the tire iron into her hand. She braced herself against the front seat and pried loose the panel beneath the steering column.

Rachel leaned into the open door. "What are you doing?"

"You're blocking my light!"

Rachel stepped back.

Allie grabbed a cluster of wires and examined them. She tore two wires free and stripped the edges with her teeth.

"Can I help?" Water was now sloshing around Rachel's ankles. Allie shook her head, and Rachel turned to see that Tavak and Demanski were now pushing hard on the trailer's rear doors. The large chains held them closed tight.

"Can she do it?" Tavak asked Rachel over his shoulder.

"If she says she can," Rachel said. "She completely rebuilt a Jeep Cherokee when she was seventeen." She was watching Allie, who was moving with the efficiency of a master car thief. Lord, she was scared.

Come on, Allie, she prayed.

The trailer submerged even farther. Water poured in from the higher side vents.

Allie picked up the tire iron, pried apart the starter assembly, and pushed the bar forward.

The Escalade roared to life.

"Get behind me!" Allie yelled as she slipped on the seat belt. "All of you. Get behind the car."

Tavak and Demanski scrambled through the calf-deep water. Demanski yelled, "Let me take the wheel!"

"No time. If the water hits the intake, we're finished!" Allie jerked her thumb back. "Get behind me. Don't argue!"

"Dammit." But Demanski turned and waded back to Tavak and Rachel behind the Escalade.

Allie gunned the engine.

Still more water poured in.

The Escalade's engine roared in Rachel's ears as the vehicle hurtled toward the locked doors.

Boom.

The doors exploded outward, and thousands of gallons of water suddenly filled the compartment. In an instant, all gravity appeared to have been suspended, and Rachel was aware of the Escalade floating in space next to her.

Allie.

Rachel kicked her feet. The still-rushing water made it impossible to move toward the door.

The Escalade's monstrous rear end swung wide, and Rachel realized it might pin her against the trailer's inside wall.

She kicked furiously. Get around it. No, not around. Normal rules didn't apply. *Over.* Get on top of it.

She pushed upward with her legs, and in a moment found her head above water, almost touching the roof of the trailer.

Allie. Must get to Allie.

Rachel moved over the Escalade's roof and thrust her face back into the water.

She opened her eyes.

Through the Escalade's windshield, there was the deployed airbag and something else. It almost looked like . . .

Allie's hair.

Shit.

Rachel reached inside the Escalade and struggled to find the seat-belt catch.

Come on, Allie. *Help me.*

The airbag and the rushing water were fighting her, jabbing and blocking with her every lunge.

Tavak was suddenly back beside her, pushing the airbag down and to one side.

Then a thin, strong hand clasped Rachel's wrist.

Allie. Thank goodness.

The seat belt loosened, and Tavak helped Rachel pull Allie out from behind the airbag.

Allie gave Rachel the thumbs-up sign, and they swam out of the trailer.

They broke the surface seconds later. Tavak came up an instant behind them.

"Thank God!" Demanski was swimming toward them.

"No." Tavak immediately grabbed Rachel. "Swim. Get as far away from here as you can. All of you." He pointed toward the middle of the lake as he gave Rachel a push and motioned for Allie and Demanski to follow her. "Stay as close to the bottom as you can. Only come up when you absolutely need to." Tavak swam back toward the shore.

"Wait." Rachel asked, "Where are you going?" But he'd disappeared beneath the surface, slicing the water with barely a ripple.

There were shouts from the truck, and Rachel spun around to see that Dawson's men were out of the cab. They lifted their rifles and opened fire.

A bullet broke the water not a foot from where Allie was treading water.

"Move!" Rachel yelled.

Rachel, Allie, and Demanski dove to the bottom as more bullets pelted the lake's surface.

SEVENTEEN

On the shore, the kid, Hannigan, turned toward Weitz. "Did we get 'em?"

"No. Keep looking."

Weitz muttered a curse as his gaze searched the waters. Kilcher would tear his ass if any of Tavak's people got away. The old man was already pissed about the casualties in St. Petersburg, and that bastard Dawson didn't seem as if he was one to tolerate failure.

"I don't see anyone. I think we got them," Hannigan said.

Weitz tried to hide his disgust. Why had Kilcher teamed him with this moron? The kid loaded himself with weapons and thought they took the place of brains. "Use your eyes, dammit. Look!"

A woman's head, hair plastered flat, broke the surface about thirty yards away.

Weitz and Hannigan opened fire.

Damn. She was gone again.

"Stay here." Weitz started down the bank at a trot. "Watch the area and see if any of them break the surface. I'll head downstream and see if they pop up there."

Shit. How could this happen? As Weitz ran through the tall grass along the bank, he could imagine what the response to his report to Kilcher would be like. Screaming expletives, humiliation, and possible discharge in front of the team. And maybe, just maybe, after half a bottle of bourbon, Kilcher would give him one more chance.

That kid, Hannigan, wouldn't be so lucky. He'd be out on his ass.

A muffled shout behind him!

Weitz ducked low and whirled with his rifle ready.

Silence.

He retraced his steps, trying his best to move silently in the tall brush.

He stopped just before he reached the clearing that he'd left only seconds before.

Hannigan was lying on his back, beside the cab, eyes open, staring blindly at the sky.

Dead.

Pain.

The gun dropped from Weitz's hands, and an icy shiver shuddered through him.

More pain.

He looked down and saw the kid's black-handled bowie knife sticking out of his own chest.

John Tavak stood beside him, water dripping from his clothes.

Tavak gripped the handle and shoved the knife deeper.

Tavak jumped onto the cab of the truck and waved an all-clear sign to Rachel, Allie, and Demanski. Satisfied that they had seen him and were swimming back, he leaped into the cab and fished through the canvas bag in which Kilcher had thrown their belongings.

He found his phone and frantically punched Ben's number.

Maybe Dawson was bluffing. He had no reason to go after Ben.

But the tightness in Tavak's stomach told him that the son of a bitch wasn't bluffing. It wasn't his style.

No answer.

Five minutes.

Dawson had said that he'd call to give the order to kill Ben in fifteen minutes. Tavak still had five minutes left.

Demanski was wading out of the water and Tavak called, "Grab your phone out of the cab.

This must be a private lake. It's totally deserted. But we don't want to stick around here and wait for Kilcher to come back. Get that security team you mentioned out here double quick and tell them to pick us up at the highway."

Demanski nodded and moved toward the cab.

Three minutes.

He hung up and dialed again.

"Come on, Ben," he muttered. "Pick up. Answer your damned phone."

CAMBRIDGE, ENGLAND
9:16 P.M.

Ben felt the vibrating phone in his pocket, but he decided to let it go to voice mail. He and Nuri were standing in the shadows of a large oak tree, watching a pair of headlights coming toward them on a campus auxiliary road.

"Is that it?" Ben asked.

"The timing is right." Nuri checked his notes. "Dr. Collier left a drive-on pass for a large delivery truck at approximately 10 P.M."

"How did you find that out?"

"I saw the list. I went to the security office and pretended to be an instructor who needed to arrange my own after-hours delivery. They pulled out the list, and they made no attempt to hide it from me."

"And why would they?"

The truck drew closer.

Ben handed Nuri a ballcap and a blue Windbreaker. "Here. These are a pretty good match for the campus security getups. And remember, we're still just fact-finding. Once we determine that the mastaba wall is here on campus, *then* we'll figure out how to take it."

"As you wish. But there's no way of knowing how long it will be here."

The phone vibrated again. The truck was almost upon them. Ben reached into his pocket and turned off the phone. "Okay, let's move."

Ben and Nuri stepped into the middle of the roadway and waved down the truck. It stopped.

Ben walked around to the driver's side window.

"Open up the back, will you?" Ben spoke in an accent he learned from watching Alec Guinness movies.

The driver glanced at the man in the seat beside him, then turned back. "We've already been cleared up front, mate."

"Sorry. We can't let any trucks through without inspecting them first. Give us a peek inside, and you'll be on your way."

"No problem."

Both men climbed out of the cab and moved around to the back. The driver pulled up the large garage-style cargo door.

Ben turned on his flashlight. "Okay, if there's a crate or packaging, I may have to ask you to . . ."

Ben shined his flashlight into the truck 's storage bed.

It was empty.

Empty, except for the two men with guns aimed at him.

Ben felt the hot, searing pain in his chest and head.

He felt the numbing coldness in his legs and arms.

Then he felt nothing.

The sun was setting when Demanski's security team dropped them off at the hotel. Allie, Tavak, and Rachel went inside while Demanski stayed behind to settle with the team leader.

Only one day, Rachel thought. Only a matter of hours, and yet it seemed as if a century had passed.

She glanced at Tavak as they got in the elevator. He'd been on the phone frantically trying to reach Ben Leonard or Nuri all the way back from the lake. "You'll let us know as soon as you hear?"

He nodded jerkily. "As soon as I know something." The door opened on his floor, and he got off and headed down the hall.

"What a hell of a day," Allie murmured.

Rachel nodded numbly. "I shouldn't have let you come with me to Russia. I should have made you stay at home. You almost died in that car."

"Knock it off, Rachel. This isn't about me. We

all came close to dying." Allie wearily pushed her damp hair back from her face. "If anyone should run the risk, it should be me. I'm the one who has the most to gain."

The hand Allie had used to push back her hair was shaking, Rachel noticed, agonized. The tremors again, more violent than she had recently seen them. "You're not well. I'm coming to your room with you."

"You are not," Allie said. "I don't want you hovering over me. I'll rest, then I'll be okay."

"And what if you're not?"

"I'll be okay," she repeated. "I'll call you when I get over this little bout. You know I'm used to handling it, Rachel."

It wasn't a little bout, and Allie shouldn't have been forced to handle this damn disease. "Let me come."

"No way. You try, and I'll lock you out."

"I'm sending you home."

"No, you aren't. I'm going on until the end. Make up your mind to it. It doesn't matter that I'm sick and sometimes have to take a few minutes' time out to be able to keep going. I helped keep us alive today. I had value." She got off the elevator as the doors opened. "But if you want to stop all this madness, I'll understand."

Rachel shook her head.

"I didn't think so." Allie started down the corridor. "Then we'll just have to work through this."

Work through keeping Allie alive until they found the cure.

Work through death and malice and Dawson, who seemed to be everywhere.

Dear God, she hoped that malice and death hadn't spread to touch Ben Leonard.

Allie called Rachel a little over an hour later. "The tremors have stopped. I'm much better. I'm going to take a hot shower, then order dinner."

"Do you want company?"

"No, I'm going to give you time to forget about my attack. I'll be much more relaxed eating alone tonight."

"You're sure there aren't any—"

"See? I'm fine, Rachel. Any news from Tavak?"

"Not yet."

"Let me know. Bye."

"Bye." Rachel hung up. Allie had sounded tired but steady, thank heaven. And Allie never lied to her. Rachel knew that she sometimes hid the symptoms of the disease, but she always told her the truth when confronted.

How many times had Allie masked the pain and exhaustion since she had started this journey?

And how much stress could she stand before she ended up in the hospital again?

Or before it killed her?

Allie had been under that ticking clock for

years, but today it seemed to be going into over-drive.

She wouldn't quit, and the only thing Rachel could do was to keep racing and try to make that clock stop.

She could do it. She *would* do it. She just had to smother the fear and forget what a disaster it had been today.

As Allie had said, they could work through this.

It was over two hours later that Tavak knocked on Rachel's door.

He looked like hell. He had obviously showered and changed, but his face was drawn and tired. "May I come in?"

She opened the door wide for him to enter. "Of course. You've heard something?"

"Ben's dead."

She had been hoping against hope, but she had known the news wouldn't be good from the moment she had seen his expression. "I'm so sorry."

Tavak nodded. "I just talked to Nuri. It was a total setup. Ben and Nuri intercepted a truck that was supposed to deliver a large item to the museum director on campus. As it turns out, the only thing in the truck was Dawson's hit squad."

"How is Nuri?"

"He wasn't hurt, but he's not good. He and Ben had become pretty close. He managed to wing one of them before making his escape." His lips twisted. "He wants my permission to track down the entire squad and take care of them himself."

"And what did you tell him?"

"I told him to go home. This isn't his battle. And Dawson is the one I want."

Rachel watched Tavak as he stared out the window. He was hurting. When she had seen the bodies of the men Tavak had killed at the lake, she had been shocked. It had seemed to come too easily to him. She had known he was a dangerous man, but she had never been brought face-to-face with that cool disregard of life and death.

But he was not disregarding Ben Leonard's death. It was obviously tearing him apart.

"Did Ben have a family?"

Tavak shook his head. "Only a brother who lives in Florida. They were never close. Two ex-wives, neither of whom wanted anything to do with him. He was a Vietnam vet, and I don't think he ever made any strong attachments since the time he was there."

"Except for you."

Tavak shook his head. "Yeah, and all I did was get him killed."

"He knew what he was doing. Even after what happened to him in the tomb in Egypt, he didn't hesitate to do another job for you."

"I paid him well."

"It was more than that, and you know it. You

probably helped make him feel alive. I'm sure he felt like he was part of something special."

Tavak managed a smile. "Maybe. He complained a lot, but no one enjoyed the thrill of the chase more than Ben."

"And he *wanted* to do this."

"I should have made Nuri send him back to that hospital. He would have been safe there." Tavak turned to face her. "Instead, I used him. Just as I used you."

"Bullshit. It was my choice. I insisted on joining you. I practically threatened you."

"Practically?"

"Okay, I doomed you to life in a federal penitentiary if you didn't make me a part of this. The point is, I took my own chances."

He was silent, staring at her. "I can't stop, Rachel. I have to go on. Dawson killed Ben, and I can't let him get away with it."

"I didn't think you'd react any other way."

"But I want you to back off. Leave it to me. A good man died today. *We* almost died today. I don't want anything to happen to you or your sister."

"Or Demanski?"

"Okay, sure. Even Demanski. I'd have a hard time living with myself."

"Then that's your problem. This isn't a game for Allie or for me. For us, this has always been a matter of life and death. Healthwise, I know Allie's on an up cycle right now."

"I'll say."

"She's not as strong as she seems. She's in her room resting right now. Sometimes she gets sick. *Really* sick. And every time she hits a rough patch, I never know if it's the one that will finally kill her. I've been feeling that way for years." She shook her head. "So bite the bullet, Tavak. We're in this for the long haul."

He nodded. "I was afraid that you wouldn't let me get away with it." He turned toward the door. "I had to try."

Because he was bleeding inside, Rachel thought.

And she was bleeding for him, she realized. She wanted to touch him, heal him.

"Tavak."

He turned to look at her.

"You come back here."

He didn't move. "Why?"

She went to him instead. "Because you need someone." She put her arms around him. "And maybe I need someone, too."

He still didn't reach out for her. "Is this an invitation?"

"Do you mean sex?" She shook her head. "Sex is about joy. If I have sex with you, I'm going to want skyrockets, not comfort. Now I want to hold you all night and we'll talk about Ben and Allie and all the things that hurt us and give us hope. Skyrockets are wonderful." She looked up at him. "But comfort is good, too."

He slowly reached out and cupped her face in his two hands with incredible tenderness. "Yes, comfort can be very good."

HOUSTON, TEXAS

Finley winced at the shit-kicking country music blaring from the speakers at Saddles, a bar known for its cheap beer, chicken wings, and almost daily fistfights. He glanced around until he spotted Carlos Dobal waving at him from a booth.

Finley walked over and sat down. "This doesn't seem like your kind of place."

"It's not." Dobal had exuded ease and confidence on the golf course a few days before, but he now appeared troubled. "I thought it would be best to go someplace nobody knew either of us. And where it would be relatively easy to spot someone else who didn't belong."

"What's the problem?"

"The problem is yours, my friend." He paused. "I did as you asked and checked with my contacts in the intelligence community. Your campus shooter was a professional."

Finley tilted his head. "A professional?"

"An assassin. Not much is known about him personally." Dobal slid a folded sheaf of papers across the table. "What little I know is here. Gaius Pelham is the name he uses most often, but nothing is known about his true identity or where he came from. But several government intelligence agencies had hired him on occasion."

"What governments?"

Dobal just stared at him.

"Mine?"

"You may wish to adjust the parameters of your investigation."

"You're telling me to back off?"

"If someone wanted to kill Rachel Kirby so much that they would engage Mr. Pelham's services, then wanted to cover their tracks so completely that they would take the risk to murder this professional killer, it seems to me that they would be capable of almost anything."

"Whose payroll had he been on? CIA? NSA?"

"It's not likely he kept a résumé. Probably everybody's."

"Shit."

"I debated with myself whether or not I should even tell you. But you have been good to me and my family, and I thought you should decide how you use the information. My recommendation is that you disregard what I have told you."

"I don't think I can do that."

Dobal nodded. "I thought that might be your response. For the moment, then, I ask that you do not attempt to contact me. I really don't want to be a part of your world right now." He smiled sadly. "Good luck to you."

Dobal slid from the booth and walked out of the bar.

MILLENNIUM HOTEL
CHICAGO, ILLINOIS

Lord, she was tired.

Allie grimaced as she gazed at her reflection in the bathroom mirror after her shower. She looked as pale and weary as she felt. What could she expect? It wasn't because she was ill. Anyone who had been through what they had today at the lake would be as sapped as she appeared.

Or maybe the illness had added to it, but she had learned to ignore those signs of weakness. As she would do now. She grabbed a towel and started to dry her hair.

"Allie." Demanski was knocking on the door of the suite.

"Coming." She wrapped her hair in the towel and quickly crossed the suite to open the door. "Is there something wrong?" Please, no more deaths. She could still see those two men lying on the bank of the lake. "Have we heard anything more about Ben Leonard and Nuri?"

"No, Tavak said he'd let us know. But I need to talk to you." Demanski strode into the hotel room and slammed the door. "Sit down."

She warily perched on the edge of a chair. "What's wrong?"

"Do you want the short list or the long list?"

"I want you to tell me why you're looking at me as if I was a criminal."

"I don't know how else to look at you. I have to walk a fine line whenever I'm near you."

"Are you going to tell me what's wrong or not?"

His hands clenched into fists. "I was scared shitless when I couldn't find you in the water. I don't like to be scared."

"Who does?"

"This was different."

"Because it was your fear instead of someone else's?"

"Yes. There's nothing wrong with being selfish. I've made a practice of it for years. I felt so damn helpless. I wasn't even the one who got you out of that car."

"You were coming back to help us."

"That's not good enough."

"It's been a long, terrible day. Spit it out. What are you trying to say, Demanski?"

He was silent a moment, then said awkwardly, "I want to be Galahad."

She covered her eyes with her hand. "Oh, God help us."

He dropped to his knees in front of her and jerked her hand down so that he could see her expression. "Don't give me that crap. Do you think I like the idea of playing the fool?"

"Then back off, Demanski."

"I can't do it," he said between his teeth. "I know you don't want to hear it, but I'm not exactly subtle. I have to be up-front with you."

"You're right, I don't want to hear it."

"Tough. Here it is anyway." He looked into her eyes. "I'm not going to say anything stupid. I like you. Hell, I may do a hell of a lot more than like you. You're funny and honest, and I want to be with you. But you keep pushing me away because you think I'm going to pity you. I *don't* pity you. Why should I? You've got us all beat. Someday, if I see you tired or fading, I'll hurt, and I'll do my damnedest to help you. But not because of pity. I'm too selfish. I'll just want to stop whatever is tearing me apart."

"There's a solution," Allie said unevenly. "You know what it is."

"That's not an option. I decided that when I couldn't find you in that damn water. So I have to find other options."

"Galahad?"

"Hell yes. You haven't seen anything like the Galahad I can be. Give me a chance, and I'll find your damn Holy Grail."

Tough and smart and yet at this moment very vulnerable. She was unbearably touched. "Maybe after you've found it, you'll lose interest."

"Then you'll have to take your chances. You don't want promises. You'll run if I don't move very carefully. So I'm creeping forward at a snail's pace."

"You're too big to creep. You'd look ridiculous."

"Allie?"

"And you'd look ridiculous as a Galahad. It's not your style. Not sophisticated enough."

"Then find me another role. Because I'm going to be around a while."

"Look, I'm having a good period right now. But it gets nasty. I never know when it's going to take me down. I could go blind, become a cripple, have brain damage, and become a vegetable."

"I'm duly warned. You're not scaring me, Allie."

"Dammit. I'm not one of your Hollywood ladies." She pulled the towel off her wet hair. "I don't glitter. Look at me. Sometimes I look pasty as biscuit dough. That's okay with me. I can handle it. I know what I am inside."

"I like biscuit dough."

"Demanski."

"And I know what you are inside, too," he said quietly. "And you do glitter."

She stared at him helplessly. He meant what he was saying, and it was hard not to let those words sway her.

She should tell him no. She didn't need a man like Demanski disturbing the tempo of her life. She had a difficult enough time riding the ups and downs that comprised her days.

But she didn't want him to go away. When she was with him, she forgot everything but the moment. Moments were important.

She said slowly, "I suppose we could try to see how it goes."

He smiled. "I suppose we could."

"And I'll never question you if you decide to walk away."

"That's very good of you," he said solemnly. "I'll keep it in mind." He sat back on his heels, gazing up at her. "Don't feel uncomfortable. We didn't commit. We just clarified." He got to his feet. "And now I'm going to find a way to prove that you're wrong about my Galahad capabilities. I don't blame you for doubting since I've not done anything impressive since I left Las Vegas. I'll have to remedy that." His brow was furrowed with concentration as he pulled a sheaf of papers out of his jacket and moved toward the computer on the desk. "Call room service and order dinner, will you?"

RURAL HALL, NORTH CAROLINA
10:40 P.M.

There was a problem," Kilcher said when Dawson picked up the phone. "Tavak and the others are still alive. I lost two men. When Weitz didn't call me to tell me that he'd completed his mission, I drove back to check."

"You idiot." Dawson's hand tightened on the phone. "What kind of blunderers did you send out with Tavak?"

"I'm not an idiot," Kilcher said. "I don't take that from you or anyone. It happened. I'll either reimburse you or work another job for you. What do you want from me?"

"I want you to erase all signs of what happened at that lake. Then I want you out of my life. And you'll damn well reimburse me." Dawson hung up the phone.

He should have handled Tavak himself. The perfect opportunity, and Kilcher had blown it. Okay, keep calm. He'd have another chance at Tavak. Right now he had to concentrate on getting that mastaba wall decoded.

He sat in the back of the company Jeep, trying to steel himself for the even greater bumps and jostling he knew were coming. It was a Jeep because no other vehicle had a chance of negotiating the hilly terrain between the tiny airstrip and Mills Pharmaceuticals' secret research center in the North Carolina mountains. It had begun to rain, and the vehicle was sliding over what passed for a road.

Damn John Tavak. It was all very well to tell himself to forget the bastard for the time being, but he was having trouble doing it.

Screw Theodore Mills and his squeamishness. Dawson should have let Kilcher do it his way. A quick burst of gunfire would have settled matters once and for all. Add ten gallons of a high-temperature liquid-combustion agent, and Tavak's merry band would now be little more than scorch marks on the face of the earth.

Next time.

The Jeep rolled to a stop outside the complex, which had been constructed for Mills Pharmaceuticals' most sensitive and important research projects. At any given time, there might be thirty to fifty researchers living on-site, totally isolated from the outside world. In the interest of security, cell-phone frequencies were jammed, and all other personal telephone conversations were monitored and transcribed. The scientists were well compensated for their inconvenience, but Dawson couldn't imagine living that way.

He climbed out of the Jeep and ran through the now-pounding rain to the entrance. He paused at a retina scanner, and within seconds, the doors slid open.

Dawson made his way to a lab at the back of the complex, and after yet another retina scan, the doors opened to reveal the Hermitage mastaba wall on a tall platform, illuminated by high-wattage lights from every direction. The walls were covered by life-size photographic blowups of the three other carved walls, and several large computer monitors were placed under each.

Dr. James Wiley stepped down from the platform and pulled off a pair of green-framed magnifying goggles. "Good evening, Mr. Dawson."

"Any progress?"

"Mostly just getting a lay of the land. Imagine my surprise when I walked in here and was shown this." He motioned toward the stone wall. "You didn't tell me I would be dealing with stolen property."

"Really, aren't all these kinds of artifacts stolen? I'm sure this nobleman didn't intend for his monument to be carted away and sold to a Russian museum."

Wiley smiled. "There's a certain logic to that argument. But this is a much bigger job than I originally thought. Your original offer, while generous, doesn't really compensate me for the sheer scope of the project."

Dawson pursed his lips. "What do you want?"

"Five hundred thousand should cover it."

Dawson stepped toward him. "You wouldn't be trying to blackmail me, would you, Professor?"

Wiley's gaze shifted hurriedly away. "No. Of course not. I just think—"

"Good. We'll discuss your total compensation when you give me results. What have you found out?"

"Well, I've been retracing your steps, seeing how you put together the pieces of the puzzle. Each piece gives you a heavily coded section that details a portion of Peseshet's cure, then a somewhat simpler section that leads us to the next piece."

"Correct."

Wiley turned to the message in flames from

Hearst Castle. "Here's the third part of our puzzle, but there are only a few characters that are legible in any of the photographs here. What I don't understand is how this led you to the Nimaatra exhibit at the Hermitage. It's obviously the next piece, but what took you from 'C' to 'D'? There's nothing here that tells me that."

Dawson should have known that Wiley would painstakingly go through every bit of the process. "You don't have to know that. I certainly have no intention of telling you. Perhaps you should realize that I have sources other than you that I can tap. Now what progress are you making on the cure itself?"

Wiley shook his head. "I haven't been able to make any headway on that yet. It's like no code I've ever seen." He gestured toward the Hermitage exhibit. "I'll focus my energies on this to find the final piece. Once we gather all the pieces, maybe it will make more sense."

" 'Maybe' just doesn't cut it. This whole thing is just an academic exercise if we don't get that."

"I understand."

"I'm not sure you do. This is a race, Professor. You're not the only ace in my deck, just the one I prefer using. It allows me a certain amount of independence from my employer that I may use to my advantage." His lips tightened. "But if you're not capable of taking me across the finish line, I'll find someone who can."

• • •

D o you know, I've never spent a night with a woman without sex," Tavak said. "It's been kind of eye-opening." He pulled her closer. "You're an extraordinary woman, Rachel."

He was the one who was extraordinary, she thought. Complex and vital and ever-changing. These hours spent together in the darkness had not been like anything she had ever before experienced. They had talked for hours, first about Ben and Allie, then they had gradually drifted into memories and an exchanging of ideas and philosophies. She had thought she knew Tavak, but she had only scratched the surface until tonight. "I don't know if that's a compliment or not. But I'll take it as one."

"It's not a compliment, it's truth." His lips brushed her temple. "You're truth. Clean and bright and without a trace of subterfuge. Do you know how rare that is?" His arms tightened. "I'm having trouble with our 'exception' relationship. I don't think I can go on with it. I didn't think I'd ever become possessive about anyone. I didn't believe I had the right. But things are changing with me."

"You've just gone through an experience that may have put you a little off-balance."

"Stop analyzing. I've already done that, and that's not the reason. I've been heading in this direction since I started thinking about you in

Kontar's tomb. I believe I'm going to have to start working to make you come along with me. If I'm lucky, you're halfway there already."

More than halfway, she thought. She had never felt as close to anyone as she had to Tavak during these hours. "We're both in an overemotional state of—"

"Shh." His fingers touched her lips, silencing her. "Give in to it, Rachel. Hear the music. I have a feeling it can lead us to incredible places."

Hear the music.

He had said that she was without subterfuge and in this moment she could not hide the truth even to protect herself at her most vulnerable.

"I hear the music," she said unevenly. "I do hear it, Tavak."

"Good." He kissed her. "That's all that's important right now. Go to sleep. There's no hurry. We can start with the slow steps and go on from there."

Rachel grabbed her buzzing mobile phone from the bedside table and hit the TALK button before she was even fully awake. "Yes?"

"Rachel, it's happening. Jonesy's doing it!"

Val's voice, Rachel realized. She snapped wide-awake. Tavak sat up in the bed next to her.

"Do you hear me? It's happening!"

"Calm down, Val. *What's* happening?"

"Something clicked. Jonesy started cracking

major portions of the code, and the rest have been falling like dominos."

"Hold on, I'm putting you on speaker. Tavak is here with me. Go ahead."

"It's looking like each one of the carvings has a different purpose. The first one presents Peseshet's treatment as an offering to the gods to allow her passage into the afterlife. The second one is an ingredient list. Plants, mostly."

"What plants?" Tavak asked.

"Simon is researching them now."

"I'm here!" Simon picked up on a telephone extension. "You'll need a botanist to go over this, but I'm afraid at least one of these plant ingredients may be extinct."

Rachel turned to Tavak. "No."

He placed a comforting hand on her arm. "It doesn't mean anything. The active ingredient is probably present in other plants."

"What if it isn't? What if after all this—?"

"Stop it. We'll make it work. Through gene splicing, cellular manipulation, whatever it takes."

Rachel nodded and tried to pull herself together. He was right. Her whole life was about solving problems, and she could solve this one. One crisis at a time. "Val, what was in the third message, the one at Hearst Castle?"

"That one seems to be about cultivating and preparing the ingredients. But it also tells you how to unlock the treatment's secret from the fourth set of wall carvings, the one from the Hermitage Museum. Any luck in finding it?"

"We've had a bit of a setback. We're having to regroup. What do we do when we find it?"

"We're working on that now," Val said. "I mean me, Simon, and Jonesy. But it looks like it involves an Egyptian sunset."

"Okay, now you're just messing with me."

"I wish I was. That part isn't entirely clear yet, but we have Jonesy mapping the relation of the sun to the mastaba wall in its position in Saqqara. We'll have more for you later."

Rachel shot a glance at Tavak. She knew that expression, intent, thoughtful. She spoke back into the phone. "Fantastic work, guys. Keep me posted." She cut the connection and turned to Tavak. "What's wrong?"

He climbed out of bed and pulled on his pants and shirt. "Nothing. Jonesy's doing a good job, but we have to offer support. We have to get that mastaba wall back."

"Any ideas?"

"No, but I'd better get one quick." He leaned forward and brushed a kiss on the tip of her nose. "Thank you."

"Thank you," she said in return. "It was a special night." So special that she wanted to reach out and hold on to it, hold on to him. "But next time, I think we'll add the skyrockets."

He went still. "Whenever you're ready."

She was ready now. But it wasn't the time. She nodded. "I'll let you know."

"Do that," he said softly.

Tavak." Demanski called him fifteen minutes after he reached his room. "I need to talk to you. I'll be down to your room in three minutes." He hung up before Tavak could reply.

Two minutes later Tavak opened the door to Demanski and Allie. "I've got an idea." Demanski strode into the room. "And I think it might work."

"Track down Wiley's plane and maybe strongarm or bribe the pilot to tell you where he flew him?"

"I suppose that's an option." Demanski's eyes were sparkling. "But I've got a better one."

"Do you?"

Allie nodded. "You should listen to him. I think it's a good idea. Demanski and I spent last night looking through the documentation that the Hermitage Museum gave him with the artifacts. That mastaba wall was X-rayed in the late nineties, and we have copies of the films. There are no hidden panels, false fronts, or anything like that. Whatever message it holds, it's somewhere on the surface."

Tavak nodded. "Like the carvings at Hearst Castle."

"Right," Demanski said. "So why go chasing after that mastaba wall . . . when we can make our own?"

Tavak went still. "And how do you propose we do that?"

"Have you ever heard of Pixel Dance Incorporated?"

"The special-effects company. They're the geeky guys who win the visual-effects Oscars every year."

"They're geniuses. I was one of their original backers, but all their revenue goes right back out to R&D and hardware upgrades. It's a terrible business. I let them buy me out for a song, so they owe me huge."

"What good is that to us?"

"They think they can help. A few of their best and brightest are giving us half a day tomorrow. We need to be at their facility in northern California at 7 A.M. tomorrow."

Tavak's excitement was growing the more he thought about it. He'd heard what miracles those techs could pull off. By God, it could work. "It's worth a shot," he murmured. "Good job, Demanski."

"Damn straight," Demanski said complacently. "And damn brilliant."

"I won't even argue with you on that point." Tavak let out a long breath. "Every minute that Dawson has those carvings that we don't, he's that much closer to getting his hands on Peseshet's cure." He glanced at Allie. "Are you on board with this?"

Allie was looking at Demanski. "Yes. Let's do it."

Demanski smiled. "Give me twelve hours, Tavak. If it doesn't work, my jet will be warmed up and waiting to take us anywhere you want to go. We'll strong-arm pilots and sundry other villains to your heart's content."

"You've got it." Tavak nodded. "Let's go tell Rachel."

EIGHTEEN

HOUSTON POLICE DEPARTMENT
CENTRAL PRECINCT

NSA Agent Wayne Norton glanced uneasily around the squadroom. He looked distinctly out of place, Finley thought, as he and Gonzalez approached him.

"To what do we owe the pleasure?" Finley asked.

"I think you know. That was a rather indiscreet message you left."

"Well, you didn't respond to any of our discreet messages," Gonzalez said.

"I'm here now." Norton sat on the edge of the table. "What do you want from me?"

"Why don't we discuss the message I left," Finley said. "We know that Rachel Kirby's shooter worked for you."

"That's not true."

"Maybe not you personally, but for the NSA. At least occasionally. He was freelance, but he did contract work for you guys."

"As a hired assassin? I'm afraid you have a rather glamorous view of my agency that's not based on fact."

"His name was Gaius Pelham. He was known as the Invisible Man because his fingerprints, DNA, and facial and dental records weren't in any public database. The agencies who used him knew who he was, though. Including yours, which is why you swooped in and took his body away when we started circulating his vitals."

Norton crossed his arms. "Ridiculous. Where do you get this stuff?"

"You're denying it, then."

"You know that I can neither confirm nor deny statements relating to the activities of the National Security Agency."

"You came down here awfully fast for something you can neither confirm nor deny," Gonzalez said.

"I need to know who is spreading this crap around."

"Then it *is* true," Finley said softly.

"Has it occurred to you that I might be interested in someone spreading disinformation? When a police detective leaves a message like that on my office phone, I have to take it seriously."

"Look at it from our perspective. Someone takes

a shot at Rachel Kirby, who happens to be involved in a project of your agency's. Then we find the shooter dead, and we have a homicide investigation on our hands. Now we have very reliable information that tells us that Kirby's would-be assassin has worked for your agency. What conclusion would a reasonable man draw from that information?"

"I can assure you that the NSA has no grudge against Rachel Kirby."

"Finally," Gonzalez said. "Something you'll go on record for."

"You obviously haven't told any of this to her. She would have gone nuclear on me by now."

"We'd like to talk to her, but she still hasn't come back into town." Gonzalez shot a glance at his partner. "We believe she could be in a great deal of danger."

Norton nodded. "Did you know she was on the Big Obukhovsky Bridge in St. Petersburg the other night?"

"During the attack?"

"Yes. My sources tell me she was right in the middle of it. It follows that if you think she could be in danger, you're probably right. So tell me where you're getting your information."

"Sorry, no can do," Finley said.

"If you're really worried about Rachel Kirby, you'll tell me."

"That's funny," Gonzalez said. "Our concern for

Rachel Kirby is a major reason for *not* confiding in you. Why don't we just cut the bullshit and try to figure out what's going on? Or is that too straightforward for you people?"

Norton gazed at them for a long moment. "You're honest cops, and I admire your initiative. I'm impressed."

"But?" Gonzalez said.

"But I've said all I'm going to say. Except that you should seriously think about giving me your source. You may soon get a call from your chief of police." He turned away. "Or you may get a knock at your door in the middle of the night and be taken somewhere depressing for a long, long time."

MARIN COUNTY, CALIFORNIA
7 A.M.

Tavak stared doubtfully at the chrome sculptures lining the outdoor entranceway of Pixel Dance Incorporated. The sculptures were of dinosaurs, spaceships, and the scores of computer-generated characters through which the special-effects facility had made its name. Tavak turned to Demanski. "Are you sure about this?"

"As sure as I am about anything." Demanski smiled. "You only have faith in yourself. I put my trust in the wonders of technology. This is the wave of the future."

"Welcome." A young man in jeans and a Hawaiian T-shirt emerged from the building. "We're honored to have you here."

Demanski smiled. "Thanks, Tillinger. It's good to be back in the place where—"

"Uh, actually, I was talking to Ms. Kirby." The young man smiled at Rachel. "You have a lot of fans in this building. Half the people here donate their unused home computer cycles to your project."

Rachel smiled. It was something she was often told when meeting people in the tech community, but she was still grateful to hear it. "Thank you."

Allie shook her head in amusement. "Freakin' computer geeks."

"My name is Mark Tillinger." The young man motioned for the group to follow him. "I'll be helping you with your project this morning."

"You're keeping early hours," Demanski said.

Mark smiled. "Actually, it's *late* hours. I haven't been to bed yet. We're running about two weeks behind on the new Spielberg film, so everybody is working crazy schedules."

Mark led them back to a workshop, where he pointed to a monitor with an image of the Hermitage mastaba wall. "I've already gotten started, using photos and X-ray images you e-mailed to me, plus a few dozen more I found online."

Rachel examined the monitor image. "This is a digital model?"

Mark nodded. "Yes. Normally, we like to do a laser scan of the original, but since that isn't an option in this case, we can use photographs. The computer can examine photographs taken from all perspectives and create an extremely accurate 3-D model. See?" Mark rotated the image on the screen.

"I've seen demonstrations of that," Rachel said. "There's a university group that's creating a 3-D computer model of the entire city of Rome just by reading vacation pictures from the online photo-sharing Web sites."

"Exactly. We're doing the same thing here. But now we're taking it a step further." Mark gestured toward the center of the workshop, where a machine with long steel rods and four massive nozzles was inlaid in a ten-foot-by-ten-foot square in the floor.

Tavak smiled. "A printer?"

"You got it. For years, industrial-design houses have used smaller 3-D printers to create architectural models, prototypes, or even reproductions of dinosaur bones. This is the biggest one in the world. If we design a digital star fighter in the computer, we can make a full-size real-life version that an actor can sit in and interact with."

"What are the model copies made out of?" Allie asked.

Mark pointed to a tank with lines to the four nozzles. "ABS plastic, but we can introduce other materials to add strength. And we can spray on a variety of textures. I take it you're looking for sandstone for this one."

"Limestone, actually."

Mark entered a series of commands on his keyboard and the nozzles flew over the center portion of the print mat. White plastic spread evenly over the mat's surface, gaining thickness with each successive pass.

"This will take a couple of hours," Mark said. "Have you had breakfast?"

Rachel pulled out her phone. "You all go ahead. I need to check on Jonesy's progress."

"We can wait. Are you sure?" Demanski asked.

"Yes. Go on."

Tavak stood over the printing device. "I'll stay here, too. We'll see you in a bit."

Rachel called the lab as soon as they left.

Val answered. "Where have you been? I've been trying to call you."

"This place probably has megaelectronic interference. Good news, I hope?"

"We're pretty sure Jonesy has figured out how to unlock the secret from that inscription. You're still going to need that mastaba wall, though."

Rachel looked at the flying nozzle spreading even more liquid plastic over the mat's surface. "In two hours, I should have it . . . or a reasonable facsimile thereof. I'll call you as soon as I get it." She glanced at Tavak as she hung up. "Jonesy's been making progress on these codes. Val should be able to transmit an updated decoding package by the time this finishes. I'll shoot them to her right away."

"Maybe not immediately," Tavak said quietly. "There's something I want to discuss with you."

"What?"

"I've been wondering how Dawson has been able to keep up with us. Even with all his resources, we have Jonesy. We should be leaving him in our dust."

"Sometimes brute-force computational power isn't enough."

"Maybe."

She stiffened. "You're saying Jonesy may be compromised?" She shook her head. "Who?"

"I don't know. But the NSA has experts whose sole profession is gathering information. I'm just inclined to be careful."

"And the NSA has a connection to Dawson?"

"I could be wrong. But before we give Jonesy a crack at this, I'd like for us to spend a few minutes writing some software routines. You can integrate it into Jonesy from here, can't you? Remotely?"

Rachel stared at him. "Yes, but I'm not going to do it until I know exactly what you have in mind."

"I didn't expect anything else. It would be hard for you to have blind trust in anyone where it concerns your Jonesy."

She stared at him for a moment. "I do trust you,

Tavak. I don't believe I've ever trusted anyone more than I trust you."

He smiled. "That's a megagift. So I'm not going to ask you for blind trust. I'll tell you why I need the software."

oly smoke."
It was slightly over two hours later that Allie stood before the mastaba-wall reproduction which, except for a slightly darker color, was identical to the original they had seen in Russia.

Tavak walked around it. "Truly amazing. The depth of the characters, the size of all of these reliefs, looks exactly the same. If they gave out Academy Awards for this sort of thing . . ."

"They do." Mark smiled. "They're called Technical Achievement Oscars. We've won quite a few."

Rachel glanced at Val's e-mail message on her phone. "Here's what Jonesy has come up with. Roughly translated, we're supposed to look at the 'shadow of a memory' as the sun's last rays disappear at dusk, then again as they reappear at dawn on the longest day of the year."

"Come again?" Demanski asked.

"Fortunately, Jonesy has already plotted it out, using the location and angle of this wall and the position of the sun in the sky during that time." She looked up. "Your cycles at work, Mark. Do you have a lighting kit handy?"

He nodded. "Sure. What do you need?"

"A high-wattage light with an eight-inch circular mask. It needs to be seven feet four inches high and aimed at the face of this wall at an almost perpendicular angle. Eighty-seven degrees."

Mark smiled. "I'll get my tape measure and protractor."

Within twenty minutes, Mark had positioned the light. Rachel tilted her head to look at the faint shadows cast by the raised carvings.

"This was sunset in Saqqara, everybody. Mark, can you turn out the other lights in here?"

Mark cut the studio lights, and the shadows became more prominent.

Tavak stepped closer to the mastaba wall. "I think that we've hit pay dirt."

"Hieroglyphics." Allie ran to the wall and traced the shadows with her fingers. "Look!"

"I see," Rachel said. "Can someone get a picture?"

Mark picked up a digital camera and snapped several shots.

Rachel looked at Val's e-mail on her phone again. "Okay, let's make a sunrise."

Mark realigned the light based on Jonesy's calculations, and a different set of hieroglyphic shadows were cast on the other side of the mastaba wall. He snapped more pictures, then printed out both sets on a color laser printer.

Rachel held up the photos side by side. "This is

incredible. There are even marks for the transcribers to indicate where the halves fit together. Together they form a complete, uninterrupted message."

Demanski turned to Tavak. "You can read this. What does it say?"

"I can't be sure," Tavak said. "We'll need to let Jonesy take a crack at it. We should get going."

Rachel studied Tavak's expression. Something was wrong.

"Thank you, Mark." Tavak shook Tillinger's hand and turned on his heel and strode out of the complex.

Rachel caught up with him as he reached the van. "Why couldn't you read it? What aren't you telling us?"

"That's not the last piece," Tavak said.

"Then what the hell is it?" Demanski asked.

"Directions."

"Directions where?"

"To Peseshet herself."

"What?" Allie asked.

"It says that she will give us the final piece in her tomb."

"Her tomb?" Rachel said. "She was murdered by the Pharaoh. She wouldn't have been given a tomb."

Tavak nodded. "It appears that Natifah, her disciple—or one of her grateful patients—had other ideas. In any case, we now have directions to the secret tomb of Lady Peseshet, overseer of women doctors." Tavak glanced back at Demanski. "Make sure your jet is fueled up and ready to go. We're finishing this where it began. We're going to Egypt."

HOUSTON, TEXAS
8:10 P.M.

Norton pressed the button to save the e-mail before pushing back his chair. The mere process of writing it had twisted his stomach. Okay, it was done. Now he could move forward.

He moved out of the office building elevator when he reached the bottom parking level and headed for his car. He'd call Simmons right away, and discuss—

"Hello, Norton."

Norton stiffened warily as he saw Robert Pierce sitting in the car next to his own. "What are you doing down here, sir?"

"Waiting for you. I agree that I shouldn't have to attend to this kind of thing myself," Pierce said. "But I'm the one who put my trust in you. I've always believed that I have to take responsibility for my actions."

"What do you mean?"

"I mean I've been waiting for you. You're keeping late hours."

"Yeah. A lot going on."

Pierce nodded. "There's trouble. We've been burning the midnight oil, too. As I told you, Rachel Kirby's computer network has been compromised. More specifically, our information has been leaked."

"Our guys cleared Tavak, didn't they?"

Pierce smiled. "I know you don't believe it's Tavak. We think it's an inside job. One of our people. I think someone panicked and was afraid Rachel Kirby would trace it back to them. She probably wouldn't have even noticed, but John Tavak's drain on her system's resources raised a red flag." He paused. "So someone ordered her killed."

Norton's brows rose. "Someone in our agency."

"That's what it looks like. Maybe someone was tapping into the processing power of Kirby's computer for their own purposes. Cracking rival governments' defense networks, banking systems, the list goes on and on. That ability could be quite valuable on the open market."

"You've got it all figured out," Norton said.

Pierce nodded. "And all that's left is to find the bad guy." He got out of the car. "But I believe we've managed to do that now."

Norton could see where this was going. His hand moved inside his jacket toward his shoulder holster. "Why, you son of a bitch. I won't let you—"

"I'm afraid you have no choice." Pierce raised a semiautomatic handgun and fired twice into Norton's chest.

• • •

Val rolled her chair across the computer lab and checked the settings on her monitor. "I don't like it."

"Don't like what?" Simon asked.

"Jonesy's taking too long with the last set of instructions."

He leaned over her shoulder. "Looks okay to me."

"Rachel will touch down in Cairo in less than two hours. I think there's more to these directions to Peseshet's burial chamber than 'step inside and turn right.' We need to be ready by the time they get there."

"What do you propose?"

Val thought for a moment. "We should take Jonesy off our other projects and channel its processing cycles here."

"All of them?"

"Yes. Until we're able to break these directions down."

"Rachel wouldn't like that. We've made obligations to the donors and the various projects in our network."

"We've been delivering everything we've promised and more."

"I agree. But think of how it looks. What if it got out that we were taking their processing cycles for Rachel's personal use?"

"Just for a few hours."

He crouched beside her. "I see where you're

coming from. I do. But that's a decision only Rachel can make."

"She would approve."

"I'm not so sure. Our donors are the lifeblood of this system. If we violate their trust, we could kill the entire project. And you and I both know that's the *last* thing Rachel would want."

She looked at him for a moment, then clucked her tongue. "Since when did you get so responsible . . . ? Okay. Rachel's decision."

"Good. For the record, I'm wildly attracted to this rebellious streak of yours. Keep it up, and you might even have a chance with me."

"You are *so* dreaming."

Simon laughed and walked away.

Val looked back at her monitor and the message cast from the shadows of the Hermitage mastaba wall. Rachel was counting on them to crack this before she journeyed into the Sahara Desert with only a vague sense of what to do. But Simon had a point. Even during Tavak's drain on their network's resources, Rachel had refused to deprive the other projects of their allotted processing cycles. The NSA took the biggest hit, followed by her own foundation.

But still . . .

Val leaned back in her chair and saw Simon working on the other side of the lab. Usually *she* was the stickler for rules, and Simon was the group's risk taker.

Not this time, she decided.

She launched the allocation protocol to direct Jonesy's processing cycles toward the mastaba wall code.

We're making good time." Demanski stepped into the lounge of his plane, where Rachel, Tavak, and Allie were seated around a small table, examining the photographic prints that made up the newest message. "Figure out anything more there?"

"No," Tavak said. "It's like all the other pieces along the way. Parts are relatively easy to understand, but other sections are written entirely in code. This area gives us the general location of Peseshet's burial chamber, but it's short on specifics. I think the rest will tell us more about what we need to know."

Rachel nodded. "I'll check in with Val and Simon when we land and see what progress Jonesy has made."

"The question of the hour is . . ." Tavak tapped the photos. "Does Dawson also have this message?"

Allie shrugged. "Look at the hoops we had to jump through. And it's not just a matter of being smart. You have to have a specific *kind* of smarts."

"Well, as excruciating as Dr. James Wiley is as a lecturer, there's a good chance he has those smarts. He knows more about ancient Nile Delta languages and customs than just about anyone. Plus, he's had more time with the mastaba wall than we've had. It's possible they've beaten us to the punch."

"We have something they don't," Demanski said. He nodded at Rachel. "You and your super-computer network."

"That's true," Tavak said. "They may still be playing catchup." He looked at Rachel. "I certainly hope so."

So did Rachel. She had been on edge since Tavak had mentioned the possibility of Jonesy being compromised by the NSA and leaking to Dawson.

Tavak glanced back down at the message. "But it might be a good idea for us to have some muscle while we're in Egypt."

CAIRO INTERNATIONAL AIRPORT
CAIRO, EGYPT

Welcome," Nuri said from the open door of a large, black-paneled van with tinted windows. "It is a pleasure to welcome you back so soon."

The van was waiting in the huge pickup/dropoff area in front of the airport after they had gone through Customs and picked up their visas at the booth. The scene appeared to be one of total chaos, with passengers and skycaps darting among literally hundreds of cabs, buses, and private vehicles.

Nuri jumped out of the van and helped Rachel,

Allie, Tavak, and Demanski load their bags into the back. Within minutes, they were on their way out of the airport.

Nuri turned around and spoke to Tavak. "Again, I am sorry for your friend's death," he said quietly. "I feel I should have done more to protect him."

"You did your best. It wasn't your job to protect him, Nuri. That wasn't what he wanted."

Nuri smiled. "That is true. Ben was a proud man."

"Yes, he was."

"I would have liked to have been able to furnish you with a larger team, but it was short notice. I think you will find we'll be capable of meeting your needs." He motioned toward the driver. "This is Abu. He was part of the team that came to your aid before, Mr. Tavak."

"I remember," Tavak said dryly. "He also did some guard duty when I was your prisoner."

Abu chuckled. "And now you are my employer. Life is strange. Nice to see you again."

Nuri pointed to the van's back row of seats, where the two remaining men sat. "And behind you are Oba and Meti. We've known each other since we were children."

Demanski drummed his fingers on the roof of the van. "Where did you get this beast?"

Nuri shrugged. "Automobile rental agency. The windows are bulletproof, and the steel is over an inch thick in places. Some diplomats and business executives—Americans mostly—insist on a vehicle like this when they visit here. It makes them feel safer even though the crime rate in many U.S. cities is much worse." Nuri turned to look at the setting sun. "We should be there in little over an hour. How long will we be at the site?"

"I'm not sure," Tavak said. "It depends on what we find when we get there."

NINETEEN

Detective Finley sat at his desk in the squad room and read the e-mail from NSA Agent Wayne Norton for a third time.

"What the hell?" Gonzalez came in holding his BlackBerry. "Did you see this?"

"Yeah." Finley was still trying to make sense of Norton's message:

Detectives Finley & Gonzalez,

I'm sending this to you because I have a great deal of respect for you both. There are not many men who would ignore threats and intimidation to do what they felt is right. Since that intimidation came from me, I have a personal admiration.

You have been very resourceful in your investigation of the Rachel Kirby shooting, and I must admit that some of the information you uncovered was a surprise even to me. I'm sure that you'll be skeptical as you read this. You probably won't believe it, but I didn't want to think you were right about the NSA involvement. Manipulating information is one thing, murder of an innocent citizen is another. I knew nothing about the attempt on her life. But it was at that point that I began to think that I had been set up to take the fall for some extremely dirty business. I wasn't going to let that happen, so I started launching an investigation of my own while I balanced very precariously on the edge of disaster.

And if you're reading this, it means that my ignorance was most likely fatal. I have placed this e-mail and accompanying attachments in a timed autosend folder that I will reschedule every six hours as long as I am able. I've used the services of Paul Simmons, one of NSA's most talented information specialists, who may also be able to bear witness. If he's still alive. In brief, I've collected evidence indicating that Robert Pierce is using our access to Rachel Kirby's data network for personal gain and attempted to kill her to avoid being discovered. She's still in great danger. Pierce will never stop.

Please exercise extreme caution in your use and dissemination of this information.

N.

Gonzalez pocketed his phone. "I just called Norton's office, but it went straight to voice mail."

"But that's nothing new. He could still be okay." Finley stood and walked to the squad room's printer. "I printed out the attachments. Let's run this upstairs and show it to the tech guys."

Val adjusted the headset as she sat down at the workstation. "Rachel, are you at the site yet?"

"We're just outside the tomb in Saqqara now. We're going in right now. Our guide had to make some arrangements with the Tourism and Antiquities Police."

"Arrangements involving an insanely large wad of cash?"

"We won't talk about that. Listen, I'll be below-ground and out of cell-phone range when I'm in the tomb. Before I go in, does Jonesy have any last pieces of information for me?"

"Yes. And Simon talked to Professor Azi for some clarification on a few things we couldn't interpret or understand. Here's what we have: 'Lady Peseshet is a guest of the gracious Donkor, maker of fine clothing for the Pharaoh.' "

"Tavak was able to read that much himself. Donkor's tomb was discovered in the 1940s, north of the Djojer Pyramid. I'm looking at it right now."

"It says Peseshet waits behind the sun for her journey to the afterlife."

"Behind the sun?"

"That's what it says. It says that those who wish to bring Peseshet's secrets to the world may do so, but they must also leave it with her to assure her safe passage. But here's something interesting. It says that anyone who breaks the seal will only be given a quarter of a summer hour to visit the great Peseshet."

"A summer hour?"

"I don't know. That's all it says."

"Okay. Thanks for your help, Val. Thanks to Simon, too."

"We'll be here if you need us."

"I'll call you when we get back up topside. Wish us luck." Rachel cut the connection.

Val pulled off her headset and turned to Simon. "Rachel is about to go in."

"Maybe Jonesy can come up with the name of a good lawyer when she gets herself arrested. I'm going to the snack bar. You want anything?"

"No, thanks."

Simon left the lab. Val launched the allocation protocol and began the task of restoring Jonesy's processing duties to the various projects. Outages were not all that uncommon due to system maintenance, upgrades, and the like, and none of the project managers had even called to complain. Val didn't think it was necessary to inform Rachel of the drastic measures she had taken, but she would note the interruption in the logs they kept for—

What the hell?

Val leaned forward and studied the screen. In the years she had been working with Jonesy, she'd thought she had seen everything.

She had never seen this.

SAQQARA, EGYPT

Tavak shined his flashlight into the tomb of Donkor. "Here we go. Time to visit the Lady."

Nuri reached over and switched off Tavak's flashlight. "Please. The Tourism and Antiquities Police were quite agreeable, but they made me promise we wouldn't turn on any flashlights or lanterns outside the tomb. We would be too easy for their superiors to spot."

"You're right," Tavak said. "My apologies." He turned to Rachel. "So according to Jonesy, Peseshet is waiting for us on the other side of the sun?"

"That's what the message says. And apparently, our invitation is only good for less than an hour."

"What do you mean?"

"The exact words were 'quarter of a summer hour.' After that, we're no longer welcome in her tomb."

"A summer hour? What the hell does that mean?" Allie asked.

Tavak led them into the tomb. "The ancient Egyptians were one of the first societies with a twenty-four-hour day. The catch is, their hours were different lengths, depending what time of year it was. During the summer, hours were more like eighty minutes."

"So we'll wear out our welcome in twenty minutes," Demanski said. "Got it."

He and Allie set off down the narrow corridor.

"Oba, Meti." Nuri gestured to the entrance. "Stay and guard here."

Tavak shook his head. "If you don't mind, they may be more useful someplace else. I've already discussed it with them while we were waiting for you."

Nuri frowned. "Where?"

Tavak produced a hand-drawn map and handed it to Oba.

Nuri glanced at the map in bewilderment. "This is a half mile from here. Are you sure this is where you want them?"

"That's where I want them." He turned to Rachel. "Do you agree?"

Rachel nodded. "Absolutely."

He smiled at her. "Thank you." He stood aside and gestured for her to precede him into Donkor's tomb. "Shall we go to see the Lady?"

The Lady Peseshet. Are you here? Are you waiting for us?

Darkness.

The flashlights cast patches of light on the walls, but the narrow path was serpentine, and they could only see for a short distance ahead of them.

She could hear Allie and Demanski ahead of them, but she couldn't see them.

Age.

Stone.

Dampness.

Flashlight beams played across the stone floors and over the carved reliefs that told the story of Donkor's life and family. Rust-colored hieroglyphics covered almost every square inch of the walls.

It had been hot outside, but Rachel was cold now.

"Okay?" Tavak was suddenly beside her.

She nodded jerkily. "It's just strange down here. I . . . feel . . ."

"What?"

She couldn't explain. It wasn't fear, but a sort of chill expectation. "Nothing."

Then suddenly they turned the corner and were in a large offering room. Demanski and Allie were standing there gazing at reliefs carved on the walls, depicting a funeral feast for the gods.

"Look how distinctively the people are dressed in these reliefs," Rachel said. "Beautiful draping."

Tavak shined his flashlight on the wall. "Donkor designed and made clothing for the Pharaoh and other wealthy citizens. These designs were probably part of his offering to the gods. A couple of these wouldn't be that out of place in department store windows on Fifth Avenue."

"Except that one." Allie directed her flashlight at a relief of a bare-chested man with a falcon head.

"That's Horus," Tavak said. He smiled as the realization hit him. "He was the sun in the sky."

Rachel swung her flashlight toward it. "The other side of the sun . . ."

Allie and Demanski were running their hands over the wall below the relief, feeling for a seam. Demanski turned back. "There's no doorway here. It's solid."

"Of course it is," Rachel said. "It was never meant to be discovered. If the Pharaoh knew that Donkor had constructed a tomb for Peseshet, it would have been dangerous for him and his family. He must have felt he owed her a great debt, so he constructed hidden chambers for her at the same time he built his own."

"We have to get through that wall," Tavak said. "Abu."

Abu slung a canvas bag from his shoulder and upended it, dropping half a dozen sledgehammers onto the ground. "Help yourselves."

As they picked up their sledgehammers, Nuri moved to the wall and drew an imaginary outline with his hand. "You want to start high and work your way down. As you dislodge the higher portions of the wall, gravity will help bring down the rest."

Allie turned toward Demanski. "Why do I get the feeling he's done this kind of thing before?"

Tavak hefted his sledgehammer and turned back to Rachel. "We don't have time to be delicate. We've talked about this. Are we still on the same page?"

Rachel knew he was speaking of the balance between possibly destroying artifacts of the past to gain the medical miracles for the future.

She didn't hesitate. She took aim with her sledgehammer and cracked the blank sandstone wall.

Tavak nodded. "Good."

They swung at the wall with their sledgehammers, and in a few minutes they had created an opening through which they could peer inside.

Tavak shined his flashlight into the opening. "It's huge," he said. "Bigger than anything up here. Keep at it."

They hit harder and more vigorously, and when a particularly large section of the wall fell, they heard a dull roar.

Tavak froze. "Stop!"

They stood motionless as the sound continued.

"What is it?" Rachel said.

Tavak shook his head. "I thought it might be a cave-in, but it's not." He pressed his ear against the wall. "I think it's sand. It's in all the walls." He turned to Nuri. "It's something we triggered."

"Like a booby trap?" Demanski said.

"The message said we'll be given a quarter of a summer hour," Rachel said. "This may be the start of it."

Tavak nodded. "Tons of sand may be being released from some kind of counterweight system."

"What happens when it runs out?" Allie said.

Tavak set the stopwatch function on his watch. "I don't know, but I don't want to be here to find out. Let's make this fast."

They crawled through the opening. Once again Rachel felt the strange sensation that had overtaken her before.

Only now did she realize what it was.

Val stared at the monitor in frustration. She had explored every adjustment she could think to make. But the readout still didn't make sense.

The usage statistics were seriously out of whack with the reports Jonesy had been generating.

Had she screwed something up?

No. Not a chance. The only way these numbers could be correct is if—

"I told you not to do that," Simon said.

Val jumped.

He was standing behind her, so close that she could feel his breath on the back of her neck.

He nodded toward the screen. "What do you make of it?"

She tried to be casual. "It's a glitch. You're right, I should have known there would be problems if I reallocated Jonesy's cycles like this."

Simon smiled. "A glitch."

"We've seen our share around here, huh?" She grabbed her keys from the desk. "I think I'm going to go outside and—"

She tried to stand, but Simon pushed her back down into her chair. "You're smarter than that. You know it's not a glitch."

He leaned close, and said softly into her ear, "Tell me what you see."

She didn't answer.

He shook her chair violently. "Tell me!"

She stared straight ahead, trying not to let him know how much he was scaring her. He knew what she was thinking. He *knew.* "I see . . . some of the processing cycles from each of these projects being rerouted."

"Rerouted *where?*"

"I don't know. But it's happening somewhere in the chain after Jonesy takes stock of where it's going. It doesn't show up in the reports." She turned and looked up at him. "It's you. That's the only way it makes sense."

He nodded.

"Why?" she asked. "You've given just as much of yourself to this project as I have."

"I got an offer."

"It must have been a hell of an offer."

"It was. And from someone who said he could make things right for me legally if the worst happened."

"Norton? That asshole Norton?"

Simon shook his head. "Norton's boss, Pierce."

Val felt her eyes stinging hot with tears. "He tried to kill Rachel, didn't he?"

"I never wanted that to happen."

"Sure you didn't."

"It's the truth. When Tavak tapped into our system, Rachel started to take a closer look at things. My contact got scared. I told him again and again that I'd take care of it, but he didn't believe me."

"If he had killed Rachel, what next? Come after me?"

"Not if I could help it."

"She created Jonesy to do good in the world. Not for whatever the hell this is."

"It's just a bunch of third-world countries fucking each other over. Spying on each other, crippling each other's economies and defense systems. Who gives a shit?"

"Rachel would. Is that all it was?"

He shrugged. "A couple companies who are willing to pay big bucks to the NSA for information."

"Like Mills Pharmaceuticals?"

Simon didn't answer.

"My God, Simon, you've been feeding Dawson the information we've been giving Rachel."

"Rachel is smart. She can take care of herself."

"Oh, yes. Why worry about her?" Val asked. "As long as they pay you, right?"

"I can use your help, Val. You wouldn't believe the money."

Val nodded. There was only one way she was getting out of there alive. Play along, say what he wanted to hear.

"How much money?"

"It could end up in the millions."

"I want a meeting with this NSA guy. I want to talk to him."

"That can be arranged."

She stood. "Call me when you find out. In the meantime—"

He snapped his arm around her neck. "You think I'm stupid?"

She couldn't breathe.

"I know you better than that, Val. I can't let you walk out of here."

She felt a darkness rising from the back of her head.

"I'm sorry," he whispered.

She was blacking out, she realized. Can't let it happen . . .

Her hands instinctively went for Simon's arm, but she felt something in her hand.

The keys.

One last chance. She pushed the keys between each knuckle and made the tightest fist she could. Then, in one quick motion, she swung her arm up and plunged the keys deep into Simon's right eye.

He screamed.

His grip loosened slightly, and she wrenched herself free and ran for the door. She pushed, but it wouldn't open.

"I locked it, you bitch." Simon cupped his hand over his wounded eye and staggered toward her. Blood ran down his cheek.

Val backed away. She pulled the printer table over in front of him and turned toward the server racks. If only she could make it to the back exit.

Simon leaped over the table, stumbled, and hit the floor face forward. Val tried to jump out of the way, but Simon grabbed her ankle and brought her down in front of him.

She screamed as Simon worked his way up her leg, pulling her back. She turned. His face was frozen in a horrible grimace, with blood still pouring from his wounded right eye.

He climbed on top of her, sat up, and reached for the broken printer. He lifted it over his head.

"No!"

The lab door splintered open.

Footsteps, then what sounded like a cannon being fired.

Simon froze. His arms went limp, and Val rolled out from under him as he dropped the printer onto the floor. Simon collapsed next to her.

Val turned toward the door. It was the two police detectives, she realized dazedly, and they still had their guns drawn.

Thank God.

"Are you okay?" Gonzalez holstered his revolver and rushed toward her. "Be still. Don't try to move."

She tried to catch her breath. "I can't believe it. He tried . . . If you hadn't been here, he would have killed me."

"Where's Rachel Kirby? Is she all right?"

Val nodded. "She's in Egypt. I talked to her a short time ago." Val glanced back at Simon's body. Blood was spreading from the bullet wounds. "He was involved in something . . . with somebody in the NSA."

Finley crouched beside her. "We know."

Her gaze flew to his face. "How do you know?"

"We received a very interesting e-mail. That's what brought us here. We could really use your help in sorting this out."

"Later." She struggled to sit up. "I have to contact Rachel. I don't know what's waiting for her down in that tomb. Simon could have—" Panic jolted though her as the realization hit home. "I can't *do* it. She's out of range. All we can do is wait."

Another world, Rachel thought as she gazed in fascination at the massive staircase leading down to a huge chamber. They had left the present behind and were now in Peseshet's world. But somehow she did not feel like an intruder.

"We have to hurry." Tavak was leading them all

435

down the staircase to the lower level of the magnificent chamber, with ceilings at least thirty feet high. The walls were covered with multicolored depictions of Peseshet in her roles as a mother, healer, and teacher of female doctors. The beams from their flashlights played across the walls, revealing still another breathtaking relief.

"It's incredible." Rachel's voice echoed in the huge chamber. She walked past the massive pillars, each completely covered with hieroglyphics from top to bottom.

"Listen," Tavak said. "The walls are roaring in here, too. Whatever we triggered, it's happening everywhere."

Demanski was ahead of them. "This way."

They were now in Peseshet's offering room, depicting another magnificent feast for the Gods, Rachel realized. On the left side, there were carved reliefs of scores of figures, both male and female, each adorned in wildly different styles of clothing. Hundreds of rows of hieroglyphics ran vertically beneath the figures.

"I think those are people she cared for during her lifetime," Tavak said. "Incredible."

The loyal subjects Peseshet had saved. The sight swamped Rachel with emotion. She made herself turn away and look at the stone pathway ahead. It was lined with dozens of huge sandstone statues. Most were representations of boats that pointed to an opening at the rear of the chamber.

She was there.

Rachel moved slowly toward the open doorway. She was being drawn deeper with each step. The pull grew stronger and stronger. The chill was gone, and Rachel was feeling an odd contentment. This was right. She was connected to this place and the woman it honored. This is where she should be.

I'm coming. I'm sorry it took me so long. Wait for me.

The rushing sand, combined with whistling pockets of air, made eerie and beautiful music in her ears.

I hear you.

"Rachel?"

She barely heard Tavak as she ducked through the doorway.

She stopped, stunned.

Not ten feet in front of her was the sarcophagus of Peseshet. The same face as she had seen on the photos of the mural in the tomb.

She moved slowly forward until she was standing before the decorative casket. Peseshet's face, while crudely painted by modern standards, reflected strong features, wisdom, and dignity.

Healer. Mother. Sage. Warrior.

Sister.

"Hello," she whispered. "We've come a long way to see you." And to honor her. To honor her mind and her soul and the boundless generosity of her heart.

"She was beautiful," Allie whispered.

Rachel hadn't even realized the others had joined her at the sarcophagus. It was strange that Allie thought Peseshet beautiful. No, not really. Strength and wisdom could be beautiful, and Allie would see that in her. "Yes, in her way, very beautiful."

Tavak had pulled out his camera and was taking pictures of a stone tablet near the sarcophagus's base.

"This has to be it," he said. "The final piece of her cure."

Rachel knelt next to it. "You're positive?"

"Yes, as far as I can be. And there's also some kind of message she had given to her students." Tavak put down the camera and gazed around the tomb. "Natifah did Peseshet proud."

Rachel nodded. "Yes, she did."

Tavak turned to Nuri and Abu. "We should take this tablet. Give me something to wrap it with."

Rachel shook her head. "No."

Tavak frowned. "What's the problem?"

"We can't take this. The directions told us to leave it with her."

Allie frowned. "But what if Dawson—"

"Let him have it. Jonesy's already cracked the code. Dawson will never have that cure before we do." Rachel looked back at the tablet. "Leave it with her."

Tavak hesitated, then nodded. "All right."

"How noble." The familiar voice that called out

from the entrance behind them was dripping with venom. "You make me sick."

She didn't even have to turn around to know who it was.

"Dawson." Tavak wheeled to look at him. "Welcome to Peseshet's world. I know how eager you were to find her."

Oba pushed Dawson into the chamber, his rifle in Dawson's back. "A delivery." Meti was right behind with Sorens in tow.

Tavak stepped toward them. "We were just talking about you, Dawson."

Meti turned to Tavak. "They were right where you said they'd be. A tomb a half mile south of here."

Nuri's brow wrinkled. "I don't understand."

"I suspected that Dawson might have had access to some of the information we had, which was provided by Rachel's computer system." He paused. "He had a source."

"The NSA," Rachel said.

"Ever since we started on this trek, Rachel's computer system has been updating the decoding software it generated for me," Tavak said. "And somehow Dawson has had access to it. So after we got the information we needed to come here, Rachel and I altered the software to direct him to the other tomb." He spoke to Oba. "Is this Dawson's entire party?"

"There were two others but we had a bit of a

scuffle. They opened fire on us." Oba shook his head. "They are no longer of this world."

"You could have told us, Tavak," Demanski said curtly.

"Why? It wasn't a sure thing. I just had to make sure we were protected."

"Very clever," Dawson said. "But it won't do you any good. I have contacts who will come down on you like a house if they don't hear from me soon."

"Really? Now who would they be? Who the hell would care if scum like you lived or died?"

"I represent cash in the till, and there's always someone who cares about money. NSA, Ted Mills." He paused. "We could make a deal."

"That's not going to happen," Rachel said fiercely. "You and your friends at NSA can't buy everyone."

"So full of faith and virtue." Dawson's gaze shifted from Tavak to her. "Corruption is everywhere, bitch, even in your boring corner of the world." He studied her expression, then started to laugh. "You didn't tell her, did you, Tavak? You wanted to protect her. You had to have put all the pieces together, but you didn't—"

"What are you talking about?" Rachel interrupted.

"A mole," Dawson said. "The most logical answer in the equation. Tavak would have gone there first."

Rachel wouldn't believe it. "No!" She looked at

Tavak. "It's not—" Then she saw his expression. "Dear God."

"I didn't want to hurt you until I was sure."

"My, my, I had no idea you could be this sentimental, Tavak." Dawson swung back to face him. "A deal?"

"No way," Tavak said coldly. "You killed my friend, you son of a bitch. You tried to kill us. You're not going to get off the hook. It stops here. You stop—"

The roaring in the walls abruptly ceased.

Rachel stiffened. The sudden silence was heavy as a hammerblow.

Then there was a low rumbling from below. The ground shook beneath their feet.

Dawson's panicky gaze darted around the burial chamber. "What's wrong? What's happening?"

Tavak's wristwatch beeped. He looked at it, then smiled at Dawson. "You read the instructions. 'A quarter of a summer hour . . .' I don't think that was just a request."

The ground shook with even greater intensity, and large chunks fell from the ceiling of the burial chamber.

"I don't have time for you now, Dawson." Tavak grabbed Rachel's hand and leaped for the door. "We have to get out. Now!"

The ceiling at the rear of the burial chamber collapsed, crushing Oba and knocking Meti to the ground. Dust and debris filled the chamber.

Sorens bent down, grabbed Oba's gun, and spun around. He was aiming at Allie, who was running for the doorway. Nuri was suddenly behind him, gripping the man's head. With one twist, he snapped Sorens's neck.

The ground shook harder. Tavak was at the entrance, shoving the others through ahead of him. He called, "Out, Nuri."

As he was about to jump through himself, he glanced back to see Dawson at the sarcophagus tearing the stone tablet from its place.

"You bastard." Dawson cradled the tablet in one arm as he turned, his eyes blazing with triumph. "I've got it. The game's not over. I'll get out of here and I'll—"

A huge chunk of the wall next to him collapsed. Dawson screamed as the barrage of stone blocks threw him against a pile of debris and pinned him upright.

Dawson stared at Tavak and started to speak. But only blood came from his mouth.

Tavak's gaze was on Peseshet's cure, still clutched in Dawson's arms. "She really didn't want you to take her tablet, did she, Dawson?"

"Tavak." Rachel grabbed his arm and pulled him out as more of the burial chamber fell. "Forget him. Get the hell out of here. Hurry! The whole place is going down."

"Tavak!" They heard Dawson's scream as they ran through the large entrance chamber.

The sculptures lining the walkway fell and shattered as the ground roiled. Chunks of the ceiling rained down like bombs from the sky.

Tavak pointed ahead. "Look!"

He was indicating the stairs, which were crumbling fast, Rachel realized. As she watched, a large section of the ceiling fell on them, completely obliterating one side.

Allie and Demanski were hesitating at the base.

Rachel pushed them forward. "Go! It's our only way out!"

The stairs crumbled further with each step, and the deep rumbling below the tomb grew even louder, filling Rachel's ears until she could hear nothing else.

Up ahead, through the clouds of debris, she could make out the hole they had made. Just another few yards.

The next step disappeared beneath her! Then there was nothing but the blackness of space.

She was falling.

Falling, then choking, from her shirt bunched up around her neck and chin.

She looked up. Tavak was on the crumbling stair above, holding her from the back of her collar.

"Cross your arms across your chest so that your shirt won't slip over your head," he shouted.

She complied, and he lifted her up until she could grip the jagged stairs. She almost lost her balance as another chunk of the ceiling fell beside her.

"I'm coming down for you."

"No!" she shouted. "Get your camera out of here. Dammit, it's the final piece of her cure."

"I'm not leaving without you."

"Do it! I'll get out on my own."

Tavak cursed, reached into his shoulder satchel, and pulled out his camera. He turned and hurled it through the opening in the wall. "There. Now I'm coming down."

The staircase buckled and tilted to one side. Tavak inched down and grabbed her wrist, but Rachel desperately held her grip on a chunk of railing. "I'm not going to let you go. Not ever. You'll have to stop holding on to that railing sooner or later. You trust me, remember?"

"Yes." Rachel took a deep breath and released her grip.

"Good." Tavak pulled her up and together they scrambled up the stairs as the cavernous room collapsed entirely. A hurricane of dust and debris blasted all around them; their faces and arms were being cut by the blast. Rachel threw herself through the opening, followed by Tavak.

Tavak bent over to pick up his camera as he and Rachel staggered for the exit. Incredibly, Donkor's mastaba was virtually untouched from the mayhem in Peseshet's tomb, though the collapse was still sending shock waves beneath their feet.

They twisted and turned through the narrow passageways.

The opening was up ahead. Rachel could see stars sparking the darkness.

A few more yards.

They burst out of the tomb. Cool night air.

Where was Allie?

There she was right ahead of them with Demanski, Nuri, and Abu.

"Keep on running," Tavak called to them. "Don't stop until you reach the crest of the next dune. You have to put distance between you and the tomb."

When they reached the dune, Allie whirled away from Demanski and ran back to Rachel. "Are you okay, Rachel? It was like a nightmare."

Rachel nodded, trying to get her breath. She turned to look back at the tomb, then glanced at Tavak.

His gaze was on the tomb but he reached out and his hand closed on Rachel's. "Yes, a nightmare. Dawson's nightmare."

The ground had not stopped shaking, and they could still hear the low rumbling.

Peseshet's voice calling like a triumphant clarion from the past?

Or the sound of distant thunder, echoing across the ages.

Dawson turned his head as another piece of the ceiling fell. He choked on blood, and his ears throbbed from the roar all around him. From somewhere in the chamber, a single flashlight still blazed, sending bizarre, angular shadows on the rubble.

He tried to move. He couldn't. There was no feeling in his legs or left arm, and his right arm was pinned under a section of the fallen wall.

He had to move. He had to get out of here.

More of the ceiling fell, splintering the sarcophagus and knocking it off its pedestal. It tumbled across the rubble, just feet away from Dawson.

Then, slowly, something emerged from the box.

Peseshet.

Dawson held his breath as the mummified remains slid headfirst down the sloping pile of debris.

Directly toward him.

The flashlight beam lit Peseshet's face, brown and leathery, as the ancient bandages caught on the edges of the broken sarcophagus and tore away. Her face drew ever closer, now inches away from Dawson's own.

God, was she smiling?

She was taunting him, he realized. Laughing at him. Mocking his helplessness. Mocking his defeat.

And there wasn't a damned thing he could do about it.

He screamed.

He was still screaming when the entire chamber collapsed on him.

EPILOGUE

Rachel climbed to the top of the hill and gazed out at the hundreds of acres below. It was almost sunset, and the late-afternoon rays fell on the earth like a benediction. Dear God, it was beautiful. Every time she came here, she went away renewed and full of hope.

"You look like a high priestess about to offer alms."

Tavak.

She stiffened but didn't turn around. "It's about time you showed up. It's been months. I thought you'd disappeared from the face of the earth."

"I had a few things to do." He joined her on the crest of the hill. "And I knew you were going to hit the ground running the minute you left Cairo."

"I did." Rachel turned to look at him. His tan was deeper, but his eyes held the same alert intelligence to which she'd become accustomed. He wore khakis and a white shirt with sleeves rolled up to the elbow, and he appeared a little thinner. Lord, she had missed him. "You're lucky I didn't try to cheat you out of your share of Peseshet's cure."

He smiled. "I wasn't worried. I knew where to find you." He gazed down at the valley below, at

447

the rows of ivy-like plants adorned with dangling clusters of berries. "No wonder you were looking like a high priestess. Is this Peseshet's magic? It's very pretty."

She shook her head. "No, it's not. It's the most beautiful thing I've ever seen."

He smiled. "I stand corrected."

"And it will be even more beautiful when we find one that actually works." Her hands clenched into fists at her sides. "And we *will*."

"I don't doubt it." He glanced back at the Dowd Agricultural Research Center, a sprawling one-story facility surrounded by farmland. "Is that your pride and joy?"

"This is only one of a half a dozen labs racing to synthesize the active ingredient of lyiathe. It's a plant that's been extinct for centuries, but it was a key ingredient of Peseshet's cure."

"How close are you?"

"Those plants down there are distant cousins of lyiathe. Future generations will be even closer. We're almost there."

"How long?"

"Six months. A year. It can't happen soon enough."

There had been considerable skepticism in the scientific community, but most naysayers were silenced when GLD Foundation researchers used Peseshet's technique to demonstrate the begin-nings of nervous-system regeneration in small mammals. With the missing ingredient, it appeared, the regeneration would continue until the damaged sections were repaired completely.

"I'm very happy for you," Tavak said quietly.

"Did you hear about Simon?"

He nodded. "I made sure I wasn't completely out of touch. I know it must have hit you hard."

"Yes, it did." Simon's betrayal and death had stunned her. There had been so few people she would have trusted with her life's work, but Simon was one. She missed his brilliance, his wit, and the humor he used to break the tension when she didn't think she could spend another minute in the lab.

She hated that those years of fond memories had been poisoned by his horrible final act. Both NSA Deputy Director Robert Pierce and Ted Mills were now awaiting trial for murder, and as angry as she was at them for hijacking her network for their own purposes, she despised them more for luring Simon down that dark path.

"How is Allie doing? When I called Val and asked where you were, she thought Allie might be with you."

She shook her head. "She's with Demanski in Nevada. They're touring the new hydroagricultural lab that he's set up. The researchers there may be even further along than this place. They're estimating four months."

Tavak chuckled. "Most guys woo women with

candy and flowers. Demanski built an entire research facility that may save her life."

"What can I say? He's a master of the grand gesture." She paused. "Why did you disappear? What was so damn important that you couldn't even wait to talk to me?"

Tavak's smile faded. "I had to arrange for Ben's funeral." He looked down at the valley. "And I had to make sure Nuri was going to be all right. I've been walking away from people I care about all my life. I thought it was time I stopped."

"But you walked away from me."

"I thought I'd give you a chance to decide if you wanted me in your life. I haven't given you much choice since I sent you that e-mail from the tomb."

"And what if I'd decided to cross you off my list?"

He tilted his head. "Have you?"

"Dammit, you left me without a word. And now you say it was some kind of test?"

"I was being noble." He grinned. "But then I got over it. So here I am like a bad penny."

"Great description."

"I thought it over, and bad pennies aren't all that bad. I may not be the most stable man in the world, but I'll spend the rest of my life teaching you to hear the music. You need someone like me."

"And do you need someone like me?" she asked unevenly.

He reached over and touched her cheek with gossamer gentleness. "Oh, yes."

She felt a melting deep within her. "It's not at all sensible. We're completely different."

He nodded. "And there will be times when you're working so hard you'll forget I'm alive, and I'll have to jar you back into my world."

"And I know you. You'll probably wander away somewhere and let me worry myself into a nervous breakdown."

"Probably. But I'll always come back. And when you need me, I'll be there." He smiled. "Think about it." He stepped back. "I want to go down to the valley and get a closer look. Do you want to go with me?"

She shook her head. "I like looking at it from up here."

"Okay." He reached into his duffel and handed her a cloth-wrapped object. "I brought you a present. It's the Peseshet letter to her students. I had it engraved on granite. I thought you'd want it to last at least another five thousand years."

She watched him move down the hill. He seemed bathed in golden light, the only vital, moving entity in the sea of plants. Yet he was casting a giant shadow before him as he had dominated and foreshadowed every moment of her life since she had met him.

She looked down at the gray granite tablet he had given her. Peseshet's message to her students delivered with the wondrous cure that ironically caused so many of their violent deaths.

My loyal and treasured students, I bestow upon you my greatest gift. You have made a solemn pledge to heal the sick, bring them hope, and give them many years of health and happiness. Your skills are a great power, and you now have a responsibility, a sacred duty, toward your fellow citizens. There are those who might wield such power as one might wield a weapon, granting life only in exchange for great riches or influence. But our calling is a nobler one, and I grant you this gift so that all people, regardless of station or personal allegiances, may benefit from our knowledge and enjoy long and fruitful lives.

Spread your knowledge far and wide, my sisters, and the citizens of the world will celebrate our skill, compassion, and boundless spirit through the ages.

Rachel smiled as the sun dipped farther into the horizon, casting dark shadows that made the plants appear like a rolling sea that went on forever. "Soon, Lady Peseshet," she said softly. "Very soon."

AUTHORS' NOTE

Although we enjoy writing stories that stretch the limits of our imaginations, the technology showcased in *Storm Cycle* is rooted in the real world. The concept of distributed computing has been around for more than a decade, and there are currently hundreds of worthwhile projects that pool the resources of personal computers and game consoles all over the globe. We encourage readers to find a cause meaningful to them (at www.distributedcomputing.info) and spend a few minutes setting up their systems to contribute cycles to a worthy endeavor. Much of this book, in fact, was written on a computer that fights disease as part of the Compute Against Cancer project.

Our characters' visit to the fictional Pixel Dance Incorporated showcases technology accessible even to hobbyists. There are several software packages that render virtual models from scanned photographs, and readers can do it themselves with a program called Photomodeler Pro obtainable from Eos Systems. A University of Washington technology group has created digital models of world landmarks based on images posted on public photo-sharing Web sites. Some of their exciting results can be viewed at http://grail.cs.washington.edu/projects/mvscpc/. And there are many firms that will, through the use of a 3-D printer, create solid objects from digital model files e-mailed to them.

Although the ancient Egyptians were just as prone to superstition and pseudoscience as many civilizations throughout the ages, they made astounding contributions to the field of medicine. And in a world where many can remember when a female doctor was a novelty, it is impressive that ancient Egypt boasted many female physicians. History's earliest known female doctor was Peseshet. Her memory was lost to the ages until archaeologist Selim Hassan discovered the tomb of her son, Akheptep, in 1929. Carvings offer only a few tantalizing details about Peseshet, including the fact that she presided over an association of female physicians. The mastaba from Akheptep's tomb now stands in the Louvre in Paris as a center-piece of its Egyptian collection.

Even though we are not privy to the specific medical advances Peseshet may have forged, modern-day researchers have made encouraging progress in the field of central nervous system regeneration. We referenced the University of Miami study to examine the regeneration effects of magnetic nanoparticles on damaged nervous system cells, but even more profound results may be forthcoming from the glial cell transplantation experiments of W. F. Blakemore and A. J. Crang, and scores of other studies around the world. Our best wishes go to all the researchers involved in such projects, and we will be the first to celebrate when this aspect of our book is rendered obsolete.

Center Point Publishing
600 Brooks Road ● PO Box 1
Thorndike ME 04986-0001 USA

(207) 568-3717

US & Canada:
1 800 929-9108
www.centerpointlargeprint.com